"A Touching and important story."
—Laila Ibrahim Amazon bestselling author of *Paper Wife*

"To read this marvelous book is to steep yourself in a magic realism narrative that is a fantastical imagining by author Kenneth W. Harmon."
—Nina Romano, Ippy Award-winning author of *The Secret Language of Women* and *The Girl Who Loved Cayo Bradley*

"I got lost in the poetic, lyrical quality of the writing, enveloped by the story, and felt if I closed my eyes I could imagine myself in Hiroshima. The narrative is lush, evocative, and surrounds the reader with the beauty of Japan and its cultural history." I give this book (a rare) 5 Stars: ★ ★ ★ ★ ★
—theBookDelight.com

"In the Realm of Ash and Sorrow is a breathtaking spiritual journey that will cause you to reconsider your view of those in the world around you and make you think more deeply about how we all treat one another."(5 stars)
—Indies Today

"A fascinating, heartbreaking read and a beautifully human balance to the often heavily militarized view of the war."
—San Francisco Book Review

"Funny, loving, and harrowing, this novel is sure to encourage you to hug the ones you love and take a chance on those you wish to love."
—Independent Book Review

"A compelling and thought—provoking novel, indeed!" (5 Stars)
—ReadersFavorites.com

"The author's research and personal knowledge of WWII, and the bombing of Hiroshima, "blast" this novel to the top of the culturally enlightened historical genre."
—AuthorsReading.Com

"An exceptional World War Two story, set in Japan that gives the reader a complete package of spectacular descriptions, history, romance, and the paranormal."
—Sublime Book Review

"If you like historical romance with a side of the supernatural...you will love this book."
—Online Book Club

"In this riveting merging of magical realism and historical fiction, Harmon goes above and beyond to portray the destruction and devastation of World War II Japan. Harmon spectacularly portrays that even amidst the horrors humans cause, there is still hope and beauty in humanity, even if just in the simple kindness of strangers." (Recommended)
—The US Review of Books

"In the Realm of Ash and Sorrow is a nuanced historical relationship story. It's a great read for anyone interested in Japanese life at that time as well as WWII fiction."
—LoveReading.Com.UK

"There is much to be admired about this book. Pre-atomic bomb Hiroshima is depicted in stunning detail. The story is interesting and enjoyable."
—Discovering Diamonds.blogspot.com

"An engrossing story that combines feelings that are terrifying, whimsical, and humorous. The words craft vivid images. It is professional researched and beautifully written. In the Realm of Ash and Sorrow has something for everybody." (5 stars)
—Book Junkie Reviews

"A magical, memorable read and one I'm very happy to give a full house of stars!"
—Reviewerlady G

"History and fiction meld seamlessly in this novel to deliver a captivating story." (5 stars)
—Literary Titan Book Reviews

In the Realm

of

Ash and Sorrow

Published by Eiledon Publishing, Fort Collins, CO.

ISBN: 978-0-578-59150-6 (Pbk)
ISBN: 978-0-578-62997-1 (eBook)
Library of Congress Control Number: 2019916602

Cover Art: Sydney Evidente
Cover Layout: Lighthouse Creative
Editing: Laura Mahal

ACKNOWLEDGEMENTS

This novel would not have been possible without the assistance of the following people: Brian Kaufman, Patricia Stoltey, Gordon MacKinney, Brigitte Dempsey, Jim Davidson, Stephanie Glick, Laura Mahal, Katherine Vasquez, Beverly Marquart, Nicole Darrow and Tim McGonagil. In addition, I want to thank my wife, Monika, daughters, Sarah, Michelle, Amanda, and Rebecca, and my mother, Jan Harmon, for their continued love and support.

To
Rebecca
With all my love
And
Patricia Stoltey
A great friend and writer

In the Realm of
Ash and Sorrow

Kenneth W. Harmon

This world—
To what may I liken it?
To autumn fields
Lit dimly in the dusk
By lightning flashes.
—Minamoto-no-Shitago

Chapter One

Death followed Micah Lund like an ever-present shadow.

It hovered in briefing rooms and Quonset huts, in the form of empty chairs and bunks. It lingered in the conversations of men tired of fighting a war. Death even invaded his sleep where, night after night, he dreamed of his brother, Levi, killed on Guadalcanal, and his mother, who died of a heart attack soon after.

Micah pressed against the hard bombardier's seat in the forward dome of the B-29 and sighed. Through the bomber's Plexiglas nose, the sapphire water of the Philippine Sea brushed past as if paint applied to canvas. Sunlight glistening upon the swells cast silver sparks. The surrounding beauty failed to improve his sullen mood. He had seen too many friends plummeting through the Japanese night sky toward an uncertain fate, toward a wave of fire rolling across bombed cities.

Behind him, Commander Adams nosed the giant plane upward. "How are we looking on those engine temperatures?" his voice crackled over the interphone.

The flight engineer responded. "Number four is a little hot, but holding at two-thirty."

The atmosphere inside the plane changed the closer they drew near Honshu. Joking and small talk stopped. Skin tightened over weary faces. The dark outline of an island appeared in the distance. Micah picked up his interphone. "Commander, we're approaching Shikoku."

"I see it. Everyone at battle stations."

As the plane passed Shikoku, the grey shape of Honshu arose from the sea. Heavy smoke blanketed the shore on the starboard side.

"Take a good look, boys," Commander Adams said. "That's Osaka burning. The 499th paid them a visit last night." He swung the aircraft to port. Below, lay the Seto Inland Sea, the passage dividing Honshu from Shikoku and Kyushu, and connecting the Pacific Ocean to the Sea of Japan. Tiny islands with sandy beaches dappled the route. "We're coming up on Hiroshima. Are you ready to enter the data into the bombsight, Lieutenant Lund?"

"Yes, Sir," Micah responded. He went to work setting the values for speed, altitude, temperature, and barometric pressure. When he had finished, Micah consulted his book of mathematical tables to synchronize the sight and aircraft speed. He paused as a nagging thought took hold, and then picked up his interphone. "Hey, Commander, why are we on a public relations mission for the Army? Aren't we supposed to be dropping bombs on the enemy instead of leaflets warning them to run away?"

"The leaflets will make their factory workers flee and hurt war production."

"Killing their factory workers will end war production."

Commander Adams smiled. "You really hate the Japs, don't you?"

"After what they did to my family? Hate doesn't begin to describe how I feel."

Hiroshima appeared ahead. Located on the broad, flat delta of the Ota River, the fan-shaped city stretched across six islands formed by seven estuarial rivers that branched out from the Ota. Green rolling hills surrounded the city. Whenever he'd flown over Hiroshima, Micah was reminded of Bellingham. An odd yellow haze hovered over the Nakajima-Honmachi district like a desert sky after a sandstorm.

Puffs of grey smoke burst beneath the plane. "We've got flak, but it's coming in low," Commander Adams said. "Switching over to bombardier control."

Micah leaned over the bombsight eyepiece. Near the bank of the Motoyasu River, the green copper dome of the Industrial Promotion Hall glinted in the sun. He adjusted the mirror that measured the changing approach angle until locating the T-shaped Aioi Bridge. A shudder tore through the bomber.

The shrill voice of the flight engineer exploded over the interphone. "The prop windmilled on number four!"

"Are we going to abort?" Micah asked.

"No," Commander Adams replied. "Stay on target."

"I can't guarantee accuracy on three engines."

"To hell with accuracy," Adams said. "We're dropping leaflets."

The bomb bay doors opened with a metallic yawn. If Micah's calculations were right, the bombs would release the instant the plane passed through a predetermined point above the bridge. The bomber lurched upward as the ordnance released. "Bombs away!" Micah said. He jerked around to follow the bombs' progress. At the precise moment, the detonating cord blew the bombs apart. Millions of leaflets scattered across the sky like wind-blown confetti. He picked up his interphone to report the leaflets' successful distribution and his nostrils twitched at the smell of something burning. Flint grey smoke filtered through the cabin.

"Set the cowl flaps on number three and pull the fire extinguisher," Commander Adams ordered. "If the fire reaches the wing spar we're dead!"

Micah eyed his parachute resting at his feet. If their plane went down, certain death awaited through beheading, torture, or starvation. He would rather die on his own terms. But now that he faced the real possibility of dying, he found his courage fleeting.

The plane continued north over the Chugoku Mountains. Commander Adams spoke into his interphone. "I'm going to turn around. If we keep heading northwest we'll reach the Sea of Japan. The Navy doesn't operate rescue subs in that area. Our only chance is to come about. If we make the Pacific, a sub or PBY might find us."

Micah coughed as the smoke intensified. His eyes watered and ached. Commander Adams completed the turn and once again they were headed toward Hiroshima—the last place Micah wanted to see. A cracking noise carried from the burning wing. He turned toward the commander whose knuckles whitened over the control yoke. Micah snatched his parachute off the floorboard. Smoke obscured everything behind the flight engineer's table.

"We're not going to make the Pacific. Sound the alarm bell," Commander Adams instructed. "Prepare to bail out."

Three short rings carried through the cabin followed by Commander Adams contacting each crewman in the forward and rear compartments to obtain acknowledgment of the order. "Lower the front landing gear." Commander Adams coughed and pointed at Micah. "As soon as the landing gear is down, you get your ass out of this plane. Don't expect a warm welcome."

The front landing gear lowered with a grinding sound. After moving a few inches, the doors froze. "Son of a bitch," Commander Adams said. "The fire must have affected the hydraulics. I want everyone to follow Micah out the bomb bay."

"We can't squeeze through the connecting tunnel with our parachutes on," Micah said.

"Take off the parachute until you enter the bomb bay, then put it back on."

Micah clutched his parachute in one hand and crawled along the floor in the direction of the forward bomb bay. He hacked after breathing in smoke. His vision turned fuzzy. Mucus streamed onto his upper lip. He inched across the floor through billowing smoke, shifting to his right at the lower gun turret. "You still here, Blevins?" Micah asked, passing the navigator's table.

No answer.

He bumped into the bulkhead and ran his hands along the steel wall, searching for the hatch that led to the unpressurized bomb bay. A blast of cold air washed over his face when he opened the hatch. Micah shoved his parachute into the tunnel and slipped in behind it. He wiggled through on his stomach, emerging in the bomb bay. The world began to spin and he closed his eyes. When his vertigo passed, Micah lowered onto the narrow ledge that surrounded the doors. Wind roared up inside the plane, threatening to suck him outside. He hesitated, his attention drawn to smoke pouring through the tunnel. Where were his crewmates? They should have been right behind him.

As Micah dipped his left shoulder under the strap of the parachute, a thunderous crack erupted throughout the bomb bay. The plane heaved over and Micah pitched into the opening. The fingers on his left hand caught the lip of a door. Steel sliced flesh. His blood painted the sky. Micah lunged at the bomb bay door and the B-29 groaned like a wounded beast and spiraled away, leaving him in space.

Micah clutched his parachute with all his strength while reaching to snag the dangling right strap. His stomach fell as if he were going down the big drop on a rollercoaster. Freezing air numbed his limbs. His fingers grazed the strap. *A little farther. Almost there.* A strong gust slammed into him. The parachute broke free and tumbled out of reach.

The ground rushed at him in a blur of green and brown. The sky shimmered like asphalt in summer heat. Micah clawed at passing clouds as if they could somehow save him. Beneath him, the buildings of Hiroshima spread toward sheltering hills. Blue rivers stitched together the islands of the city like threads in a quilt. Overhead, the blazing sun dimmed and a curtain of darkness closed over him.

Chapter Two

The *fūrin* swayed in the morning breeze, producing a gentle tinkling sound. Kiyomi Oshiro smiled at the glass wind-bell. She would have waited until summer to hang the *fūrin*, but Ai insisted they put it out early. For once, Kiyomi was glad she gave in to the whims of her eight-year-old daughter. The pleasant chiming took her mind off the war. Kiyomi draped the last of the family's futons over the veranda railing. The white bedding sagged as if they were *Yūrei*—the ghosts exhausted after a night of haunting. She held little hope that the futons would be fresh when she arrived home from the factory.

Yellow dust rose from Kakō-machi, where mobilized students worked to tear down houses and create firebreaks near the prefectural government offices. The sight sickened her, as did the dirty stench and taste of grit on her tongue. Two kites flew in from the distant blue hills. The hunters fluttered over the city with cries of "*Pi-yoroyoro, pi-yoroyoro.*" The shadows of the Kites passed across the *shōji* paper and Kiyomi remembered an old proverb: when the shadow of a bird falls upon the sliding paper door, guests will come.

Ai emerged from the *doma* in her socks. She carried her *geta* in one hand, her canvas emergency supply bag in the other hand. Before Kiyomi could scold her, Ai spun around and shouted into the house, "I am going."

Ai faced her with a sheepish grin. "So sorry, Mama."

"Let me guess. You're running late because of your grandparents?"

Blood rushed into Ai's cheeks, turning them a soft pink. Kiyomi couldn't help but smile as she stared into the dark, trusting-eyes of her daughter. She longed to reach out and pull Ai against her. To feel her heartbeat and warm breath. To smell the flowery scent of her velvet hair. To hold on forever. "Do you intend to spend the day in your socks?"

"Please forgive my mistake." Ai dropped the *geta* onto the veranda with a thud, slipped them on, then straightened like a soldier coming to attention. "I'm ready."

Kiyomi's jaw clenched as she inspected her daughter. Ai should be wearing a sailor suit to school, not baggy grey *monpe* and wooden clogs. The war turned them all into peasants. She brushed a hand over the small wooden plate attached to Ai's sash, engraved with Ai's name and address to help authorities find Kiyomi in case they became separated during an air raid. "Do you have your first-aid supplies?"

Ai held up her emergency bag. "Packed and ready."

"And your padded hood?"

Ai gazed at her sandals. "At school."

"You forgot to bring it home? What would happen if Mister B returned to drop bombs? Your head needs protection."

"Please forgive my carelessness." Ai looked up, her eyes seeking compassion.

"You're apologizing a great deal this morning." She held out her hand. "Come along."

Kiyomi unlatched the side gate and led Ai onto Tenjin-machi Road. They walked hand in hand along the quiet street, past houses and small shops. Cramped buildings formed a narrow passage, their somber wooden walls and black tiled roofs adding to the wartime melancholy.

"I had a nightmare last night," Ai announced.

"The same dream as before?"

Ai nodded. "Someone chases me through the dark house."

Their *geta* tapped on the street, the sound echoing off the latticed windows.

"Mama?"

Kiyomi gave Ai a reassuring smile. "When I was your age, I too suffered nightmares. My Uncle Hideo, told me evil spirits cause bad dreams. He said whenever I awakened from a bad dream, I should ask *Baku*, the eater of nightmares, to devour the dream. This will turn the nightmare into a good omen."

"Is that true?"

"You must try to find out."

"All right. I'll try, Mama."

They turned onto Nakajima-Hondori Street in the direction of Motoyanagi-machi and the Honkawa River. The street once bustled with traffic coming from the Old Sanyo Highway. Shoppers had crowded the many businesses. Now, *kanban* fanned and snapped in front of empty buildings, the shop signs advertising what had once been Hiroshima. They passed the shuttered Yano Shoe Store, Sawamura Print Store, and Ōmoto Lacquerware. Kiyomi paused outside the closed Tada Bookstore, recalling the many hours spent browsing through books. Mr. Tada smuggled her a copy of *The Makioka Sisters* before government censors forced the novel off the market a second time.

Mr. Hamai swept the sidewalk outside his barbershop. His was one of the few businesses to survive the war cuts. He smiled at their approach.

Kiyomi stopped in front of him and bowed. "Good morning, Mr. Hamai."

Mr. Hamai brought the broom to his chest and bowed. "Good morning, Kiyomi-san, and Ai-chan, and what a fine day it is."

"How is business?"

"Business is most favorable. Thank you for asking, Kiyomi-san."

"Good day," Kiyomi said and bowed again before walking past.

Ai leaned close and whispered, "Why is Mr. Hamai's shop still open when so many have closed?"

"Stores cannot stay in business if they have no products to sell. Men still need haircuts."

An army truck rumbled along the street, tires stirring up dust. Soldiers with tired faces stood in the back. They looked nothing like the proud men who once marched through the streets of the city toward Ujina Harbor and war—cheered on by admiring crowds waving rising sun flags.

At the former Matoya Clothes Store, Kiyomi steered Ai into the alley that led to her school. The alley swallowed the light and a chill moved through Kiyomi as she ruminated on Ai's question. Typically, Ai never asked questions about the war, as if avoiding the subject would make it go away.

The sky opened at the end of the alley. Warm sunlight greeted them. To their left, a cemetery stood in silent repose, black headstones absorbing the morning light. To their right, young life celebrated a new day on the playground of the Nakajima National School. Children's laughter and shouting filled the air. The two-story wooden structure fanned out into an L shape. A section of the playground had been converted to a victory garden. The playground appeared larger with the children grades three and above evacuated to the Shōhōji Temple in Mirasaka-chō. Boys sheathed in air-raid hoods resembled miniature samurai warriors as they wrestled. Other boys spun tops or shot marbles. Girls played oranges and lemons, *Janken*, or stood watching the boys and chatting.

Ai pulled back.

"What is it?" Kiyomi asked.

Ai's focus drifted to the playground, then back to her. Questions moved across her black eyes.

"Is something wrong?"

"Norio bragged about his father. He said he's a war hero."

"*Hai*. He's a naval commander."

"And my father?"

Kiyomi wavered. She hated lying to her daughter but her in-laws had insisted this was the best course of action. "He vanished while fighting in China. Why ask now? We've spoken of this already."

Ai kicked a rock, sending it on a chattering journey. "Was Jikan my real father?"

A flutter traveled through Kiyomi's stomach as if a hundred butterflies took flight. She had anticipated this day would come, only . . . not this soon. She feigned ignorance. "I don't understand your question."

"I heard *Baa-baa* and *Ojiisan* talking. They said my father came from Tokyo."

"*Hai*. We met before the war."

"You were married?"

"We never married."

"Why?"

Kiyomi jerked on Ai's arm to get her moving. "We'll have this conversation another day."

"Did you love him?"

Kiyomi remembered the warmth of his lips in the darkness of Hibiya Park. A muscular hand working under her blouse, soft fingers climbing her ribcage. Months later she stood alone on the Ryōgoku Bridge beneath a full moon. A dagger in her hand shimmered in the darkness as a voice inside her head steered her away from the unseen world.

"He was a good man," Kiyomi lied for the second time that morning. She motioned with her chin at the silver moon necklace around Ai's neck. "He gave me that."

Ai fingered the tiny moon resting at the base of her neck. The necklace had always been her most prized possession. "You loved each other?"

Kiyomi sighed as her daughter's repeated questions weighed on her. This wasn't the time to have such a discussion.

"Baa-baa says you're possessed by a worm."

Kiyomi blinked. "A worm?"

"*Hai*. The worm of depression."

Kiyomi choked back laughter. "The worm of depression? Nonsense. I can never be sad as long as I have you for a daughter."

"Mama, will the war ever end? I want to go to the horse market."

"The horse market? In Shiraichi?"

"*Hai*."

"Why do you want to go there?"

"To eat the cotton candy."

"Cotton candy, *eh*?" Kiyomi grinned at her daughter's innocence. "We must be patient, my love. We fight for the Emperor. The Emperor alone decides when the war will end."

"Miya says the Americans will be here soon."

Kiyomi stopped and looked around to make certain no one listened. "Never repeat that to anyone. Listen to only half of a person's talk. The mouth is the gate of misfortune."

"I understand, Mama."

At the edge of the schoolyard, Ai raised the flap on her emergency supply bag. "What did you pack in my bento box?"

"What would you like me to pack?"

Ai tapped a finger against her lips. "How about *tendon*?"

"I see. So, I must travel to the ocean and catch shrimp, then hike into the hills to find wild vegetables."

"That would be most agreeable."

Kiyomi's hands fell to her sides. "How about a rice ball?"

A veil of disappointment moved across Ai's face. "Again?"

"Better than having the worm of depression."

Ai smiled and bowed. "Sayōnara, Mama."

Although customary to leave a child with a bow, Kiyomi leaned down to kiss Ai on her cheek. "Sayōnara, my love."

As Ai melted into the crowd of children, Kiyomi thought of the cherry trees that grew along the banks of the Honkawa River. She pictured the blossoms, falling like pink snowflakes to settle upon the placid water, and remembered how they floated out to the welcoming arms of the sea.

Chapter Three

Kiyomi's shoulders sagged when she reached the Aioi Bridge tram stop where commuters squeezed together on the concrete platform. If she didn't catch a streetcar soon, she'd be late to her job at the Tōyō Kōgyō factory. Not that they would fire her. The government needed every able-bodied worker it could get. But her supervisor, Mr. Akita, might try to humiliate her in front of the other workers in an attempt to bring her to tears. She wouldn't cry. No man could ever make her cry again.

The people on the platform were united in their misery. Most were women in their twenties and thirties, dressed in baggy *monpe* and blouses, with dark crescents under their eyes and hollow cheeks. The few men in the crowd wore the government-recommended khaki uniforms with puttees and army caps. The men shared the women's malnourished appearance. No one spoke, as if they were guests at their own funerals. Kiyomi missed how things had been before the war, back when women breezed along the sidewalks in western-style dresses or kimonos—their hair in curls, lips bright with lipstick. Once the government decided all things western were evil, that dresses and kimonos represented unnecessary extravagance, it had the *Kempeitai*, the military police, pressure women into wearing the work clothes of farmers.

The crowd swayed like stalks of wheat against the wind, heads turning in the direction of Falconer Town. A blur of apricot and hunter green caught Kiyomi's attention; a streetcar rattled on the rails, its trolley pole popping against overhead wires. People on the platform straightened in anticipation of boarding but the streetcar, overflowing with passengers, blew past without stopping.

Kiyomi tightened her grip on her emergency supply bag and advanced onto the bridge. She paused halfway across to look out over the Motoyasu River, palms resting on the rough concrete handrail. A cool southern breeze carried the salty tang of the Inland Sea. An old man stood on the sandy riverbed, casting a leaded net into the water with a splash. Closer to the bridge, a woman knelt at the river's edge to check an eel trap. Crows settled on the roofs of the buildings crowding the stone embankment that marked the division between river and city, voicing their complaints with harsh cawing. An oyster boat glided toward the bay. Two fishermen propelled the boat with long poles, their skin a rich mahogany from hours spent on the waves. Farther out, the white sails of fishing boats billowed against the yellow haze like Bedouin tents brushed by desert winds.

If she remained on the bridge, she could almost forget the troubles of the world, but the First Noble Truth declared life was full of suffering, and so it was for her. Kiyomi remembered her conversation with Ai. Surely her in-laws hadn't meant for Ai to hear about Kiyomi's old lover. It was, after all, their plan to hide the details of Kiyomi's past from Ai. Why would they change their minds now? Angered by their betrayal, heat rose into her face, but she tempered this feeling by taking a deep breath and focusing on the scene in front of her. *Mono no aware*, the impermanence of things, yes, this is what captured her eye as she created a memory of the morning. Would cherry blossoms be less attractive if they were a long-lived flower? Would this river and these people move her soul if she didn't know they would one day vanish upon the wind? Life was an illusion, nothing more.

She resumed her journey. The Tōyō Kōgyō factory stood miles away in Fuchū-cho. With luck, she could be there in less than an hour. To the east, brilliant sunlight slanted onto the green summits of Tanna Mountain and Shira Mountain. Hiroshima came alive with the rising sun. People crowded the sidewalks, most heading to factory jobs. The clacking of their *geta* filled the air like the tapping of woodpeckers. On the road, streetcars went by with a grinding of steel. Military trucks rumbled past, belching exhaust clouds that carried the stench of burnt motor oil and left a smoky taste on her tongue. There were no cars, due to the gasoline shortage, but the street remained congested with evacuees. Entire families trudged along behind handcarts while others rode in horse-drawn wagons, their wooden wheels creaking as the horse's hooves clopped in rhythm to the song of the *geta*. Men on bicycles weaved between the pedestrians. Most rode on rims because their tires were worn beyond repair. The evacuees headed toward mountain villages where family awaited. The government discouraged the practice and deployed soldiers to turn people back. As more cities suffered incendiary attacks, the military found it impossible to stop citizens from fleeing. Hiroshima had been spared the horror of firebombing, but no one expected this to last.

A line stretched from the entrance of the food distribution center. What did people wait for on this day? Maybe rancid sardines or brown rice. The government had long ago stopped rationing the more popular white rice. With the food situation in their own house growing more desperate, Kiyomi questioned why her mother-in-law, Sayoko, refused to stand in the distribution line. Did her swollen pride keep her nose lifted above her empty mouth? Kiyomi could endure whatever hardship resulted from her mother-in-law's laziness but to make Ai suffer was incomprehensible.

She had been walking an hour, her legs burning with fatigue and hunger slicing through her belly like a dull blade, when the shrill blast of an air-raid siren erupted across the calm morning. Birds recoiled from the shrieking alarm and flew off toward the hills. On the sidewalk, people stopped and gaped at the sky. A bomber had struck the city two days prior and the memory of that attack left citizens rattled. Three women hurried past toward a shallow ditch. Two men huddled in the trench waved the women over. "Hurry! Hurry!"

Kiyomi continued walking. If the Americans arrived in force, a trench offered no protection but she might survive if she reached the factory.

The deep droning of a B-29's engines approached from the bay. Kiyomi squinted against the sun. A lone bomber flew in the direction of the city, aluminum fuselage shining, and contrails stretched out behind it like white serpents. Antiaircraft guns on Mount Futaba boomed. Shells exploded across the sky in bursts of grey and white but nowhere near the American plane. Kiyomi tracked the bomber's path toward the Aioi Bridge. An image of Ai outside on the playground flashed through her mind. Blood drained from her head leaving her lightheaded. She leaned against a telephone pole. Black sticks tumbled from the bottom of the B-29.

Bombs!

She glanced down the empty sidewalk, resisting the urge to run back to Nakajima-Honmachi. Would she be cradling her dead child before the day ended?

The bombs broke apart, filling the sky with leaflets, and Kiyomi relaxed. The B-29 flew past the city moving northwest, black smoke marking its passage. Had the army guns managed to hit the great machine? As she neared the East Hiroshima Freight Yard, leaflets fluttered onto Hiroshima. Kiyomi stopped. She considered the leaflets surrounding her. Should she dare read one? The *Kempeitai* arrested any person who read a message from the Americans. Satisfied no one watched her, she knelt to pick up a leaflet. One side featured the image of B-29s dropping bombs and the names of a dozen cities, including Hiroshima. The other side had words written in Japanese.

Read this carefully as it may save your life or the life of a relative or friend. In the next few days, some or all of the cities named on the reverse side will be destroyed by American bombs. These cities contain military installations and workshops or factories which produce military goods. We are determined to destroy all of the tools of the military clique which they are using to prolong this useless war. But, unfortunately, bombs have no eyes. So, in accordance with America's humanitarian policies, the American Air Force, which does not wish to injure innocent people, now gives you warning to evacuate the cities named and save your lives. America is not fighting the Japanese people but is fighting the military clique which has enslaved the Japanese people. The peace which America will bring will free the people from the oppression of the military clique and mean the emergence of a new and better Japan. You can restore peace by demanding new and good leaders who will end the war. We cannot promise that only these cities will be among those attacked but some or all of them will be, so heed this warning and evacuate these cities immediately.

Kiyomi gnashed her teeth. *Lies. All lies.* Where were the American humanitarian policies when they burned Tokyo and killed her aunt and uncle? They did not wish to injure innocent people? Then why kill thousands of mothers and their children and old people who could hardly move, let alone lift a rifle?

"Put that down! Put that down!"

A man in civilian attire ran at her waving his arms. Sweat glistened on his brow. Kiyomi let the leaflet slip from her grasp.

"They're bombs," he said, his voice rising. "A new paper bomb that explodes in your hand."

"Please excuse me, so sorry."

"Did you read it?"

Kiyomi shook her head. "Why would I want to do that?"

"Are you certain?"

"Of course. I must leave now. I'm late to work." She hurried away from the man, glancing over her shoulder to make certain he didn't follow. Around her, people emerged from their hiding places. Their faces held curious amusement as they followed the swirling leaflets. The air raid sirens stopped. The groaning and banging and straining of industry returned as people resumed their routines. Kiyomi thought about Ai. Did Mr. B frighten her as it passed? Ai was such a brave girl. Kiyomi smiled while imaging Ai standing on the playground shaking a fist at the American airmen.

She cinched her emergency supply bag tight against her shoulder and picked up her pace. The sun climbed over the surrounding hills bringing warmth to the streets. Sweat trickled down her temples. Kiyomi stopped. Her mind raced as she tried to comprehend her sudden apprehension. Air raid sirens began to scream once more. A B-29 flew toward the city from the north with thick black smoke trailed out behind it. Something red flickered over the wing. *Fire!* Yes, it was fire. How was this possible? People crowded onto the sidewalk. Their faces betrayed shock. No one believed the powerful Mr. B could be humbled.

She continued toward the factory, her trepidation growing with each step. Kiyomi gasped and covered her mouth as the B-29 broke apart. She forced herself to look away because to observe felt indecent. But her curiosity pulled with magnetic force, raising her eyes to the scene above her. Kiyomi's attention shifted from the dying aircraft to a solitary image captured in the bright morning light—a dark spot growing larger with each passing second. A man falling through the sky. "My god," she whispered.

The airman clawed at the air as if expecting a ladder to materialize. She debated turning away from the unfolding horror but this seemed dishonorable. The man might be her enemy but he deserved respect for his courage.

She followed his path to a vacant lot, not fifteen meters away, where *Kabocha* vines snaked across the dry ground. He arrived without a sound, his body thumping against the earth, then leaping upward as if launched by a spring, before settling amongst the vines. Kiyomi crept closer. Her heart thundered like a *Taiko* drum. Her skin crawled and tingled. When she reached the lot, she expected to see a bloody pile of flesh, not an intact man. She moved within a few meters of the airman. He had hair the color of ripe wheat. His eyes were as blue as the sky. Prior to the war, she danced with Americans at the Nichi-Bei Dance Hall in Tokyo over the objections of her aunt and uncle. She found Westerners fascinating, despite their strange odors and brazen manners. The fallen airman was the most attractive American she had ever seen. *Have I lost my senses?* The sound of pounding footsteps came rushing up behind her. Four *Kempeitai* ran toward her, waving their batons. "Get away! Get away from him!"

Kiyomi faced the airman and put her raised hands together. "Peace be with you."

"What are you doing?"

She faced the nearest *Kempeitai* officer who glared at her through narrowed eyes. "Nothing."

Another *Kempeitai* pointed his baton at her face. "Did you pray on behalf of this man? He's our enemy."

She knew they could drag her off to a dark cell, but guessed the *Kempeitai* men would be too caught up in the turmoil of the moment to want to mess with her. "I'm on my way to work."

"Where do you work?" one of the men inquired, his mouth curled into a snarl.

"Tōyō Kōgyō factory."

"You live nearby?"

She shook her head. "Nakajima-Honmachi."

"You walked this far?"

"The streetcar didn't stop."

"You shouldn't be here."

Kiyomi bowed deeper than the men deserved. "So sorry, please excuse."

"Go now," an officer commanded.

She bowed again, then dared reproach by glancing over at the fallen airman one last time, before hastening away from the *Kempeitai* men.

Chapter Four

Darkness enveloped him in a state of limbo. How did he arrive in this black void? The mission. Hiroshima. What else? Micah rapped knuckles against his forehead. *Think. Think. There has to be more.*

A sound emanated from the darkness. Distant, then growing louder. Gentle pattering. He strained to recognize the source. Could it be … rain? His body trudged forward, but he couldn't feel the ground. Grey light bled through the dark ceiling. *The sky?* The surrounding landscape emerged and took on form. A forest bathed in white mist that hovered near the ground. Towering Douglas fir and Western Hemlock—ancient sentinels of the natural world—mounted the slate-colored sky.

Micah cupped his hands around his mouth and called out, "Hello? Hello? Anyone there?"

No answer.

Cold raindrops splattered against his face. *Am I back in Washington?*

Birds chirped in the trees. A deer leaped through the mist. He shouted once more and again was answered with silence. *I need to find a landmark to tell me where I am. Maybe I'm in the Snoqualmie Forest. Where is Mount Baker? I should be able to see the mountain.* He squatted beside a creek and splashed cold water on his face. A memory flashed through his mind. An engine fire. Smoke flooded the forward compartment of the bomber. Had to escape. *But how?* Crawl. He had crawled through smoke and fire until finding the tunnel that led to the forward bomb bay. Yes. He had gone into the bomb bay. The plane broke apart. He dropped outside without his ... parachute. No. This was wrong. It had to be wrong.

Micah had explored for what seemed like hours when the ground began to shake. Pinecones scattered across the forest floor twitched. Shrieking birds burst from trees in a blaze of colors. The tremor intensified and he pitched onto his knees.

An earthquake?

Wood cracked and splintered. The giant trees vibrated, faster and faster until their trunks blurred, and the ground around them erupted in craggy blocks. Tree roots, like arteries connecting to the heart of the earth, tore out of the dirt. The roots shimmied about like spider legs climbing a web. Trees threw off dirt showers as they ascended en masse. Boulders and ground cover ripped from their anchorage in a thunderous roar along with screaming animals.

The forest swept upward, leaving behind a barren plain. Micah failed to notice his body rising. He moved slowly at first as if caught in a gentle updraft, but soon his body picked up speed and he soared higher until finding himself surrounded by flying trees.

Wildlife swirled around him like debris caught in a tornado. A rabbit looked him in the eye and said, "Did you do this?"

Micah blinked. *Did that rabbit just talk to me?*

"Something wrong with your hearing?"

"I'm not sure."

"Figures," the rabbit said and turned away.

The forest soared beyond the clouds, into a brilliant luminescence that grew brighter and brighter. Heat cascaded over his body. Around him, trees burst into flames, scarlet and golden fire dancing through space. Above the inferno, the light erupted into a blinding flash.

Micah slammed into something hard and stopped.

He found himself on the ground, enveloped by green vines. Someone stood nearby—a woman. He pushed up into a sitting position and took in the view. Buildings encompassed by distant green hills. *Bellingham?* No, not Bellingham. Something odd here, but he couldn't place it. He eased onto his feet, his body swaying. Three men came running down the road. Olive uniforms. Wooden clubs. Flesh the color of potato skins. Eye openings compressed. They shouted in a language he'd heard before but didn't understand. *Think. Think. What could it be?* And then it hit him and his stomach clenched.

Japs.

The soldiers drew closer and Micah thrust his hands skyward. The men rushed up to the woman and started talking. When their conversation ended, the woman walked away.

The soldiers brushed past, their attention drawn to something behind him. Micah turned and spotted the body of an American airman. His throat and stomach burned as if he'd swallowed a red-hot coal. The soldiers ignored him as they pointed at the body and laughed. *Bastards.* Micah inched sideways for a better look. As the face of the dead man came into view, he trembled. *No. This isn't possible.* But there was no escaping the truth. The body was his own. *Oh, Jesus. What the hell? I'm dead? I can't be dead.* And yet, in his heart, Micah knew the truth. The soldiers paid no attention to him because they couldn't see him. He surveyed the road and spotted the woman in the distance. Something told him to follow her.

Chapter Five

By the time Kiyomi reached the factory on the shore of the Enko-Gawa River, her thoughts lay scattered like puzzle pieces waiting to be connected. In her mind, she pictured the dead airman. Kiyomi wished she could have studied his eyes longer. What would they reveal to her? This man was her enemy. He would kill them all given the opportunity and yet, she could not bring herself to hate him. Perhaps this was due to the nature of his death. He had to be terrified as the earth rushed toward him. She knew she shouldn't care, but her capacity for empathy did not die when the drums of war sounded.

Miko, the old guard, greeted her at the gate with a bow. His once portly frame had diminished due to food rationing. "Good morning, Kiyomi-san."

Kiyomi returned his bow. "Good morning, Miko-san."

"Did you see the B-29?"

"*Hai.*"

"You think the Army brought down that monster?"

"I cannot say," Kiyomi said, before continuing to the factory.

The Tōyō Kōgyō plant manufactured everything from aircraft parts to the Type 99 rifle. Kiyomi worked in a section that produced rifle barrels. She paused at the entrance to the factory floor. Her colleagues were hard at work operating their machines. Gears whirled with a metallic squeal. The air reeked of sweat and machine oil. Patriotic posters hung from the grey walls with slogans such as *One hundred million hearts beating as one, the eight corners of the world under one roof,* and *We'll never cease fire till our enemies cease to be!* The words lost their meaning once the struggle against starvation commenced. She hastened to her assigned locker to stash her bento box and emergency supply kit. Before she could get away to her lathe, Lee-Sam Yoo stepped in front of her with a broad grin on his face.

"Are you well today, Kiyomi-san?"

The company had constructed a two-story dormitory near the beach and brought in Korean workers to make up for the absence of Japanese men drafted into military service. Because the Koreans were the only young men available, some of the Japanese women took an interest in them, and vice versa. At one time, Lee-Sam had been enamored with Kiyomi, but she did not reciprocate his advances. Although she found him somewhat handsome, with his strong jaw and sharp eyes, she knew nothing positive could come out of such a relationship.

"*Hai.* I'm fine. Thank you."

"You are pale this morning. Have you eaten?"

She found his question irritating. Lee-Sam knew of the food shortage in Hiroshima, and rumor had it the company fed the Korean laborers better than what the average Japanese person received. She smiled to mask her petulance. "I had a long walk. I feel better now."

"I have extra food if you're hungry?"

Her stomach growled at the thought of eating, but she wouldn't wear his *On*. She would not be indebted to him. "Thank you, Lee-Sam. I've brought my lunch."

He stepped aside to let her pass. Haru followed her progress with inquisitive eyes. She left her station and approached Kiyomi, a grin on her face. Kiyomi knew Haru fancied Lee-Sam. She hoped Lee-Sam wasn't aware of Haru's infatuation. Like many of the women who worked in the factory, Haru was a war widow. Her husband, Masa, died most gloriously at Midway according to the Naval Department. Kiyomi had her doubts.

"Good morning, Kiyomi-san."

Kiyomi stopped at her lathe machine. "Good morning, Haru-san."

"Did you see the bomber crash? Everyone cheered."

Kiyomi checked to ensure the spindle work had the cup center embedded, and the tail, stock, and tool rests were clamped leaving clearance for the rotating stock. "I heard about the plane. I didn't see what happened."

"How could you not see? The bomber went down over the city."

"So sorry. My mind remained with Ai."

Haru offered a weak smile in response and Kiyomi knew she wouldn't criticize her for worrying about her child.

"What is this?" Mr. Akita crept up behind Haru.

Haru's eyes widened at the sight of their supervisor. "So sorry, Mr. Akita-san. I'll return to work."

Mr. Akita puffed out his chest like a rooster spoiling for a fight. A diminutive scarecrow with fierce black eyes, Mr. Akita never passed an opportunity to stress his authority. "Why are you away from your machine, Haru-san? Are you bored working on behalf of the Emperor?"

Haru's cheeks bloomed red. Mr. Akita had questioned her sense of duty and Haru could not save face. "So sorry," she said in the frightened voice of a child. "I did not mean to offend."

"The Army drafts my workers and what am I left with? Old ladies and schoolgirls. It takes ten of you to do the labor of one man." His attention shifted to Kiyomi, but before he could speak, the sound of chanting echoed throughout the building.

The mobilized students from the Hiroshima Girl's Commercial School marched into the factory, dressed in matching navy long-sleeved blouses with white collars over lighter blue *monpe*. They wore white headbands with the rising sun emblem in the center. A nametag over their left breast and an armband on the left side identified them as members of the school corps. Their smooth young faces shined with optimism. They believed with hard work the war could still be won. The girls chanted, ". . . for the purpose of victory, for the purpose of victory."

"They may not produce like a man, but at least they bring energy to their work." Mr. Akita stabbed a bony finger at Haru.

"Which is more than I can say for you." The scarecrow continued down the line, snapping off commands as he went.

Haru glanced at Kiyomi before returning to her machine. Haru kept her head low, the red remaining in her cheeks.

Kiyomi pitied Haru, but she had no time to dwell on the matter. Instead, she was thankful the chanting students spared her from Mr. Akita's wrath. She went to work rifling a barrel. She had been operating her machine a few minutes when a chill crept across the back of her neck. Kiyomi peered over her shoulder and saw no one. She went on working but the cold sensation never left her. It wrapped around her shoulders like a winter breeze.

At lunch, Kiyomi sat alone at the end of a long table. Typically, she sat with Haru, but on this day, Haru joined Lee-Sam. Jealousy stoked a fire in Kiyomi's heart as they talked and laughed. *Why do I feel this way? I have no interest in Lee-Sam or any other man.* Kiyomi opened her bento box which contained a rice ball wrapped in wilted *Amanori*. With this diet, she would be a pile of bones in no time. Her thoughts turned to the American airman. She tried to clear the image of his death from her head without success. Instead, she developed questions as if playing a game. Did the American come from a small town or a big city? A place like San Francisco perhaps. Did he have a wife? A big round woman with heavy breasts who rolled through life like a tsunami or someone petite who floated through rooms as a wisp of smoke? Was her hair the color of summer wheat or as black as the night? A dull pain resonated throughout Kiyomi's heart when she imagined the airman holding a child. Children were the real victims of war. So many orphans, so many dreams scattered as windblown ash.

By the time her shift ended, Kiyomi's sweat-dampened blouse stuck to her flesh, and the muscles in her arms and legs smoldered. She willed her feet to shuffle toward the door. Head low, she made her way to the nearest tram stop. On a nearby street, soldiers chased after blowing leaflets. Eyes closed, she tried to steal a moment of sleep.

"Kiyomi-san, I had hoped to find you."

She opened her eyes to discover Umi beside her. Umi belonged to the student group at the factory. Umi had a broad, plain face and pleasant disposition. She lived in Otemachi and often accompanied Kiyomi during the ride home. On most days, Kiyomi enjoyed their conversations, even though Umi spoke with the naiveté of youth. In a few more years the words coming off Umi's tongue would be darker and less hopeful. After all she had experienced, Kiyomi wanted to be alone. She needed to envision herself at the sea under a night sky, floating on her back, a mere speck in the darkness, stars twinkling above her.

"How are you, Umi-san?"

A streetcar arrived with the hissing of brakes. Kiyomi fell in behind four women who waited to board. Umi joined her. "A most exciting day, *neh*?"

Kiyomi knew Umi wanted to discuss the bomber, but Kiyomi remained quiet as she boarded the streetcar. The streetcar driver was a girl no older than Umi. The Hiroshima Electric Railway Company trained schoolgirls to operate their streetcars because male drivers had been drafted into the military. She acknowledged them with a subtle nod. The passengers sat with their heads bowed, the effects of hunger and fatigue tearing down their fortitude. When the war with America started, and the Army rolled to victory after victory across the Pacific, the people of the nation walked proud. The impossible became possible. With cities reduced to wasteland and hundreds of thousands of civilians killed, what had once been righteous seemed foolish and misguided. But she could never share this sentiment. To do so in front of the wrong person might lead to arrest and prison. She must at no time doubt the mind of the Emperor. The Emperor knew the best course for Japan and her people.

Kiyomi took a seat near the front of the streetcar. Umi sat beside her, an optimistic smile lifting the corners of her mouth. The tram jerked ahead, a jolt traveling from the rail, up through the seats.

"The tide of war is turning," Umi announced in a voice that carried throughout the streetcar. "When we shot down that bomber today, it was a sign. You'll see."

Iwo Jima lost. Okinawa under attack. And Umi wanted to discuss signs. Kiyomi remained quiet and stared out the window.

The May sun had swung westward and settled above the mountains.

"Did you notice Haru and Lee-Sam together at lunch? I could never be with a garlic-eater."

"I didn't notice them."

Umi tugged on an earlobe. "I have a secret. Would you like to hear it?"

Kiyomi forced herself to nod. *"Hai,* if the secret is about you."

"I'm not a gossip."

"Of course," Kiyomi said. Looking at Umi's face, she noted the flushing of her cheeks and the glimmer in her eyes and realized Umi's secret must be both personal and a source of great satisfaction. "What's your secret?"

"I'm in love with a boy from my neighborhood. His name is Yōshio. His parents are merchants. They own a furniture store. It's closed now."

"Does Yōshio feel the same toward you?"

Umi pressed a hand over her heart and sighed. *"Hai.* Isn't it wonderful?"

Kiyomi found herself at a loss for something to say. Having only once experienced what she considered at the time to be love, she hardly thought of herself as an expert on the subject. "I'm happy for you, Umi-san."

Umi babbled on about her boyfriend and their future plans together. They would wait until the war ended to get married. She would then move into his parents' house and help with their business. She'd give Yōshio many sons. When the streetcar reached Umi's stop, she kept talking all the way out the door. After Umi left, and the streetcar resumed its journey, an elderly woman glared at Kiyomi and shook her head. Kiyomi turned to watch Umi until she vanished between two buildings, all the while thinking how sad the world had become when another person's happiness became the source of antipathy.

Chapter Six

Kiyomi found Ai waiting with her teacher, Mr. Kondo, on the playground. Mr. Kondo was an older gentleman who left instruction of militarism to the younger teachers. He once told Ai children should learn the beauty of poetry, not the follies of government policy. Kiyomi was surprised Mr. Kondo hadn't been arrested on account of his pacifist beliefs. Mr. Kondo held something in his hands for Ai to see. Mr. Kondo and Ai looked up as she approached. Ai beamed. "Look, Mama."

Kiyomi bowed. "Good evening, Sensei-Kondo."

Mr. Kondo's wrinkled hands unfolded to reveal a black and yellow *Chou*. The delicate butterfly kept its wings still as if this would make it invisible to the giant creature that held it captive. "It flew onto my hand while we discussed Matsuo Bashō's poem, 'Taking a Nap.' Have you heard it?"

"Many years ago, as a child," Kiyomi said.

"Basho's poetry stirs my soul." He brought his hands closer to Ai. "Shall we release our friend?"

"*Hai,*" Ai said. "She has been a most splendid guest."

Mr. Kondo beamed. "How do you know the *Chou* is female? Did she whisper this into your ear?"

"She is delicate like a girl. Boys are grasshoppers and spiders."

Mr. Kondo chuckled. "You are a keen observer of life, little one." He raised his open palms. "Here we go." The butterfly fluttered off into the gloaming.

Kiyomi held out a hand for Ai. When her daughter's tiny, warm-fingers wove between Kiyomi's, a feeling of contentment rose inside her. She bowed again to the wise teacher. "*Arigatō*, Sensei-Kondo."

He returned her bow. "It's my pleasure. Sayōnara, Kiyomi-san. Sayōnara, Ai-chan."

Mother and daughter headed home in the inky darkness. Before the Americans arrived with their powerful war machines, lamps and lanterns cast squares of red and yellow light onto the streets and alleyways. People did their shopping at night because prices went down. At the public market, fishmongers displayed what remained of their catch. The pungent odor attracted neighborhood cats who sat in the darkness and meowed. Grocers sold eggplants, cucumbers, potatoes, and lotus roots. Merchants displayed shoes, furniture, or clothes. Now the night brought impenetrable gloom due to blackouts. Bats fluttered through the murky sky joined by ghostly moths. Factory workers returned home, their movements slow and mechanical.

"Did you have a good day at school?"

"We went to the playground for spiritual training."

Kiyomi's eyebrows went up. "Oh?"

"We practiced using wooden swords and spears in case the enemy arrives."

"Did you enjoy that?"

"The boys did. I would rather draw pictures."

Kiyomi squeezed her daughter's hand. "Me too."

"Mr. B flew over today. Did you see it?"

"*Hai.* I saw it."

"The Americans dropped leaflets again. A boy picked one up. He was taken inside and did not return."

"I'm glad you were not foolish enough to do the same thing," Kiyomi said while recalling her own irrational behavior.

A thin band of sunlight rested on the western mountains by the time they arrived home. "I cannot wait to bathe," Kiyomi said, unlatching the gate. "I smell like a dead fish rotting in the sun."

"You smell good to me," Ai said.

"If you're trying to get a bigger dinner portion, it just might work."

Kiyomi growled under her breath upon seeing the futons draped over the veranda railing. Laziness infected Sayoka like a virus. "Could you help me with the futons?"

"Why must we always carry them into the house?"

Kiyomi wondered the same thing but, rather than voice displeasure, it was her duty to prepare Ai for her future life. "Your grandparents provide us a home. They love you. It's a little thing to help them with chores, *neh*?"

Ai released Kiyomi's hand and went to the nearest futon. Ai's turned-down mouth and slumping shoulders told Kiyomi her daughter understood what was expected of her as she grew older. "First, our shoes," Kiyomi said. They stepped past the *shōji* and paused at the earthen-floor entry. They removed their *geta* and arranged them in a neat line alongside the sandals of her in-laws. Next, they put on their house slippers before returning to the veranda.

Ai grinned as Kiyomi helped her fold the first futon. "We can pretend the futons are clouds and we are carrying them to their beds."

"Clouds, *eh*? You have a wonderful imagination," Kiyomi said.

They each lugged a futon into the house. The screens that divided the rooms stood open. Banri sat inside the parlor on a pillow, hunched over his writing desk, his attention on whatever sutra he copied from the *Tipitaka*. With his bulbous head, receding hairline and folds of wrinkled skin at the base of his neck, he reminded Kiyomi of the *gama-gaeru* toad in the garden. Sayoka sat nearby holding a book of poetry. In Kiyomi's eyes, her mother-in-law resembled a cunning snake, with her thin face, piercing black eyes, and long neck.

"I have come back!" Ai shouted as she followed Kiyomi across the *tatami* mats.

Banri looked up and smiled. "You have returned."

Kiyomi compelled a smile onto her lips. How could her in-laws sit in the same spot all day? Didn't they know a war was going on?

"How was school?" Sayoka asked.

"We saw Mr. B. The bomber was noisy like a crow."

After storing the futons in the cupboard, Kiyomi led Ai back to the veranda to collect the remaining two. She closed the *Amado* that sealed up the house at night, the wooden screen clicking into place. Electric lamps inside the house stood dark while a kerosene lantern glowed white on a nearby table. *Another no—electricity day.* With all the windows and screens enshrouded by blackout curtains, shadows permeated the rooms. A thread of black smoke weaved upward from the lantern's dome and gave the air a fetid stench that called to mind an unused room buried in dust. Light ascended into the rafters where a pair of house swallows had built their nest. Her aunt told her birds flying inside a home brought good luck. Kiyomi wished this were true.

Sayoka beckoned Ai to sit beside her. "I've missed you." She placed a hand on Ai's shoulder before returning it to her lap. Her attention shifted to Kiyomi. "After dinner, can you dust the house? And do something with that awful brown rice?"

Kiyomi hid her resentment and offered a quick bow. *"Hai.* I'll prepare the bath water now." *Prepare bath. Cook dinner. Clean the house. Pound the rice. I'm a slave to unrelenting masters.*

Sayoka called out in a cheerful voice, "Remember, happiness is measured by sacrifice."

Kiyomi fought back mounting anger as she entered the bathing room. She used balls made of half-burnt embers collected from the stove to stoke a fire in the copper charcoal box under the bathtub. Soon, steam rose out of the deep wooden tub constructed from a barrel. She set out towels, razors, a basin of room temperature water, and cloth bags containing rice bran and caustic soda that served as soap. With everything ready, Kiyomi reentered the living room and informed Banri.

He pushed off the floor, his knees crackling. A raspy cough escaped his throat followed by wheezing in his chest. He faced her and bowed. *"Arigatō,* Kiyomi-san."

Banri had always treated her well. He showed her respect, unlike Sayoka. Kiyomi feared her father-in-law's strength was declining at a time they needed him to be strong. She picked out a book from her *Tsuzura* chest and returned to the living room to read to Ai, only to find her mother-in-law talking with her. Kiyomi simmered with indignation as she lowered onto a nearby pillow. Book open, Kiyomi pretended to read while Sayoka spun a tale of adventure from her youth, something about being caught on a neighbor's fishing boat in a typhoon. *Pure nonsense.* When Banri emerged from his bath, Sayoka left Ai with the promise of finishing her story. Ai covered her mouth and yawned, which made Kiyomi smile.

Kiyomi took Sayoka's place beside her daughter. Exciting story, *neh?* Raging storm, monster waves, demons from the deep."

Ai giggled. "You're silly."

"I've brought us a book." Kiyomi held it out for Ai to see.

Ai's eyes grew wide. "*The Adventures of Tom Sawyer* by Mark Twain. Is it all right to read an American book?"

"Why not? I read many books by American writers before the war and I remained Japanese."

Ai giggled once more as she snuggled against Kiyomi.

Kiyomi had reached the part where Tom painted the fence when Sayoka returned. She tucked the novel under her arm, knowing Sayoka wouldn't approve of her choice. Kiyomi had hid her books in the attic when the *Shisōbu* confiscated all things Western, but Sayoka turned over Kiyomi's collection of Jazz and Swing records to the Thought-Police. Kiyomi never forgave her. She gracefully unfolded from the floor and sauntered to a storage trunk where she stashed the book under her wedding kimono. "I'll hurry in the bath," Kiyomi told Ai.

"Do not hurry for me," Ai said.

Inside the bathing room, Kiyomi employed a straight razor to shave her cheeks and neck. Kiyomi next slipped out of her clothes and ladled water over her head and body. After washing with soap and rinsing off, she dipped a toe into the steaming water but pulled back when a rush of cold air swept over her shoulders making her shiver. With a determined breath, she entered the tub and sat. Searing water enveloped her. She drew her legs to her chest and closed her eyes. Frigid air lingered around her head, raising hairs on the nape of her neck. What did it mean? Had a *Yūrei* latched onto her soul? Could it be Jikan or Yutaka returned from the battlefields of China? When Kiyomi was a child, her mother, Ameya, took her and her siblings to the public bathhouse. They were taught nudity was a natural state and no cause for embarrassment. You trained yourself not to be conscious of it. But this experience proved peculiar. Alone, yet not alone, under the observation of an invisible guest, Kiyomi found herself mindful of her own nakedness. She stood, a chill passing over her, and hurried to dry off with a damp towel. Kiyomi slipped into her *yukata*, pulling the plain cotton kimono tight against her body.

She called for Ai to join her. Ai enjoyed a bath and approached the room with anticipation. Her joy vanished when she looked up at Kiyomi. "Is something wrong, Mama?"

How could she explain her concern without frightening Ai? "Can we make it a short bath tonight?"

"*Hai,* Mama."

The chill in the airlifted and Kiyomi realized the ghost that haunted her wouldn't remain inside the room while Ai bathed. Why would a spirit be uncomfortable at the sight of a child's body?

Ai flattened a hand against her tight belly. "Mama, my stomach hurts."

"I know," Kiyomi said as she lathered Ai's hair, "mine also hurts. But we must endure the discomfort, for that's what the Emperor requires of us."

"Will we have more food soon?"

"I don't know. But we must do our best." With widespread hunger in the city, the tears of Hiroshima were hidden behind thousands of closed doors.

After helping Ai bathe, Kiyomi went into the kitchen where a cockroach scurried across the earthen floor. She choked back her revulsion and cooked *nukapan,* made of fried wheat flour and rice bran. *Nukapan* tasted bitter and smelled like horse dung but would keep them alive. She served the family on lacquer trays inside the living room. They sat on pillows in a semicircle. Before picking up their chopsticks, they said "*Itadakimasu,*" to give thanks. The family ate in silence as usual, but Banri turned on the radio to listen to government war broadcasts. When the announcer reported Imperial forces on Okinawa had killed eighty thousand American officers, Banri huffed. "If the Americans can absorb such losses and continue fighting, how are we to defend the homeland from invasion? Not even our brave kamikaze can stop the enemy's advance. No divine wind will save Japan."

Sayoka sat openmouthed with her chopsticks paused at her lips. Ai looked from person to person with eyes that sought the truth. Kiyomi envisioned a postwar world in which American soldiers occupied Japan. Was this even possible? Hadn't the government vowed to fight to the last person before allowing that to occur?

"I have my beer ration tickets from the Industrial Association," Banri said. "Maybe I'll line up tomorrow at the beer hall."

Kiyomi pressed her lips together to mask her displeasure. *We're running out of food and he will line up for beer. Typical man.*

When they finished eating, Kiyomi and Ai carried dishes into the kitchen. Ai nudged her elbow as they placed bowls in the sink. "Is it true, Mama? What Ojiisan said about the war? Will Japan lose?"

After Singapore fell, the possibility of defeat seemed as remote as the stars. The Japanese military appeared invincible. As the war progressed and the tide turned against Japan, the government's lies became the truth, phony victories accepted as fact, until the truth crawled out of the darkness and denial became the lie. Now the government spoke of the Japanese people dying together, in a final stand against the barbaric enemy, but there would be no one left to fight if they all starved to death before the invasion arrived.

Kiyomi touched Ai on the cheek. "We don't know what the future holds. Let us live each day in the best way possible. No matter what, I'll always be here for you."

The uncertainty left Ai's eyes and she smiled. "And I'm here for you."

"Kiyomi-san," Sayoka called from the living room. "Could you please join us? We have something to discuss with you."

Kiyomi's tongue clicked on the roof of her mouth. "She must think these dishes can clean themselves."

"I can wash them, Mama."

"No, that's unnecessary. Fate is not ours to change."

"What does that mean?"

"The future is a winding road, but it's the road we must travel." Kiyomi shooed her toward the living room. "Go and draw me a picture. Something pretty."

"A plum blossom?"

"*Hai.* That would be lovely."

Inside the living room, Banri and Sayoka knelt on their cushions. One of them had lit a second lantern and glowing light spilled across the tatami mats, bringing out their greenish tint. Banri waved Kiyomi to an empty cushion. Kiyomi eased onto her knees, reading the faces of her in-laws, but their expressions told her nothing. Ai sat nearby at the writing desk, head tilted toward the adults to catch their conversation.

They sat in silence for several minutes before Banri asked, "How are things at work?"

His question struck Kiyomi as odd, seeing as he never took an interest in her affairs outside the house unless they involved procuring food. "We are busy."

"*Hai.* I'm sure you are." Banri cleared his throat. "We've been contemplating the world to come. Despite the war, we must look to preserve the Oshiro family lineage."

Her father-in-law's words traveled through her brain like a meandering river. Where did they lead? What was their purpose?

"We have sacrificed both of our sons for the Emperor," Banri continued, "therefore, we intend to adopt a son to carry on the Oshiro name."

"A wise plan," Kiyomi said while wondering where they would find a suitable man in Hiroshima with the majority away fighting.

Sayoka leaned closer. "And you will marry him and provide the family with a grandson."

Blood drained from Kiyomi's face. *I should have anticipated this*. It made sense for Banri and Sayoka to want an heir and who better in this war-torn land to provide this blessing than her? She was a captive surrogate, a prisoner to circumstance. A nervous tremor raced through Kiyomi's hands, which she forced deeper into her lap. *I must not show them anything.*

"As you have noted, Jikan died while fighting for his country. It's not proper that I remarry," Kiyomi said.

"Trust us to know what is best," Banri said.

"I'm not worthy of this honor."

"Acceptance is the key to a contented heart," Sayoka said.

A contented heart? What do you know about my heart? My heart hasn't been contented since arriving in Hiroshima.

"We've noticed," Sayoka went on. "Your *Ki* has closed these past months. A new husband could lift your spirits."

Kiyomi weighed Sayoka's words and found them preposterous. Kiyomi had been down this path before, pressured into a loveless marriage due to her incongruous behavior. Must she continue to pay for the mistake of giving her heart away so easily? She recalled a drunken Englishman at the Nichi-Bei dance hall who asked her to be his wife. Westerners had no appreciation of duty or obligation, but they could surrender their hearts to the emotion of love. Why must her own people take the joy out of relationships? There had to be more to life than producing sons and groveling before mothers-in-laws.

"And what if something were to happen to us?" Banri offered. "With a husband, you and Ai could remain here. You would be protected."

"There are only old men in the city."

"There are younger men," Sayoka said.

"None that would bring honor to your family."

Banri sat back on the pillow, his face reddening. "The five worst maladies that afflict the female mind are indocility, discontent, slander, jealousy, and silliness. The worst of them is silliness. A woman should cure them by self-inspection and self-reproach."

Kiyomi's eyes narrowed at Banri. "You believe I'm acting silly?"

"*Hai*," Sayoka answered.

Banri pulled the last of his *Kinshi* cigarettes from its pack. He used a match to light the cigarette, took three puffs, and exhaled a grey cloud. "It's most unfortunate what happened to Jikan. He could have been a good husband for you."

Kiyomi recalled Jikan being an awkward lover, more interested in drink and gambling than his wife. Jikan gambled away much of the family's wealth before their arranged marriage. If her aunt and uncle knew the truth regarding the Oshiro's financial state, they never would have consented to the match, scandal or no scandal.

"Kiyomi, you must know your place in this family."

She stared straight into Banri's eyes, a terrible act of rudeness that appeared to unnerve him because he could not maintain eye contact. "I'm a *mibōjin*. Do you not realize how difficult it is for a war widow to remarry? And I'm twenty-eight. What worthy man would want someone so old?"

Banri massaged his chin. "*Hai.* You are old for a bride."

Sayoka dismissed their concerns with a wave of her hand. "Let us worry about that. We'll find a good *Nakōdo*. A matchmaker who understands our needs." She smoothed the front of her kimono. "Your karma and your shadow are always there, Kiyomi."

Kiyomi recalled an old proverb as she thought about a *Nakōdo* choosing a husband for her. The joys and sorrows of a whole life depend on a stranger. "I apologize if I've offended. You have my best interest at heart."

"Best to remember your obedience."

Kiyomi bit her tongue to keep from responding. She pushed off the floor and bowed to her in-laws. "With your permission, I'll clean the dishes now."

"*Hai.* Go clean the dishes," Banri said. "We'll talk more on this later."

Kiyomi padded across the living room in measured steps that revealed nothing of her feelings. Inside the kitchen, she gripped the side of the sink so hard her knuckles whitened. *Remember your obedience, she says. How can I forget when she reminds me daily?*

After finishing in the kitchen, Kiyomi spent the remainder of the evening polishing the woodwork inside the house. Ai studied her with pity in her eyes, and it hurt Kiyomi to think her daughter already knew so much about the pain of living. When all the wood had been polished, Kiyomi brought out the futons. She turned to Banri. "Ai and I will go to bed now."

"Goodnight, then."

"Come along, Ai," Kiyomi said. They moved into the adjoining room. Kiyomi closed the *shōji*, the sliding paper door offering little in the way of privacy. She snuggled under the covers of her futon and turned to face Ai.

"Mama, what is—"

Kiyomi touched a finger to Ai's lips and gestured at the *shōji*. "We must whisper."

Ai nodded and Kiyomi removed her finger. "Mama, do you want a new husband?"

Kiyomi stroked a finger along Ai's cheek, warm as sunshine and soft as a downy feather. She remembered holding her for the first time in the hospital, thankful her baby was a girl. If she delivered a boy, the Ito family would have claimed the child as their heir and taken him away from her. Nothing or no one would take Ai from her. *Ever.*

Ai scooted closer. "You look sad, Mama."

"The face is the mirror of the heart."

"So, you are sad?"

"Have you heard the term, *amae?*"

"What does it mean, Mama?"

"The sun cannot hold back the rain, and even if it could, the sun would not, and do you know why? Because the rice must have both sun and rain to grow. People are like rice in that respect."

Ai pushed her bottom lip out to one side as she puzzled over Kiyomi's words.

"There is a difference between desire and reality," Kiyomi went on. "We dream of love. Reality does not match the dream. I will marry whomever your grandparents find for me to marry because I'm obligated to do this. They have provided us with a home and will continue to let us live here. You'll finish school and become a smart girl. Smarter than me."

"But you went to college, Mama."

"*Hai.* Three years. And I would have finished if I hadn't fallen in …"

"What, Mama?"

Kiyomi forced a smile. "Nothing. Try to sleep. We have much to do in the morning."

Ai rested her head near Kiyomi. "Good night, Mama. I love you."

"And I love you, little one."

Kiyomi closed her eyes. She breathed in the scent of Ai's skin, which reminded her of a warm *Taiyaki* filled with chocolate cream. Kiyomi sighed. To contemplate the future while a war raged was foolish, and yet, she found herself brimming with ideas. She longed for love, as much as anyone, and fantasized about living her life with a man worth dreaming of. Sayoka would tell her those ideas were the thoughts of a child and she must accept her place in the world. Kiyomi hated the world and her place in it. If not for Ai, she would have been a memory long ago.

The *shōji* slid open and Banri stood in the aperture with wide fearful, eyes. "The radio reported American bombers are on a course from the Bungo Channel north toward Hiroshima Bay. Please hurry."

Kiyomi shook Ai's shoulder to awaken her. "Ai, we must go into the shelter."

Ai groaned as her eyes fluttered open. "I'm so tired."

"I know. We all are. Now come on."

Kiyomi helped Ai to her feet. Hand in hand, they hurried into the kitchen where Banri and Sayoka waited. Outside, an air raid siren screamed. The shelter consisted of a hole dug in the kitchen floor, three feet deep. Banri mounted a steel plate against the wall nearest their heads to prevent a cave in. He lowered into the hole and held out a hand to Sayoka. Next came Ai, followed by Kiyomi. Once inside the hole, they slept on their sides, bodies pressed together. Sayoka rested an arm on Ai's shoulder. It took all of Kiyomi's resolve to not push Sayoka's arm away.

It didn't take long in the confined space until the temperature started to rise. Banri, Sayoka, and Ai drifted into sleep, but Kiyomi struggled to relax. Sweat beaded on the back of her neck. Hunger made her stomach shrivel and ache. Muscles on fire from a hard day of work burned to cinders. When they first used the shelter, she dreamed the hole was a grave. Worms burrowed out of the dirt and crawled down her throat. The worms devoured her from the inside. Now, with the heat rising and the wailing siren tearing through the walls, she thought about the airman. She remembered how he fell from the sky without a sound. Brave for an American. She pictured the shape of his face, the tone of his skin, the half-closed eyes that looked onto the world and saw nothing. A chill settled over her and Kiyomi knew the *Yūrei* had returned to enter the grave of the living. *Go away and haunt someone else. Do it now or I will drive you away!*

Chapter Seven

Micah sat on the kitchen floor staring at the family inside their hole. How could anyone sleep through the blaring of an air raid siren? He let out a breath. Why did he continue to breathe, and why did he feel tired? Was it like this for everyone when they died? He retained his senses, yet he knew he was dead. When he started to follow the woman he could not feel his feet, but in time the ground returned. His reflection did not appear in windows. The wind moved through him as if he were made of smoke, but when he touched a hand to his chest he felt solid. Everything around him appeared a little sharper, more vivid, the green of distant hills richer, the blue of the sky more pronounced. He was trapped in a state of limbo and it filled him with resentment and rage. Where was the miraculous Heaven promised by Father Olson? The sparkling angels with their beautiful music? His personal visit with Jesus? Why weren't his mother, brother, and grandparents there to greet him? Curiosity opened Micah's eyes to the world around him. Isolation brought him to the edge of tears.

He recalled falling through the sky without his parachute, but not hitting the ground. There had been a forest. Trees tore loose from the earth and soared into the sky, and he traveled with them. Was any of it real? And then he arrived in this place. Hiroshima. Home of his enemies.

The woman. The factory. Memories arrived in bits and pieces, information jumbled and out of order. When he first noticed her standing over him, Micah sensed a connection between them. Was it the pity her eyes betrayed or the idea she could somehow see past his body, to the man who lived an unseen life. He had trailed her to the factory. A large facility he recognized from aerial reconnaissance photos as Tōyō Kōgyō, manufacturers of aircraft parts and military rifles.

At first, sounds were amplified. The clanging and whining of machines and the workers' voices hummed inside his head. As the day progressed, the sounds softened, and the humming stopped. He remained close to the woman. She kept her head down, even while eating lunch. Her body sagged as the day progressed until it appeared she would melt into the floor.

When the woman left the factory, he followed her onto a streetcar, where she talked to one of the schoolgirls. Why couldn't he understand their conversation? Wouldn't the language here be universal? But where was here? He clearly didn't belong in the same plane of existence as the living.

He trailed the woman to a school where she met a little girl. Together, they journeyed through alleyways no wider than his parent's garage door back home. Buildings constructed of grey wood, with pitched roofs covered in dark tiles, stood inches apart. He called to mind Bellingham with its wide streets and bright houses with large fenced yards, and big trees shading lawns. He observed nothing green here.

A smattering of people navigated the streets and alleyways, but the ones who did lumbered with their heads down. The bleak atmosphere created a mood of depression more severe than any he experienced under the winter skies back home. By the time they reached the woman's residence, he believed he'd been sent to hell. They passed through a squeaking side gate that opened onto a dirt yard. Compared to the narrow streets and compressed houses, the yard seemed enormous. An ornamental garden featuring a willow tree bowing over a pond stood at the rear of the yard. Orange and white fish swam near the surface.

Shadows filled corners and blanketed the rafters of the home. Dark curtains covered screens that formed the outer walls, no doubt to help create a blackout condition in the city. If the bombardier can't see the target, he can't hit the target. But the radar on a B-29 allowed the bombardier to place their ordinance without a visual reference. The Japs could wrap a black curtain over the entire city and it wouldn't do any good. If Lemay wanted Hiroshima to burn, the city would burn.

The woman and her daughter entered another room where two older residents, a man, and woman, awaited. Were these the woman's parents? Micah thought back to his Japanese Studies class at Western College. What had his professor said? Japanese women married and moved in with their husband's families? Yes, that was it. These people must be the woman's in-laws. The rooms were void of furniture. *How strange.* Furniture crowded each room of his childhood home. The man carried an air of dignity. He dressed like the majority of men Micah had seen on the streets in a khaki-colored shirt and trousers. His head belonged on the body of a larger man. He conveyed physical strength, but his skin had taken on an ashen hue as if he suffered from a hidden malady. The woman wore an unadorned kimono wrapped tight around her slender waist. Her black hair was pinned up revealing a long neck. Her face pinched into a sneer aimed at the younger woman.

The family greeted each other in a stiff, formal manner. No hugging or kissing. Smiles were reserved for the child. He found their behavior odd. Back home in Washington, his family traded warm greetings with hardy embraces, kisses, and laughter.

After her mother-in-law addressed her, the younger woman made her way toward the back of the house. She went straight into a small room with a planked floor and paneled walls. She lit a fire inside a copper box under a wooden tub. Steam rose from the water's surface, condensation beading on the walls and ceiling.

Micah remained inside the living room as the in-laws bathed, but followed the younger woman into the bathroom. His voyeuristic behavior felt wrong, but the urge to watch her overruled reason. She picked up a straight razor and proceeded to shave her face. *Odd.* She next removed her scarf, pulled a pin at the back of her hair, and shook it loose. Long bluish-black hair cascaded to slender shoulders. She slipped out of her clothes and his jaw went slack as he took her in. The woman's beauty affected him the way a sunrise over Mt. Baker had affected him. She had parchment-colored skin, flawless except for a tiny mole on her left breast. Her slender neck brought to mind Benlliure's *Cleo de Merode*. Micah's gaze traveled to the patch of dark hair feathering out between her legs. He wanted to touch her so badly his fingers tingled and ached with anticipation. Women had always puzzled him. Back in Bellingham, he had many opportunities with women but these moments always ended the same—with him alone under the moon. "Can't let 'em scare you," his older brother, Levi, used to say. Micah knew the day had come when he must move past his fear so it was with a native beauty on Saipan that he made love for the first time. He no longer found women as mysterious, but they still terrified him.

The woman sat on a stool and dipped a ladle into a basin of water. She brought the ladle over her head and allowed the water to pour across her scalp. After washing her hair, she proceeded to clean her body. Dirt and grime fell off in black rivulets. It was then he noticed her eyes. They expressed sadness as if witness to acute misery, and yet, they also conveyed a sense of mystery and devotion, and he envisioned walking beside her along a mountain trail as dawn arrived in golden waves.

As she eased into the steaming water, he noticed the tautness of her skin, how her stomach concaved and her ribs lay exposed. *She's starving to death*, he thought, the idea filling him with trepidation. He tried to shake his unease by reminding himself she was the enemy. She worked in a factory producing rifles meant to kill his countrymen. Why should he care if she suffered? But the more he considered the matter, the less like an enemy she seemed. After all, his own sister helped to build the planes used to bomb her people. *Her people? I must be losing my mind.*

At one point, she spun around as if startled, water splashing over the side of the tub. She stared straight at him, her eyelids opening wide, her lips parted. Did she detect his presence? Soon after, she hurried from the tub and dressed.

When the younger woman took her daughter for her bath, Micah remained inside the living room until they returned, then followed the woman into the kitchen, but unlike any kitchen, he had ever seen, with no refrigerator, oven, or stove. An opening in the ceiling allowed smoke to escape. Black soot caked the overhead beams. The room had an earthen floor, with a rectangular pit dug about four feet deep. He stood over the hole and scratched the back of his neck while trying to imagine what purpose it served. The woman used a charcoal grill to prepare their dinner, which she served on small lacquer trays. Their meager ration could not sustain a child, let alone an adult.

After eating, the family gathered to talk. The older man spoke first. Whatever he said struck the young woman hard. Her jaw flexed. Her hands trembled over her lap. When the conversation ended, the younger woman rose from her pillow with the splendor of a blossoming flower and went to work cleaning. She polished cabinets and beams. Inside the long hallway, she buffed the planked floor. Her face held a grim resolve as she worked. At the end of the passage stood a ladder. He followed her up into a storage room. An odd assortment of items lay stacked against the wall. Paper umbrellas, hand-held fans, porcelain bowls, lacquered Buddha, and a stack of bamboo rafts.

The woman lifted a rag to one of the beams, then slumped onto the floor. She folded inward, her bowed head between rolled shoulder blades. Her eyes moistened as if she might cry, then she drew in a breath and pushed onto her feet. By the time she finished working, a sheen of sweat glistened on her brow. When Kiyomi returned downstairs, the older woman contemplated her with a gleam of satisfaction in her eyes.

Later, they closed a screen to divide the living room, the in-laws sleeping on one side, the woman and her daughter on the other. They stretched out heavy blankets and lay on the mats covering the floor. After whispering their thoughts, the younger woman and her daughter closed their eyes to sleep, the daughter's head resting near her mother's head. The tenderness of the moment had a strange effect on him, and his mind drifted to the incendiary raids he had taken part in against other Japanese cities. Micah retreated to a corner and sat. His body felt heavy as if cement coursed through his veins. Maybe if he slept, when he awakened he would be in Heaven with his family. But what if he didn't deserve to be in Heaven? What if he was being punished for the things he did in the war? *I have to quit thinking of them as people*, he reminded himself. *They're my enemy*. And yet, it was difficult to see an enemy in the face of a child.

As the woman and her daughter drifted into sleep, the screen flew open and the father-in-law entered. He spoke in a rapid voice and whatever he said made the woman jump up. She woke the girl and together they trudged into the kitchen. Air raid sirens commenced wailing across the quiet night, cutting right through the paper screens enclosing the house. Was this the night Lemay chose for Hiroshima's destruction? One by one, they descended into the hole in the floor. Micah couldn't believe how they managed to squeeze inside the confined space. He hovered over the hole and peered down at them. As the siren continued to blare, the family somehow went to sleep. All but the younger woman. She remained awake, staring straight at him as if she knew he were there.

Chapter Eight

The younger woman awoke before dawn. She eased out of the hole in the floor, careful not to wake the others. Her face appeared drawn, the skin under her eyes discolored and baggy. No surprise. The air raid sirens had wailed throughout much of the night. She massaged fatigue from her eyes, her fingers long and graceful like those of a piano player. Micah remembered his mother playing "Greensleeves" on the piano in the parlor. She would play the song over and over, the melody floating up the stairs and into his bedroom where he pressed a pillow against his ears to block out the sound. He would give anything to hear her playing "Greensleeves" now.

The woman tip-toed into the living room, her movements precise and measured, the house quiet except for the chirping of the nesting birds. Inside the bathing room, she used a damp towel to wash. At one point, she spun around and faced him, knocking the razor onto the floor. She stared straight at him and once again, he was certain she could sense his presence.

She changed into baggy work clothes and pinned her hair up beneath a scarf. He had seen too much of her to be fooled by an ugly disguise. While she might project an image of unpretentiousness, what lay beneath the carefully crafted persona was the most beautiful woman he'd ever seen.

When she left the bathing room, he expected her to return to the kitchen; instead, she climbed into the upstairs storage room.

Light seeped through the latticed windows, turning the room a soft grey. The air smelled like the inside of a dusty steamer trunk opened for the first time in years. She knelt in front of two altars. One stood about five feet and was constructed from black and gold lacquer. The other altar was smaller, made from untreated wood, darkened with age. She used matches to light incense on the taller altar, clapped her hands once, and bowed her head.

The portraits she prayed before each featured a Japanese man wearing an army uniform. Micah guessed their ages around thirty. The man on the left had a moon face with sharp, focused eyes. The other man had a gaunt face. A white scar marred his chin.

Back downstairs, she opened up the house. Screens rolled opened with a clicking sound and sunlight spilled inside. She returned to the kitchen and stood over the hole, staring at her sleeping daughter. Kneeling, she shook the girl's shoulder and spoke to her in a soft voice. One by one, the rest of the family stirred from their dreams.

After preparing their breakfast she packed two lunches. When her daughter finished eating, she helped the child dress and put up her hair. The girl hugged her mother twice and Micah found this touching. Mother and daughter then gathered the bedding and draped it over the porch railing. He remained on the veranda when they went back inside. A rumbling carried from the south, followed by a loud cracking. The sound reminded Micah of a giant Douglas fir felled by lumbermen. In the distance, yellow haze rose over tiled roofs. The same haze he had noticed on the previous day.

The woman and girl emerged from the house. The girl yawned, which made her mother yawn. Exhaustion molded their faces into drawn masks as they plodded toward the gate. At first, Micah kept his distance, until he remembered he was invisible to them.

The streets and alleys contained little traffic when the woman and girl set out, but gradually, more people ventured outside. Most were women, all dressed in the same style of ugly work pants. Where were the colorful kimonos he had seen in photographs? The elegant ladies with hair swept off their slender necks, secured by elaborate combs, paper umbrellas shielding their fair skin from the sun. The woman and her daughter stopped a few times along the way to greet someone with a bow and a smile.

When they arrived at the girl's school, the woman struggled to let go, her eyes fixed on her daughter's face. Her anguished expression reminded him of the look on his parent's faces as they sent him off to war.

On the streetcar ride to the factory, she kept her head down except on two occasions when she glanced at the aisle where he stood. He had ridden on the streetcar in Bellingham numerous times, but the atmosphere here proved oppressive. Passengers slouched, their focus on the floor. He understood their anxiety, with city after city reduced to ashes in their empire. Was Hiroshima the next to burn?

Inside the factory, she operated a lathe that bore out rifle barrels with a high-pitched metallic shriek. After a while, he grew restless and decided to explore the city. Outside, he squinted against the bright light. Humidity wrapped around his face. To the southwest, the yellow haze spread upward from the city, staining the blue sky. He glanced back at the massive factory complex. Why hadn't the facility been targeted for bombing along with the rest of Hiroshima? Every major offensive launched by the Imperial Army began with the embarkation of troops from Ujina Harbor and reports that the Japanese Second Army had moved their headquarters to Hiroshima circulated amongst the aircrews on Saipan. What stopped High Command from ordering an attack on the city?

Micah walked down to a river where an old man sat on the bank, fishing. The air carried the pungency of salt and something rancid, like drying kelp. In the distance, the outlines of buildings spread across the horizon, but here, far from the heart of the city, a stillness pervaded.

He left the old man and headed toward the harbor. The water of the Inland Sea beckoned as sunlight flashed on the surface. Black-headed gulls floated on the wind where the river and sea melded. An Osprey circled above the gulls, and a greenish-blue kingfisher patrolled the grassy shoreline. The sea lapped onto the beach and foamed around his shoes. A pair of white sails floated past like low-lying clouds. Dark-skinned men worked the boats, steering them toward open water. *Fishermen.*

Micah recalled the last outing on his Grandfather Finn's troller, seven months prior to the war breaking out. He had recently graduated from Western College and looked forward to time off before he applied for a teaching job. Levi talked of moving his family to Seattle and the brothers knew this might be their last great adventure together.

The original plan was to head south to warm California waters, but when they reached Cape Flattery, their Grandfather had a change of heart, as trollers often did, and steered them north toward British Columbia's Inside Passage. "The chinook are swarming around Port Alexander," he insisted, and who were they to question a man with over sixty years of experience? After sailing through the Dixon Entrance into the Gulf of Alaska, they turned in the direction of Port Alexander.

Heavy clouds, the color of river stones, greeted them on the morning of the fourth day. Grandfather Finn carried a mug of coffee and a hard muffin to his chair on the flying bridge. With his weathered face and silver mane snapping out behind his slicker, he resembled a Viking raider. He took a sip of coffee, steam curling around his hawkish nose, then shouted as if addressing a room filled with people, "Ain't enough that a fisherman knows the surface of the sea. No, he must know what lies beneath as well. Rocks waiting to rip out the bottom of your boat. Sunken reefs and submerged snags. He understands the hidden landscape of his fishing grounds the way a farmer knows his fields." After another sip of coffee, he added, "I pity the poor souls who work regular jobs. I'd rather spend a day fishing in freezing rain than sit behind a desk."

The damp air smelled of ancient places, hidden caverns and inlets once visited by Tlingit warriors before the Russians arrived with their guns and smallpox. The troller's engine shook to life with a throaty grumble and Grandfather Finn steered them out into the bay. Seabirds appeared all around the boat—Black– and white-bellied petrels and brownish shearwaters, riding the current and screeching while anticipating a meal of discarded fish guts.

He and Levi went to work lowering the trolling poles, keeping the ends of the lines in the cockpit. After the fishing line was payed through a clothespin, they attached the heavy lead weight known as a cannonball. Next, they lowered the lightest leads, the twenty-five-pounders on the main lines, and then snapped on the leaders containing spoons and bait. After the light leads were out, they followed with the fifty-pounders.

With the tag lines set, they settled near the main hatch to wait for the telltale jerk on the poles that indicated a catch. Condensation pearled along the bulwark. A flock of migrating geese split the sky, their honking reverberating across the quiet morning. A sharp breeze sent a chill through their slickers and caused the spring lines to vibrate and hum. As the troller moved ever westward through low fog that shrouded the water, they appeared to be flying. Levi grinned as he tapped out a cigarette. "This is the life, eh brother?"

Micah tried to push this memory aside as he dipped a hand into the warm water of Hiroshima Bay. He wished Levi was there so he had someone to talk with. He wanted to go home and bask in the splendor of a sunrise over the Cascades, swim in the frigid water of Lake Whatcom, roam the streets of downtown Bellingham, and most of all, see his father once again. Micah sighed as he stared at the serene bay. "This is some life, Levi. We're both dead. God knows where you are. As for me, well, what can I say? This is what I get for wanting to see Japan after the war. I'm seeing plenty of Japan now."

Chapter Nine

Micah spent the afternoon exploring Hiroshima with the goal of gathering data on the Japs' military strength. He reasoned Bomber Command hadn't ordered an attack on the city due to a lack of intelligence. If he could pinpoint the location of enemy strongholds and get this intelligence to the planners on Saipan they might take action. He paused in the middle of the Aioi Bridge and stared out over the Motoyasu River. A day earlier he had targeted the bridge, now he moved through the world like a breeze.

He meandered along the top of the river embankment, hands in his pockets. Each river in the city had a stone embankment built along the riverbed. Stairwells allowed access to the river below. Black and grey clouds sweeping in from the mountains threatened rain. Across the river, shadows crept over the dome of the Industrial Promotion Hall. Men wearing Western-style suits went in and out of the building.

Micah made his way to the riverbed. An old woman brought a young girl onto the sand. At the bridge, the woman stooped over and plucked grass from the sand which she placed inside a basket. Micah recalled roaming the shore of Bellingham Bay with his grandmother, Molly, turning jagged rocks that sliced their fingertips in order to capture tiny crabs. Micah turned to leave and a voice called out, "Hey you!"

A Japanese man wearing a white long-sleeve button-down shirt and khaki trousers stood on the deck of a fishing boat anchored at a nearby pier. He appeared to be staring straight at him. Micah started toward the stairs when the man shouted again.

"Hey you, American. Come over here and join us."

Micah faced the boat. "You can see me?"

The man smiled. "Of course."

A sharp pain splintered across Micah's forehead as he made his way to the boat. The idea of being alone made him melancholy. The idea of being with others in this place left him unnerved.

A second Japanese man sat on a barrel holding a brown bottle. Both men appeared to be in their late twenties or early thirties. The one who called to him had short hair, combed and parted. Black-framed glasses perched at the end of his nose. Behind the lenses, dark eyes projected confidence. He resembled an academic, his skin fair, and hands unscarred. The sitting man wore a sleeveless undershirt and shorts. Dark curly hairs covered his wide sloping shoulders. The greasy hair on his oversized head dangled like ivy vines. He possessed the belly of a sumo wrestler and skin the hue of an acorn. His bear-paw hands bore numerous scars on the knuckles. A strange bluish glow surrounded both men.

Micah climbed onto the boat. The sampan rocked and creaked as the river lapped against the wooden hull. A single sail nestled against the mast set atop a small structure in the center of the craft that resembled a child's playhouse.

The standing man extended his hand. "Frank Natsume. Pleased to meet you." He gave a sideways nod toward his shipmate. "This lug is Oda Baba."

Oda raised the bottle. "Welcome aboard, American."

Micah shook Frank's hand, surprised to find it warm and Frank's grip strong. "Micah Lund."

Frank folded his arms over his chest. "We watched your plane go down. I'm sorry about your friends."

"It's war," Oda said. "People die in wars." He belched.

"Don't mind, Oda. He was born rude." Frank pointed to one of the barrels. "Take a seat."

Micah lowered onto the barrel. Downriver, the old woman and child vanished into the darkness under the bridge. A streetcar rattled across the top. He cleared his throat. "How can—"

"We see you?"

Micah nodded.

"Because, like you, we're dead."

"Oh."

"Did you believe you're the only one in your condition?"

"I hadn't given it much thought." On the opposite side of the river, a group of small white birds pecked at the sand. "Why do I feel alive?"

"You have much to learn," Frank said.

"So, so much," Oda added before taking a swig from his bottle.

"Did my crewmates die in the crash?"

"How many men are on a B-29?"

"Eleven."

"I counted ten *Hitodama*."

"*Hitodama?*"

Oda ran a hand over the stubble on his chin. "He doesn't know what a *Hitodama* is."

Frank straightened. "Of course. How foolish of me. When a person dies, their soul exits the body in the shape of a bluish ball of light we call a *Hitodama*. The souls of your crewmates flew off in the direction of the sea. I'm assuming toward a final resting place. If they had been Japanese Buddhist they'd have traveled north to Mount Osore on the Shimokita Peninsula."

Micah's left eyebrow went up. "Mount Osore? What's that?"

"You keep forgetting he's not Japanese," Oda said.

"Yes. So sorry. Mount Osore is a volcano. According to some Buddhists, the soul travels to Mount Osore where it enters the Pure Land through the crater."

"And the Pure Land is?"

"What Christians would call Heaven?"

Gulls hovered near the mast of a nearby boat, their cries rising over the tranquil river. Watching them, Micah thought about Bellingham: the family home overlooking the bay, paper mills and factories on the shoreline belching smoke into the grey sky, the scent of pine carried on an autumn breeze, eating a peppermint cone at Moody's Ice Cream Shop as Levi flirted with pretty girls.

"Where are we? This isn't Heaven."

"Hiroshima."

"Why are we stuck here?"

"I'm too much of a sinner to go anyplace else," Oda replied.

Frank stood. He gripped the gunwale and surveyed the river. "I died in November of Forty-Three from typhoid fever."

"My wife killed me," Oda said.

"You were murdered?"

"Tell him the truth, Oda-san."

Oda shrugged. "What's the truth?"

"Oda's wife caught him in bed with her sister. She ran into the kitchen for a knife and chased him around the house. Oda's heart couldn't take the strain."

"I was doing her sister a favor. No man wanted her."

"And look what that got you?"

Oda hugged the bottle against his chest. "At least I have my sake."

"When did you die, Oda?" Micah asked.

"Long time ago. Before the war."

The sudden realization he could be stuck here forever sent a wave of panic through Micah.

"Where are you from, Micah?"

"Bellingham."

Frank sat up straight. "Bellingham ... Washington?"

"You know the place?"

"Why sure. I was born and raised in Seattle. Ever hear of JapanTown?"

"You're an American?"

"As American as Babe Ruth." Frank smiled.

Micah found himself liking Frank more and more. At last, someone he could talk to. "Are more Americans here?"

"You mean Japanese-Americans?"

Micah shrugged.

"Thousands of us."

"You don't say? Did they migrate here after Pearl Harbor?"

Frank struggled to suppress a smile.

"What's so funny?"

"You talk as if we're enemies of the United States. We're loyal Americans. We traveled to Hiroshima for various reasons; visiting relatives, going to school, and so forth, and got trapped here once the fighting broke out."

Micah worked this information over. The Japanese citizens in Bellingham declared they were loyal Americans right before they were shipped off to camps. He didn't believe them, but hearing the same words from Frank seemed different. "My father drove me and my brother to Seattle to watch the Rainiers at Sick's Field. After the game, he took us to a restaurant in JapanTown, said they had the best soba noodle bowl."

"Do you recall the name of the restaurant?"

"I can picture the restaurant. Cramped. Smelled spicy. Man … something."

"Maneki?"

"Yeah, that's it."

Frank beamed. "I used to eat there all the time."

Oda rocked onto his thighs. "I am Japanese from Japan. A real Japanese man, not some foreign transplant."

Frank rolled his eyes. "Here we go."

"What's your story, Oda?" Micah asked.

"My story?"

"Where are you from? I mean, other than Japan."

"You want to know about me?" Oda's eyes drew down.

"Sure. Why not?"

Oda hawked up phlegm and spat into the river. A line of spittle trailed from his bottom lip. "Don't know why the dead need to spit. Don't know why the dead need to do a lot of things we do. Some trick God played on us. The priests promised more than this."

Micah leaned back on the barrel. "Priests?"

"Oda was raised a Christian."

"And look at me now. Jesus doesn't visit me. He doesn't drink with me. If a priest were here, he would drink with me." Oda took another gulp of sake.

"You were going to tell me your history," Micah reminded him.

"Was I?" Oda lowered the bottle. "Why should I tell you anything, American? You were dropping bombs on me."

"Bombs? No. We weren't dropping bombs. Those were leaflets."

"What's a leaflet?"

"You know, papers."

"Why drop papers?"

"To warn the people of Hiroshima to leave before we returned and dropped the bombs."

Oda grunted. "Why would you do that? Don't you want to kill people?"

Micah let out a breath. "I used to think so."

"You are confused, Micah-san." Oda smacked his lips and settled back on the barrel. "So, you want to know about me? Fine. I was born on the island of Seijima. White beaches. Pine trees. A tiny village consisting of four buildings. My father fished. His father fished. I fished." He took another drink, his eyes moist as he escaped into memory.

"When I was young, I'd go out on my father's boat with my friends. We caught octopus.

To catch an octopus, you look into the water and see Mr. Octopus asleep or in front of his cave. Then you lower a pole with a red flag on it."

"To make the octopus mad?"

"No. Octopuses are gentle. You put down the red flag because octopuses love the color red. Mr. Octopus loves it so much, he hugs that flag and won't let go. If we caught a big one, we'd bring it into the boat, then take turns putting Mr. Octopus on our backs like a knapsack. He'd wrap his tentacles around us and we'd dive into the sea."

"Didn't the octopus attempt to escape?"

"Oh no. Once they grab onto something, they don't let go. Mr. Octopus would then start swimming, shooting water out behind him while attached to our backs. Imagine having your own personal motor. The octopus swam fast but we could guide him back to the boat. If Mr. Octopus frightened, he'd release his ink and we'd surface as black as an African. We played all day, taking turns, our backs spotted from the suction cups. When we finished, we carved up Mr. Octopus and ate him. Those were fine days."

"I'm sure the octopus had a great time," Micah said.

"We never hurt turtles. Turtles represent long life. If we caught a turtle in our nets, we carefully removed him, then gave the turtle sake to drink. We released the turtle after he drank, and that happy old turtle dove under the water then resurfaced to bow to us."

"Oh, Oda-san," Frank said with a groan.

"It's true," Oda insisted. "You would not understand because you are not a real Japanese."

"A real Japanese? Both of my parents are Japanese, as were their parents."

"They are real Japanese. They were born in Japan. You were not."

Frank rolled his eyes.

"If you died on the island, how did you end up in Hiroshima?" Micah asked.

Oda scratched his big belly. "After I died, I stayed at home, but living with my wife proved impossible. The smell of her cooking. Terrible. The strange men she made love to. Disgusting. So, I hitched a ride with a shrimper to Hiroshima."

An idea came to Micah and he pushed off the barrel. "When the war ends, I can catch a ride back home." He turned to Frank. "We can go together. Back to Washington State."

Frank's eyebrows twitched as he thought. "It would be nice to return to Seattle and see my family, even if they couldn't see me." His face darkened. "Are the rumors true?"

"What rumors?"

"That all the Japanese-Americans were rounded up and placed in camps."

Micah's gaze sank to the deck. "It's true. The government gave them one week to sell their possessions, then took them into custody."

"And you supported that?"

"Hell, we all wanted the Nips gone after Pearl Harbor. Everyone hated them. Everyone still hates them."

"Nips. Japs. You toss around those words rather casually. A man's skin reveals nothing of the man beneath it."

"Don't forget what happened at Bataan," Micah said.

"What happened at Bataan?"

"After we surrendered, the Japs murdered thousands of American and Filipino prisoners. They've been doing that crap across the Pacific. I heard they slaughtered thousands of Filipinos before Manila fell. Men, women, and children, made no difference to them."

Frank studied the river, a wounded expression on his face. "War is a terrible endeavor. Japan was foolish to start one against a country with greater resources. And if what you say is true, then I suppose they deserve what's coming to them. It's karma. But it wasn't old people or women and children who committed those atrocities. Some actions cannot be justified, and in the end, I fear we've lost all hope of salvation."

"You reap what you sow," Oda said.

"Do you want to see Hiroshima destroyed?" Frank asked.

Oda held up the bottle and peered into the amber colored glass. "Magic bottle in my hand, tell me the fate of my Japan." He waited a few seconds and brought the bottle down. "The bottle says it's for drinking, not for fortune-telling."

Micah smiled.

Frank removed his glasses and tapped a temple tip against his bottom lip. "When it comes to judging people in this war, you must use your heart and not your head." He put his glasses back on. "Tell me, Micah, are Japanese-Americans still held in camps?"

"No," Micah said. "The government released them. They even formed a unit of Japanese soldiers who are fighting the Germans."

"So, if I return, I'll find my family in Seattle?"

"Political groups in Washington State prevented the Japanese-Americans from returning to their old neighborhoods. The last I heard, none of the Japs ... uh, Japanese ... returned to Seattle."

"I would expect as much," Frank said. "Even before the war, when I applied for a teaching position at Seattle College, the administration never took me seriously because of my race."

"You wanted to teach? Me too. I graduated from Western College with a degree in education."

Frank smiled at this. "So, Micah, what have you been doing with yourself since your arrival?"

Behind Frank, a young boy led an elderly man down the stone steps to the riverbed. The boy knelt and placed a toy boat with a white sail on the water, then waved as the current pulled it toward the sea.

"I explored the city today. I'm still not accustomed to being dead."

"You worry someone will see you?"

"Silly, I know."

"Actually," Frank said, "You can be seen."

"Are you serious?"

"Other spirits can see you, of course, but so can the living under certain circumstances. You might appear to a powerful psychic. People less gifted will see you as a shadow, or experience you as a cold breeze."

Micah remembered the woman's behavior in the bathing room. Did she sense his presence?

"But no worries," Frank continued. "If the spirit of a Japanese person sees you, they won't be alarmed. They'll recognize you're dead and consequently, of no threat to them."

"Are there many spirits in the city?"

"I wish my wife's spirit was here. I would make her miserable." Oda yawned and stretched.

Frank's tongue clicked on the roof of his mouth. "Now, Oda-san, you know your wife isn't dead."

"I could make her dead," Oda said.

"If we ever leave this realm, you're going straight to hell."

"I've been there. It's called marriage."

Frank looked back at Micah. "To answer your question, yes, there are spirits here, but the majority do not remain when they die." Frank reached out a hand. "Pass me that sake, Oda." Frank took a long pull, then held the bottle out to Micah. "Go on. It won't kill you."

"You're a funny guy," Micah said, taking the bottle. He swallowed three gulps, the rice wine burning as it raced down his throat. "Not bad." He offered the bottle to Oda, who accepted it with a grateful smile. "If we want something, like food or a drink, all we need to do is imagine whatever we want and it appears?"

"We don't need food or water to survive, of course, so I can't tell you what purpose they serve. Perhaps to ease our transition into the afterlife."

"If I think of Ingrid Bergman, she will appear to me?"

"Old girlfriend?"

"You don't know who Ingrid Bergman is? She happens to be one of the most popular actresses going."

Frank shrugged. "I don't believe it works the same way with people. Especially the living."

"Just as well. I couldn't do anything if she did appear."

Oda pointed the bottle at Frank, sake sloshing onto the deck. "Tell him, Frank."

Frank tapped a finger against his lips.

"Tell me what?"

"It's possible," Frank said, "for a spirit to have sexual relations with another spirit. From time to time, I go and visit Ikumi, a former geisha from Kio."

This revelation set Micah's mind in motion. The idea of spirits engaging in sex went against everything he'd been taught in church.

"He's taking the news well," Oda said, with a grin. "But you would need to find yourself a Japanese girl, Micah-san. Not many white ladies die around here."

"Can we have relationships with the living?"

Frank's right eyebrow arched over his glasses. "A sexual relationship?"

Micah waved a hand before him. "No. No. Not that. I mean, is there a way we can communicate with the living? To get to know them?"

"Did you have someone in mind?"

Micah pictured the woman he had followed home. "No. I was just curious."

"I too would be curious about such things," Oda said.

Frank thrust his chin toward Micah. "You were going to tell us what you saw on your expedition through the city."

Micah struggled to purge the image of the woman from his mind. Teeth clenched, he willed himself to forget her. "The Tōyō Kōgyō factory."

"What else did you see?"

"A large build-up of troops. I noted the location of their bases and their anti-aircraft batteries."

"You explored the city to discover the location of the Japanese military? What are you going to do with this information?"

Micah hesitated to say more, then remembered Frank was an American. "If I get this intelligence to HQ on Saipan, they could use it to plan their attack."

"Their attack? As in, bomb Hiroshima?"

"There must be a reason we haven't hit Hiroshima. Maybe they don't have the intelligence they need."

"And how will you get this back to Saipan?" Frank asked. "You are, after all, quite dead."

The boat creaked as the river slipped past. On the far bank, the boy and old man reached the top of the stairs. Overhead, the swirling clouds took on an ominous character. Micah couldn't look Frank in the eye. He felt moronic for having proposed he could relay intelligence back to headquarters. Frank must have sensed his discomfort because he added, "I'm not ridiculing your intention, but do question your motive. The war's over for you, Micah."

Micah thought of Levi meeting his end on Guadalcanal. How did he experience the afterlife? Did he float through the jungles without a purpose, a mere shadow carrying the gelidity of the grave? No. It wasn't like that for his brother. He traveled beyond this realm, into the embrace of a loving God. Levi deserved Heaven.

Frank rested a hand on Micah's shoulder. "Come. Let me show you another side of the city. The side you failed to notice."

Chapter Ten

Frank led him off the boat and into the city. With Frank as his guide, Micah's irrational fear of the living Japanese disappeared. He breezed past a group of soldiers standing outside a building smoking cigarettes as if they were old friends of his. Yellow haze continued to rise like factory smoke in the direction of the harbor, but Micah didn't see any smokestacks. He drew abreast of Frank and gestured at a wooden house. "They wouldn't burn so easily if constructed from stone or brick."

Frank smiled. "True. But in Japan, they have many earthquakes. A wooden house can be rebuilt in days."

"Not after the B-29s get done with them."

Frank's smile went away, replaced by a look of sad resignation. "I'll bet you wouldn't feel that way if we were talking about Bellingham."

Micah remained quiet. What Frank wouldn't understand was the aching in the breast of Americans after Pearl Harbor, when their hearts were torn out and crushed by Japan's treachery. Frank had been away from Seattle too long.

Frank pointed to a pile of red and white balls stacked outside a house. "You see those? They're filled with sand. When the bombers come, people are supposed to put out fires by throwing them at the flames. And those cement cisterns filled with water? For bucket brigades. But everyone knows these things won't be effective against the power of incendiary bombs. How many people died in the first raid on Tokyo? Ninety thousand? If the B-29s come to Hiroshima, it will be the death of this place."

Frank led him onto a bridge. He walked to the center and stopped. Micah recognized it as the Motoyasu Bridge from surveillance photos. The Motoyasu River slipped past, the surface of the water placid in the dusky evening. Thunder rolled through the clouds. Lightning flashed over blue hills. A feathering rain began to fall. Cool, but refreshing. "It's strange how we can feel things like rain," Micah said, joining Frank at the guardrail.

"The dead experience the same things as the living. Even pain."

"We can feel pain?"

"Touch a flame and you'll feel its heat, but the sensation quickly dissipates. And you won't die here, Micah. Dunk your head in the river an hour and see what happens."

The grey sky threatened to overwhelm the city, but to the northwest, a hint of white light dared to rise on the horizon.

"When I visited Hiroshima as a boy, we swam in the river when summer arrived. We'd take turns jumping off the bridge to impress girls."

"Did it work?"

Frank grinned. "No." He pointed to the far shore where the incoming tide consumed the sandy riverbed. "At low tide, we played baseball on the riverbed. The other boys chided me for saying the New York Yankees were the best team in the world."

"Well, it's true. I mean, come on, Ruth, Gehrig, DiMaggio. Who's better than that?"

"In their eyes, the Hiroshima Carp."

Micah imagined Frank playing baseball on the riverbed. He could almost hear the smack of the ball into leather, and the crack of the bat as a hit sailed into the sky.

A woman emerged from the grey mist in a solid black kimono, swaying from side to side as if blown by the wind. She held something in her hands, and tears ran in crystal runnels down her cheeks.

A sense of unease overcame Micah as she stepped onto the bridge, and he could tell Frank felt the same way from his hard gaze and flexing jaw. He leaned toward Frank. "Who is she?"

"I don't know. But she's wearing a funeral kimono."

The woman, who appeared to be in her mid-twenties, drew alongside Frank and pressed against the railing. She had concaved cheeks, hollowed eyes, and pallid skin. She raised trembling hands to her lips and murmured something in a quaking voice. The woman opened her palms and tiny pieces of paper fluttered out, floating to the river below.

"What's she doing?" Micah asked.

"Praying on behalf of her dead child. Those papers she's dropping either bear a picture of *Jizō*, a Buddhist bodhisattva who protects children, or an inscription that says, 'For the sake of ...' with the soul name the Buddhist priest has given her child."

"What does she keep saying?"

"*Namu Jizō, Dai Bosatsu.* It means, 'Do not miss it.' You see, she believes the water flows down to the shadow world and through the Sai-no-Kawara, where *Jizō* is. If *Jizō* finds her papers, he will keep her child safe."

The woman finished releasing the papers. She remained a while, her gaze fixed on the river, then shambled away, fading into the gloom.

"I wonder what killed her child."

"It's the war. People are starving and there's much sickness. A million pieces of paper could float to *Jizō* and it still won't save them." Frank's expression took on a new resolve. "Let's go. We have much to see."

They crossed the bridge and entered a neighborhood Frank called, Sarugakucho-Saiku-Machi. The farther they ventured, the more familiar the surrounding area appeared to Micah. "I've been on this road. I traveled on it yesterday in a streetcar."

"It's one of the main roads in the city. You probably noticed the Division Commander's Quarters while you were out scouting."

Fat raindrops pattered the sidewalk. On the road, a slow current of men, women, and children traveled through the downpour in wagons, carts, and on bicycles. Their faces were grim masks. Their dark eyes lifeless with despair.

"Are they evacuees?" Micah asked.

"Your leaflets have been effective. Of course, for every person who flees, more refugees flood into Hiroshima from cities destroyed by fire. The evacuees might find peace in the countryside, but not food. A person can starve at the edge of a bountiful sea, or in the middle of a rice field." Frank pointed to a long line of people outside a building. "They wait to get food, hoping the government will save them. What is one life worth to a government responsible for the deaths of millions?"

Frank led him to Hiroshima Castle. The ancient structure stood among groves of bamboo and dwarf pines. The castle, built in shades of white, black, and grey, stared down on the city. Raindrops dappled the green water of the moat. An old man sat at the edge of the moat with his legs dangling over the side. He used a pole with a crooked nail attached to a string to snag frogs. His mouth cracked into a wide smile with each frog he captured.

"When you see the castle, you see a military command center. I see history."

Micah stared up at the castle. "It reminds me of a temple."

"Does Bellingham have any buildings this magnificent?"

"No. Nothing like this."

"The castle is over three hundred years old. I'd hate to see it destroyed by bombs."

Two green-headed ducks swam past water-lilies floating on the surface of the moat. The frogs croaked as the old man shoved one into a quivering canvas bag.

The rain slowed to a drizzle as they joined a throng of pedestrians. Women hid from the rain beneath brightly colored paper umbrellas. Power lines crisscrossing over the street produced a soft hum. A streetcar rattled past. The rain brought out the earthy scent of nearby hills. If not for the appearance of the people, Micah could be in downtown Bellingham. He'd never given much thought to the civilians who suffered during incendiary raids. No one in the squadron did. To humanize the victims would raise the question of morality, and yet, it was their sense of morality, and superiority, which made them hate the Japanese. The Japanese weren't decent, God-fearing people, they were cold-hearted killers, primeval beasts who stalked the darkness, waiting for an opportunity to taste blood. But as Micah walked among them, he didn't see beasts.

Levi never hated the Japanese. Even after Pearl Harbor, his attitude was, "Let's get this over with," more than, "let's kill those Nip bastards." In high school, Levi had a crush on a Japanese girl named June Tomoda. "So what if she's Japanese," Levi said. "A pretty gal is a pretty gal. I'll bet her lips are as sweet as the lips of any white girl. Don't close yourself off to possibilities, Micah. Taste what the world has to offer."

You kept your mind open while they closed your eyes forever. What am I to think, brother? Accept that I'm stranded amongst our enemies, like the missionaries of old who came to save these people? You always had the answers. Where are you now when I have so many questions?

The dark clouds drifted eastward, taking the rain with them, and the sun dipped toward shadowed hills, casting a sheen over the damp streets. As they walked, Frank explained the eccentricities of Japanese culture.

"The Japanese have a structured society with many rules. You may have noticed how they bow when greeting each other. They must know to whom one bows and how much one bows. And they do not show expressions of regret, disappointment, or embarrassment. They smile to hide their true feelings. Things they pronounce publicly are known as *Tatemae*. Things connected with the heart and senses which are hidden are called *Honne*. Most of their elementary school years are spent learning how to be a good citizen and take one's proper station."

"Christ almighty, how do you get to know these people when they hide what they're thinking?"

"It's not easy. Especially with the women. They will talk to each other, but keep quiet whenever a man is around. And if a Japanese woman does talk with you, they don't always say what they mean."

"Sounds like women back in the States."

"Yes, some of them. There is a Japanese term that applies to their women, *Ishibotoke mo mono wo iu*. It means, Even a Buddha will say things on occasion."

"Did you follow all these rules back home?"

"Are you kidding? I grew up listening to Dick Tracy and eating hot dogs. I'm more American than Japanese, I just don't look the part."

As they approached the Aioi Bridge, Micah recalled briefings on Saipan. Sometimes the officer in charge would refer to the Japanese as sub-human, vermin, or worse. None of these terms seemed to apply to Frank or the citizens of Hiroshima. *Stop being an idiot*, he told himself. *A lot of good American boys are feeding the worms because of these bastards. But were they all bastards? Did all Japanese hate Americans? Did they all want to see America destroyed?* Micah sensed he already knew the answers which meant he had been lied to by his superiors. A sea of flames rolled over Japanese cities, and he had helped start the fire. What had Oda said? "This is war and people die in wars." Could it be that simple?

"I passed over this bridge yesterday when I followed her home."

Frank shot him a questioning glance. "Who are you talking about?"

Micah hesitated.

The air remained damp and heavy with the smell of rain. Micah jammed his hands inside his pockets. "I stayed in the house of the first person I saw after my death. A woman who works at a factory. She has a daughter in school. They live with a couple. She doesn't get along with the older woman."

"Must be her mother-in-law. A Japanese mother-in-law is notoriously venomous to their son's wife. I'll bet this woman you followed is a war widow. She must live nearby."

Micah remembered the woman praying before the photographs of the two men wearing uniforms. He found himself jealous of the men in the pictures.

"Are you all right, Micah? You look pale."

"How are the dead supposed to look?"

Frank gave a quick shrug. "Like the living I suppose. At least to each other."

"The afterlife is not what I expected."

"Was your life before death what you expected?"

Stars awakened in the evening sky, their fire traveling billions of miles to wash over Hiroshima. A vivid white moon joined the stars, hovering above the harbor. Micah soaked it all in as he considered Frank's question. What kind of life would he have enjoyed if not for the war? A career in teaching? Marriage and children?

"Why do our hearts beat? Why do our lungs breathe air? We're dead to the world, and yet, I feel more alive than ever."

"I can't provide the answers you seek. But this is your life now. Maybe when the war ends you can catch that boat back to America. Or maybe you'll find yourself in new circumstances."

"There must be some purpose for my being here."

"I stopped searching for my purpose long ago. Instead, I live my life as best as I can. If there is to be more, then so be it. But if this is my final destination, I'm prepared to carry on. What else can I do?" Frank waved Micah forward. "We should keep moving. There are things I need to show you."

They entered the Nakajima Honmachi District, which Frank explained was the heart of Hiroshima. "There are many temples, shrines, geisha houses, *Kabuki* and *Noh* theaters, and shops." Night settled over deserted streets and alleys. A rat scurried outside a house. Moths fluttered through the air. "Prior to the Doolittle Raid, lantern light shined on each street. Residents ventured out at night to shop and attend plays and movies. Now Hiroshima is a tomb."

Frank paused outside a temple. "You should have seen the neighborhood when I was boy. I had so much fun here. The *chindon-ya* man settled on a corner to announce a new bill at the theater or cinema house, or to advertise a special sale. He'd play his samisen, bang his drums, and rattle his bells. Not to be outdone, the *kamishibai* beat his wooden clappers to attract children. We'd gather around as he set up his wooden frame on the saddle of his bicycle. He'd open a box and sell candy, then give a paper show."

Frank resumed walking. The enveloping night swallowed his features until all Micah could see was his silhouette and the flicker of white that encompassed his black pupils. An eerie silence amplified the scratching of rats, and bat wings whipping the air. "You used to hear dogs barking but dogs are mute inside a starving stomach."

Their journey ended at a pile of shattered wooden planks, beams, and roof tiles.

"What's this?" Micah asked.

"The government has recruited students to tear down houses and businesses to create firebreaks. Some of these houses belonged to families for hundreds of years. This destruction creates the yellow haze that fills the sky during the day."

"Why doesn't the government surrender before the city is destroyed? The people must grasp that the war is lost?"

Frank bent over and picked up a piece of broken tile. He stared at the tile before tossing it on the rubbish heap. "A lot of Japanese were shocked when the government announced the country had gone to war with America. 'How can we win against a country with superior technology?' they asked. And there wasn't a deep-seated hatred of Americans back then. Many of my Japanese friends loved jazz music and American movies. But the government controls everything through secret police and the press. They hid the truth when Japanese forces lost battles until the mounting death toll could no longer be explained through broadcasts claiming the men died bringing glory to the Emperor. The only ones who believe such nonsense are the young people."

"And that's why the young people tear down the buildings?"

Frank removed his eyeglasses and pinched the bridge of his nose. "Yes. The government exploits their naiveté." His shoulders rose and fell with a deep sigh. "You would think in the afterlife, eyeglasses wouldn't be necessary." He put them back on and faced Micah. "I don't want to see Hiroshima reduced to ashes and I don't want my relatives to die. This is why I needed you to see the city through my eyes. As you said, the war is lost. Why must Hiroshima join the list of incinerated cities? What purpose could that serve? Hasn't there been enough suffering on both sides?"

Micah had seen post-bombing photographs of Tokyo, block after block turned into a barren wasteland. He didn't want Hiroshima to share Tokyo's fate. Frank was right when he said the war had ended for him. He must find whatever peace he could. "Can we leave now?"

They walked without speaking. No light. No sounds. It was as Frank had said, a tomb where people lived as if they had already died. A flaming blue ball streaked northward leaving behind an arched trail.

"Is that a—"

"*Hitodama.* Yes. Someone has died. *Hitodamas* are a regular visitor to the night sky of Hiroshima. Let us pray their numbers decrease in the coming months."

Frank led him to a merchant house. He pointed at the building. "Is this not your home?"

Micah studied the house. Although it resembled the other structures, he was certain the woman waited inside. "How did you know?"

"I just knew," Frank answered. "As you will from now on." In the pale light of the moon, a smile played on Frank's lips. "I would offer to let you stay with us, but something tells me you would decline. I understand. If I were in your shoes, I'd choose to stay with the woman. You're always welcome to visit us."

Micah gestured toward the house. "How can I learn their names?"

"The people you're staying with?"

Micah nodded.

"Listen to their conversations. They use honorifics at the end of their names. I'm, Frank-san, and you, Micah-san."

"Around here, they'd call me bastard-san."

Frank laughed. "Maybe. They use other honorifics as well depending on the situation and person they are speaking with. Chan is added to a child's name. In time, you'll pick up on their language."

"Time is the one thing I have."

Chapter Eleven

A shadow flashed overhead, drawing Kiyomi's attention from the picture Ai was coloring. The spirit had remained inside the house six days. *Why?* And why was she the only person who noticed the apparition? Surely, Banri or Sayoka experienced cold drafts whenever the spirit came around. If Ai was aware of the *Yūrei*, she said nothing. *What must I do about this intruder?*

Kiyomi covered her mouth to yawn. Her empty stomach ached as if a band of goblins had slipped inside and hollowed her out with shovels. Her bones and joints hurt whenever she moved. She accepted this as the price of serving the Emperor. But Ai shouldn't have to go through such torture. Ai never complained, but Kiyomi noticed her wince with hunger pangs. Ai's watery eyes and heavy eyelids struggled to stay open. Every night, air raid sirens blasted like wind whistling through mountain passes. Sometimes they went off during the day. How could they endure this torment? And now a spirit haunted them. What did it want?

Banri groaned as he leaned toward his writing desk, his brush hovering over the paper he worked on. A strange odor wafting from his skin reminded Kiyomi of seaweed drying in the sun. Sayoka knelt on a nearby pillow reading the *Kokin Wakashu*, her bony fingers fanning each page with care.

Banri coughed and blood pressed into his cheeks.

"Are you all right?" Kiyomi asked.

Sayoka glanced up from her book. "He's fine."

"It's the war," Banri said. "We are told to support the Emperor. We are told we'll be victorious. How can you fight without food in your stomach? How can you work? How can you go to school? The neighborhood association is supposed to provide rations. Where are the rations?" He straightened on his pillow, his back creaking like the wooden screen frames swelling in summer heat. "Army officers eat. The police eat. Wealthy merchants in Kio eat. But we must starve. It's not right. And if the radio reports are true, Okinawa will soon be lost. What then?"

Sayoka lowered her book. "You must not talk this way."

Banri's attention shifted to Kiyomi. "I have spoken with Nobu and Rei Takada. They will join us for dinner tomorrow to discuss our plan to adopt a son for you to marry."

Kiyomi's head bowed as his words sank in. She didn't want a new husband. She hadn't wanted her last husband. But what could she do?

"We must have food if we're to have guests," Sayoka said.

Kiyomi did not look up. "Perhaps I can barter something."

Sayoka's left eyebrow arched. "What is left to barter? We've traded most of our kimonos and lacquer goods. We even traded our dining table."

In her mind, Kiyomi pictured her wedding kimono buried at the bottom of the storage trunk. At the black market, the kimono might be worth something. It meant nothing to her.

"When will the association bring food again?" Sayoka asked.

Banri pushed off the floor, his knees joining his spine in a symphony of crackling. He stood doubled over, his chest heaving. He remained in this position until his breathing slowed, then he straightened. "I don't trust, Masa," Banri said. "He's supposed to distribute food equally but gives the Mori family the largest share. He even claims a share for Sora and Tadao."

Sayoka's brow wrinkled. "What? His dead relatives receive food?"

"Our food," Banri said.

Sayoka glared at Kiyomi. "Kiyomi does not work tomorrow. She can go to the food distribution center in the morning. She'll need to leave before sunrise to secure a place near the front of the line. Ai can stay with us."

"And if they have nothing at the distribution center?" Kiyomi asked.

"Then try the black market at the Kio Station. You must have something of value to trade?"

What does she mean by saying that? Is Sayoka implying I would sell my body to acquire food? Never. But if I did, whatever food I brought home would be eaten by me and Ai. The old hag wouldn't taste a bite.

Ai tugged on the sleeve of Kiyomi's kimono. "Mama, can we visit the garden?"

"At night?" Sayoka said. "With the mosquitoes? Crazy."

"Can we, Mama?"

"*Hai.* But only for a short time."

Ai stood and held out her hand. Her tiny warm fingers slipped into Kiyomi's grasp like a key joining a lock. They stole across the tatami mats without a sound and went outside. The sky above them was a canvas of colors, ribbons of violet, amber, blue, and orange intertwined amongst the darkening clouds. Ai grinned. "I want to draw that sky."

"I'm sure you could," Kiyomi said.

They strolled to the courtyard garden. The branches of an old *Yanagi* drooped toward the pond. Her aunt told her a *Yanagi* possessed the power of haunting. If the branches were cut, blood flowed from the gash. The pond appeared black and lifeless, but a multitude of sounds arose from the surrounding plants: croaking frogs, chirping crickets, the stirring of willow leaves in the soft spring breeze.

"When I was a girl, we had a pond in our yard, but much larger than this one with turtles, lizards, and a blue snake."

Ai's grip tightened on her hand. "Are they going to make you get married?"

"A family must have an heir. If I can help—"

"It's not fair!" Ai said and jerked her hand away.

Kiyomi stared at her empty hand. The sudden loss of Ai's touch felt as if they'd been torn apart forever. Did Ai believe she was betrayed? Did she feel jealous at the thought of her mother sharing her affection with someone new?

"What if you don't love this man? What if you give him a son and the boy is a monster?"

"I cannot see into the future," Kiyomi said.

A tear glistened upon Ai's cheek. "What if you love him more than you love me?"

Kiyomi slipped an arm around Ai's waist and drew her close. "I'll never put anyone ahead of you."

"I'm scared, Mama. I still have bad dreams. I asked *Baku* to eat them, but his stomach must be full." Ai focused on Kiyomi's eyes. "Are we all going to die?"

"We all die eventually."

"I mean in the war?"

"That's not going to happen. I will not lose you."

Ai pressed her cheek against Kiyomi's shoulder. "I want to go with you tomorrow."

"To the distribution center?"

"*Hai.*"

"You heard what your *Baa-baa* said. I must leave while it's still dark outside."

"Please take me."

"I must travel a long way."

"My legs are most capable for such a journey."

Kiyomi smiled. "*Hai.* I do believe they are." She glanced over her shoulder at the house. "Your *Baa-baa* and *Ojiisan* will be angry."

"*Baa-baa* is always angry with you."

A soft chuckle escaped Kiyomi's throat. "She has a most unpleasant nature."

"Please, Mama. Please take me with you."

Kiyomi closed her eyes and listened to Ai breathing. "Of course you can come with me. I still have some control over my life."

Chapter Twelve

When the mournful wailing of the air raid sirens ended, Kiyomi awakened Ai. Eyes half-closed, she dutifully followed her mother out of the kitchen hole. Banri and Sayoka stirred but remained asleep. Kiyomi brought Ai to their futons and helped her settle beneath the heavy blankets. They needed to leave soon, but for now, she'd allow Ai to sleep, only not in the hole. No. They had spent a lifetime in the dirt, living like moles afraid of sunlight. Kiyomi laid beside her and stroked her daughter's sunken cheek. Ai needed food. She was starving before her eyes. Mosquito netting enclosed the room in white walls. Kiyomi wished she could walk past these walls and enter a place where there was no war, no hatred, and no hunger. A place where cherry blossoms never fell from the branch.

The mosquito netting rippled and a chill brushed across her face. *The ghost has returned.* As determined as she was to remove the presence from their lives, she found it oddly comforting to have the spirit close by in the darkness, as if it were an ancestor watching over them.

Kiyomi closed her eyes. Her thoughts veered from the *Yūrei* to her arranged marriage. What kind of man could the matchmakers find for her to marry? A hunchback? A beast with fangs and claws? She smiled as absurd images played through her mind, but her smile turned upside down at the notion of becoming chained to this man. She used to envision returning to

Tokyo with Ai when the war ended. She imagined them living with her aunt and uncle until finding a place of their own. After finishing college, she would start a new career. And if the right man happened along, someone who could love Ai as his daughter, she might marry. Those fantasies died in the fires of the American bombs. She had no family. No home to return to. Only ashes and tears. Her future, it seemed, was in Hiroshima.

Kiyomi snuggled against Ai who snored, her lips fluttering. She traced a finger over Ai's eyebrows, tiny hairs bristling at her invasion. She remembered seeing her daughter for the first time at the hospital in Tokyo. In the days leading up to the delivery, fear ruled her heart. Was she prepared to be a single mother? The shame of her pregnancy and abandonment continued to sting. She came to doubt her ability to ever move beyond the social stigma placed upon her. Her aunt offered comforting words meant to ease her anguish. Nothing worked. Kiyomi fought her labor as if she could hold back the delivery by the force of her will. She might as well have been trying to turn back the sea.

When the nurse brought Ai into her room, and she viewed her tiny face cocooned in a pink blanket, Kiyomi's resistance shattered. Overcome with joy, she felt selfish for having contemplated suicide. Ai deserved all the happiness she could find. Bonded by a dark history, they must work to climb into the light.

The night passed slowly with the mosquito netting dancing all around her. Heat and humidity impregnated the air. When the swallows chirped inside their nest, Kiyomi knew it was time to leave. She shook Ai's shoulder until her tired eyes opened. "Are we going now, Mama?"

"*Hai.* We must be quiet and not wake your grandparents."

"I will be a butterfly and float out of the house."

"That's a good plan, little butterfly."

Ai stood. Kiyomi brushed a hand down her daughter's side, sharp rib bones rippling the flesh on her palm. Anger and frustration threatened to crush Kiyomi's spirit. If Sayoka were awake, she would say it could not be helped and Kiyomi should accept things as they are. *Stupid woman.*

Kiyomi helped Ai into her *monpe* and a clean shirt. A tiny smile fluttered at the corners of Ai's mouth.

"This is an adventure for us," Ai whispered.

Kiyomi dressed herself, then gathered a wicker basket. "Are you ready?"

"I'm ready."

They slipped out of the house, pausing to collect their *geta* at the *doma*. The city slept beneath shimmering stars, a half-moon reflected in puddles. A breeze carried the lingering scent of the rain. Their *geta* tapped on the road, the sound echoing far into the darkness.

"Later, will you help me make a *Teru-teru bozu?*"

It pleased her that Ai wanted to make a sunshine doll. They had always made one together before the rainy season set in. This once, not even the trials of war could triumph over the innocence of youth. "We'll hang it from the tree in the garden."

"*Hai.* And I'll chant for fair weather."

Kiyomi squeezed her hand. "Remind me when we get back home."

A side gate creaked open and a man wearing all black emerged from a yard carrying a bulging *furoshiki* sack. He paused upon seeing them and touched a finger to his lips. *A burglar.* The war had turned Japan into a country of thieves. He was a young man, perhaps in high school. Shame marked his face before he turned and vanished into the darkness.

"He scared me, Mama."

"He won't hurt us. He is a coward. What he does is bad, *neh*?"

"*Hai.*"

Bats darted through the shifting light in pursuit of moths and mosquitoes. Frogs croaked along the riverbed. To the east, a thread of orange stitched sea and sky. A dull ache traveled through Kiyomi as if a fox nibbled on her bones. The lack of adequate food steered her toward an early grave. She could accept this for herself, but not Ai. *I must find her more food. If Sayoka's house falls into disarray, if her futons rot with the spring rain, so be it. Ai will not die.*

They ventured onto the Motoyasu Bridge, mist steaming from the damp pavement. Kiyomi stopped at the midpoint and turned to Ai. "We should eat, *neh*?"

"My stomach is most eager to have food."

Kiyomi reached into the basket and produced two rice balls. "I'm sorry I have nothing better to offer."

"At least we have something," Ai said as she peeled seaweed off the rice ball. "When the war ends, we'll have better food."

"*Hai*. Remember the red bean, rice, and pumpkin squash we had for New Years a few years ago?"

Ai licked a grain of rice from her upper lip. "I missed not having *shiohi-gari*."

Kiyomi's guilt intensified at the idea of Ai sitting at home while her friends went with their families on the annual low tide gathering of shellfish. Why couldn't she have gotten off work? *Damn this war.* "We'll go next year. I promise."

Ai stared at her geta. "I shouldn't have complained."

The new day arrived, the waking sun stretching across the river turning the surface golden. Water slapped against oyster boats, their slender masts groaning. A tern glided out from beneath the bridge, cutting a wake through the polished water. Kiyomi closed her eyes and breathed in the morning smells of Hiroshima. The crisp scent of the river, a hint of salt drifting in from the sea, and the bitter fetor wafting from streets where torn-down buildings lay shattered. How much longer could the war go on? How could Japan win? Did she even care about victory anymore when the struggle to survive was punctuated by moments of intense hunger? Their bodies wilted like dying flowers. How much longer must she lie to her child with the promise that things were going to get better? The war made liars of them all.

She opened her eyes. Ai continued to stare at her *geta*. "You need not apologize. I too missed sharing *shiohi-gari* with you."

"What is this, Mama?" Ai retrieved two slips of paper pasted to the bridge railing by the rain. She straightened and held out her hand.

Kiyomi's heart filled with anguish as she read what was written on the papers. She pictured the woman who brought the offering, face drawn and pallid, eyes glassy with rising tears, kimono as black as the void that filled her soul. The woman's pain became her own as Kiyomi studied Ai and worried that one day she could be the one standing at the edge of the world, tiny papers of hope slipping from her grasp. Kiyomi forced a smile. "I'm not sure what these papers are. Perhaps we should let them fall into the river."

"You drop the papers, Mama."

Kiyomi chewed the inside of her lip as she contemplated the task ahead of her. *I don't want to do this,* she thought, all the while knowing it was proper that a mother complete the task for another mother. *I should be honored. These papers might be the key to keeping her child safe in the Sai-no-Kawara.* Kiyomi leaned over the bridge railing and opened her hand, the tiny papers fluttering off her palm toward the river below. "We should finish eating."

Horse hooves clopped on the road, accompanied by the creaking of wood, and the thud of something heavy. Dozens of people emerged from the darkness. Stick figures with vacant eyes, despair and fatigue weighing on their faces. Some rode in horse-drawn carts. Most walked. Kiyomi brought her rice ball down to her side. Ai followed her lead. She leaned close to whisper. "Are they evacuees, Mama?"

"*Hai.* They are fleeing into the countryside."

"To escape Mr. B?"

Kiyomi rested a hand on Ai's shoulder. "And to find food."

"I hope the Emperor is able to find food."

Tears welled in Kiyomi's eyes. *If only the world could be as innocent as its children.*

The procession passed in silence, their heads hung low. When the last of the evacuees cleared the bridge, Kiyomi said. "We must hurry and finish eating."

Ai held out her rice ball. "May I save the rest until later?"

"*Hai.*" Kiyomi took the rice ball and returned it to the basket. It saddened her to know the rice balls were all she could offer her daughter. Ai took hold of her hand and they set off. The sun climbed higher and around them, a blanket of grey settled over the tranquil city. A group of young people uniformed in black shirts and pants approached from the far side of the bridge. The boys shouldered axes or carried hammers. They marched with heads held high. Students on their way to tear down buildings and clear the road to create firebreaks. They still believed in victory. And why shouldn't they, when the alternative offered a future as bleak as the retreating night? What was to become of Japan if they lost the war? Would the Americans destroy every reminder of their heritage? Every temple. Every castle. Would they castrate Japanese males to eradicate the Japanese race from the world? Some of Ai's teachers taught that American's ran over captured Japanese with tanks, or mailed home the skulls of dead Japanese soldiers' as souvenirs. Kiyomi had her doubts. The Americans she knew before the war didn't strike her as barbaric. Still, if Japan were to lose the war, the Japan of old would cease to exist.

Kiyomi pulled Ai against the bridge railing to let the students pass.

Umi emerged from the crowd with a broad smile. "Kiyomi-san, is that you?"

"Good morning, Umi-san. Where are you headed?"

"Clearing rubble from Kawauchi-mura."

"I didn't know you worked with the Student Corps."

"There is much to be done if we're to be victorious, *neh?* Did you hear we might be moved into the factory?"

"All the workers?"

"The students. Mothers are to remain at home with their children." Umi turned to Ai. "You must be proud of your mama, working to help the Emperor?"

Ai nodded.

"Where are you heading at this hour?" Umi asked.

"Food distribution center," Kiyomi answered.

"Must have food in our bellies if we are to work, *neh?*" The students approached the far side of the bridge. "I better hurry and catch them. Sayōnara, Kiyomi-san. Sayonara, Ai-chan." Umi joined the other students.

"She is funny," Ai said.

"Oh. In what way?"

"She smiles all the time."

"Since when is a smile a bad thing?"

Ai bowed. "Please forgive me if I've offended you."

"There's nothing to forgive."

Surrounding buildings took shape as shadows retreated. A voice on a radio delivered a scratchy propaganda message. People exercising behind a courtyard wall responded to the instructions by chanting, "Annihilate America and England, one, two, three." Did these people still believe Japan remained capable of annihilating her enemies? With the world reduced to ash and sorrow, it was difficult to recall the government's purpose for going to war. What had they hoped to accomplish?

The broadcast started at six each morning, which meant they were running late. "We must hurry," Kiyomi said, quickening her pace.

Kiyomi's heart sank when they reached the food distribution center, located inside a red brick building on Aioi-Dori Street near the old Fukuya Department Store. A long line snaked out from the back door where handouts were made.

"There are so many," Ai said in a quiet voice.

"*Hai*. But we must make the best of the situation, *neh?*"

Kiyomi steered Ai to the back of the line. The woman in front of them turned to stare at Ai. She managed a weak smile then presented her back. The war took the best from people, leaving behind empty shells. They were all ghosts with no sense of reality. Time meant nothing here. Having food meant everything.

The door of the food distribution center yawned open and a man stepped outside holding a clipboard. He had the face of an accountant and ink blackened fingers. He wore a Western-style suit. A fedora crowned his head. The man focused on his papers, then at the starving souls before him. "We have wheat flour and sardines. Nothing more."

What could she do with flour and sardines? Ai tugged on her sleeve. "Mama?"

Kiyomi patted her arm. "We'll have food. That's what matters."

"*Hai*. But what if the sardines are spoiled again?"

"We'll have food," Kiyomi repeated.

The line crept forward, the government man taking the name and address of each person who received food before waving them toward soldiers who waited with rations. To the west, a line of churning grey clouds edged closer with the threat of rain. Sweat beaded over Kiyomi's shoulders and trickled in hot rivulets toward her waist. A rancid smell greeted their noses as they drew closer to the building. Ai pinched her nose and turned away. Despair coursed through Kiyomi at the sight of her daughter suffering, followed by intense anger.

"Kiyomi-san, is that you?"

Miyuki Okada strolled their direction, wearing a luxurious peach-colored kimono decorated with a cherry blossom pattern. A pale green *obi* brought out the vividness of the peach. Her hair was swept up into a *marumage* and held by tortoiseshell clips. She moved with the elegance and grace of a refined woman of means. The soldiers eyed Miyuki with disdain but did not approach her. The Okada family owned a factory that produced military uniforms. Prior to the war, Miyuki's husband did business with Banri, and still considered him and Sayoka friends, despite the decline in Banri's fortune.

Miyuki stopped near Kiyomi, her face relaxed, a gleam in her eyes. "Ah, Kiyomi-san, it is you. And with Ai-chan. She is getting so big." Miyuki's chin rose and her nostrils flared as she sniffed the air. The stench of the sardines erased her pleasant expression.

Kiyomi kept her gaze low but from the corner of her eye caught the people in line glaring at Miyuki. Their mouths were tight, their expressions hard, for they could see her cheeks were full and flushed, not sunken and ashen like their own. Miyuki's money shielded her from the trials of war and they hated her because of this. So much hate, it encompassed them like the air they breathed.

Kiyomi bowed, knowing the action would further ostracize her with those waiting for food. "Good morning, Miyuki-san."

Miyuki dipped her head. "Good morning, Kiyomi-san, and Ai-chan."

"You're looking well, Miyuki-san," Kiyomi said, then immediately regretted her word choice.

Miyuki took in the scene around her. "How are things in the Oshiro household? I heard Banri is not well."

Kiyomi tried to conceal the surprise from her face as she questioned how Miyuki knew this. "Thank you for asking. Banri has a cold."

Silence hung over them but Miyuki's eyes told Kiyomi she knew Banri's condition was more serious than a cold. "Have you tried *tamago-zake*? The Okada family has been using it for centuries to treat colds."

Sayoka wanted to try the hot sake and egg mixture, but in Hiroshima, eggs were rarer than gold. "We haven't tried *tamago-zake*. Thank you for the suggestion."

"My servant will be visiting her mother in Nakajima-Honmachi soon. I'll instruct her to deliver an egg to the Oshiro household."

Kiyomi bowed again. "*Arigatō.*"

"How is Sayoka-san? It's a tragedy she lost both of her sons defending the Empire."

Before Kiyomi could respond, Miyuki added, "And you a husband."

Ai pressed against her hip. Kiyomi placed a hand on Ai's shoulder and squeezed. Miyuki's eyebrows raised at this public show of affection.

Air raid sirens shrieked across the quiet morning, the sound bouncing off buildings and rattling Kiyomi's bones. People looked skyward. Voices spoke in rapid, frightened tones. The soldiers abandoned their posts and scurried toward the food distribution center. No one in line fled. It was better to meet death head-on in a wall of flame than die slowly from hunger.

Miyuki stood fast, a hand to her chest. "We'll confront this challenge together, *neh*?"

Kiyomi tried to speak but her tongue lay paralyzed by fear. Not for herself, but for Ai. She scanned the surrounding buildings. Where could Ai hide? Where would she be safe when the bombs rained down? As if reading her mind, Ai hugged her waist and said, "I'll stay with you, Mama." Kiyomi leaned over to kiss Ai's hair.

The familiar sound of B-29 engines rose above the sirens. Antiaircraft guns boomed across the city. Puffs of flak erupted in the sky. The ground shook beneath their feet. "There," a man shouted and pointed to the south. Dozens of bombers sliced through the clouds, their aluminum fuselages shining. Long contrails streamed out behind the planes in white ribbons. "They will burn us all," an old woman cried. Kiyomi remembered the newspaper photographs of Tokyo after the firebomb raid in March. Block after block of scorched earth. Buildings flattened. People burnt to ash, including her aunt and uncle. If this was to be their end, she prayed death came quickly. Ai didn't deserve to suffer. No child deserved to burn.

Kiyomi looked at Miyuki. "You do not need to be here. Protect yourself. We must stay. We must keep our place in line."

Miyuki brushed a loose strand of hair behind an ear. "Where would I go? How can I save myself? Throw money at the American bomber crews? No. I'm here and this is where I'll remain. Should I die, it will happen in good company."

Kiyomi bowed. "You honor me, Miyuki-san."

"Don't thank me for saying what's true. Besides, they're not here to bomb Hiroshima. You'll see."

Puzzled, Kiyomi watched the bombers as they reached Koi. "How can you be certain?"

"I've heard General McArthur's mother is Japanese and her family lives in the city."

"And this is why the city has been spared?"

"*Hai*," Miyuki said. "I wish I knew the name of her family. I would give them food and beg them not to evacuate."

The sound of the B-29's engines filled the sky like an approaching storm. Ai pressed her face against Kiyomi's side. "I'm frightened."

"They will not attack," a man said. "The Americans want to turn Hiroshima into a resort for their troops after the war."

The bombers continued flying northward.

"See?" he said. "What did I tell you? No bombs are falling."

Kiyomi remembered her aunt saying how the people in Tokyo used to go outside and watch the B-29s. Their bombs sailed so far off target, nobody worried. The people mockingly referred to these attacks as mail runs. No one in Tokyo called the attacks mail runs anymore.

When the bombers cleared the airspace over Hiroshima the people in line relaxed. The air raid sirens stopped and quiet returned to the morning. Kiyomi raised Ai's chin with a finger. "The Americans are gone. You need not be afraid."

"They could have killed us."

"*Hai*," Kiyomi said, "but they let us live, and so we will."

The door of the food distribution center reopened and the man with the list stepped outside, accompanied by two soldiers. "Go home," the man called. "There is no more food today." He spun about and hurried inside the building, the soldiers banging the doors closed behind them.

The crowd stood in stunned silence as they absorbed the news. No food. That's what the man said. How could they survive without food? The calm lasted a few seconds, replaced by angry shouts and shaking fists. A man snatched a rock off the ground and hurled it at the building. Others joined in and soon rocks, boards, and sand balls banged against doors and cracked windows.

"We should leave," Miyuki said with urgency in her voice.

The sound of pounding boots carried from the street. Six soldiers rushed the mob, rifles thrust out with bayonets attached and ready to kill.

"Too late," Miyuki whispered.

An officer strolled up behind the men. His eyes narrowed into black slits. "Everyone stop what you're doing!" The officer stepped in front of his men and assessed the situation. His right hand traveled to the hilt of his sword. The sight of the officer's hand on his sword produced quiet gasps. "You're a disgrace. A disgrace to your families. A disgrace to your country. A disgrace to yourselves and a disgrace to the Emperor." The first three examples appeared to have little effect on the crowd, but upon hearing the name of the Emperor, heads bowed in unison. "I should arrest you all," the officer went on. He withdrew his hand from the sword and pointed at the road. "Leave now while you can. Anyone who remains will be taken into custody."

Miyuki tugged on Kiyomi's sleeve. "Follow me."

On Aioi-Dori Street, a black limousine sat beside the curb. A man wearing a chauffeur's uniform stood outside. The driver straightened upon seeing Miyuki. He bowed. "Are you all right, Miyuki-sama? You should have let me accompany you."

"I'm fine," Miyuki said. "A woman my age knows how to take care of herself. Would you mind waiting in the car while I talk with my friend, Kiyomi-san?"

"Of course." He bowed and stepped around to the driver's side of the car and climbed inside.

"He's a good man," Miyuki said. "He fought in China."

"Oh," Kiyomi said, surprised to learn Miyuki's driver had served in the army.

"Something happened to him," Miyuki went on. She pointed to her head. "Inside his mind. He witnessed things that changed him. Terrible things."

Kiyomi wished Miyuki would stop talking about the war in front of Ai. Despite government censors, rumors spread of Japanese soldiers slaughtering Chinese civilians in Nanjing. She recalled reading Ishikawa Tatsuzo's novel, *Living Soldiers,* before the Special Higher Police began ripping out pages from the book. Tatsuzo, an eyewitness to the Nanjing incident, described cruel behavior by Japanese soldiers. It couldn't be true. No. How could the men who served the Emperor with honor conduct themselves in such a manner? Lies. The stories had to be lies. If they were true, the Japanese people had lost their moral compass.

"It's by the mercy of the gods he has recovered at all." Miyuki turned to look out on the street where civilians were emerging from shelters. "I was on my way to see a friend," Miyuki said without looking at Kiyomi. "That's how I came to pass the food distribution center. She owned a kimono shop before the war. Now I'm her only customer. So sad." Miyuki considered Ai, her dark eyes softening. "You need food."

Kiyomi's toes and fingers tingled with unease. Where was Miyuki going with this?

"You've met my daughter, Keiko?"

"*Hai.* One time." Kiyomi remembered their brief encounter at the market. Keiko, who was three years her junior, came across as spoiled and undisciplined, her nose so high in the air it could touch the clouds.

"Keiko works at the Kikusui Ryokan at 3-chome Otemachi. Do you know it?"

Kiyomi nodded. Members of the Imperial family had stayed at the Kikusui Ryokan. Former Prime Minister Tōjō visited the hotel last year.

"She works in the kitchen. Go around to the back entrance. Knock. When someone answers, tell them to summon her. When Keiko appears, ask her for food. Mention that I sent you."

No. Kiyomi would not wear the *On* for Miyuki or worse yet, Keiko. The debt would crush her spirit into dust. "*Arigatō-gozaimasu*, Miyuki-san," she said and bowed.

The muscles in Miyuki's face pulled tight as she stared into Kiyomi's eyes. "Please, Kiyomi-san. Do this. It's not about obligation or debt. Just once, cast aside the chains of decorum."

As Kiyomi studied the approaching storm, a fist squeezed her empty stomach, waves of pain spreading throughout her body. "I understand," she said and bowed again.

Miyuki set off toward her car, a ghost of Japan's past in her ornate kimono. Around her, people in peasant clothes went to work for the Emperor. The contrast was as striking as the dark clouds to the west and the bright sky hovering over Hiroshima. Kiyomi held out her hand. "Come, Ai-chan, we must find food."

They meandered in a daze past buildings that once housed restaurants, and vacant lots stripped of vegetation. If there was a way to make rocks edible, Kiyomi would have filled her pockets. Ai kept her head down, dragging her *geta* over the concrete. Kiyomi led them to a place where houses had been destroyed to create a firebreak.

The ominous clouds swept across the western section of the city with black curtains of rain. "I've heard pigweed and trefoil grow amongst the rubble," Kiyomi said, scanning the piles of debris. She released Ai's hand. "Wait here. I'll search." Kiyomi picked her way through the remnants of shattered lives without spotting anything. The storm arrived as she returned to Ai, cold raindrops splattering them. *I should have brought an umbrella.* Ai hugged herself and shivered. Rain plastered her bangs to her forehead. "Let's check at the river," Kiyomi said. She pressed a hand between Ai's shoulder blades and steered her away from the ruins.

Near the Motoyasu Bridge, Kiyomi guided Ai onto the riverbed. Raindrops splashed across the surface of the river, pitting the green water. Their *geta* sank in the wet sand. Tired muscles protested with each step. Rain drummed oyster boats tied near shore with a steady, tap-tap-tap. "I don't see anything," Ai said in a dejected voice.

"Let's go under the bridge," Kiyomi said.

It was good to be out of the rain, even if their clothes were soaked through. Kiyomi sank to her knees and probed the sand. She wiggled her fingers beneath the coarse surface. "If I had a shovel, or an old writing-brush and trowel, I would find something."

"I'm so hungry, Mama."

As Kiyomi read Ai's eyes, downcast, yet trusting, she felt like a failure. What kind of mother allowed their child to starve? "If I dig I might find clams. You enjoy clams, *neh*?" Kiyomi clawed at the sand, scooping it by the handful, grains working under her fingernails and stabbing like knives. "I must dig deeper. *Hai*. I can go deeper. You'll see." She hollowed out sand, her hands disappearing into the hole. She dug until water seeped from the ground and stopped her progress. "No. No. I must find food. I must." Kiyomi ladled out water and tossed it aside, but the hole continued to flood. Her eyes filled with tears. Her fingers turned raw from digging. "There must be something. If I keep digging. There must be." She pulled back and buried her face in her palms, too ashamed to look at her daughter.

"It's all right, Mama," Ai said. "We can go to the hotel. There might be food for us. We must try."

Kiyomi brought down her hands but kept her eyes closed. "*Hai*. You're right, my love. We must try." A chill swept through her damp clothes, seeping deep into her bones. She would wear Miyuki's and Keiko's *On* the rest of her days, a small price to pay for Ai's survival.

On a good day, with the sun blazing overhead, and their stomachs filled with food, the trip to the Inn would have taken a few minutes, but the cold rain accompanied by starvation made the journey seem long. Each step brought new pain. Each raindrop served as a reminder of their condition. When they arrived at the Kikusui Ryokan, Kiyomi sensed the weight of the sky upon her shoulders. The repainted signboard outside the white building identified the facility as an assembly hall for military officers. What if she got arrested for loitering? What would happen to Ai?

Kiyomi gestured toward an alley at the side of the building. "We'll try there. Maybe the alley goes through to the rear of the building."

The smell of spicy food wafting from the inn gave Kiyomi hope. A man sat on the covered back step, smoking. A most unpleasant looking fellow with a shaved head and leering fish eyes. The white uniform of a cook stretched tight across his oversized belly. Grease stains speckled his apron. Kiyomi leaned toward Ai. "From the size of his stomach, we know where all the food in Hiroshima has been going."

Ai covered her mouth and snickered.

"Unfortunately, we must talk to him. With any luck, he won't turn into a monster and devour us. There appears to be room for the both of us inside his stomach, *neh?*"

Kiyomi drew a breath to steady her nerves and released it. "Let's go."

The man tracked their progress. As they drew closer, he flicked his cigarette into the yard. Kiyomi bowed. "*Kon'nichiwa.*"

He looked them over, his right eye twitching. "Why are you here? This facility is for Army officers."

"We're here to see Keiko."

"Keiko, huh? She expecting you?"

"Not exactly."

He raised off the step with a groan. "What's your name?"

"Kiyomi Oshiro. This is my daughter, Ai."

"You look half-dead. When did you last eat?"

Humiliated by her state, Kiyomi averted her gaze. "This morning."

"I will find Keiko," he said and disappeared inside the building.

"Are you all right, Mama?"

No, I'm not all right, Kiyomi thought, a sentiment she could not share with Ai. "*Hai*. Thank you for asking. You mustn't worry about me."

A short time later, Keiko stepped onto the porch wearing a purple kimono with a white lily pattern. She had a wide face with a touch of pink in her cheeks and pouting lips. Keiko folded her arms over her chest. "I was told you needed to see me?"

"*Hai*. I'm Kiyomi Oshiro and this—"

"I know who you are."

The tone of Keiko's voice told Kiyomi they would be lucky to come away with anything; still, she must try. "Your mother told us to come. She said you might be able to help."

Keiko's left eyebrow arched. "How do you know my mother?"

"She is a friend of my in-laws, Banri and Sayoka Oshiro."

This news produced a frown. "What is it you want?"

Kiyomi hesitated. She would rather climb into a pit filled with venomous snakes than ask Keiko for assistance. I wouldn't be here if not for Ai, she reminded herself. "Miyuki-san said you might have food."

Keiko continued to frown. "You do realize the military has taken over this inn?"

"I would not ask if—"

"I could lose my job. I could be arrested."

"We do not want to bring trouble on you. Perhaps we should leave."

Keiko's attention shifted to Ai. "Wait here," she said. Keiko spun about and disappeared into the building.

Kiyomi stared at the closed door. What was Keiko up to?

"She is a pretty lady," Ai said.

"Even the prettiest shoe makes a sorry hat."

"What does that mean, Mama?"

"Don't expect much from Keiko."

The door reopened and the man from the porch emerged carrying two porcelain bowls. Steam curled over the edges. A spicy scent caught Kiyomi's attention. He motioned with a sideways nod. "Come inside. Eat." He led them into a narrow hallway with a hardwood floor. The mauve-colored walls held paintings of flowers in vases. "I have no chairs," the man said. "Better than standing in the rain, *neh?*"

"*Hai*," Kiyomi said.

"Here," he said, handing them the bowls. "Soba noodles."

A tear rolled onto Kiyomi's cheek as she stared into the bowl. She brushed it aside, hoping he hadn't noticed. "*Arigatō.*"

He massaged the back of his thick neck as he watched them. When they continued to stare at the food he said, "Eat. Eat," then threw up his hands and hurried off.

"Is it all right to eat?" Ai asked.

"*Hai,*" Kiyomi answered.

They ate in silence, the warm broth a gift from the gods as it trickled down Kiyomi's throat. The sound of men laughing carried from another room, along with the clinking of glasses, the slurping of food, and belching. Kiyomi ignored the distraction, content to watch Ai savor her meal. When they finished eating, Ai held out her bowl. "Should we leave now?"

Kiyomi stared down the empty hallway. "I guess it will be all right to leave the bowls on the floor." Ai knelt and placed her bowl on the hardwood without making a sound. "I had hoped Keiko would bring us more, but at least we got something."

Ai flattened a hand against her stomach. "I'm still hungry."

"*Hai.* Me too." Kiyomi held open the door. "We should head home. Your grandparents will be disappointed, but some things cannot be helped."

The wind picked up and the rain blew sideways. Kiyomi took hold of Ai's hand. "Please forgive me. I should have brought an umbrella."

"There is nothing to forgive," Ai said. "The rain is good for flowers. Maybe it is good for us too."

"For someone so young, you are always teaching me."

They set off across the yard. Cold rain slashed at their faces. "Kiyomi. Wait. Please."

She stopped and glanced back at the building. Keiko stood on the porch holding a basket. Ai shrugged. "The prettiest shoe is good for your foot."

Keiko held out the basket. "It's not much. Some uncooked noodles. A chunk of salted dolphin. So sorry, you'll get used to the taste. A dozen oysters. Kelp. Radishes. And some apples. It is the best I could do."

Kiyomi accepted the basket and bowed. "I'm indebted to you."

"No," Keiko said. "You owe me nothing."

Kiyomi bowed again. "*Arigatō-gozaimasu*, Keiko-san."

"Sayōnara, Kiyomi-san. Sayōnara, Ai-chan. Good luck."

Keiko's act of kindness lifted Kiyomi's spirits. She smiled at Ai as they returned home. When they neared the Motoyasu River, Ai squeezed her hand and said, "Do you hate the Americans?"

Kiyomi recalled newspaper photographs of Tokyo after the bombing. She wanted to hate the Americans for what they had done, then remembered watching the airman die. "I do not want to hate anybody, but the Emperor has made America our enemy."

"I wish the Emperor would change his mind. I'm tired of the war."

"Me too," Kiyomi said. She reached inside the basket and withdrew an apple. "I don't think anyone would care if we shared one, *neh*?"

The apple crunched as Ai sank her teeth into the skin. She pulled back with a piece in her mouth and began to chew, apple juice streaming onto her chin.

Chapter Thirteen

Evening rain pattered across the tile roof. A raw dampness pervaded the walls and crawled over Kiyomi's flesh, making her shiver. Too cold for June. Much too cold. The rainy season had begun. Day after day of steady downpour awaited. She brushed mold from their shoes. Tobacco turned musty. Books mildewed. The tatami mats and all their clothing became sodden. Kiyomi sat on a cushion inside the *Sakinoma*, the principal parlor for entertaining, surrounded by her family and the matchmakers hired to find her in-laws a son, and her a husband. Kiyomi's legs were rusted springs after spending the day traveling through town with Ai in search of food. A sharp pain drilled beneath her left breast. Each breath caused the discomfort to radiate outward. Flies buzzed around their heads, drawn by the putrid smell of cooked dolphin. The swallows stirred inside their nest, making an occasional chirp.

Nobu Takada and his wife, Rei, were known throughout Hiroshima for their matchmaking abilities. Some people suggested the couple possessed magical powers allowing them to pair up partners as easily as pairing sake with an accompanying dish. Sayoka told Kiyomi to think of the Takadas as a road to a brighter future. The image that came to Kiyomi was a road leading to the edge of a cliff. She guessed the Takadas to be in their fifties. Nobu's head was as round as a melon. Grey hair tickled the tops of his protruding ears. Rei's large eyes didn't miss anything. Lips the color of a Füji apple formed a permanent pout.

Rei bit into the dolphin. Her nose wrinkled before she swallowed with a loud gulp. "A most interesting meal."

"Dolphin," Kiyomi said.

"I see," Rei answered, shifting her chopsticks to the steamed kelp.

"They serve fried dolphin with mayonnaise at the beer hall," Banri said.

"What I wouldn't give for a beer right now," Nobu added.

What I wouldn't give for a different life, Kiyomi thought.

Beside her, Ai jerked away from one of the flies. She smiled at Kiyomi and said, "Thank you for this most delicious meal."

Warmth spread throughout Kiyomi's chest. "You're most welcome."

"So, Sayoka-san," Rei said, pushing the meat around the bowl with her chopsticks, "would you say Kiyomi is a good cook? Men desire a wife who can prepare edible food."

Sayoka contemplated her food. "With my assistance, she's improving."

"Did you assist with this meal?"

Sayoka hesitated then said, "Kiyomi prepared dinner on her own."

Kiyomi gnashed her teeth. *How dare Sayoka say such a thing? When I arrived from Tokyo, she couldn't boil a shrimp. With her assistance, I'm improving. Ha.*

"I suppose we must be grateful for any food we receive in such times," Rei said.

Kiyomi glared at the matchmaker even though she knew her action would be considered rude. Rei was nothing more than a nasty little spider who crawled out of the darkness to bite.

Banri shifted on his pillow. "Did you know Kiyomi attended the university?"

"Women who are intellectual are not so graceful or elegant at heart." Rei fanned herself. "A woman's good personality shows when she doesn't know too much about the way of things." She turned to Sayoka. "Do you agree?"

"*Hai,*" Sayoka said. "Intelligence is not the most desired quality in a woman."

If that was true, her mother-in-law possessed the most desired quality. Kiyomi chewed the inside of her lip as she struggled to control the anger boiling deep inside.

The room turned silent. Heads bowed in proper etiquette. Even Ai knew not to stare into the faces of the adults. The buzzing of the flies intensified. The rain continued to tap on the roof. Kiyomi closed her eyes and drifted back into a distant memory, sitting on the veranda of her uncle's house in Tokyo beside her aunt. Summer rain coming down in gentle waves as they sipped hot tea. Her life was simple then, moments of discovery and wonder, the warmth of security, and the feeling of being loved. Now the rain served as a reminder of how much she had lost and how much there was to lose moving forward.

"Will we ever taste white rice again?" Rei sighed.

Kiyomi opened her eyes in time to catch the matchmaker rubbing her belly with a wistful gleam in her eyes. Most of the food before her remained untouched. Clearly, the spider had already taken plenty of victims if she could pass on a meal.

"*Hai,*" Sayoka agreed. "Sometimes the ration rice is mixed with soybeans and tastes most unpleasant. Nothing we eat has *awai.*"

Rei nodded. "No depth."

"Food doesn't reach Hiroshima because of the American submarines," Nobu said.

"And no soldiers are departing through the Gaisenkan," Banri added.

"*Hai,*" Nobu said. "The soldiers are not leaving through the Hall of Triumphal Return as they did earlier in the war. Now they are filling our inns and houses, eating what food is left."

"Soldiers cannot leave for battle, but too many are returning inside white boxes. We don't need more ashes. We need sustenance." Banri drew in a breath and exhaled, air escaping his lungs with a noticeable wheeze. "Ah, but what is it our government tells us? 'We will not want a thing until victory.' Victory is a mountain we must climb. A mountain whose slopes are slippery and treacherous, and whose summit is shrouded in mist."

Silence returned to the house. Kiyomi raised her head to consider the faces of their guests. Where did they stand on the war? If they did not share Banri's sentiments, would they report him to the *Kempeitai?* Would the police arrive during the night to arrest Banri? To arrest them all?

Rei glanced at her husband from the corner of her eye. Nobu massaged his chin, the atmosphere inside the room growing tense. Nobu sat up straight and announced, "The spirits of our ancestors will not win this war. *Kami* spirits will not protect our country. Tearing down houses to create firebreaks will not save Hiroshima from the Americans' wrath."

The strain that had bubbled to the surface of the conversation disappeared into the darkness of memory. Kiyomi glanced at Ai and smiled upon seeing her daughter's empty plate. When the matchmakers left the house, she'd salvage what she could from Rei's bowl and give it to Ai. What the spider refused, the butterfly would enjoy.

"When do you think the guests from America will visit Hiroshima?" Rei asked without seeming to direct the question toward anyone in particular. Women didn't discuss the war in the presence of strangers, and Rei appeared to catch her mistake, her chin dipping toward her chest, and a blush spreading across her cheeks.

A fly landed on Kiyomi's arm. The fly's legs made her itch, but Kiyomi resisted the urge to swat the insect.

"When the Americans arrive, we'll be prepared," Banri said. "Our neighborhood association has ordered us to go into the mountains and gather pine needles, which we are to burn when Mr. B appears."

"For what purpose?" Nobu inquired.

"The smoke from the pine needles will make the city invisible to the bomber crews."

Nobu chuckled without reserve, his upper body quaking. Even Rei and Sayoka found humor in the idea, laughing behind their hands. Kiyomi sat stone-faced. She couldn't laugh in the face of death and suffering. Not with Ai beside her, innocent and vulnerable to the madness of adults.

Nobu motioned toward Banri with a thrust of his chin. "Now that Germany has surrendered, how is Japan to win with the entire world aligned against us? The government would have us fight to the last man if the Americans invade, which they are sure to do. 'The honorable death of one hundred million.' Absurd."

"*Hai,*" Banri said. "How can we win against an enemy whose manufacturing capabilities far exceed our own? The Americans fill the sky with their bombers. Japan cannot defend herself. Are we to commit *seppuku* like the Samurai of old?"

"What will happen if Japan loses the war?" Sayoka whispered in another slip of etiquette. Kiyomi knew the thought of defeat had been on their minds, but to utter the words felt sacrilegious as if Sayoka had breached a dam and washed them all in sin.

No one spoke for a long time and then Rei said, "They will force us to eat terrible American food. Hot dogs and hamburgers. And drink Coca-Cola all day."

"And watch their gangster movies and read their preposterous books," Sayoka said.

"It would be the end of our national existence," Banri chimed in.

"I like American food and Coca-Cola," Kiyomi blurted. She squirmed under the glower of the other adults and quickly added, "Of course, their food is not as good as ours."

Rei's eyes narrowed on Kiyomi as if she were a cockroach that needed crushing. She shifted her attention to Banri and Sayoka. "The Americans are barbaric. Look at how they treated their slaves and Indians. They cannot be trusted. On Guadalcanal, they ran over Japanese prisoners with their tanks."

Banri left the gathering. He returned with his *Tabako-bon.* After repositioning himself on his pillow, he retrieved his pipe and leather pouch from the small wooden box. He packed the bowl with tobacco, then used a match to fire the cut leaf. "Our government promised great victories. Eight corners of the world under Japanese rule. Now they cannot even feed our people. It's shameful." He handed the pipe to Nobu who accepted the offer with a bow.

"If Japan does lose, at least we will be released from the rule of militarism," Nobu said.

"I wish our enemy would differentiate between civilians and soldiers," Rei said. "Why must we suffer their anger? Why must we burn?"

"Why should the Americans do this when our own government refuses to separate combatants from noncombatants?" Banri answered. "Civilians on Okinawa strap bombs to their bodies and dive under tanks. We are all their enemies. To win a war, you kill as many of your enemies as possible. If Japan were in a more favorable position, our bombers would strike Los Angeles and San Francisco with no regard for civilian victims." Banri accepted the pipe back from Nobu with a slight bow.

Banri's opinion of Japanese morality weighed on Kiyomi. The Japanese cause was true. The Japanese soldiers acted with honor. She needed to believe this. But in her heart, the war was no longer about causes or honor. There was no cause worth the suffering Japan now endured, and no honor in watching starving children plead with their eyes for a scrap of food.

The evening spiraled into an abyss and discussion of the war threatened to undermine the purpose of the Takada's visit. As if sensing this eventuality, Rei leaned toward Banri and said, "Will you reopen your shop after the war?"

Banri glanced at Sayoka and then back at Rei. "*Hai.* With a new son at my side, we will reopen."

"Our business will blossom when the soldiers return," Nobu said. "There are few good men left in Hiroshima."

A burning pain stitched under Kiyomi's ribs. She bit her tongue to absorb the discomfort. If what Nobu said were true, why wouldn't Banri and Sayoka wait until the war ended to find their heir? Were they hiding the truth about Banri's health from her?

Ai yawned and covered her mouth. She kept her head low, a blush in her cheeks. Kiyomi couldn't help but feel pride at the conduct of her daughter. She was growing up too fast. Soon she'd move into a world where boys received all the privileges, and Ai would be expected to submit to their whims while she prepared for her future role of wife and mother. Japan needed girls to marry young and bear many sons to fight on behalf of the Emperor. Kiyomi hated the system. She hated the unfairness and limited opportunities for women. Perhaps Banri was right when he said if the Americans won the war it would be the end of Japanese culture. There were customs in her country that needed to change. Maybe the Americans would be the ones to bring these changes about.

Rei sipped her tea. The bitter taste did not appear to agree with her palate, for her lips puckered and she clanged the porcelain cup onto its saucer. "There is something I must ask. Was Kiyomi a good wife to Jikan?"

The question stunned Kiyomi. *Why would Rei ask such a thing?*

"Good in some ways," Sayoka said. "In other ways, Kiyomi needs improvement."

How could the snake say such a thing after everything I've done for them? Sayoka should crawl off into the night with the spider. Let them enjoy each other's company.

"Hmm," Rei said and tapped a finger against her chin. "Interesting." She brought her hand down. "Is Kiyomi a hard worker?"

"When she decides to work."

Kiyomi's hands curled tight. *Sayoka calls me lazy while she spends her days sitting on her bony bottom. What if I poison the snake? Would anyone miss her?*

"Does Kiyomi know her place?"

"She is like most women her age, somewhat willful. But all in all, she appears to understand her obligations."

Rei accepted the information with a subtle nod. "There is much to gain from a successful union. Your new son will become heir and entitled to your estate. The Oshiro name will live on. You'll have someone to aid you with your business. Kiyomi will no longer be a widow. Her bed will once again be warm."

Rei dipped her chin to stare at Kiyomi through her eyelashes. "But he'll expect much from Kiyomi. She must be a good cook. She must keep a clean house. Kiyomi must fulfill her obligations as a mother and give him a son. And she must do all these things willingly, with grace and humility."

It suddenly occurred to Kiyomi what was transpiring. Rei questioned Kiyomi's character to signal Banri and Sayoka that they might have to settle for a man with lesser qualities if he were to marry such a flawed woman. By acknowledging Rei's concerns, Sayoka made it known they understood Rei's position and were willing to accept whomever the matchmakers could find under these difficult circumstances. In truth, the situation had nothing to do with Kiyomi's abilities and everything to do with a shortage of suitable male candidates.

Rei lowered her fan and turned to Ai. "Ai is a well-mannered child."

Kiyomi smiled inwardly at the compliment. She went to respond but before the words could leave her tongue, Sayoka said, "I have worked hard to prepare Ai for her future life." A flame traveled up Kiyomi's neck and into her face. *How dare she claim responsibility for Ai's upbringing? All she does is fill her head with nonsense.*

Rei ignored Sayoka's remark. She gestured toward Ai and said, "Do you enjoy school, Ai-Chan?"

Ai raised her head long enough to nod.

"What is your day like at school? Who is your favorite *Sensei?*"

"We exercise in the yard. Chant things about the war. Practice fighting with spears. It's not fun. Mr. Kondo's class is fun. He reads poetry and tells stories."

"I remember Mr. Kondo," Nobu said. He has been at the school forever."

"What would you like to do with your life when school is finished?"

Ai glanced over at Rei. "Draw pictures."

"Don't you want to get married and have children of your own?"

"I would rather draw pictures."

Banri chuckled behind a fist, which turned into a raspy cough. When he stopped coughing, he said, "You have plenty of time until marriage, little one."

Rei considered Ai with a critical eye as if judging her as a future client. "You should take Ai to a physiognomist. They can tell you what vocation is best suited to a girl of her abilities."

Kiyomi said nothing, believing the idea ridiculous, but Sayoka responded with exuberance. "You are most wise, Rei-san. Sometimes a mother is blinded by her love and cannot see the road ahead."

"Kiyomi strikes me as a good mother," Nobu said and rubbed his eyes.

"We must hope she is a good mother and wife," Rei said. "You can't polish a tile into precious stone."

"This is true," Nobu agreed. "No branch is better than its trunk."

Their use of proverbs confused Kiyomi. What were they trying to say? Did they consider her an unfit mother? A woman undeserving of happiness? And what did Nobu mean by no branch is better than its trunk? She came from a successful family of merchants and academics. More successful than anyone present at this dinner.

"You are from Tokyo, correct?" Rei asked.

"*Hai*," Kiyomi said.

"I have always found *Edokko* to be ..." Rei tugged on an earlobe. "How to put this? I have always found Tokyo-ites to be like dogs that don't know to come in out of the rain. Their heads are full of fanciful ideas. But they can be taught. *Hai*."

"So sorry my background offends your sensibilities," Kiyomi said in a clipped tone. "Perhaps if I had been raised in Hiroshima, you would find me more acceptable? Then I would not be a dog in your eyes."

The room went quiet. Sayoka's face turned ashen. No doubt she believed Kiyomi had ruined their chances to adopt a son. Banri's expression remained calm as he tapped burnt tobacco from the bowl of his pipe. Nobu studied the rafters as if trying to distance himself from the fray. To Kiyomi's surprise, Rei's lips formed a quiet smile. If she was angry, she kept it hidden.

"We must be careful when arranging a marriage," Rei said. "Our job is so tiring and important. If we shirk that responsibility, our souls at death are reborn into the bodies of slugs."

I wish you both would turn into slugs right now, Kiyomi thought.

"It must be difficult to arrange a marriage under our present conditions," Banri said. He returned his pipe to the *Tabako-bon*.

A cloud of smoke hovered near the ceiling, overwhelming the room with an earthy scent.

"We're not able to follow tradition," Rei said. "There are no elaborate *mi-ai* planned. Once we find a suitable candidate, you'll arrange a meeting at your house. He might object to the match after meeting Kiyomi. She is older than the average bride and stands like a crane. Men do not want to look up at their wives."

Sayoka let out a melodramatic sigh. "*Hai.* It's most unfortunate about Kiyomi's height. Men prefer their women to stand on shorter legs."

Kiyomi smoothed her palms over her thighs. It was true her legs were longer than those of the average Japanese woman, but no man ever complained about them. If anything, her height provided more flesh for a curious tongue to explore. Rei and Sayoka were jealous because their stubby legs brought them closer to the ground.

"Do you want the wedding ceremony to be held at a temple?" Nobu plucked a roll of skin at the base of his neck.

"That's not necessary," Sayoka answered. "And Kiyomi wouldn't need to wear a white kimono. She won't be leaving her family. There's no need to mourn."

Ah, but I will mourn, Kiyomi thought. A thousand tears will form in my eyes, but I will swallow them before they can fall. You will never know the sorrow that rules my heart.

"And no need for a honeymoon," Rei said.

Kiyomi found herself nodding. She stopped before anyone else noticed. What did or did not happen on her wedding night was no one's business but her own.

"How long will it take to find someone?" Sayoka asked.

Nobu's lips moved from side to side. "Hard to say. We will try to find the most suitable man. There's much to consider. In a world of sparrows, do not expect an eagle."

Banri coughed into a fist. "As far as payment we—"

"Pay when you can," Nobu said. "If you are like us, the head of your association is always asking you to buy war bonds, *neh?* Blood from a stone."

"*Hai.* When the war ends, things will improve."

Nobu pushed off his pillow, body trembling, and face as red as a *Daruma* doll. He cleared his throat. "I believe we are finished with our business. Thank you for the most interesting meal." He bowed. Rei joined him and also bowed.

They paused at the entrance of the house. Outside, the rain arrived in pale curtains. Rei opened her umbrella and glanced back at Kiyomi. "Perhaps you should evacuate Ai into the country with the other children."

Kiyomi bowed. "Ai is too young to be sent away."

"I'm certain the government would make an exception if pressed."

"I've heard the children sent into the mountain temples are miserable. They must forage for their food. Girls cry themselves to sleep and wet their futons. No, Ai is better off in Hiroshima with her family."

"*Hai.* You may be right. Goodnight everyone. Sayōnara."

No sooner had the Takadas disappeared through the gate when Sayoka pressed close to wrap Kiyomi in her coils. "Why did you say you enjoy drinking Coca-Cola? Are you trying to sabotage our plans?"

Kiyomi debated her response. The proper thing would be to apologize, but she wasn't in the mood for proper. "I like Coca-Cola. After the war, I will drink Coca-Cola, and so will my daughter."

Sayoka's eyes flared. "What? Why … I can't believe you—" She turned to Banri. "Help me here."

Banri gestured for them to come inside. "It has been a long night."

Sayoka gaped at her husband as she hurried past, her kimono rustling on the hardwood floor.

Banri dipped his chin. "Kiyomi-san. The wind tosses waves and bends trees, but it doesn't move mountains. Become a breeze."

Later, after she cleaned the dishes and put them away, Kiyomi snuggled beside Ai in their futons. Ai turned to face her and Kiyomi detected worry in her daughter's eyes. "What's bothering you?"

Ai sucked in her lips, which gave her the appearance of a mouthless doll. Kiyomi grew impatient when Ai remained quiet. "Ai-chan, you must tell me your thoughts."

Ai reached out to touch Kiyomi on the cheek. Her soft, warm fingers removed the tension from Kiyomi's mind. "I didn't like those people. We don't need their help."

"You may be right, but I'm in no position to go against the wishes of your grandparents."

Ai pulled back her hand and blood pounded past Kiyomi's ears. They remained this way a long time, the rain drumming on the roof and mosquitoes buzzing outside the netting.

"Are you going to send me away to the temple? I don't want to leave."

The joy and heartache that accompanied raising a child welled up inside Kiyomi as she contemplated Ai's words. Kiyomi wished she could keep Ai this way forever. Young and vulnerable. Dependent on her for almost everything. But that would be impossible. Time stopped for no one. And yet, in her mind, she could imagine them together in this perfect moment for eternity.

"You are staying with me. Always."

A smile passed over Ai's lips. "Mama, why do we have a ghost in the house?"

The nerves in Kiyomi's body smoldered. "What do you know of this?"

"I'm not afraid."

"You're not?"

Ai shook her head. "I've seen him."

Kiyomi blinked as she absorbed this information. "What do you mean? You have seen his shadow?"

"No, not a shadow. A person."

Then he is a man, as I suspected. Kiyomi captured a strand of Ai's hair and let it slip through her fingers. "Do you recognize this man? Is he Jikan or your Uncle Yutaka?"

"No, Mama."

"Are you certain?"

"He's an American."

Chapter Fourteen

Time rushed past like fast-moving clouds, sunrises, and sunsets—a blur. The rain settled in. Monotonous. Cold. Falling in immense drops that exploded on roofs and sidewalks. According to Frank, it was June. June already? Impossible. It seemed only yesterday Micah had been aboard the *Tasty Topekan* with the rest of the crew, cutting jokes and dreaming of home. *Home.* The word lived inside Micah's brain as a cancer. Longing to return to Bellingham brought him pain. Hiroshima was his home now.

Micah settled into routines as he did in the military. In the morning, he watched the woman and little girl prepare for their day. After listening to their conversations, as Frank suggested Micah believed he knew their names. The woman was Kiyomi, her daughter, Ai. Kiyomi's father-in-law was Banri and her mother-in-law, Sayoka. Their calm approach to everything from dressing, styling their hair, and eating astonished him. When he was the girl's age, their house had turned into a circus each morning. They wolfed down their breakfast. Syrup dribbled on his chin and a milk mustache painted his upper lip. His mother shouted instructions. Battles ensued over bathroom privileges. Water splashed. Toothpaste smeared porcelain. He jostled with Levi over the comb and tube of Brylcreem. Somehow they managed to rush outside right as the school bus arrived. Inside the Japanese house, each movement appeared calculated, rehearsed. No one shouted. No one dashed about like a wild man from the jungle.

Most mornings, he stayed with Ai at her school for a few hours. The school program was odd, yet predictable. Frank told him the older children were evacuated into the country. The little ones left behind received a heavy dose of combat training. Thrusting spears twice as long as their bodies at imaginary soldiers. Wrestling. Inside the classroom, Ai paid little attention to her teachers. She stared at the window with dreams in her eyes. Sometimes she drew pictures of flowers and animals. Once, she drew a scary elongated figure cloaked in a flowing robe, with bony arms, no legs, and no face. Did the picture represent him? There were times Ai acted as if she could sense his presence. She would stop whatever she was doing and search the surrounding air, then smile before returning to her work.

Kiyomi intrigued him. She also sensed his presence, but, unlike Ai, Kiyomi's reaction revealed her apprehension. Her dark eyes dilated. Her lips parted with a quiver. Why did she fear him? Surely she recognized that he meant her no harm. He stopped following Kiyomi to her factory job because the clatter of war production filled him with despair. Besides, he was more interested in her when she returned home. His heart ached with yearning as he watched her. Why? What was it about this woman that made him feel this way?

On some days, Micah explored the city. He came to know the people of Hiroshima. He observed their movements, their habits; workers' morning commute to factory jobs, student volunteers assisting soldiers in the destruction of buildings, hammers pummeling the visages of the old city, wooden beams cracking under the blows of axes; people desperate for food falling into long lines, faces void of hope turning skyward as formations of B-29s passed overhead.

On the Honkawa River, near the Hiroshima Prison, a man fished from dawn until dusk. He cast his line into the translucent water and waited, his expression never changing. Even when the tide ebbed, leaving his bait stranded on dry rocks, he sat and stared, waiting. In Otemachi, Micah came across a woman sitting outside a house with a baby. The woman couldn't have been more than twenty-five, yet the war had taken a terrible toll on her appearance. Dark crescents underlined her lifeless eyes. Skin hung from her bones. She pressed the baby to her sagging breast in an effort to nurse, but the baby squirmed and cried as it failed to find nourishment. It was the same all over Hiroshima. Broken and desperate people struggled to survive while the tragic war raged on.

Micah's thoughts returned to Kiyomi. Her image floated before him throughout the day like a neon sign advertising a vacancy. A vacancy for what? A place in her life? Stupid, he knew, when they were separated by more than race, nationality, or a devastating war. If only he could talk to her somehow. Now, sitting inside the living room of Kiyomi's home, his back against the wall, a mere shadow in the darkness, he watched Kiyomi and Ai sleeping. *Maybe I should leave*, he told himself. *Travel across Japan and find someone else to haunt. I could scare Emperor Hirohito into ending the damn war.*

As he mulled over his future, Ai sat up from the floor, surrounded by a blue band of pulsating energy. She pushed off the floor and ambled toward the screen that divided the rooms, passed through the screen without pausing, and disappeared. *What the hell just happened?*

He stood and walked over to them. Ai lay pressed against Kiyomi's spine, her chest rising and falling with each breath. *If she's here, who did I see passing through the screen?* An idea blossomed inside his mind. Did Ai's soul leave her body? And if so, could he interact with her?

Micah found Ai outside sitting by the pond. She stared at the black water, oblivious to the rain. *Should I approach her? No. I need to see Frank.*

Micah hurried from the yard to find Frank. Having never traveled around Hiroshima at night, he had no idea what to expect. As soon as he stepped onto Tenjin-machi Road, a soft gasp left his throat. Despite the blackout and the persistent rain, people walked on the road, each one surrounded by the same bluish-glow as Ai. An older man stopped in front of him and bowed. "Good evening," he said before continuing on his way. *He could see me. And he spoke in English. How strange.* As he made his way toward the river, Micah found himself greeted by more spirits. They bore not a trace of animosity, as if the war meant nothing to them. Why didn't they hate a man who had fire-bombed their country? If he were in their in shoes he would ... no, he wouldn't hate them. After living among the Japanese over a month, he no longer despised them. He abhorred the soldiers who slaughtered innocent civilians and prisoners of war, but these were not those men. These were husbands, wives, parents, grandparents, and children too young to comprehend what drove adults to destroy the world.

Micah found Frank and Oda onboard the oyster boat, passing a bottle of sake. The spirit of a plump Japanese woman sat on Oda's lap. Her kimono gaped to reveal ample cleavage. Her moon face held wide-set eyes and a pleasant smile that showed off her teeth.

Frank raised the bottle in salute. "Ah, Micah-san. So good to see you. I didn't think you came out at night." He pointed the bottle toward the woman. "This is Momo, a friend of Oda's."

Oda squeezed Momo against his belly, making her giggle. "Momo has a big round bottom, a rare quality in a Japanese woman. Most have skinny bottoms. She is a cherry blossom."

Micah faced her and dipped his head. "A pleasure to meet you, Momo-san."

She leaned close to Oda's ear and whispered, "He's polite for an American."

Oda tipped back his head and roared. "Ha. He has you fooled with his charming ways. It's an American trick."

Frank passed over the sake and belched.

"You're drunk," Micah said.

"No." Frank thrust an empty hand toward Micah. "Here, have a drink."

Micah sighed. "Can we take a walk? I must ask you something."

Frank's eyebrows raised when he noticed the bottle was missing. "Oda is a thief."

"*Hai*," Oda said. "Tonight, I will steal Momo-san's virtue."

"Virtue? Momo-san?" Frank slapped a knee. He turned serious under Oda's glare. "*Hai.* I see your point. Momo-san is most virtuous."

"Frank?"

Frank leaned closer to Micah and tilted his head. "When did you get here?"

"We were going to take a walk?"

"Right. A walk." Frank bowed to Oda. "Goodbye, my friend. Goodbye, Momo-san's virtue."

She giggled once more, oblivious to Oda massaging one of her breasts.

Away from Oda and the sake, Frank sobered with remarkable speed. He opened his mouth as they walked, catching rain on his tongue. "So, Micah, what questions do you have?"

"I saw her."

"What? Who?"

"Ai. I watched her spirit leave her body. You never told me this happened."

Frank stopped outside a shuttered bicycle shop and leaned against the wall. "You never asked."

"Can we—"

"Yes. We can interact with the spirits of the living."

There was a chance now, a chance to learn more about Kiyomi and for her to get to know him. Micah imagined himself talking with Kiyomi. *Would she even want to talk to me? And if she did, would I answer her or stand there like an idiot?* As if reading his thoughts, Frank said, "Having feelings for a living person outside of your family is never smart. You'll end up with a broken heart."

"Why do you say that?"

Frank lit a cigarette. "A living spirit forgets everything that happens in this realm. Whatever experience we have with them vanishes the instant they awaken."

"They forget everything?"

"Hard to develop a relationship under those conditions."

Why shouldn't he become friends with Kiyomi? Yes, her beauty enchanted him, but there was so much more to her than that. He admired her strength and how she cared for Ai. He sensed a strong passion for life within her heart. But how could he express this to Frank?

"Does this happen to all living people?" Micah asked.

"It does. And to us as well."

"What do you mean?'

Frank blew out a cloud of white smoke that fizzled in the rain. "We don't travel outside our spirit bodies, of course, but there are times when we sleep, we go to different realms, and see other spirits."

"I could visit my brother?"

"It's possible." Frank flicked his cigarette into the darkness. "There are some people who seldom experience astral projection."

"What does that mean?"

"You might never catch Kiyomi's spirit outside her body."

"I didn't come here about—"

"Yes you did," Frank said and grinned. "I can't imagine you'd come outside in this soup, all fired up with questions if they were about the child."

Micah joined Frank on the wall. Raindrops emerged from the darkness in silver ribbons. He opened his mouth to speak, but nothing came out.

"You still think you're going to be friends with Kiyomi, don't you?" Frank shook his head. "I've warned you about Japanese women. If you're in need of company, I'm sure Momo has a dead friend."

Micah stared past him in the direction of the house. "I should go."

"You didn't hear a single word I said, did you?"

"I heard what I wanted to hear."

Chapter Fifteen

A biting wind blew in from Canada tearing through the protection of his winter coat. Evergreen trees scattered throughout the Bayview Cemetery swayed in opposition, refusing to relinquish their hold on the fragile earth. Beside him, his grandmother, Molly, studied the headstone of her sister, Rose. His grandmother's eyes drew tight. Wrinkles fanned along her temples. A tremor pulsed along her upper lip. The salty pungency of Bellingham Bay filled the morning air. Micah thought of his grandfather, Finn, alone on his troller. Passed out. An empty bottle of Irish whiskey rolling across the cabin with each slap of a wave against the hull. Finn said Irish whiskey was the one good thing to come out of that god-forsaken land.

His grandmother showed up at his parent's house before sunrise. Her sniffling pulled Micah from a dream. He crept onto the staircase to draw closer to the parlor. The voices of his parents and grandmother carried throughout the quiet house. His grandparents had argued once again. No surprise. His grandfather became a mean old bear when the seasons turned against him and he was forced to remain on land. When the conversation dragged on, Micah retreated to the room he shared with his brother. Levi sat up in bed when Micah returned. "They fighting again?"

"Yeah," Micah said, crawling under his covers.

"Predictable as the sunrise. Well, you'd better get some sleep. She always expects you to accompany her to the cemetery after she and grandpa have a row."

Micah had just closed his eyes when his mother shook his arm and said, "Your grandmother wants you to—"

"I know, I know," Micah said with a groan.

"It's a big responsibility for a boy your age."

He focused on his mother's concerned face. "I'm fourteen. I can handle it."

Standing beside his grandmother at the cemetery, he wished he had put up more resistance. Why did it always have to be him who accompanied her? After his grandmother whispered her problems to her dead sister, she turned toward him and said, "You know why your Aunt Rose never married?"

He often pondered this. Unlike her mother and sister, Rose was petite, with fair skin and rich green eyes. Strawberry red hair framed her face. She shattered the dreams of many men in Bellingham who imagined themselves her partner.

"I'll tell you why," his grandmother went on. "Back in the old country, Rose fell in love with a Protestant boy from Galway. Son of a merchant. Handsome fellow. Tall. Black hair." His grandmother sighed. "Rose should have known better. No future for a Catholic girl in an arrangement like that. The boy's parents rejected her of course. Broke her heart. Poor Rose never recovered. Foolish girl."

His grandmother scraped a shoe over the frozen ground.

"Don't know why I come out here. Talking to ghosts like I do. And even if Rose could answer me, which she can't, she'd be a fine one to hand out advice." She took hold of his arm and squeezed. "Folks should stick to their own kind, know what I mean? A farmer wouldn't mate a Clydesdale to a Shetland pony, now would he? Find yourself a smart girl, but not too smart. Your father's a businessman, so it's all right if her family has some money, but not too much money. Irish would be all right, but we have tempers, let me tell you. A Norwegian such as your father might be best. Don't get lost in a fantasy of love. Be practical. Be smart. Think of your heart as a box filled with gold coins. You wouldn't share that treasure with just anyone would you?"

This childhood memory played through Micah's head as he sat on the floor watching Kiyomi sleep. He had grown weary with anticipation as he waited for her spirit, or Ai's, to leave their bodies. A week had passed since he observed Ai outside her body. The idea of forging a relationship with Kiyomi and Ai gave Micah a sense of purpose. He had developed feelings for them, especially Kiyomi. In his mind, he pictured them as lovers, forbidden kisses shared in the moonlight. Whenever this happened, the gruff voice of his grandmother spoke to him. "Micah, I thought I told you to stick to your own kind? She's Japanese. You want to end up like your Aunt Rose?" His teeth gnashed as he silently answered his grandmother. "I don't care if she's Japanese. She's beautiful. And why does it matter how I feel? I'm dead. I can do whatever the hell I want. And this is what I want. God help me, but this is what I want."

He tried to forget about the war and his role in it, but the constant air raid sirens and passing B-29s in the night sky made this impossible. The conflict was not a dream or conjured from a fairytale. Kiyomi and her family suffered because of it. Misery and starvation were the new emperors to rule their lives. But something other than the war seemed to be crushing Kiyomi's spirit. He had noticed a change in her demeanor ever since the strange couple visited. Her gaze seldom rose from the floor unless she was alone with Ai. And when she did look up, her eyes conveyed consternation.

There had been no air raid sirens on this night and the family retired to bed early. Kiyomi and Ai fell into a deep sleep. Mosquitoes buzzed outside the mosquito netting. The birds scratched around their nest. Micah paced. A part of him wanted to visit Frank and Oda, but he would never leave the house knowing the spirits of Kiyomi or Ai might appear anytime.

The family had been asleep a few hours when a fuzzy blue glow appeared over Ai. Her spirit partially emerged from the shell of her body, only to sink back out of view. He wrung his hands over his lap. Would this be the night he had been waiting for?

Ai's right arm shot up, fingers spread as if she waved at someone. After a few seconds, her arm went down. "No, no, no,"

Micah said. *This is never going to happen. I'm a fool for thinking otherwise.* He pushed off the floor and left the room. Outside, he stood near the small garden at the back of the yard. A soft breeze tinkled the glass wind chime hanging above the porch. With the city blacked out, stars revealed themselves in flashes of brilliant light. They floated across the blackness like a phytoplankton bloom stretched across the ocean. *The burning of the sea.* Micah jammed his hands inside his pockets. He had never felt so alone in his life. Something stirred the leaves beside the pond. A toad the size of his fist hopped into a swath of moonlight. The toad made a loud noise that reminded Micah of his grandmother belching.

"He's an ugly one."

Micah whirled around to find Ai's spirit standing behind him.

"Don't you think he is ugly?" she pressed.

"In my book, he's the ugliest toad I've ever seen."

Ai blinked. "What book is that?"

"Uh." He scratched the back of his neck. How to explain American slang to a Japanese child? "Not a real book, you see. If I were to write a book detailing the experiences of my life, this toad would qualify as the ugliest one I've seen."

"You should write this book. Mama used to keep a diary before she started working at the factory. Sometimes she told me stories about things that happened when she was a girl." She moved past him, went straight to the toad, grabbed it, and held the beast high in the air. "He scares me sometimes. But not now." Ai studied Micah. "You're the ghost that watches over us."

"How do you know that? Can you see me?"

She placed the toad in the pond and stepped away. "Sometimes I can. Sometimes you're a black cloud." Ai moved closer, her chin raised. Her head moved from side to side as she examined him. "You don't look like a demon."

"Why would I look like a demon?"

"One of my teachers, Mrs. Hada, said all Americans are demons."

"Why would she say such a thing?"

"Americans killed her husband on Iwo Jima."

A thin grey cloud slithered across the black sky. A bright star beamed like a magnifying glass capturing the sun. Of course, she would think of Americans as demons, the same way he used to demonize all Japanese. The war stole their humanity. Micah gazed into Ai's questioning eyes. "War is a terrible thing. I wish our countries had never gone to war against each other."

"Me too. Then my stomach wouldn't hurt all the time."

"You don't get enough to eat."

"We had plenty to eat before the war. Mama is a great cook. She made us *okonomiyaki.*"

Awkward silence settled between them. He had so many things he wanted to ask her, but where to begin? She took a step toward the porch and he thrust out an arm to stop her. "Do you enjoy going to school?"

Ai stared at his arm until he brought it down. "You watch me at school sometimes?"

"I hope you don't mind. I was curious about how they taught classes in Japan. You see, prior to the war, I planned to be a teacher."

Ai smiled. "You were going to be a teacher?"

"Yes. I was about to start my first job at Custer Elementary School when Pearl Harbor was attacked."

She stared at her feet and in a small voice said, "We stole your dream from you."

"A lot of dreams died on that day, including the dreams of many Japanese."

Ai raised her head. "Why are we fighting? Some of my teachers try to explain. Their words give me a headache. I want to learn things. I want to be smart like Mama."

"Is she an educated woman?"

"Mama went to the university in Tokyo."

"She's from Tokyo, not Hiroshima?"

"She moved here when she got married."

"To your father?"

"No. He lived in Tokyo."

"Oh. I see." Micah massaged his chin. "Your mama has been married twice?"

She grinned. "Haven't you learned anything since living with us?"

"I couldn't understand what you were saying."

"But you're speaking Japanese."

"No. You're speaking English."

Micah remembered what Frank had told him. In the spirit realm, people shared a universal language. "Does your mama ever come out with you while you're sleeping?"

"Where does she come?"

"You know," Micah said, "to the place you are now."

"*Hai.* We live here."

"No. No. Not Hiroshima. I mean here, at night, while you sleep."

"Am I asleep?"

Behind Ai, the toad splashed through the pond. Micah knew it was pointless to discuss their condition. She wouldn't remember the conversation upon waking. Besides, he still wasn't sure he understood what had happened to him since his death. "Maybe I'm the one who's asleep," he said.

"Would you like to play a game?"

"Sure. That'd be swell."

"What is ... swell?"

He stepped closer. "It means, very good."

"Ah. I see. *Hai.* A game would be swell." Ai thrust out her arms. "How about *janken?*"

"I'm afraid I don't know that game."

"It's easy. I'll teach you." She made a fist with her right hand in the palm of her left hand. "Like this."

"All right," he said, mimicking her actions.

"Now we both say, *Saisho wa guu.*"

"Why are you speaking in Japanese?"

Her eyebrows knitted. "I'm not sure. I was remembering how we say this in Japanese. Should I try again?"

"Please."

Ai's lips pressed together as she concentrated. "Let me see. Um. Here goes. Say, 'starting with rock'." She beamed. "I did it!"

"Yes." He smiled at her. "Starting with rock."

"Now we say, *Janken pon*, and ..." Her lips flattened into a grimace. "I did it again."

"That's all right. I can remember that one. *Janken pon*. Now what?"

"We make our move," Ai said, and flattened her closed fist over her palm. "See? Paper covers rock."

"Yes. I see. This is rock, paper, and scissors. We play the same game back in the States. What happens if we tie?"

"We say, *Aiko deshō!*" She grunted. "I mean, uh, it seems like, uh, it seems like a tie. *Hai*. That's what we say. And then we do our next move. Do you follow me?"

"The terminology is a little different, but yes, I believe I can manage."

They launched into the game, hands flying over open palms, voices shouting their intentions, laughter filling the void separating them. Ai played with unmatched precision, outwitting his strategy over and over as if she could read his thoughts. By the time they finished, the sky had lightened to a soft grey. She held a hand to her chest. "You play well for a beginner."

He chuckled. "So, I'm a beginner?"

Ai appeared horrified. "I didn't mean to offend. So sorry."

"No. No," he said, waving a hand before him. "You didn't offend me. Against someone as skilled as you, I must seem like a beginner."

The tension left her face and she bowed. "We'll play again sometime."

"I look forward to it."

Ai's attention shifted to the sky, then over to the house. "I must go now." She hustled across the yard and onto the porch.

"Wait!" he shouted.

She stopped and glanced over her shoulder. "What is it?"

"Is your name, Ai?"

"*Hai.*"

He repeated her name, allowing the word to roll off his tongue. "It's good to meet you, Ai. I'm Micah."

"Ah. Micah-san."

"Should I call you, Ai-chan?"

She giggled behind a fist. "*Hai*. I'm a child."

"And your mama's name is Kiyomi?"

Ai nodded. "Mama's name is Kiyomi. My grandfather is Banri. My grandmother is Sayoka."

"They are the ones you live with?"

"*Hai*." She smiled and waved. "Sayōnara, Micah-san." And with that, she hurried inside the house.

Micah stared at his hands, remembering the time spent playing the game. His body tingled all over, he couldn't feel the earth under his boots, and for a moment he imagined he could float skyward to join the last of the evening stars. "Kiyomi," he whispered, then grinned like a schoolboy with a crush.

Chapter Sixteen

Kiyomi stood at her lathe inside the factory. Her hands operated the machine independently of her mind, which traveled far from the grinding and groans of the factory floor. She remembered walking Ai to school. Ai seemed unusually happy despite her hunger and the menacing grey clouds. And even when the clouds opened up, and a steady drizzle forced them under their umbrella, Ai continued to beam. She had to discover the reason for Ai's giddiness before leaving to work, otherwise, she would fret all day over the unanswered question.

"You're filled with joy it seems."

"I spoke with our ghost," Ai said in a cheerful voice.

Kiyomi stopped. She grabbed Ai's arm and steered her to the side of the alley. Ai's expression turned serious. "What's wrong, Mama?"

Kiyomi was both curious and frightened by the thought of Ai communicating with a spirit. What if the spirit was evil? She had to know more. She had to protect her child. "When did you talk with this spirit?"

"Last night."

"Inside the house?"

"In the yard. We played *janken*. It was fun."

Kiyomi pulled back. She tried to hide her astonishment but was certain it marked her face. "And where was I while this happened?"

"I think you were inside the house sleeping."

A gust of wind blew the umbrella forward and cool rain feathered across her neck. Kiyomi steadied the umbrella over their heads. "You must have been dreaming."

"No. It was real."

Kiyomi realized nothing could be said that would convince her daughter the entire incident was a figment of her imagination. But what if it was real? What if Ai did interact with a spirit?

"You don't need to be afraid, Mama. He's nice."

Kiyomi shook her head as if waking from a dream. "What? Who?"

"Micah-san. He's the ghost." Ai's smile returned. "Micah-san is American. He flew on Mr. B."

Kiyomi placed a hand on Ai's shoulder and squeezed. "If this ghost is real, we must not talk to him. And promise me you'll not mention him to anyone. Do you understand?"

"He watches over us. He's probably watching us now."

Kiyomi glanced over her shoulder, searching the air as if expecting to see something. "We cannot have the ghost of an American inside our house. It's dangerous. And it's dangerous to talk of such things. Promise me you'll keep your tongue silent."

Ai hesitated, her expression changing from confused to resolute. Just when Kiyomi thought her daughter might rebel against her instructions, something she had never done before, she said, "*Hai.* I won't talk about Micah-san to anyone." Ai's grip tightened on her emergency supply bag. "May I talk to you about him?"

Kiyomi brought back her hand. "This ghost scares me."

"Why?"

"He came here to kill us, Ai-chan. He's our enemy."

"Not anymore. Micah-san told me he wishes America and Japan had never gone to war."

"He said this?"

"*Hai.*"

Unable to find a response, Kiyomi steered Ai back into the alley and continued to her school.

On the streetcar ride to work, Kiyomi relived her conversation with Ai. Why would an American settle inside their house? What did he want? As the streetcar rattled along, Kiyomi bolted upright, drawing the attention of her fellow passengers. Kiyomi's cheeks burned. "So sorry," she said. They glared at her with disapproval before turning away. When the fire left her face, Kiyomi returned to the idea that shook her to the core. The ghost had to be the American she watched fall from the sky. She experienced the odd sensation of coldness on her skin that day at the factory and later at home. She detected the spirit's presence while she bathed, only to have the feeling leave when Ai bathed. An American would be embarrassed by a child's nudity. Why did he follow her? She exited the streetcar and headed to the factory gate.

Raindrops splashed in surrounding puddles. The air carried the scent of trees and wild grasses. As she neared the gate, the answer came to her and Kiyomi stopped. She had been there when the American's spirit awoke from a place of darkness. She was the first person he saw, naturally he would bond with her. But why did he remain inside their house? And why didn't his spirit travel to whatever Heaven he believed in? She recalled she had found him attractive. Warmth returned to her face.

With her mind lost in a haze of questions and concerns, Kiyomi found work difficult. Adding to her complications, she hadn't eaten anything of substance in two days. Hunger wormed into her brain. Her head throbbed and each step sent waves of pain crashing through joints and muscles. She needed to concentrate to keep her chin off her chest. Inside the lunchroom, Kiyomi caught her reflection in a mirror and gasped at the sight of her greying skin and dull eyes. What man could be attracted to such a woman?

As she struggled to focus on her work, Kiyomi thought about Ai. Having the spirit of the American airman inside their house couldn't be good for her. Kiyomi needed to find a way to make him leave. She couldn't risk having him influence Ai's impressionable mind with odd American ideas. The temple. *Hai.* She must go to the temple and talk to a priest. If he performed an exorcism, the American would flee and never return. She must see a priest right away. Her hand slipped off the lever and the lathe stopped spinning. Kiyomi grabbed onto the base of the machine, her body betraying her at a time she needed strength.

Haru watched with concern. She craned her neck to check the area around her, no doubt looking for Mr. Akita, then asked in a voice that carried over the factory sounds. "Kiyomi-san, are you sick?"

Haru's question caught the attention of Umi and Lee-Sam. Kiyomi lowered her gaze to avoid their eyes. "I'm fine," Kiyomi lied. The room blurred around her.

"Kiyomi-san?" Lee-Sam called. "Do you need to go to the clinic?"

Kiyomi backed away from the lathe. She took a step toward Umi and the floor rushed at her face.

She found herself standing at the edge of a mountain stream, the surrounding countryside bathed in dozens of green shades. The stream bubbled clear around ancient stones. Sunlight beamed through trees in golden shafts. The American stood at her side. He was smiling and she couldn't help but think he was as golden as the sunlight. "I won't hurt you," he said. "You or your daughter. Please believe me."

Kiyomi blinked. The factory ceiling rose over her. The cold factory floor greeted her spine. Something warm cocooned her head. A hand stroked her hair. She blinked again to bring everything into focus. She was on the ground, her head resting on Haru's lap. Lee-Sam and Umi knelt beside her with worried expressions. "What happened?"

"You fainted," Haru said. "Fortunately, you didn't hit one of the machines."

Lee-Sam touched her shoulder. "Are you hurt?"

Her head ached as if stepped on by a giant, but otherwise, Kiyomi felt no worse than she did before blacking out. "I'm fine."

"You're not fine," Umi said. "When did you last eat?"

"I'm fine. Please help me stand."

"You must go home and eat," Umi said. "You'll get hurt if you stay here."

"*Hai,*" Haru said. "Can you take her to the streetcar?"

"What's going on?" Mr. Akita loomed over Lee-Sam. "Why have you stopped working?" His cold dark eyes shifted to Kiyomi. "And why is Kiyomi-san on the floor?"

"She's not feeling well," Haru answered.

Mr. Akita huffed. "No one is feeling well. Get her on her feet and back to work. I will not tolerate laziness."

"No," Umi said, rising from the floor. "Kiyomi must go home. I will escort her to the streetcar."

Blood rushed into Mr. Akita's face. He shook a fist at Umi. "How dare you contradict me, you stupid girl!"

"You are the one being stupid," Umi responded.

Workers across the factory gasped. Mr. Akita growled between clenched teeth. "I will fire you."

Umi opened her mouth to respond and Lee-Sam blurted, "Umi-san is right. Kiyomi must go home. She cannot work if she's sick."

"That's enough, garlic-eater."

Lee-Sam glared at Mr. Akita. Kiyomi patted Haru on the arm. "Please, Haru-san, help me onto my feet. I have caused enough trouble."

"See," Mr. Akita said. "Kiyomi-san knows she's all right."

Umi took a step toward him. "She is leaving. I am taking her to the tram stop. Fire me if you want. I can find another job."

Mr. Akita's face transformed into a fierce Kabuki mask, his eyes burning with rage, his nostrils flared. No one on the factory floor challenged his authority, least of all, a young girl. Silence spread through the building as lathe machines stopped spinning. Workers gaped at Mr. Akita. What would he do to the rebellious teenager? Slap her? Scream in her face? Make good on his threat to fire her?

Shame weighed on Kiyomi's shoulders like a heavy stone. It was her fault if Umi got fired. She should have eaten something. She shouldn't have fainted and drawn unnecessary attention to herself. Kiyomi knew she must take responsibility for her actions. If anyone should be fired, it was her. Mr. Akita turned toward the factory workers. "What are you looking at? Everyone back to work this instant. You're a disgrace to the Emperor." When heads across the factory bowed and the metallic whine of the lathes resumed, Mr. Akita faced Umi. "You take Kiyomi-san to the streetcar. Don't waste time."

"*Hai.*"

Mr. Akita took three steps, then stopped to look back at Umi. "And if you ever talk that way to me again, I'll have you arrested." He stomped away, shouting at workers to get busy as he passed.

"Stubborn old goat," Umi said.

"You are very brave," Lee-Sam told her.

"Or very dumb," Haru added, which made Umi smile. Haru helped Kiyomi stand. "You must take better care of yourself."

"*Hai,*" Kiyomi agreed. "I have a lot on my mind. But that's no excuse for my ignorance. So sorry."

"No apology needed," Haru said. "Go home. Rest. Eat something."

"I'll be right back, then we can leave," Umi said. She headed toward the lockers.

Kiyomi motioned with her chin at Umi. "She is strong for someone so young, neh?"

"Young and foolish," Haru said. She sighed. "I wish I were more like her."

"I'm glad you're not like Umi-san," Lee-Sam said. "You would be fired and I would have no one to talk with at lunch." He smiled before walking away.

Haru's eyes flashed at Kiyomi. "Don't say anything."

"It isn't my place."

Umi returned carrying her bento box. "Are we ready?"

Outside the factory, the storm had passed and brilliant sunshine hurt Kiyomi's eyes.

"It's a sign," Umi said. "We'll have victory over the Americans."

Kiyomi wanted to tell her it was a sign the rainy season had drawn to an end and nothing more, but she kept silent.

The clear sky brought birds over the Enko-Gawa River. Black-winged gulls fluttered above the water and squabbled along the riverbed, filling the air with their chatter. Ducks swam near shore. In Kako-machi, students continued to destroy buildings to make firebreaks, the disheartening yellow haze they created rising unabated without the rain. Umi walked beside Kiyomi with a hand on her shoulder. Exhausted and worn-down by hunger, every muscle in Kiyomi's body burned and her head throbbed where it had struck the floor.

Umi opened her bento box and removed a rice ball. "Here, eat this."

Kiyomi hesitated, not wanting to wear Umi's *On*, but the idea of putting something in her aching stomach overpowered her reservation and she accepted the food with a bow. "Thank you, Umi-san. One day, I'll repay your kindness."

"You've always treated me as an equal and not some immature schoolgirl with a head full of fanciful ideas. For this, I am grateful."

"No one else in the factory would have stood up to Mr. Akita the way you did. That took great courage."

"Mr. Akita is a nasty little worm. We grovel before him because that is what the Emperor requires. By the time the war ends, Mr. Akita will have made many enemies, *neh?*"

Kiyomi wanted to bite into the rice ball but eating while walking was rude. "How are things with your boyfriend?"

"Good. We hope to marry before he's drafted into the army."

They approached the streetcar platform, crowded with morning commuters. "Maybe the war will end soon."

"He's willing to fight and die for the Emperor."

Kiyomi choked down the words she longed to say while thinking, youth are easily fooled.

Umi helped her onto the platform. People turned to watch them. Kiyomi averted her gaze, ashamed of her weakness. "Are you all right?" Umi asked.

"*Hai. Arigatō*, Umi-san."

Umi glanced back in the direction of the factory. "I'd better return before the worm starts to miss me. You should stay home tomorrow. The war's not lost if Kiyomi Oshiro misses a day of work."

"I'll consider it."

Umi smirked. "No, you won't." She skipped off the platform with the vigor of a child and hurried down the road.

Umi was long gone by the time the clanking streetcar arrived. Kiyomi took a seat beside a white-haired woman. The woman hunched over, her arms and shoulders drawn inward as if she had been doused with a bucket of ice water.

The streetcar jerked forward. Sunlight beamed through the front windshield making Kiyomi squint. She caught the old woman staring at the rice ball in her hand. "Would you like half?" Kiyomi asked.

"*Arigatō*. You are most kind."

Kiyomi carefully tore the rice ball and handed half to the old woman who brought it against her chest. "For my husband. He is dying." Purple veins pulsed across the tops of her hands.

Kiyomi settled back in the hard seat. Outside the streetcar, evacuees crowded one side of the road. On the opposite side, refugees from bombed cities shuffled into Hiroshima with dirty faces and eyes that stared straight ahead but appeared to see nothing.

"They'll find no peace in Hiroshima," the old woman said. "Our time is coming. Only fools believe the city will be spared."

Kiyomi pictured Ai sitting inside her classroom. She didn't deserve to die in this senseless war.

"Do you have children?"

Kiyomi nodded. "A daughter."

"Keep her safe at all costs. She must be your purpose for living. You and your daughter must become your own country. No more Japan. No more Emperor. Just the two of you surviving this madness."

Kiyomi remained quiet. The old woman turned toward the window. Eyes closed, her breathing slowed. The old woman was asleep when the streetcar arrived at the Aioi Bridge stop. Kiyomi debated waking her. She wanted to say something about the woman's husband and thank her for her words of wisdom. Instead, Kiyomi slipped into the aisle without a sound and left the old woman to her dreams. Dreams, it seemed, were the only place where a person could find peace.

Kiyomi entered the Nakajima-hon-machi District. Her plan was to visit the *Jisenji* Temple and speak with the temple's head priest. A group of laughing boys chased each other on the deck of the Harbor Police boat moored on the Honkawa River. Next to the police station, army officers went in and out of the Aioi Shokudō cafeteria, while at the Koizumi Pediatric Clinic, a woman exited holding a young boy. Across the road, a light burned inside the Ohtu Uchimi Yakuten Pharmacy. Soldiers milled about the Kikkawa Inn next door.

These streets and alleys had become the landmarks of Kiyomi's life, points that grounded her to the reality of what was expected from her. Each house and business with their unique sounds and smells. Smiling shop owners with courteous bows and greetings. Now it felt as if she were a visitor to an unfamiliar place. The war shuttered doors. It emptied businesses of merchandise. Young men who worked in the shops, restaurants, and theaters had gone off to fight leaving haunting memories. The people left behind moved in a daze, fraught with apprehension. Would the Americans firebomb Hiroshima? Of course. When? Soon. It must be soon.

By the time Kiyomi arrived at the temple, she wheezed with each breath, and the muscles in her calves compressed into hard knots. Whatever energy she obtained from eating half a rice ball was gone and she wanted nothing more than to sleep. Kiyomi knew she must take Ai and forage for food outside the city. She had nothing to offer the black marketers except her body and while she would sacrifice anything to keep Ai from starving, including her dignity, Kiyomi wasn't ready to take that step.

Kiyomi entered the temple grounds. The bronze statues that once decorated the path had been requisitioned, removed, and melted into cannons. Gingkō trees grew broad and tall in the grassy areas, leaves rustling in the summer breeze. Kiyomi dug into her pockets for coins to toss into the wooden offertory box. Her search produced a 1 *sen* piece. Kiyomi remembered an old saying her aunt taught her, *The judgment of Hell depends on the amount of money offered.* Would *King Yama*, Judge of the Dead, condemn her to Hell for her meager offering? Kiyomi tossed the coin into the box where it made a lonely rattling sound, then joined her hands and bowed. When she arrived at the front of the *Butsuden*, Kiyomi struck the gong suspended by a rope, a rich metallic note rising into the air, then again pressed her palms together and bowed.

She climbed stairs leading into the main temple, her body like melting clay. The interior smelled of fresh cedar, incense, and weathered tatami mats. Beams had turned a molasses brown from smoke and incense. The air became heavier and shadows lengthened. The sound of her tapping *geta* echoed along adjoining corridors. Reverend Ichiro approached from a side room. He stopped upon seeing her and waited. Kiyomi went to him and bowed. "*Kon'nichiwa, Sensei*-Ichiro."

He returned her bow. "*Kon'nichiwa*, Kiyomi-san. How may I be of assistance?"

"I'm looking for Sensei-Saito."

His eyebrows raised. "Is this something I can help you with?"

Kiyomi feared disrespecting Sensei-Ichiro but knew only the head priest could help her. "I must see Sensei-Saito."

The priest studied her eyes, his expression unchanging. "I'll take you to him."

Outside, they traveled the path leading to the *Butsunichian* subtemple. Gravel crunched beneath their *geta*. Birds chattered in nearby trees. Cicada screeched. Sensei-Saito sat on a concrete bench near the garden. He had served as the temple's *jushoku* for as long as Kiyomi could remember. His eyes were closed. His chin raised toward the sun. Sunlight glistened on his shaven head. For a man in his seventies, his face bore few wrinkles, and his copper skin remained unblemished. He had a strong square jaw and piercing black eyes. Despite his intimidating appearance, he spoke with a comforting voice. As they drew closer, Sensei-Saito lowered his chin and stared at her. Her pulse quickened. A restrained smile passed over his mouth and he stood.

Reverend Ichiro bowed. "Please pardon the interruption. Kiyomi-san would like a word."

Sensei-Saito faced her. "You wish to see me, Kiyomi-san?"

She swallowed hard and bowed. "*Hai*. Sensei-Saito. So sorry to bother you."

"Thank you, Reverend Ichiro." He waited until the younger priest was well down the path, then motioned her to sit on the bench.

Kiyomi sat with her knees locked together and hands on her lap. She yawned, heat rising into her cheeks. Sensei-Saito remained quiet, his gaze traveling across the temple grounds to the pond where a duck launched into the sky with a thrashing of wings. Kiyomi watched him from the corner of her eye. She knew better than to speak before he was ready to listen. Her palms perspired. Bright sunlight stabbed her eyes. The longer he made her wait, the more nervous she became. He will think I'm a fool, she decided.

"You appear troubled, Kiyomi-san. Your face is flushed. An artery throbs in your neck."

Kiyomi shifted on the hard bench. "I had an accident at work."

He leaned toward her, his eyes drawn down. "An accident?"

"I fell."

"I see. You appear to be starving. That is no accident." He sat up taller, the sleeves on his plum-colored robe dragging across his thighs. "The war casts a cold shadow. Did you know some Buddhist monks volunteered to serve in the army? How can you believe it's wrong to take life and then agree to kill? We do this for Japan, they say. Is Japan the master of humanity? Is Japan the creator of the universe?" He shook his head and sighed. "So, Kiyomi-san, what brings you to me on this hot summer day?"

"We have a ghost inside our home."

His hands tented in front of his chest. "And how do you know this?"

"Um … well, there are times an icy chill appears inside the house. Unexplained shadows move about."

"So you believe a *gaki* or *jikininki* inhabits your in-laws home? How do Banri and Sayoka feel about this?"

Kiyomi stared at the ground. "They don't know."

"You haven't mentioned the ghost to them?"

"No."

"Small dishonesties and lies lead to big ones and final disaster."

She looked up at him. "They don't seem to have noticed the ghost."

He pulled back. "You're the only one who sees the spirit?"

"Well . . ." Kiyomi debated whether or not she should mention Ai.

"You have been experiencing a great deal of stress, *neh*? A shortage of food. The prospect of remarriage."

"You know about that?"

He smiled. "I'm wise and all-knowing."

"Oh."

"And Rei Takada likes to talk."

With so much uncertainty surrounding her possible marriage, why would Rei Takada want to gossip about it? Wouldn't this hurt the matchmaker's chances of finding her a suitable husband, or was Rei casting a wide net in hopes of snaring whatever poor soul passed by?

"Tell me, Kiyomi-san. Did your aunt in Tokyo tell you *obake* tales on warm summer nights? Ghost stories do awaken the mind to possibilities, *neh*?"

Kiyomi's resolve crumbled. *He believes I'm insane or possessed by a fox. He'll report my condition to Banri and Sayoka. I'll be shamed.*

"Cold drafts and strange shadows hardly qualify as evidence of a haunting."

"Ai has seen the spirit. She has spoken with him. He's an American."

Sensei-Saito sat up straighter. His eyebrows furrowed as he considered a juniper tree. He stared at the tree for some time. Wrinkles formed at the corners of his eyes and then relaxed. His lips pressed into a flat line. "Ai told you this?"

"*Hai.* This morning as I walked her to school."

"She's a child. Children have big—"

"She knows his name," Kiyomi blurted. "It's Micah-san."

Sensei-Saito leaned onto his thighs, resting his chin on his palms. "Why would an American ghost haunt your home?"

"Do you remember when Mr. B went down over the city?"

"About three months ago?"

"*Hai.* I watched one of the crew fall to his death. I stood over his body."

"And you believe his spirit has attached itself to you?"

"At first, I thought it might be the ghost of Jikan or his brother, but over time, I realized this wasn't the case. Now I'm afraid. Not for myself, but for Ai. If she does, in fact, communicate with this American, what influence will he have over her?"

"You believe he will corrupt her mind?"

"America is our enemy."

"We're at war with ourselves, Kiyomi-san. The Emperor invited the Americans to bomb us when we attacked Pearl Harbor."

She tried to conceal her surprise by willing her body not to tremble. How could Sensei-Saito speak of the Emperor this way? Did he not fear arrest? "My mind is too simple to consider such matters."

He chuckled. "I have known you five years. Your mind is far from simple."

"Can you help me?"

"You want me to come to the Oshiro's home and perform an exorcism?"

"*Hai*. On Saturday."

His left eyebrow went up. "Why Saturday?"

"Banri and Sayoka will be visiting her family Saturday morning. It's the only time they will be gone from the house."

"I hear Banri is not well."

"This is true."

He massaged his chin. "I don't like secret plans."

"This is for their own good," Kiyomi insisted.

"And for your own good as well, *neh?*"

She remained quiet.

He pushed off the bench, his shoulders squaring as he drew in a breath. "I will come to your home on Saturday and perform an exorcism."

Kiyomi stood, a smile on her face. "*Arigatō*, Sensei-Saito."

"I do this for Ai," he said. "While I personally do not believe the spirit would harm her, I can see how your distress at his presence might. Ai doesn't need more to worry about in these already difficult times. Your focus should be on feeding your daughter, not lingering ghosts."

"*Hai.*" Kiyomi bowed. He turned to leave and she called to him, "Sensei-Saito."

"Yes?"

"I want to ask you something." Kiyomi massaged the back of her neck. "Lately, I keep having the same dream."

"Divination is not my specialty."

"I know," she went on, "but I was hoping to hear your thoughts."

He faced her and cleared his throat. "Go on."

"In my dream, I awaken on a bright day, such as this one. I go outside, then I see them."

"See what?"

"Crows. They are everywhere, covering the roofs of houses, and filling the sky. They screech at my arrival. The sound is a hammer to my head."

"Crows are said to be evil omens that bring ill-fortune. Let us hope your dream is not a glimpse of your future."

Chapter Seventeen

Micah waited for the family to fall asleep inside the hole, hoping the spirits of Ai or Kiyomi would venture outside their bodies. Air raid sirens wailed. Aircraft flew overhead, their engines filling the sky with a mechanical roar. After some time had passed, and the air raid sirens fell silent, he gave up and left the house. Summer heat washed over his face as he stepped into the yard. He missed the cool rain that kept the heat at bay. The rain had come to an abrupt end, replaced by fiery winds sweeping in from the mountains. Growing up in Washington State, he was accustomed to cool summers and feathering rain.

He left the yard and traveled to the riverbank. Along the way, he passed a number of Japanese spirits on the street. They glowed like blue flames and greeted him with smiles and bows. Strange, he thought, how contented the dead appeared to be. In Hiroshima, it was the living who suffered.

Micah sat on the stone steps that led to the riverbed. Moths flashed through beams of moonlight. Crickets chirped from their hiding places. The Motoyasu River ran calmly toward the sea, gently sloshing the hulls of resting oyster boats. As he watched the serene river, Micah thought about Levi. He remembered a fishing trip they went on the summer before Pearl Harbor. Levi stood on the bank of the Nooksack River showing his son, Aaron, how to cast a fishing line. The river ran swift and green with white caps snapping against rocks. "If a fish bites, he's going to yank hard on your line. You've got to hang on tight," Levi said. Aaron looked up and nodded. "Yes, Daddy. I'll hold on."

Micah stared at his shoes with a bitter frown. He pictured Aaron standing alone on the riverbank holding his first catch with no one there to praise him.

When he first arrived in Saipan, he imagined what his homecoming would be like. His father standing on the lawn of their house under a pewter sky, a trembling smile on his lips. His hair, thick and brown at the beginning of the war, now thin and streaked with grey. Anguish reflected in the dusky blue of his eyes. "You'll never be truly home, Micah. The war has carved out a piece of your soul and you'll never get it back."

Micah raised his eyes to the night sky. "The war carved out more than a piece of my soul, Dad. It took the whole damn thing."

"Micah-san?"

Ai stood behind him wearing a pale blue kimono. "Good evening, Ai-chan. I'm happy you could join me. Did I say that right?"

"*Hai.*" She came alongside him. "Who were you talking to? Another ghost?"

"I was talking to my father."

"Is he alive?"

"I believe so. He lives in Bellingham, Washington. That's where I'm from."

"Is he a soldier too?"

"No. He's too old to fight in the war. My father owns a business on the waterfront. He repairs boats."

Ai stepped onto the riverbank. She approached the dark river and knelt to touch the water. "The a*yu* are swimming to the sea."

Micah joined her at the water's edge. "*Ayu?*"

"Little fish from the mountains. They pass through Hiroshima this time of year."

"I see."

"Would you like to join them?" she asked.

"What do you mean?"

"Swim." Ai bent over to grab the bottom of her kimono, which she raised above her knees. She stepped into the river, black water swirling around her ankles.

He reached for her. "Ai, wait."

She laughed. "The water is not deep." She moved away from him, pushing toward the middle of the river.

Micah hesitated. Walking into the river at night seemed crazy, but he had to remain with her. He inched into the water. A chill traveled up his legs. "What are we doing here?"

Ai grinned and held out a hand. "Are you ready to swim?"

"Do I have a choice?" he asked, taking her hand.

"No." She dropped into the river pulling him down with her. "You're all wet, Micah-san."

He brushed water off his face. "Ha. Ha. Very funny."

Ai lunged forward and began to swim. She traveled about fifty yards and stopped. "Look at the *ayu*," she said. Hundreds of tiny silver fish flashed through the water all around them. Micah opened his mouth to comment but before he could speak, Ai plunged back into the river and resumed swimming. The *ayu* swam up close as if he were one of them, their cold scales rubbing against his body. Ai paused again. Water droplets cascaded from her black hair. She pointed at the shimmering white moon. "Do you see it?"

"What? The moon?"

"The rabbit on the moon. He's pounding *mochi* with a mallet."

"I don't see a rabbit," Micah said, "but I do see a man in the moon."

Her left eyebrow went up. "Why is there a man in the moon?"

"Not a real man ... more like ... we see a man's face on the surface of the moon."

Ai giggled behind her hands. "You're silly, Micah-san." She dove into the water and went on until she reached the point where the river merged with the sea. Waves lapped against her, making her bob like a buoy. The silhouettes of abandoned merchant ships lined the harbor. "Come on," Ai said, "we'll catch a ride."

"Catch a ride? Where? Into the sea? It's not a good idea to swim too far. There could be sharks."

"They won't bite us."

"The sea is deeper than a river."

"*Hai.* And you're bigger and stronger than me, so you should have no problem swimming in the sea." Ai swam away and Micah groaned before following.

As he moved beyond the river, warmth surrounded him as if he'd been swaddled in a blanket. The smell of salt hung in the air. Ai swam a short distance and stopped. She raised her chin and wailed, "Ah-oooh. Ah-oooh."

"What are you doing?"

"I'm getting our ride," she said. "Ah-oooh. Ah-oooh."

Micah scanned the surface of the sea as he tread water. "What are we looking for?"

"Be patient, Micah-san."

"I am patient. I just wish I knew what we're doing."

"There!" she shouted and pointed ahead of her.

A smooth round head broke the surface of the water. Grey with black eyes. A small whale or dolphin. The creature dipped out of sight, then resurfaced in front of Ai. "Micah-san, this is my friend, Hoshi. He's a finless porpoise."

Micah blinked rapidly as he stared at the porpoise. "Uh … hello … Hoshi-san."

"Hello, Micah-san," the porpoise responded in a nasally voice.

"I must be losing my mind. I could have sworn that porpoise talked to me."

"Haven't you ever talked to animals?"

"I used to talk to our dog, but he never answered me." Micah tried to snap his wet fingers. "Wait! I did talk to a rabbit once."

Ai smiled. "The rabbit on the moon."

"I'm not sure about that, but he was flying."

She flattened a hand on Hoshi's flank and swung herself onto his back. He gave a little shake and lifted her up until only her legs remained submerged.

"You want me to climb on him?"

"Don't you want a ride?"

Micah inspected the porpoise. "Are you sure he's big enough for both of us?"

"You'll be a feather," Hoshi said.

"This is so weird." Micah made his way around to Ai. He swung his leg onto the back of the porpoise and slid off. "How do I get on?"

Ai held out a hand. "Let me help you."

He accepted her hand and climbed. "Whoa ... whoa ... whoa, I'm slipping." Micah slid off, splashing face first into the sea. He surfaced and smacked the water. "This is impossible."

"Try again," Ai said. "But when you climb on, dig in with your thighs. It won't hurt Hoshi."

"She's right," Hoshi said. "I won't break."

"One more time." Micah reached for Ai's hand and swung over Hoshi's back.

"Use your legs," Ai said.

He pressed his thighs against the cool, slick flesh of the porpoise and brought his full weight onto its back. His body rocked unsteadily and Micah thought he would fall again, until settling against Ai. "I got it."

"Put your arms around me and hold on."

He wrapped his arms around her slender waist. "I'm ready."

And with that, Hoshi set off, slow at first, his body gliding near the surface, before picking up speed. Micah grinned as they cut through the waves, Hoshi's body rising and falling like a carousel horse. He traveled farther into the Inland Sea, past the floating *torii* gate of the Itsukushima Shrine and slumbering black islands. Overhead, stars appeared to swirl and dance to an unknown symphony, spinning pinwheels that cast golden sparks. Hoshi slowed to a stop. "Look at them," Ai said pointing to the stars. "Don't you wish it could always be this way?"

Micah wished she could enjoy moments like this while awake, but the magic of this place, like the magic of dreams, faded with the birth of each sunrise. And yet, if Frank was right, and the visitors to this plane forgot what they experienced, why did Ai remember how to call Hoshi? And why did she remember Micah's name?

"Ai, I have a question for you."

"All right."

"When you wake up, do you remember what happens here?"

Ai brushed hair back from her face. "Some of it. I told Mama about you."

"Oh. How did that go?"

"She went to see a priest at the temple."

"A priest? Why would she do that?"

"He's coming to the house to do something."

"To do what?"

"Make you leave."

Micah let this sink in. He assumed the priest would perform a ritual akin to an exorcism. What would happen if the exorcism succeeded? Where would he go? The thought of being away from Ai and Kiyomi made his chest hurt. He wasn't ready to move on. Not when he was close to getting to know them.

"Do you want me to leave?"

Ai laid a hand on his arm. "If I wanted you gone, you wouldn't be here with me. Hoshi doesn't give rides to just anyone."

"This is true," Hoshi said.

Micah patted Hoshi on his flank, which was cool as a milk bottle delivered on the porch during winter. "I appreciate that, buddy."

"We should go back," Ai said.

"If that's what you want."

"I would rather stay here, but I can't."

"Hey," Micah said, "would you like to meet some friends of mine?"

"Are they as nice as you?"

"Oda drinks a lot of sake, but he's harmless."

"Where do they live?" she asked.

"On an oyster boat between the Aioi Bridge and Motoyasu Bridge."

"I will take you there," Hoshi said.

Hoshi swung about and headed toward Hiroshima. As they pitched on the waves, Micah went over the questions he had for Frank. To have a relationship with Kiyomi, he needed to grasp the principles governing interaction between the living and the dead. *Relationship*. He let the word linger and then laughed inwardly. How was he going to have a relationship with her? A woman who wanted him gone *posthaste*.

Ai glanced back at him. "Are you all right, Micah-san?"

"I'm fine."

"There's sadness in your eyes. You must miss your family? I would miss my family if they were gone."

"Yes. I miss them sometimes. Love is defined by how much it hurts us."

She appeared confused.

"I mean, the more we love someone, the more it hurts to lose them."

Ai nodded. "Then we must try our best not to lose them."

"Yes. That's a wise plan, Ai-chan."

Hoshi entered the current of the Motoyasu River, a*yu* parting around him. The luminous moon edged closer, watching over the city with a sharp eye. A glowing lantern on an oyster boat highlighted the silhouette of a slender man. Frank. Before Micah could tell Hoshi this was their boat, the purpose shifted course and headed straight toward the oyster boat. As they drew near, Frank's head swiveled and he eyed them with amusement. "A little night swimming, Micah-san?"

Hoshi came alongside the boat. Frank reached for Ai and lifted her onto the deck. "And who do we have here?"

Ai kept her gaze low. "My name is Ai."

"Are you going to help me up?" Micah asked.

Frank looked at Oda who caressed a bottle of sake. "I don't know. Oda-san, what do you think? Should we welcome Micah-san aboard or send him back to sea?"

Oda rose from his barrel and burped. Ai chuckled and he blushed. "Please excuse my rudeness, Ai-chan."

"You are forgiven," she said.

Oda waddled to the gunwale, his stomach shaking. He leaned over and extended a hand. "Come on, Micah-san."

Micah landed on the deck with a thud. His clothes were dry as if he had never been in the water.

"How are you, Hoshi-san?" Oda asked.

"I'm well, Oda-san. Would you share your sake with me?" Hoshi opened his mouth and Oda poured sake down the creature's throat. Hoshi flopped into the river, water splashing onto the deck. "You thought only turtles enjoyed sake."

"No. No," Oda said, "I never thought that. Even Micah-san likes sake and he's an American."

Micah noticed for the first time how small Hoshi was. He estimated his body to be six feet in length, and his weight no more than two hundred pounds. How could he carry a full-grown man? Perhaps in this magical place, God endowed animals with supernatural abilities, including the capacity to reason. They certainly didn't waste time waging war and dropping bombs.

"Well, goodbye then," Hoshi said.

Ai leaned against the gunwale to wave. "Sayōnara, Hoshi-san."

Micah stepped in front of Frank, hands on his hips. "I have questions."

"So do I, but first, introductions are in order." He bowed to Ai. "I'm Frank. The big lout with the sake is Oda."

"I'm master of this boat," Oda said, returning to his barrel.

Frank rolled his eyes. "So, Ai-chan, how do you like having Micah-san in your house?"

Ai grinned. "He is a quiet ghost."

Oda scratched the stubble on his chin. "Does your mother like having him around?"

"She has arranged an exorcism," Micah said.

Frank and Oda exchanged bemused smiles. Frank turned to Micah. "To drive you from their home?"

"That's right."

"Damn, Micah-san," Oda said, "What did you do? Pinch her butt while she slept?"

Ai giggled again.

Frank sighed. "Oda-san, please. She's a child."

"He doesn't offend me," Ai said.

"See," Oda said. "She's not offended. I like this girl."

"Back to my questions," Micah said.

Frank folded his arms over his chest. "What do you want to know?"

"You told me a living person doesn't remember what they experience when they're outside their body. Ai does. She knew my name. She recalled swimming with Hoshi in the sea. Why did you lie to me?"

"I was trying to protect you, Micah."

"Protect me ... from what?"

"From your wild expectations. Yes, the living do visit us, and sometimes they recall those encounters, but the distance between us is as vast as the ocean. It makes no difference what happens here."

"It makes a difference to me."

"You have no future with her, Micah. Why can't you accept that?"

Ai edged closer to Micah. "Are you talking about Mama?"

"There you go," Frank said. "See what you've done."

Ai continued to stare and Micah fumbled to find the proper response. Should he admit his attraction to Kiyomi? She probably wouldn't have liked him when he was alive, let alone dead. This whole thing was madness. He should listen to Frank and walk away. And yet, his heart screamed for him to stay, to get to know Kiyomi better, to let nature take its course as the four seasons swept across the waiting earth, the cycle of life raising and resolving mysteries along the way. As he opened his mouth to speak Ai blurted, "Mama is getting married."

Micah's core pulled down to the deck. His hopes and dreams crushed by her words.

"Baa-baa and Ojiisan want to adopt a son," Ai continued.

"Who wants to adopt a son?" Micah asked.

"Her grandparents," Frank said. "Do your grandparents want an heir?"

"Both of their sons died in China. Mama is to marry this man and give them a son."

Micah massaged his chin. "This is an arranged marriage?"

"*Hai*," Ai answered. "Mama isn't happy."

Micah turned toward Frank feeling vindicated, as if Kiyomi's unhappiness was a welcome mat outside a front door. Frank shook his head, but Micah didn't care. Kiyomi didn't want this marriage. He had a chance. But for what? An impossible relationship? He shifted his focus to Ai. "Do you want your mama to remarry?"

"She should choose her husband."

"Arranged marriages have been a tradition in Japan for hundreds of years," Frank said.

"Don't listen to him," Micah said. "Love comes from the heart, not a business deal set up by meddling parents."

Ai smiled at his words, and her reaction sent a wave of warmth rising from his chest.

"Micah, you're heading into dangerous territory."

He ignored Frank and turned to Ai. "Perhaps I can help you. Would a potential husband want to move into a house that's haunted?"

"Micah, no!"

"Good plan," Oda said. "Scare him away before anything is arranged."

A grin flickered over Ai's lips. "Could you do that?"

"I don't know. I could try. You could help me."

Ai tapped a finger against her lips. "You want to be with Mama?"

"I want to be her friend."

"She might not like you."

"But you like me, don't you?" he asked, in a voice that sounded a little too desperate.

"*Hai*. But I'm a child. She's an adult. Mama needs more than a friend to ride on Hoshi with her."

Frank stood with his chin thrust out as if staring down a classroom of naïve students. "Ai can teach you a thing or two, Micah."

Silence settled over the group. Micah stared at the lantern hanging from the mast. A glow spread out from beneath the lantern, bathing the deck in a soft red. Mosquitoes buzzed around the light. As he gazed into the pulsating color, Micah could almost hear the hiss of the propane lantern his family took on camping trips.

Deep in the Washington woods, cloaked in darkness so thick the world vanished beyond the glow of their fire, they sat on rocks and stared into the crackling flames, the smell of wood smoke heavy in the air. A fuzzy glow settled over the boat. Frank and Ai faded like rainbows dissolving into the sky after a storm, until all he could see was a campfire painting the black canvas of a surrounding forest.

"I know I told you not to be afraid of women, Micah. I just didn't think you'd wait until you were dead." Levi whittled a piece of wood, the blade of his knife capturing firelight which sparked prismatic colors along the edge.

His father sat nearby sipping from a mug of coffee. "Micah always was a little slow to move on things. It took him a month to work up the nerve to ask Jenny Guthrie to homecoming."

"And then she turned me down," Micah said, another black mark in his book of memories.

Levi sheathed his knife and snatched a stick off the ground. "That's because it took you so long to ask her." He poked the stick into the fire and stirred the embers.

His mother, who sat near the lantern reading the latest novel from Willa Cather, paused to peer over the top of her book. Her eyes held the tough love only mothers knew how to wield—a sword that cut but never scarred. "And now look at you, Micah, falling for a Japanese girl after what they did to your brother."

"Kiyomi's nice, Mother. You'd like her."

His mother returned to her book. "The Japs killed Levi, that's all I know."

"*She* didn't kill Levi."

His father poured the last of his coffee on the ground, then banged out coffee grounds on a rock. "It's your afterlife, Micah."

"Hell's bells," Levi said. "If you like this Kiyomi, be her friend. Nothing wrong in that."

"Be her friend," Micah repeated. He stared into the leaping flames and nodded. "Yes, I can do that. It's a start."

Micah looked up to find everyone on the oyster boat staring at him. "What?"

Frank pushed back his glasses. "Enjoy your trip?"

"My trip?"

"You've been standing there in a daze for over an hour."

Micah turned to Ai for confirmation.

"Don't worry, Micah-san, Oda-san has been teaching me how to burp."

"A most useful skill," Oda said.

Frank massaged the bridge of his nose. "It's called dimensional travel. We all experience it. Even the living. We might go back in time to relive an important event, or forward into what could have been a possible future."

A glimpse into a possible future seemed cruel, especially if that future revealed a life filled with love and happiness. "I was with my family. We were sitting around a campfire talking about Kiyomi."

Ai's mouth fell open. "About Mama?"

"Yes. About your mama."

Oda pointed the sake bottle at him. "And what did they tell you?"

"That I should be her friend."

"I agree," Ai said.

"And not interfere in her personal affairs," Frank added. "The dead can influence the living if we whisper into their ear while they sleep. Whatever we say plants a seed in their subconscious."

"Nonsense," Oda said. "I whispered into my wife's ear for years and nothing happened."

"What did you tell her?" Ai asked.

Oda beamed like a madman who saw the world beyond the bars that constrained him. "I told her to jump into a volcano."

"Oh, Oda-san," Frank groaned.

"He's funny," Ai said, chuckling.

"*Hai,*" Oda agreed. "I've been telling Frank I'm funny for years."

"Ai-chan, what are you doing!" Kiyomi stormed toward the boat. In the waves of moonlight spilling around her, her cheeks appeared fuller, and her breasts swelled against the cloth of her kimono. Nervous energy raced to the tips of Micah's fingers and toes. Frank and Oda eyed her approach with caution and admiration. Ai smiled as if taking part in a game.

Kiyomi marched up the narrow gangplank and stepped onto the boat. She searched each of their faces with fire in her eyes before glaring at Ai who continued to smile. "Why are you here with these men?"

"We went swimming," Micah said.

"I know who you are," Kiyomi said. "You're the American I watched die. You're the one who haunts our home and torments my daughter."

"His name is Micah-san," Ai said. "He's nice."

"I don't care if he's nice." She faced him. "Leave us alone, Micah-san. You will not corrupt Ai with your strange American ideas."

"Please, Mama, he means us no harm."

Kiyomi whirled toward Ai. "Hush. You are young and foolish. You don't know of what you say. He's our enemy. He flew to Hiroshima to kill us. Stay away from him."

Ai pushed out her bottom lip and folded her arms over her chest. "He doesn't want to hurt us now."

"And stay away from these two as well," Kiyomi said, looking from Frank to Oda. "They have no honor."

"Now wait a minute," Frank said, stepping toward her. Kiyomi pointed a finger at him and Frank retreated like a schoolboy before a bully.

"Ai is my daughter. You will respect my wishes." Kiyomi held out her hand and Ai sighed before taking it. Kiyomi hustled down the gangplank, towing Ai behind her.

Micah sank onto a barrel.

"She's a looker," Frank said, taking another barrel. "I get the attraction."

"Holy mackerel. I've never seen her act this way. She's usually passive and quiet."

Frank and Oda burst out laughing.

"What did I say?"

"While they're alive, Japanese women behave that way," Frank said.

"Some of them," Oda corrected.

"But here," Frank continued, "where they no longer feel constrained by expectations, a Japanese woman can roar like a lion."

Micah stared into the darkness, trying to catch a glimpse of Kiyomi and Ai, but they were nowhere in sight. *She won't get rid of me so easily. Not until she gets to know me.*

Chapter Eighteen

Kneeling on a pillow inside the living room, Kiyomi watched Ai and her best friend, Jun, work on a school assignment, a drawing that represented the spirit of Japan. According to Ai, the boys drew pictures of soldiers with crazy eyes, or Zeros blasting Mr. B from the sky. Ai and Jun drew *Sakura.* Ai's cherry blossoms cascaded against a background featuring Mt. Füji. Kiyomi couldn't help but smile. It was the first time she had smiled in days, unable to forget her disturbing dream. In the dream, she found Ai onboard an oyster boat with three men. One was the American she watched fall from the sky, the ghost Ai called Micah-san. The dream had been so lucid it felt more like a memory. This made her uneasy and she counted the days until the priests would perform an exorcism.

With the house opened up, pale afternoon light filtered in and a soft breeze explored the rooms, bringing with it the earthy scent of the garden. In addition to her anxiety over the dream, Kiyomi fretted because Banri and Sayoka had gone to meet the Takadas who claimed to have news regarding an adopted son. Compounding her distress was a nearly empty cupboard and Banri's failing health. He coughed throughout the night, a sucking wet sound that reminded her of walking through mud.

"*Kon'nichiwa*, Kiyomi-san."

Jun's mother, Chuya stood at the *doma* removing her *geta*. Kiyomi met Chuya shortly after moving to Hiroshima. They became instant friends, watching their daughters grow from wobbly toddlers to proper young ladies. Chuya taught Ai the story about the rabbit on the moon.

"*Kon'nichiwa*, Chuya-san. Come inside. Please."

Jun looked up from the floor and waved. "We are making pictures for school."

"I see," Chuya said, glancing over Jun's shoulder. "You and Ai have drawn beautiful flowers."

Jun and Ai beamed with pride before returning to their work.

"Please sit," Kiyomi said motioning toward a cushion.

"We can't stay long."

"The war takes everything from us, including time," Kiyomi said.

They settled on their pillows, backs straight, hands folded over their laps. Chuya's gaze sank to the *tatami* mats. The skin under Chuya's eyes was puffy. Fine wrinkles emerged at the corners of her mouth. "What's wrong, Chuya-san?"

Chuya closed her eyes. When she reopened them, they were moist with tears. "We're evacuating Jun to the country. To the Miyoshi Temple."

Kiyomi glanced at Ai, who stared at Chuya with an open mouth. "When?" Ai asked.

"Tomorrow morning."

Jun put down her pencil and reached out to lay a hand on Ai's arm. "I wanted to tell you."

Ai resumed drawing without comment.

"I thought the government wouldn't authorize the evacuation of girls as young as Jun."

"This is true," Chuya said. "However, Jun has an older cousin who has agreed to watch over her. We are going to come for her when summer ends and move together into my uncle's house in Asa-chō. If you have relatives in the country, you should do the same. The city is no longer safe."

As Kiyomi studied Ai stretched out on the floor, she recalled the photographs of Japanese cities burnt to ashes. A crow cawed from the garden. The sound reminded her of her strange dream. What were the crows trying to tell her? She had to protect Ai at all costs, but how?

"Perhaps you should send Ai to the temple?"

"We have no one at the temple to watch over her," Kiyomi said.

"Can you take her somewhere?"

"There is no place we could go. And Banri isn't healthy enough to travel."

"You could leave your in-laws in Hiroshima. I am certain they would understand."

"No. They would not," Kiyomi said.

Chuya bowed her head. "*Hai.* You are right. So sorry for mentioning this."

"No need to apologize, my friend. Your heart is in a good place."

Chuya smiled. "You are kind for thinking so."

Sayoka and Banri entered the yard.

"We should be leaving," Chuya said, standing. She turned to Jun. "Tell Ai-chan goodbye."

Jun pushed off the floor, bringing her journal with her. Ai remained on the mats, her focus on her drawing. Normally, Kiyomi would have scolded her for acting rude; however, she knew this was Ai's way of expressing her sadness.

Jun stood over Ai. She pushed out her bottom lip and offered a subtle nod. Clearly, Jun understood what Ai was doing. "Sayōnara, Kiyomi-san. Sayōnara, Ai-chan."

Ai remained quiet, refusing to look up from her journal.

Chuya took hold of Jun's hand and bid them both farewell. At the *doma,* she greeted Banri and Sayoka, pausing to exchange pleasantries before leaving. Ai set down her pencil and rested her head on her arms. Sayoka entered the room with her chin thrust out. She glared at Ai and her face pinched. "What's wrong with Ai?"

"She's tired," Kiyomi said.

Banri knelt on his pillow. "I hope she's not getting sick," he said and coughed.

Sayoka lowered onto her pillow and gestured for Kiyomi to sit.

"We have wonderful news, Kiyomi-san," Banri said, retrieving his pipe.

Kiyomi sat on her pillow. Ai appeared to have fallen asleep.

Banri produced his tobacco pouch and filled the pipe bowl. He struck a match and took fire to the tobacco. "The matchmakers have found someone."

Kiyomi remained quiet. What quality of man could this be? She felt certain if he were a fish, he'd be released back into the sea.

Banri inhaled, his cheeks concaving, then blew out smoke. "You know Mitsuyo Hata?"

Her chest ached as if Banri had chiseled off a piece of her heart. Yes, she knew Mitsuyo Hata. Jikan introduced them when she first arrived in Hiroshima on a visit to the Industrial Promotion Hall, where Mitsuyo worked as an accountant. Mitsuyo had studied her from behind thick black glasses. His head appeared too small for his body, a surprise given Mitsuyo's slight frame and spindly legs. Despite his frail appearance, Mitsuyo had been a fine athlete. A champion swimmer in school. And Kiyomi knew him to be a kind and decent man, someone who would treat Ai with the respect she deserved. But Kiyomi couldn't shake the memory of neighborhood ladies laughing behind Mitsuyo's back when he joined the army. They said he resembled a boy wearing a costume in his uniform. In the Philippines, shrapnel tore into Mitsuyo's side. He returned from the war a cripple. Unable to straighten, he walked hunched over, taking small steps. He reminded Kiyomi of the stick insects that clung to tree branches. She had seen him standing on the Aioi Bridge watching boys swim in the river, a look of longing on his face. The sight always saddened her.

Despite his physical shortcomings, Kiyomi understood why her in-laws would be interested in Mitsuyo. A college graduate with financial experience, Mitsuyo had a head for business. No doubt, Banri saw him as someone who could restore the family's fortune. And with his gentle nature, Mitsuyo would respect Sayoka's place in the household if something happened to Banri. But what quality of sons would he produce? And given his physical limitations, was he capable of pillowing her?

"Kiyomi?" Banri's voice pulled her back into the conversation.

"*Hai.*"

A frown settled upon Sayoka's mouth. "Did you not hear Banri's question?"

Kiyomi's scalp tingled. "*Hai.* So sorry. I do know Mitsuyo."

Sayoka continued to frown. "Well? What do you think of him?"

Kiyomi hesitated while searching for the proper response. Mitsuyo would never make her heart flutter like a butterfly's wings. His face would never appear in her dreams. Kiyomi feared a life of regret if she accepted this match, but what could she do if Banri and Sayoka were determined to adopt a son, and Mitsuyo proved to be their best choice? If she refused, her in-laws could put her and Ai out on the street. Where would they live? How could they find food in a city where people were starving? The situation proved intolerable, yet she found no solution to her dilemma.

"Mitsuyo is an honorable man," Kiyomi said.

Sayoka grunted. "Is that all you have to say?"

"He suffered a serious war wound."

Banri pointed the stem of his pipe at her. "What are you suggesting?"

Kiyomi's gaze fell to her lap. "Are you certain he can provide a son?"

The question remained unanswered, making Kiyomi believe her in-laws had never considered the matter. Finally, Banri said, "Mitsuyo is coming over for dinner on Saturday. You can ask him that question."

Heat traveled up from Kiyomi's chest and settled in her cheeks. Why did Banri defer such an important and delicate question to her? They were, after all, the ones who wanted an heir. "With your permission, I will prepare dinner."

"*Hai*," Banri said, his voice gruff. "The kitchen is a good place for you."

Kiyomi bowed before rising from the floor. Her face continued to burn. *The kitchen is a good place for you? What does that mean?* They asked her opinion but gave her no voice. She had no control over her own future. Kiyomi searched through their meager supplies. It didn't matter what they had planned for her. Without more food, they would be dead before the month ended.

Kiyomi prepared soup flavored with a few wilted bean sprouts. Ai sighed upon seeing the soup. She kept her face downcast to try and hide the disenchantment in her eyes. After dinner and her evening chores, Kiyomi had Ai help her close up the house, then spread their futons. Ai was quick to snuggle under her covers. She closed her eyes, pretending to be asleep.

Kiyomi reached out to stroke her hair. "It hurts having Jun leave, *neh*?"

Ai remained quiet.

"Please, Ai-chan, talk to me."

The swallows chirped inside their nest. Wind rattled the screens. The mosquito netting billowed like sails catching wind, but only ghost wind blew inside the house.

"None of it's fair. Jun leaving. Your marriage to Mitsuyo."

"You were listening to our conversation? I thought you were asleep?"

"I wish I had been," Ai said.

"What would you have me do?"

Ai's eyes opened. "We should do what Chuya suggested and leave the city."

"Impossible."

Ai propped up on an elbow. "Why is it impossible? Must we stay so you can marry Mitsuyo?"

"I have obligations."

"But you don't want to get married."

"You're young. You don't understand. Besides, you cannot move into the country unless you have a place to go. We know no one outside Hiroshima."

"Ojiisan and Baa-baa are wrong to make you get married. The war can't last forever."

The war can't last forever. If only this were true. But at that moment, it seemed as if the war would go on and on without end. Did the generals even remember why they went to war? The screen opened and Banri appeared, his eyes flashing fear. It was a look she had seen far too many times.

"Bombers are approaching. Hurry."

Kiyomi stood and held out a hand for Ai. "You're right. This can't go on forever."

Air raid sirens began to howl.

As they climbed into the hole, Kiyomi experienced the cold draft that now accompanied these moments. *Why won't you find peace, American? We have nothing to offer you. Surely Heaven awaits.*

Chapter Nineteen

Micah left the house after the family fell asleep. While being near Kiyomi brought a feeling of satisfaction, it was tinged with sadness, for he could find no way to narrow the divide between them. Outside, a star-filled sky greeted him, the surrounding air heavy with heat and humidity. He had no particular plan. No place to go. He left Nakajima-Honmachi and crossed the Aioi Bridge. Below, the river traveled with quiet purpose reminding him of the night he sat beside Whatcom Creek with Levi and watched the Aurora Borealis. Bands of green and violet light had dipped toward the ground before surging back into the heavens. "Can you imagine what the first people on earth must have thought when they saw this?" Levi asked. "God did this for us, Micah. He shines down his light to show us the way."

Micah had never considered himself particularly religious, but under this blackest of Japanese skies, he found himself wishing God would shine his light down again.

The main road through Hiroshima congested closer to the hills. Evacuees crowded the sidewalks. Entire families shuffled along in silence, their possessions in sacks or suitcases. They weaved upward into the countryside in long single file lines.

A sound rolled across the dark sky. Droning. Mechanical. Men brought carts to a stop. Bicycle riders braked. People stood with their eyes trained to the south where a formation of B-29s appeared on the horizon. The evacuees watched in silence. There were no screams or shouts. No mad dashes toward ditches. Children nestled against their mothers. His thoughts turned to Kiyomi and Ai hiding in their hole and he could see their futures unfolding as if watching a movie. Bombs rained onto their home. Fire blocked escape to the river. They screamed in agony as flames overtook them. Micah jammed his hands into his pockets and hurried toward their house while monitoring the bombers' progress.

Not tonight. Please, God. Let them pass tonight.

Searchlights probed the darkness. Anti-aircraft guns boomed and spat fire. Micah hustled along the sidewalk. He tried to imagine what Kiyomi was doing. Would she remain inside the shelter? What if she was still asleep? She had slept through air raids before. If they were asleep, he would have to awaken them somehow. The hole was a death trap.

He spotted Kiyomi, alone on the Aioi Bridge, eyes wide, head turning from side to side as if she searched for something. A bluish glow surrounded her and Micah recognized this was her spirit. Micah walked straight to her.

"You," she said, brushing hair from her face.

He bit his lip while considering his response. *I'm not going to be afraid of her. I'm not going to be afraid of her.* His fingernails dug into his palms. *Who am I kidding? I'm terrified.*

"Why are you here? Are you following me?"

"I'm not following you. You're following me."

She blinked rapidly.

"Is something wrong? You seem distressed."

Kiyomi gazed beyond the river toward Nakajima-Honmachi. "No ... yes. I'm ..."

"Looking for Ai?"

Desperation emerged in her eyes. "Have you seen her?"

"No."

Kiyomi seized the bridge railing and squeezed.

"How do you know Ai is missing?"

She glanced over her shoulder. "What are you saying?"

Micah tugged on an earlobe. *How can I explain this in a way that makes sense to her?* "Well ... uh ... what I mean is, we're in the realm of spirits, so how did you know Ai is missing?"

Kiyomi whirled around to face him. "You believe I'm an ignorant woman?"

Micah took a step back, feeling like a zookeeper who had accidentally released a hungry tiger. "No. That's not what I—"

"You died. I watched it happen. Of course I know we're in the spirit realm. You must think I'm a fool."

"A fool? No. I don't think that at all."

She waved a finger at him. "A simple woman who cooks and cleans all day without a serious thought in her head?"

"I never said—"

"Don't presume to know me," she pressed.

He found himself smiling.

Her eyebrows went up. "Why are you smiling?"

"I'm sorry. Would you rather I frown?"

"Please excuse me. I don't have time for this conversation."

Micah considered telling her she had nothing to worry about. What harm could come to Ai's spirit in a place where she rode on the back of a porpoise and swam with fishes? Instead, he said, "May I ask you something?"

"What is it?"

"When you awaken, do you remember what happens here?"

Kiyomi turned from him. "I have no memory of you other than watching your death. But Ai seems to remember you. She mentioned your name."

Micah knew Kiyomi was lying. She had recognized him the moment she saw him approaching.

"Why do you haunt us?"

"I have nowhere else to go."

Wrinkles creased her brow as she appeared to be working through something.

"I would never hurt you or Ai."

Anger flashed over her face. "That's a lie. You flew on Mr. B."

"You know I did."

"What was your job?"

"On board the bomber?"

"*Hai*. On board the bomber. What did you do?"

Why did she have to ask me this question? "I was the bombardier."

"What does that mean? You were responsible for dropping the bombs?"

"I entered the information into the bombsight to direct the bombs and then released them."

"You bombed Tokyo?"

"I did bomb Tokyo."

Kiyomi nodded as if his confession reaffirmed a question in her mind. "With incendiary bombs?"

Prior to his death and subsequent rebirth in Hiroshima, he didn't give a damn what anyone thought about his role in the war, but her questions probed like a surgeons blade exposing a cancer, and to admit his part in the firebombing campaign left him vulnerable and guilt-ridden.

"That's right," he said.

"My aunt and uncle died in that attack. They burned alive. You did this."

"Yes," he whispered.

"And now you say you won't hurt us."

"I can't hurt you. I'm dead."

"But you would try to kill us if you were alive."

How to defend what could not be defended? How to justify an action that no longer made sense to him? "It was never my job to kill civilians. We tried to hit military targets."

"But you knew civilians burned?"

He deserved her wrath, but this didn't make it go down any easier. "Yes. I knew they burned."

Kiyomi bore into him with a critical glare. "That makes you a murderer."

"And what would you call the Japanese soldiers who raped and slaughtered in Nanjing and Manila? How about the American prisoners they murdered on Bataan?"

She averted her gaze. "I do not know of these things."

"Well I do, and so does the rest of the world, and it filled our hearts with a terrible rage."

"Must we continue this conversation?"

Micah wasn't surprised Kiyomi avoided the subject of Japanese atrocities, but instead of holding it against her, he decided to move on. "We should talk about something other than the war."

"Let us find Ai. Then you leave."

Overhead, the B-29s moved away from the city heading north. He watched until they vanished in the darkness, then turned his attention to Kiyomi who waited. "I'd like to, believe me." The lie came off his tongue awkwardly, the words forced, and he could tell from her reaction she wasn't convinced by his declaration. To overcome his embarrassment, Micah steered her back to the subject of Ai. "Where might Ai have gone?"

Kiyomi touched her cheek. "I'm not sure. Maybe Nigitsu Park."

"All right. Let's go find her."

She hesitated as if waiting for him to go in front of her.

"Kiyomi-san, you must lead. I don't know the way."

Kiyomi gave a quick nod and set off at a brisk pace. At first, he was content to follow and watch the sway of her hips, but as he trailed her through dark alleys Micah pulled closer until they walked side by side.

The air raid sirens stopped and spirits crowded the roads. An older couple sat watching the moon. A man carrying a lantern stopped every few yards to call out a name. Kiyomi appeared oblivious to it all, her focus on getting to the park. She pointed ahead. "See the prefectural office? We're getting close. Ai likes to pick wildflowers in the Yorakuen garden."

The park was located across the street from the government building. Kiyomi hustled onto a trail leading into the park and waved him forward. "Hurry, Micah-san."

They searched near the pond, inside the pagoda, and at the playground where spirit children laughed and played games. Kiyomi pressed a hand against her forehead. "Where could she be?"

"Is there anywhere else she likes to visit?"

"Nowhere close," she said.

He touched her arm, marveling at the softness of her skin. "Ai is going to be all right."

Kiyomi stared at his hand before pulling back her arm. "I must find her."

Micah scanned the surrounding area. "If I were Ai, where would I want to …" An idea came to him and he nodded. "It makes too much sense," he said.

"What are you saying?"

"I might know where she is. Can you get us to the river, near the bridge?"

She studied him through narrowed eyes. "Which bridge?"

"The Motoyasu Bridge."

"Near your friend's oyster boat?"

"Hey, I thought you didn't remember anything that happened here."

Kiyomi stared at her slippers. "I might remember some things." When she looked up, her features had softened in the moonlight, as if she had removed a mask of bitterness and mistrust. "I must find her. Please help."

"Of course I'll help you."

She appeared pleased by his words. Another small victory in his battle to win her trust.

He trailed her to the river and down the stone steps to the riverbed. The river rippled past, moonlight bringing out the silver scales of the *ayu* near the surface. Darkness shrouded Frank and Oda's oyster boat. Where had they gone?

Kiyomi surveyed the riverbed. "What now?"

"I must do something. You'll think I'm crazy."

"You are crazy."

"Thanks a lot," Micah said. He cupped his hands around his mouth and let out a long, "Ah-oooh. Ah-oooh."

"What are you doing? Have you lost your mind?"

"Calling someone," he said. "Ah-oooh. Ah-oooh."

Kiyomi glanced over her shoulder toward the steps. "Do you want the *Kempeitai* to hear you?"

"The *Kempeitai*?"

"Military police."

Micah smiled at this before arching back his head. "Ah-oooh. Ah-oooh."

Kiyomi stepped closer and grabbed his arm. "This is madness."

"Don't worry, no one can hear us." He resumed his strange call without success. Micah lowered his hands. "Maybe Ai isn't here."

Kiyomi pointed at the river. "Micah-san. Look! Look!"

Hoshi glided near the surface of the river with a smiling Ai on his back like a circus performer. Ai waved as they drew closer. "Mama! Micah-san!"

Kiyomi plunged into the river. "Ai! What are you doing? Come here now!"

Micah joined her, cool water rising over his thighs. "She's all right. Hoshi is a friend."

"Who is Hoshi?"

Micah pointed at the approaching porpoise. "He's Hoshi."

"I don't understand."

"You will."

Hoshi slowed as he drew closer, water swishing away from his flanks. Ai slid off his back and patted him. "*Arigatō*, Hoshi-san. Once again, you have given me a nice adventure."

"Once again?" Kiyomi said, reaching for Ai. "You've ridden him before?"

"Many times," Hoshi said.

Kiyomi's mouth dropped open. "He can talk." She turned to Micah. "He can talk."

"He can do a lot more than that," Micah said taking her by the elbow. "Hello, Hoshi-san."

Hoshi raised his head out of the river. "Hello, Micah-san. We missed you tonight."

"You've ridden on him too?" Kiyomi asked.

"I'm sure Hoshi would be happy to give you a ride one day. Won't you, Hoshi-san?"

"I would be honored to carry the mother of Ai."

"Pet him, Mama."

Kiyomi hesitated. "I don't know if I—"

"He doesn't bite," Micah said.

Micah released her elbow and Kiyomi edged toward Hoshi who viewed her approach through a gleaming black eye. When she reached him, Kiyomi flattened a hand on his flank.

A joyful smile lit up her face. "His skin is smooth like a river stone and as cool as a mountain stream." A breath caught in her throat.

"What is it?" Micah asked.

"I had a memory," Kiyomi said, "from my childhood. I see myself riding on the back of a porpoise like this. It's so clear. So vivid. The moon. The stars. The spray of the sea upon my face." She glanced up at Micah. "You don't think I—"

"Traveled into the spirit realm as a child and rode on a porpoise such as Hoshi?"

"*Hai.*"

"Why not?"

She turned back to Hoshi. "I would be honored to ride you one day."

"Ai-chan will teach you how to call me," Hoshi said. "Micah-san has already learned this. We heard him calling from out in the bay."

"He is loud," Ai said and giggled behind her hands.

Kiyomi pulled back and glanced over her shoulder at Micah with wonder in her eyes. She patted Hoshi. "You take good care of Ai. For this I'm grateful."

"Ai is my friend," Hoshi said.

"And Hoshi is my friend," Ai said. She moved alongside Kiyomi and bent over to kiss Hoshi on his bulbous head.

"I must be going," Hoshi said. "Sayōnara."

"Sayōnara, Hoshi-san!" Ai shouted as he circled about and headed toward the bay.

When Hoshi disappeared into the darkness, Kiyomi rested a hand on Ai's shoulder. "You scared me. I awakened to find you gone. What would I do without you?"

"So sorry. I didn't know you missed me."

Kiyomi kissed Ai's hair. "Let us go home."

"Can we stay with Micah-san?"

"That's not a good idea."

"He's kind to me. We swim together. Please."

Kiyomi stared into her daughter's eyes as if searching for an answer in their liquid blackness. "All right. For a little while."

Micah held out a hand. Kiyomi wavered before accepting it. When his fingers closed over hers, like the petals of a tulip turning inward against the first hint of moonlight, he felt satisfied. There were no fireworks exploding inside his mind. No eruption of emotion. As he guided Kiyomi onto the riverbed, a sense of peace moved through him.

She released his hand when they cleared the river, but the action was measured, without a trace of anxiety. They strolled along the riverbed in silence, the river singing an ancient song performed long before men dreamed at the water's edge. The moon shined down a spotlight to light their way. Dark buildings crowded the riverbank, but these belonged in another world, separate from their tiny space. Ai walked in front, pausing to examine something.

"Ai is a beautiful girl," he said.

"Are you certain?"

Her response puzzled him. "Of course. You don't believe me?"

"She is Japanese."

"Yes. She is."

Kiyomi's gaze fell to the sand.

"Am I not supposed to admire anyone who is Japanese?"

"You surprise, Micah-san."

He hoped she meant this in a good way. "Am I the first American you've ever met?"

"I lived in Tokyo before the war. I danced with American sailors. They were mindless but fun, and smelled like *natto*, made from fermented soya beans."

"Sailors huh? No wonder you think so little of Americans."

Her attention shifted to the Industrial Promotion Hall across the river where moonlight danced upon the building's dome. "Hiroshima was a nice place before the war. Not refined like Tokyo. No. But charming. I hated the city when I moved here but, in time, learned to accept her. Hiroshima is beautiful, *neh*?"

"In some ways, it reminds me of Bellingham."

"Is that where you're from, Micah-san?"

"Yes. Bellingham, Washington."

"Ah," she said. "Near the capitol? Have you met President Roosevelt?"

Ai paused to stare at the moon. Micah glanced at Kiyomi who waited patiently. "You're thinking of Washington D.C. I live ... lived, in Washington State on the opposite side of the country."

"Oh. I see."

"Don't feel bad. A lot of people confuse Washington State with Washington D.C."

"I don't feel bad," she said.

"Hell, I took a Japanese Culture class in college and almost everything they taught us was wrong."

"I also went to college," Kiyomi said with pride.

"You strike me as an intelligent person."

A smile blossomed on her lips. "Tell me about your hometown? How does it remind you of Hiroshima?"

Ai pointed at the water. "See the *ayu*? We should catch them."

"They are smart fish," Kiyomi said. "No one is catching them during the day." She looked up at him. "You were telling me about Bellingham."

"Bellingham's a harbor town. The shore is lined with all kinds of businesses. Lumber mills. Canning factories. Ship builders. A large fishing fleet operates out of Bellingham. Downtown is quaint. Not as big as Hiroshima. Outside of town, there are many farms. Mount Baker towers over Bellingham. It's a big volcano. Taller than Mount Fūuji."

Kiyomi cocked her head. "Taller than Fūji-san?"

"Yes. And Mount Baker remains snowcapped year–round."

"Did you ever climb the mountain? I wanted to climb Mount Fūji-san but women are not allowed."

He let this sink in a moment and began to understand why Japanese women acted so differently in the spirit realm. "Levi kept after me to climb Baker. I finally agreed once I graduated high school."

"Who is Levi?" Kiyomi asked.

"My older brother. He died on Guadalcanal."

Her chin dipped toward her chest. "I see. You must hate Japan for taking his life."

"I did," Micah admitted. "Not anymore. My hatred died with me when I fell out of the sky."

"There's been too much hate."

Micah reached out to grab her arm and Kiyomi's eyes opened wide. "I want this war to end. I want it to end before you and Ai are hurt." He released her arm.

Kiyomi's attention shifted to Ai, then back to him. "America will bomb Hiroshima?"

"I'm not sure why we haven't already bombed the city."

"We have been bombed twice," Kiyomi corrected. "Once by Naval planes. And once by a single bomber."

"When we bombed Tokyo, we used over three hundred planes. That's what's coming to Hiroshima."

Her eyes took on a wounded appearance. "There will be nothing left. Everyone will die."

"What would you do if Hiroshima is attacked?"

"To escape?"

"Yes."

"Is that possible?" Kiyomi asked. "So many died in Tokyo."

"Do you have a plan to get away?"

"Our neighborhood association gave us bamboo rafts. If Hiroshima comes under attack, we're to make our way to the river. Once in the river, we're supposed to float out to sea. Foolish, *neh*?"

"If you get caught in a raid, you hit the water as fast as you can and get on those rafts. If you can make it to the sea, you might live. If you stay inside the hole in your kitchen, you will die." He massaged his chin as he contemplated the best course of action for her. "I saw families fleeing the city during tonight's warning. Couldn't you do that?"

"Those people live on the outskirts of Hiroshima, close to the hills. We live in the heart of the city. We would not have time." Kiyomi turned to watch Ai skipping stones. "My friend, Chuya, is evacuating with her family into the countryside. They will be safe from the bombs."

"Then you should take Ai and do the same thing."

"We cannot," Kiyomi said, her voice barely rising above the passing river.

"Why not?"

Kiyomi cupped a hand around her mouth and called to Ai. "Come, Ai-chan. We must leave."

"Can't you stay a little longer?"

"No. We must go." Kiyomi stepped closer. She searched his face as if burning it into memory. "You're not the devil I imagined you to be, Micah-san."

Micah jammed his hands inside his pockets as he watched them leave. *Maybe I'm worse than a devil. Much worse.*

Chapter Twenty

Anguish swept through Kiyomi's heart at the sight of her grieving daughter lying on the floor, her head resting on a tearstained pillow. Kiyomi wished she possessed magic that could take away her daughter's sorrow. It would require more than a comforting word or warm embrace to lift the dark thoughts from Ai's mind. Earlier, they had been at the Hiroshima Station with the rise of the sun. Sweat beaded on the brows of everyone gathered near the steam train. Grey clouds puffed from its smokestack. The atmosphere was thick with excitement, fear, tension, and heartache. Fathers and grandfathers stood motionless with faces carved from stone. Mothers and grandmothers dabbed at their eyes with cloth to hide tears from their children. The jaws of the women trembled in anticipation of what was to come, and in their hearts, they all asked the same question: "How can I survive the absence of my child?"

The children were organized by school and grade. Teachers scolded older boys who acted as if they were embarking on a grand adventure, shouting and laughing with abandon, while the girls joined their mothers and grandmothers in quiet reflection, sharing their misery and tears. Kiyomi remembered how Ai pressed against her hip, attention fixated on Jun who sobbed into her palms as Chuya tried to console her. Ai's hand clutched and released the skin on Kiyomi's lower back, but her face revealed nothing. Her emotions were locked deep inside and this caused

Kiyomi more distress than if Ai had broken down into a weeping wreck. Finally, the station master called, *"Miyoshi! Miyoshi!"* on his loudspeaker and teachers herded the children toward the train. At that moment, a strange calmness moved through the crowd as if everyone understood their duty to the Emperor. With a final sniffle, the women and girls stopped crying. Chuya squeezed Jun's hand and leaned over as if to give her a kiss, only to pull back at the last moment. "Be brave, Jun. Remember, we'll be coming to get you in a few weeks after we've arranged everything with the relocation office." Jun turned to Ai and they stared at each other in meditation, no doubt revisiting memories of swimming together in the river, watching cherry blossoms quiver in a breeze, or laughing as co-conspirators at a joke adults wouldn't understand.

Jun boarded the train with her head hung. She paused on the steps to look back and offered a half-hearted wave accompanied by a brave smile, then disappeared inside.

Ai released her hold on Kiyomi and stood with her hands balled into fists, her mouth drawn into a flat line. "It's not fair," she said and turned away.

The train whistle screamed, the sound vibrating across the platform. Parents and grandparents waved as the train chugged into motion. And as she observed them swallow their despair, knowing each of them would do anything to change their fate, Kiyomi found herself agreeing with Ai's assessment of the situation. How could anyone take pleasure from war? And how could the Japanese people continue to endure what could not be endured?

Back home, as Kiyomi wondered if there was anything she could do for Ai, she noticed *Sensei*-Sato and Reverend Ichiro strolling across the yard toward the veranda. They wore dark brown ceremonial robes and moved with determined purpose. Perplexed, she tried to guess why they had come, and then it hit her: *the exorcism.* "Ai-chan, the priests are here. You must get up to greet them."

Ai brushed tears onto the back of her hand. She rolled onto her side and glared at Kiyomi. "Why are they here?"

"To remove the ghost from our house."

Ai pushed off the floor and stood. "I don't want them here."

"Hush," Kiyomi said. She shuffled toward the *doma*, arriving as the priests removed their *geta*. "Good morning, *Sensei*-Sato. Good morning, Reverend Ichiro."

Sensei-Sato stared past her into the house. "You didn't tell them about the spirit, did you?"

"So sorry. Please excuse my ignorance, *Sensei*."

Sensei-Sato cleared his throat. "I would have preferred Banri and Sayoka had knowledge of the situation since they are the masters of this house, but what is done is done. We're here to eradicate this troubling spirit, and that's what we will do. Agreed?"

"*Hai*," Kiyomi answered.

They walked into the living room, where Ai stood with her hands locked to her sides. She bowed and greeted the priests formally. Both men offered approving smiles. Ai then turned toward Kiyomi, her expression hard and venomous. Kiyomi moved alongside her and placed an arm on her shoulder. "What's bothering you?"

"This is all wrong," Ai said, then shrugged out from beneath Kiyomi's arm.

Kiyomi's arm dangled in space like a dying branch. She grimaced and hoped the priests' wouldn't notice her anguish.

Ai covered her mouth and leaned into Kiyomi to whisper, "Remember, Mama. If you remember you'll know why I'm upset."

Sensei-Sato produced a *bokken* from a bag he carried and handed it to Reverend Ichiro. Reverend Ichiro faced Kiyomi and held out the flat piece of wood with a ball attached to it. "The sharp clicking of the *bokken* has a powerful effect on spiritual beings," he explained.

Sensei-Sato carried a stone the color of a rain cloud and wore a circular piece of iron over his knuckles. "We will go from room to room chanting from Lotus Sutra. Do not follow."

Kiyomi bowed. "*Hai*. We will remain here."

Father Ichiro fell in behind *Sensei*-Sato and they set off. Both men chanted while *Sensei*-Sato clacked the iron across the stone, producing sparks, and Reverend Ichiro snapped the ball against the *bokken*. They moved at a deliberate pace, pausing at each corner, their eyes rising toward the ceiling before continuing around the room. When the priests disappeared into the kitchen, Ai reached out to tug on Kiyomi's sleeve. "Don't you remember anything, Mama? Micah-san? The spirit world? Me riding on Hoshi?"

Kiyomi massaged her brow. "I'm so confused. What is it I'm to remember?"

"Micah-san is the spirit who lives with us. An American airman. He's not evil. Why are the priests trying to drive him away?"

"I … think …" Kiyomi pressed a hand against her stomach as a wave of nausea rolled through her. The sounds of the iron striking the flint, the ball clacking on the *bokken*, and the priests chanting grew louder. Kiyomi looked at Ai, who watched her through imploring eyes. "I'm not sure."

"Micah-san's hair is the color of wheat and his eyes are like the sky."

An image flashed through Kiyomi's mind. It was night in the city and she walked beside a tall man wearing a khaki shirt and trousers. He was talking to her. What did he say? Wait … she remembered now. Bellingham. This was his hometown. There were lumber mills and canning factories. *Hai.* What else? A volcano … Mount Baker. He said it was taller than Füji-san. Kiyomi clutched Ai's shoulders and brought her face close. "I recall Micah-san. *Hai.* I witnessed his death."

A smile warmed Ai's face. "He's not our enemy, Mama. Why must he leave?"

"Because he …" Kiyomi's chin dropped to her chest.

"What, Mama?"

"He doesn't belong here."

"Micah-san is my friend. I've lost Jun to the war. Now I must lose Micah-san. Why? What are you afraid of?"

"I don't know," Kiyomi whispered. "Losing you. *Hai.* I'm afraid of losing you."

"Tell the priests to leave. Tell them they are no longer needed."

"It's too late."

Ai's hard glare drilled into Kiyomi. "If they drive Micah-san from our home, I won't forgive you." She retreated to a far corner where she plopped onto the floor, arms folded over her chest.

A feeling of hopelessness took root as Kiyomi studied her daughter. What if she carried through on her threat and held a grudge forever? They had always been close, their bond a shield against the pressures of the world. Kiyomi remembered her aunt coming to her with the news that Kiyomi's mother had died. "It's always this way for a Japanese mother," her aunt said. "They can never hold the hand of their daughter long enough. It's not our fate."

The clacking *bokken* pulled Kiyomi from her memory. Inside the hallway, the priests disappeared in the direction of the stairs. Kiyomi stepped in front of her daughter. "I would never hurt you intentionally. You must believe me."

Ai crumbled under the weight of the moment. She leaned onto her thighs, hands covering her face. Tears rolled out from beneath her hands. "I'm sorry, Mama. Please forgive me."

Kiyomi knelt beside Ai and drew her close. "It's strange that we recollect our experience with a ghost, *neh?*"

Ai rested her head on Kiyomi's chest. "*Hai.* But I believe Micah-san is here for a reason."

The priest's clacking and chanting carried from upstairs. Kiyomi kissed Ai's hair. "I had not considered that."

Ai pulled back. "Don't you believe it's possible?"

Kiyomi brushed a tear from Ai's cheek with the back of her hand. Why did Micah remain with her? Ai was right; there must be a reason. "*Hai,*" she answered, "it's possible."

The priests continued with the exorcism until they passed through every room. The house turned quiet. *Sensei*-Sato led Reverend Ichiro into the room. Kiyomi pushed off the floor and bowed.

Sensei-Sato retrieved his bag, "We have cleansed this house of the inferior spirit."

Kiyomi glanced over at Ai who glared at the priests, then at *Sensei*-Sato. She bowed again. "*Arigatō, Sensei*-Sato."

He returned her bow. "You should have told your in-laws about the spirit."

Ai rose quickly, her face flushed. "Pardon, *Sensei*-Sato, how can you be sure the spirit is gone?"

The old priest smiled. "I have performed many exorcisms, Ai-chan. You must trust me. There's no longer a spirit in this house."

"Aren't you happy?" Reverend Ichiro asked.

Ai looked at her socks.

"We are most grateful," Kiyomi said, moving alongside Ai.

The priests slipped into their *geta* and left the house. When they disappeared through the gate, Ai set off toward the kitchen. She went from room to room looking high and low. Kiyomi waited patiently for Ai to finish her search. After several minutes, Ai returned with a smirk on her face. "Did you find something?"

"*Sensei*-Sato is wrong. There's still a spirit inside this house."

Chapter Twenty One

Micah blinked as the room came into focus. He sat up and yawned. To his left, Kiyomi and Ai slept on the floor. Behind them, white mosquito netting cascaded from the ceiling like water spilling over a crest. He massaged his eyes. How long had he been out? The last thing he remembered, two men wearing fancy robes strolled through the house making a terrible racket. Micah yawned again.

"Ai said you were still here."

He turned toward the voice. Kiyomi's spirit sat a few feet away, her legs pulled under her. She wore a pale green kimono with her hair pinned up. Being this close to her made his body tingle with excitement. To have these thoughts about Kiyomi seemed preposterous, but he could no more control his feelings than a bombardier could control the flight of a bomb once it left the airplane.

"I'm not sure why I fall asleep. You wouldn't think the dead needed rest."

"We worried the priest drove you away."

"Those two fellows who were here earlier?"

"They came to—"

"Get rid of me."

"*Hai.*"

"I seem to recall Ai mentioning that." Micah massaged the back of his neck. "You had them here because I scare you?"

"You used to scare me. Not anymore."

He sensed a door had opened. There was a chance now. A chance for them to draw closer. Micah glanced over at Ai asleep, then back at Kiyomi. "Why was Ai crying earlier?"

"There's only sorrow in war."

"The girl at the train station. She was a friend of Ai's?"

Kiyomi raised her eyes a moment before looking away. "You followed us to the station?"

"I hope you don't mind. There's not a lot to do around here."

"I don't mind."

Kiyomi shifted her weight and started to rise off the floor. Sensing she was about to leave, Micah thrust his chin in the direction of the screen and said, "Can we go sit in the garden?"

Kiyomi's right hand brushed over the floor as if smoothing out a wrinkle. "*Hai.*"

Micah stood and held out a hand. She ignored the gesture and walked away. He trailed her through the mosquito netting, then passed through the sliding screen that divided the room. Kiyomi wasn't a woman who could be rushed into anything. This realization left him confused, but his growing excitement pushed the confusion aside. Micah hoped he wouldn't say anything Kiyomi might find offensive. In the past he told women the wrong things, sharing his mind as if expecting them to fall in line with his hopes and dreams. "You can't hurry a woman into making a decision," Levi warned him, "and the ones who can be hurried aren't the kind you'd bring home for Sunday dinner."

A peaceful night greeted them, the only sound the chirping of crickets. Stars dappled the dark sky. Kiyomi sat on a large rock near the pond. Micah sat across from her. With the sun gone, the sweltering heat diminished, but the air remained warm and moist. Fish swam near the pond surface, producing quiet splashes. A tickling breeze carried the dank smell of the riverbed and swayed a smiling ghost doll tied to the branches of the willow. Micah watched Kiyomi in fleeting glimpses, careful not to overwhelm her with his enthusiasm. If she were an American woman, he would have pulled her into a conversation, but he knew from careful observation Kiyomi could sit in a room with other people for hours and not say a word. And so they sat in silent rumination, him stealing glances at her face, marveling at her unblemished skin, and the way she kept her focus on the ground, yet seemed aware of everything transpiring around her.

Micah wrung his hands. He had so much he wanted to ask, so much to learn, but where to begin? He was starting to believe they would pass the time in silence when he noticed the moon glowing overhead. "The rabbit is working hard tonight."

Kiyomi followed his gaze to the glowing orb.

"It's a beautiful night," Micah said.

"*Hai.* Moonlight sweeps over the pond in white waves. The stars burn bright."

"I meant because there isn't an air raid."

"Oh," she said, her attention returning to the ground.

"Ai told me your husband died fighting in China. I'm sorry."

"Why do you feel sorry for me? He was your enemy."

"I suppose. But now you have no one and your in-laws are forcing you to remarry. It doesn't seem right."

"Ai says too much. It is not her place to discuss such matters."

"But this involves her too. I mean, this man would be her stepfather."

"Ai cannot put her own interests first. She must subordinate her will to her duties to the Emperor, her family, and her neighbors."

The subject of arranged marriage upset her. He needed to steer their discussion in another direction, but he would never know her heart unless he asked the difficult questions. "She also told me you want to find your own husband."

Kiyomi's head came up and she glared at him as if he had crossed a line with his inquiry. She quickly looked down. "Sparrows know not the dreams of swans."

"What does that mean?"

"It's not easy for a widow to marry in Japan. She remains faithful to her deceased husband." Kiyomi pressed a hand against her forehead, her eyes half-closed as she concentrated. "If I refuse to marry the man my in-laws have chosen for me, they might force us to leave their home. Where would we go? There's nothing left for me in Tokyo."

"You should be able to choose the person you want to marry. We're not living in the dark ages for Christ's sake."

"You judge things from a narrow and limited experience. In Japan, we are taught to not be self-serving, unlike Americans, who think only of making money and admiring their virtues."

"I'm sorry," he said. "I had no right to question your position in this matter."

Her eyes widened in surprise. She met his gaze for several seconds before lowering her head. "And I should not have spoken so harshly of your countrymen."

This moment wasn't going the way he had hoped. His words should have been chosen more carefully. He should have considered their effect upon her. After this night, she would never want to see him again. The familiar feelings of failure and loneliness that had dogged him all his life returned in spades.

"Are you married?"

His eyebrows went up. "What?"

"I asked if you are married. Does someone wait for you at home?"

"No. There's no one." Heat crept up the back of his neck, his admission serving as a reminder of previous missteps. His family never understood why he couldn't find a nice girl to settle down with. His mother relished the role of matchmaker, steering a steady stream of Scandinavian and Irish girls his direction. Grandfather Finn took a different approach to the problem. "Micah," he said, "women are like fish. If you want to catch a certain type, you've got to use the right bait."

"Why haven't you married?" Kiyomi inquired.

Now it was his turn to stare at the ground, all the time wishing he could dig a hole and bury himself in it. "I don't know. I suppose I was too busy with schoolwork."

"Don't women in your country find you attractive?"

His head came up. "Do you find me attractive?"

Kiyomi remained quiet, her shoulders rolling forward as if she tried to hide within herself.

Her silence heightened his sense of self-deprecation and he languished at the idea that she recognized every flaw in his character. He berated himself for asking her such a stupid question. Of course she didn't find him attractive . . . she wouldn't even look him in the eye.

"Are you from Tokyo originally?" he asked, to change the topic. Kiyomi straightened and met his gaze before looking away. Micah could tell from the way her eyes widened and her lips ticked up that this subject pleased her.

She stared at the pond as if expecting to pull memories from the dark water. Micah slumped on his rock. He would never get her to open up to him. He pictured Frank and Oda sitting on their boat, getting drunk without a care in the world. Maybe he should join them, instead of burdening himself with the same problems that haunted his old life. *Haunted. Ha!* What a word for a ghost to come up with.

"When I was a young girl, we lived in a house in the Nihombashi District. Nihombashi was the heart of the Low City, with many temples, shrines, and academics. My father, Daichi, worked as a professor of mathematics at the University of Tokyo. Our home had a fine garden with evergreen trees, granite rocks, white butterflies, and a large pond. Inside the house, tall shelves held books. Sometimes my father took me on his lap and we read together. My favorite stories were Western fairy tales. Of course, I also heard Japanese fairy tales: *Peach Boy*, *The Crab and the Monkey*, *Tongue-cut Sparrow*, and *The Flower Blooming Old Man*. I snuggled against my father's chest the way a baby bird snuggles into the downy softness of a nest. He smelled of pipe smoke and wore thick black glasses. This I remember.

"My mama, Ameya, stood tall and straight like a pine tree surveying the forest. She had the most expressive eyes, long thick eyelashes, and beautiful eyebrows. She was always cooking, sewing, or housecleaning. Mama moved with a natural grace, her hands swimming through the air as she beckoned me and my older sister, Fuyuko, to her side.

"When Fuyuko and I weren't scaring each other in ghost play, we would accompany our mother on shopping excursions." Kiyomi looked up and he could see a glow of contentment in her eyes. "There were no sidewalks so we'd stroll in the middle of the road, dodging the *kurumaya* men who dashed past pulling their rickshaws. People walked shoulder to shoulder. Mothers with babies on their backs, little girls with dolls tied to their shoulders, businessmen, students, coolies, and peddlers. Sometimes at night, after my father returned from work, we all went shopping or to the theater. We drifted in and out of soft yellow light spilling onto the street from windows. Night peddlers filled the air with their cries; hot soba men: fortune-tellers, the sellers of rice wine, sweet amber soup, love papers, and diving papers. And rising above it all was the great bell of *Tokoji* with its gentle resonance." Kiyomi turned toward him. "I wish you could have seen it, Micah-san."

But I have seen it, from eight thousand feet, the city on fire like a forest ravaged by lightning.

Kiyomi's mouth tightened and her shoulders slumped as her attention returned to the pond.

The sudden shift in her demeanor confused Micah. Before he could ask her what was wrong she said, "The earthquake changed everything."

Her eyes closed and her upper body bowed over her thighs. "I was at school that day. My parents had taken Fuyuko to get a pair of eyeglasses. When the ground ripped apart with a terrible roar, my family took shelter in the former army clothing depot. Firestorms broke out. A fire tornado engulfed the building my parents had taken refuge in. Forty thousand people were incinerated inside the store. Forty thousand in one building, including my parents and Fuyuko." Kiyomi covered her face with her hands, her body rocking.

Micah wanted to go to her. He longed to put an arm across her shoulders and bring her against him. But it was too soon. Much too soon. Instead, he gave her time to grieve, and when she lowered her hands he said, "I can't imagine such devastation."

Kiyomi stared at him with a puzzled expression as if she wasn't sure she had heard him correctly.

He had said something wrong, but what was it? And then it hit him. The firebombing raid. Block after city block reduced to ash. Ninety thousand killed in a single night. He could do more than imagine such devastation. He had been the cause of it.

"I had nothing," she continued. "No family. No home. What was to become of me? It was raining on the day my Uncle

Hayato and Aunt Natsumi arrived to welcome me into a new life. I knew little about them, other than my uncle operated a warehouse on one of the canals that specialized in processing fish." Kiyomi massaged her brow. "They were quiet people with good hearts. Because they weren't able to bear children, they viewed my addition as a blessing. But despite their best efforts to provide all I needed, my aunt and uncle could not stop tears from staining my pillow each night. And when we celebrated *Obon*, and they assured me the spirits of my family had come home to be with me, I never believed it. My parents and sister remained as distant as the moon and stars."

Kiyomi picked up a stone. She brought it near her face, studying the rock the way a person examined the purity of a diamond. She let the stone slip from her fingers. "I attended the university after high school, my goal to be a journalist. You see, as much as I loved Japan, I dreamed of leaving her. I imagined myself landing a job with a newspaper in a foreign city. New York. Paris. Rome. It didn't matter where as long as I was out of my homeland. In Japan, I was broken in spirit, living in the shadow of a past that offered only sorrow. A foolish plan, *neh*? But all I could think of was escaping the pain. And then I met Shigeo Ito."

"Who's Shigeo?"

"Ai's father."

Jealousy swept through Micah's heart like a fire hunting oxygen. Kiyomi gave him no reason to feel this way, no cause for expectation, and still, her words cut through him. Kiyomi glanced over as if anticipating his response, but he remained silent, refusing to let her share in his distress. Micah felt the familiar sting of rejection. He had lost count of the times a woman had broken his heart because his shyness, had seemed immature to their way of thinking.

Micah clenched and unclenched his hands in an effort to control his raging emotions. He needed to eradicate the jealousy that threatened to derail his plans. He cleared his throat and said, "I'd like to hear about him. How did you meet?"

She blinked several times, clearly confounded by the change in his demeanor. "Are you certain?"

"Yes. Please."

Kiyomi's face relaxed, her focus shifting to the pond, then back to her feet.

Overhead, clouds uncovered the bashful moon. Micah looked down and was surprised to find Kiyomi staring at him. She averted her gaze and Micah reminded himself to ask Frank why Kiyomi wouldn't maintain eye contact with him.

"I met Shigeo in college. He was covering a communist party demonstration for their newspaper, *The Red Flag*. What I remember of that day is people shoving and shouting and waving banners. Police arrived. Protesters were beaten and arrested. Those were dangerous times, Micah-san. The nationalist government went after anyone who opposed them. But Shigeo didn't care. He came from a wealthy family and knew his father's money bought him protection. As I turned to leave, Shigeo caught me by the arm and asked to take my picture. I should have refused. But no. I was irrational. Shigeo's smile removed the doubts from my mind. The heart makes poor decisions."

She stared at her hands while silently meditating, as if debating how much of her past to share with him. The cricket's song trailed off, but the frogs continued filling the night with music. Kiyomi closed her eyes and massaged her temples. "Dating in Japan is governed by tradition. If Shigeo had asked my uncle for permission to court me, my uncle would have refused. You see, it would not have been acceptable for him to accept Shigeo's request without a proper introduction by a go-between, such as a respected elder or relative. Passion ruled our hearts and filled our minds with a fire that could not be contained. I wanted to be wooed by a man of my choice, tradition be damned."

Her eyes opened and she brought her hands to her lap. "At first, our relationship was simple, and in some ways, traditional. We'd visit the Mukōjima Embankment and watch the collegiate boat races. In midsummer, we celebrated the river opening on the Ryogoku Bridge, watching fireworks fill the night sky with bursts of color. Canopied boats choked the river, their lanterns turning the surface red. Everyone clapped and smiled in the moments the fireworks lit up their faces, and between the explosions, the singing of geisha filled the air. We were surrounded by strange magic that turned us into mindless fools.

"Things changed after that. We drew closer. Each day we met at Lafcadio Hearn's grave before setting off on a grand adventure."

"I'm familiar with Hearn," Micah said. "As I recall, he was a Greek who settled in western Japan. He married a Japanese woman, took a Japanese name, and wrote several books about the country. I read *In Ghostly Japan* for a college class."

Kiyomi smiled before continuing. "We resided in the floating world, taking pleasure from life and each other. Sometimes we visited the Imperial Museum. We'd stroll through rooms filled with national treasures, lingering in shadows to partake in forbidden activities."

She turned quiet once more. When she spoke again her voice sounded strained. "Autumn brought changes. Each morning I awoke feeling ill. I recognized what was happening and knew I must tell Shigeo. He appeared happy to hear of my pregnancy. He told me he wanted us to marry and promised to discuss the matter with his family."

"Did he?"

Kiyomi glanced at him before looking down. "What?"

"Did Shigeo discuss it with his family?"

"*Hai.* The Ito family wouldn't allow Shigeo to marry someone outside of a traditional arrangement. My heart shattered at the news." She brushed a hand across her cheek as if capturing a tear.

Micah remained quiet as she battled to regain her composure.

She sat up straighter. "Shigeo said we would not let his family keep us apart. And so we agreed to meet one night on the Ryogoku Bridge where we had so many memories and take our own lives, knowing we would be reunited in Heaven." Kiyomi stared at her lap.

As Kiyomi's past swallowed her like quicksand, Micah pictured Ai, the girl who drew beautiful pictures of flowers and taught him to ride a porpoise beneath the stars. He couldn't imagine the world without her smile and yet, her future had almost been stolen from her. The thought made him shudder.

The glass bell tinkled on the veranda, the gentle sound lifting Kiyomi's eyes for a moment. "I had everything I needed on that bridge: a full moon as lucid as a pearl drawn from the sea, a warm breeze to caress my face, and the black river stretched before me like a road toward the future. I had everything I needed except for Shigeo. He never arrived."

She drew in a breath and released it with a wounded sigh. "Something must have prevented him from coming. Maybe his parents discovered our plan. *Hai*. There had to be a reason he didn't show up. I hurried home dispirited but hopeful. Shigeo would contact me. He would find me in the library at school, pull me into a dark corner, and explain why he didn't show up. Only, it didn't happen that way. Days passed without seeing him. At first, I assumed Shigeo's family kept him from me. I created elaborate stories inside my head. What if Shigeo was injured in an accident? He could have a broken arm. Two broken arms. Two broken arms and a broken leg. In my fantasy, Shigeo's injuries became increasingly severe until at last, I was certain he had fallen into a coma. Believing this brought little solace, but at least Shigeo had not betrayed me. No. He would never do that. Shigeo would recover and then we would carry out our plan."

She rapped knuckles against her forehead as if trying to hammer a memory from her mind. "I ran into Shigeo at school. He was with a young woman. They were smiling and laughing. I played a fool. I cried. I wailed like a child. 'Why, Shigeo, why didn't you come to me?' He told the woman to leave before meeting me with a dispassionate gaze. His soul turned as black as his eyes. 'Did you believe I would throw my life away for you?' Shigeo asked." Once more, Kiyomi brushed a hand over her eyes.

Micah wanted to say something to her, to offer comforting words, but he needed to hear the rest of her story and she must work through her pain if she were to continue.

The moon and stars appeared to nod as if agreeing with Kiyomi's account, their luminescence fading for an instant before returning. The same moon and stars that witnessed the scene on the bridge. Props from Kiyomi's tragic past. Constant reminders of a life she might have known.

"What did you do?" Micah asked.

She studied his face, then turned away.

"You don't have to tell me more if you don't want to," he said.

She glanced his direction but kept her gaze low. "To answer your question. After Shigeo rejected me, I was filled with dread. How could I tell my aunt and uncle what had happened? What future could I have? And so I returned to the Ryogoku Bridge, to the moon and stars, and the summer wind, and the black river waiting to carry me home."

"You went to kill yourself?"

Kiyomi hugged herself and rocked back and forth. "*Hai,*" she blurted as if the word were a blade that carved out her heart. "If I killed myself, it would clear my name of the shame I had brought to my family. Suicide would be an honorable and purposeful act." Kiyomi sniffled again. "But as you know, I couldn't go through with it. As I stood on that bridge, dagger in my hand, I swear my unborn child sang to me. It was the most beautiful sound I had ever heard. How could I silence such a voice? I left the bridge and carried my shame to my aunt and uncle, who embraced me with tears on their faces. Why? Why did they love me after what I had done?

"It wasn't until I delivered Ai that I understood my family's reaction. Gazing into her trusting eyes, thankful for the song Ai sang upon the bridge, I learned forgiveness was a thread that bound a life to a life. The gift of love was the greatest honor a person could bestow."

Jesus H. Christ, what's with these people? If he had killed himself each time a girl had rejected him, he would have died a dozen times over.

"Our ways must seem strange to you, *neh?*"

Micah knew better than to criticize Japanese customs if he wanted Kiyomi to finish her story. "What happened after you gave birth to Ai?"

Kiyomi's eyebrows knitted and a V-shaped wrinkle creased her forehead. "You surprise me."

"I hope in a good way?"

"Like a sudden storm that catches a farmer unprepared."

Micah crossed his legs. "I'll take that as a yes." He smiled.

Kiyomi stared at her lap. She drifted into familiar silence, allowing the night creatures to fill in the void.

"I had to leave school," she said. "My dream of becoming a journalist died. But I was satisfied. *Hai.* Being with Ai made me most happy. After feeding, Ai would fall asleep against my chest. I sang to her. Songs about mountains, butterflies, and cherry blossoms. Sometimes I stroked her eyebrows or kissed her cheek over and over. I did not deserve her and feared losing her. Ai became my life. My aunt and uncle believed I needed a husband. A marriage would help restore my honor. A business associate told my uncle of a family in Hiroshima who wanted a wife for their youngest son. He said the Oshiros were a fine merchant family. And so it was arranged. The Oshiro's traveled to Tokyo for the wedding and I met my husband, Jikan."

"You never loved him," Micah said.

Kiyomi's head dipped lower. "The matter of love was never a question to be answered. I needed to focus on the serious side of life. Being a good wife. Providing the Oshiro's with an heir."

"But you wanted to love Jikan. You hoped that was possible."

"When I met Jikan, I knew I would never love him. My heart remained locked and he did not have the key. This must sound foolish."

"No. Not at all."

"The train ride to Hiroshima was one of the saddest events of my life. Things got worse after we arrived. Jikan had run up gambling debts. He did not have a mind for business. The family fortune declined."

"Your mother-in-law is a piece of work," Micah said.

Kiyomi's brow wrinkled. "Piece of work?"

He ran a hand over his jaw. How to explain this? "Uh, you know ... difficult."

"*Hai.* Difficult."

A white snake swam across the surface of the pond, scattering fish in its wake. When the snake slithered out of the water and disappeared under a bush, Kiyomi sighed. "Sayoka must exert her dominance over me. I must know my place. This is the way of things."

"An American woman would never put up with that."

"I'm not an American woman."

Micah wanted to tell her that beauty and grace could be found in women of all nationalities and races, but kept the words hidden, fearful she would misinterpret their meaning. But what did he intend with these thoughts? If the circumstances were different, and they were both alive back in Bellingham, would he be interested in dating Kiyomi? Moonlight bathed her face, bringing out the contour of her jawline and the gentle slope of her nose. Hell yes, he told himself, he would definitely be interested, but would she feel the same way toward him? He screamed internally, frustrated at allowing himself to get caught up in an impossible situation.

"I slipped into a deep melancholy," Kiyomi went on. "I had no friends in Hiroshima. No life. Dreams of returning to Tokyo occupied my mind. And then Jikan received the red paper announcing his entry into the army. It shames me to admit I rejoiced in his absence. And when Jikan went missing in China and was assumed dead, no tears touched my cheeks."

"Why did you remain in Hiroshima?"

"I weighed leaving but knew such an act might bring dishonor onto my family. And besides, I had a child to consider. Banri and Sayoka provided us with a home and treated Ai as if she were their granddaughter. It would have been selfish of me to take Ai from them."

"And now you will marry to provide the Oshiros an heir."

"I'm obligated to do this."

"Do you love the man they've chosen for you?"

"A Japanese woman is not allowed to—"

"Do you love him?"

"Mitsuyo is a good man. He—"

"That's not what I asked."

Kiyomi glared at him. "You will never receive an answer by interrupting me."

Heat spread across his cheeks. "You're right. I'm sorry."

Her attention returned to her lap. "Mitsuyo is a good man. A war veteran. He works as an accountant for the government."

"He sounds like a good man," Micah answered, forcing the words out of his mouth.

"Mitsuyo cannot see his hand in front of his face, so he wears thick eyeglasses. He walks hunched over because of a war wound. The Oshiros expect him to provide an heir but I don't—" Kiyomi opened her eyes and sat up straight. "To answer your question, Micah-san, I stopped looking for love a long time ago. When Mitsuyo comes to our home, I will accept his marriage offer because I must. I don't expect you to understand."

He wished he could find the words that might give her hope. He wished he could plant the seed of possibility inside her mind where it would grow and open her eyes to the changing world. The war had to end soon and with Japan's defeat, their old customs would die, including arranged marriages. If Kiyomi held out a little longer, she might have the freedom to make her own decisions. *But why torment myself with thoughts of being with her? It's not good for either of us.*

Kiyomi slowly rose from her rock. In her pale green kimono, she resembled a delicate blade of grass. "I must return to my body. I will awaken soon."

"Why so early?"

"Ai and I are going out into the country to find food. We'll be gone a couple of days."

What would he do with himself during their absence? The idea of sitting around drinking sake all day with Frank and Oda was not appealing.

"Will you be joining us?"

Micah tried not to smile, but his effort proved futile. No matter, Kiyomi was staring at her slippers. "Would you like me to come along?"

"*Hai*," she answered, then hurried past him and disappeared inside the house.

Chapter Twenty Two

Kiyomi awakened Ai before dawn. After gathering their supplies, they shared an apple. Ai yawned and covered her mouth.

"So sorry," Ai said, her eyes widening the way a child's did when they were embarrassed.

The last thing Kiyomi did was fold her wedding kimono and place it in a wicker basket on top of a dozen good luck talismans. Women sobbed at the black market as they traded their favorite kimonos for food. Kiyomi would surrender a lifetime of tears to put food inside her daughter's stomach.

Darkness cloaked the city. Kiyomi held Ai's hand as they traveled in the direction of the Hiroshima train station. It wasn't long until other people appeared—branches whittled down to twigs by hunger—hair brittle, eyes clouded and lifeless. Evacuees carrying bags and suitcases were joined by women carrying baskets or *furoshiki*. The women trudged forward with grim determination. Kiyomi knew these women planned to gather or trade for food in the country. Every day, hundreds of women traveled outside Hiroshima in a desperate quest for survival. Because of this, Kiyomi believed the only way she could succeed was to venture farther than the others. With any luck, she might stumble upon an isolated farmer willing to barter. In any case, she was prepared to gather edible wild plants along the way; whatever it took to keep Ai from starving.

A throbbing settled in Kiyomi's head. Her legs became numb. Between working at the factory and the almost nightly air raid sirens, fatigue took up residence in her body like an unwanted visitor. On this morning, she was more exhausted than usual, as if she had been awake all night. Low clouds settled over the surrounding blue hills. Kiyomi imagined the clouds as fluffy pillows for her to rest on. Lying beneath the sun, she would sleep twenty years like Rip Van Winkle. What world might she awaken to? Surely the war would be over. She pictured American soldiers marching through the streets of Hiroshima as a band blasted patriotic music. Red, white, and blue bunting displayed on stores and houses. Japanese children waved at the troops while nibbling hot dogs and drinking Coca-Colas. In twenty years, Ai would be a grown woman with a husband and children of her own. Kiyomi pictured herself playing with her grandchildren and smiled. But what about her? Would she be married to Mitsuyo, carrying on the Oshiro lineage? She saw him returning home from his job, hunched over a cane, his dull eyes crossed behind a thick pair of eyeglasses. At night, he would drag his aging, crippled body over to her, demanding she please him. The thought of making love to Mitsuyo caused the pain inside her skull to spread, burning a path along every nerve.

Ai squeezed her hand as they passed the train station, crowded with evacuating students and their families. In the hard grey light, they were silhouettes, mere shadows swaying in the cool breeze sweeping in from the Sea of Japan. Shadows that disappeared in the blossoming light of the sun as if they had never existed.

Outside the city, the road became packed dirt. Shuffling feet, animal hooves, and wagon wheels stirred up dust. Traffic thinned as people headed in different directions. Kiyomi was envious of the families who had relatives waiting for them. They would have a roof over their heads, a fire to warm their bones, and food to quiet their rumbling stomachs. By now, the sun had awakened, rising above the sapphire water of the inland sea. Searing rays beamed onto their bodies. Kiyomi's knees trembled as heat settled across her shoulders. Sweat glistened on her forehead and pooled in the pits of her arms, making her itch.

"Look at the butterflies, Mama," Ai said, pointing at dozens of white and yellow butterflies. "I wish we could bring one back to Sensei Kondo. He would be most pleased."

Kiyomi nodded while thinking, only a child would notice butterflies as hunger devoured them from the inside.

Mid-morning, they reached the mountain pass leading to *Takata-gun*. The narrow rocky path branched off the prefecture road and twisted deep into the surrounding hills.

"We must climb, Mama?"

Kiyomi stroked Ai's hair. "*Hai*. Are you up to it?"

Ai's gaze traveled to the green hills. "You can count on me."

"And you on me," Kiyomi responded, which filled Ai's eyes with a contented glow.

Kiyomi moved onto the pass, disheartened to see that a number of the scavenging women followed. The pass ascended toward a grey mountain that eyed their trespass with contempt. Fire spread over Kiyomi's thighs. Her brain demanded rest, but her heart refused to stop. Ai struggled behind her, face blanched and glistening with sweat. The trailing women stretched down the slope in a ragged chain, gasping breaths escaping their lungs. Overhead, the sun floated higher into the translucent sky. The trail dipped into a ravine where the surrounding hills funneled the sun's heat, turning the passage into a furnace. Kiyomi's sweat-dampened shirt clung to her body. The itching in her armpits intensified.

Kiyomi held out a hand to Ai. "Would you like to stop and eat?"

Ai grasped her hand. "Can we wait for a better spot?"

"*Hai*. This place feels like Hell, *neh*?"

The trail moved out of the ravine and into an area of rolling hills dotted with *Icho* trees, their fan-shaped leaves rustling in the warm breeze. Purple *ajisai* and lavender grew on the grassy slopes, joined by proud sunflowers standing tall in the heat. Bees buzzed around flowers, getting drunk on nectar. The flower's sweet perfume drifted onto the path. Cicadas screeched from the tree branches.

They arrived at a fork in the trail. A *dōsojin* stood under the branches of a *momo* tree with an image of Buddha inscribed on the stone tablet.

"What's that for, Mama?"

"The *dosojin* serve as village guardians." Kiyomi considered the trail leading away from the pass. "There must be a village nearby."

The scavenger women caught up to them. Several of the group took shelter under the peach tree. A few plucked leaves off the branches and pressed them into pockets.

"Why did they take leaves?" Ai asked.

"My aunt told me the leaves of the *momo* tree possess power that brings happiness to people."

Ai glanced at the tree, then back at her. "May I take a leaf?"

Kiyomi had long given up on finding true happiness, but she would not steal the longing from her daughter's heart. "Can you reach one?"

Ai frowned. "I'm not a baby."

While Kiyomi smiled at this, inwardly she crawled under a blanket of despair, saddened by the realization that her time with Ai was fleeting. "*Hai.* You can take one."

Ai released Kiyomi's hand and ventured over to the tree. Ai returned holding two leaves, a triumphant smile warming her face. "I got us both a leaf."

Kiyomi accepted the leaf as if it were made of gold and kissed it. "The magic of the *momo* tree must be real. I already feel happier."

After a short rest, all the scavenger women except one headed off along the path leading to the village. The women hadn't gone far enough. Farmers were under tremendous pressure from the government to supply the military food, and because of their close proximity to Hiroshima, Kiyomi assumed these villagers received a steady stream of visitors seeking to barter. What could these women offer the farmers that they hadn't already acquired?

The remaining scavenger woman stood under the shade of the peach tree, observing them from the shadows. She stepped out into the light. The skin on her face was pulled tight like a piece of wet leather left to dry in the sun. Her sunken eyes resembled black marbles that had rolled through dust. Shafts of brittle hair sprouting from her scalp failed to conceal patches of wrinkled flesh where hair had fallen out. A damp shirt swallowed her shriveling torso. Kiyomi pitied the woman, whom she guessed to be in her fifties.

She tottered onto the trail, her legs swaying like wind-blown grass, and stopped near Kiyomi. "I'm Fuka. Do not fear me."

Kiyomi rested an arm on Ai's shoulder. "I'm Kiyomi from Nakajima-Honmachi, and this is my daughter, Ai."

"I have a son, Ko, in the city. He is five. We live in Otemachi, near the electric substation."

Kiyomi was stunned to hear Fuka had such a young son. "How old are you, Fuka-san?"

Fuka hesitated, then blurted, "Twenty-four last month."

Kiyomi realized there was no hiding the consternation that widened her eyes and parted her lips. She drew from the well of sorrow buried in her chest, the troubled water rolling through every fiber of her being like a tsunami. How could Fuka be so young and have the appearance of an old hag? The cruelty of war knew no limits.

A crow flapped onto the *dosojin*. The evil bird stared at Fuka with its black demon eyes and cawed, the high-pitched sound echoing across the wild landscape.

"I must find Ko food," Fuka went on. Her eyes glistened with tears. "He is so …" She stared at the ground.

"We also have come for food," Kiyomi said. "Would you like to join us?"

Fuka sniffled and brushed away tears. "Are you certain?"

Kiyomi looked at Ai, who nodded, then back at Fuka. "*Hai.* We would be honored."

"You are most kind."

Fuka joined them on the pass, walking a few paces behind. As they journeyed westward, Fuka told them her life story. Born in Hiroshima to a metal worker, she left school at the age of twelve and found herself in an arranged marriage at the age of fifteen to a man ten years her senior. Having no experience with men, Fuka was terrified of her husband, but soon discovered he was a gentle, caring man. In time, she fell deeply in love with him. Fuka gave her husband two sons. The oldest son died at the age of six from typhoid fever. Her husband received the red card notifying him of his obligation to report to the army in 1941. His ashes arrived home two years later. Her in-laws did the best they could for Fuka and Ko, but they were old and penniless. Little by little their food supplies dwindled until at last, they survived on whatever rations their association provided. Ko had developed a cough in the spring. He grew weaker each day. Fuka knew she must find food. She went to the black market and offered men the use of her body. The men laughed and sent her away. Now she hiked the mountain pass in the hope of finding a sympathetic farmer.

"There are edible plants we can gather," Kiyomi said.

"Can you show me?"

"*Hai*. If you're willing to work, you'll return to Hiroshima with a full basket."

"I'll work like an ox pulling a plow if it brings my son food."

The narrow pass ascended higher and higher until Kiyomi believed she could almost reach out and touch the clouds, before plummeting at a sharp grade. Her legs went numb, her muscles transformed into jellyfish floating in a sea of blood. Ai pushed onward with grim determination. Fuka labored to stay with them, and many times they stopped until she could catch up. Rivulets of sweat trickled down her temples. Her face turned the hue of a snow-capped peak. Short, raspy breaths escaped her lungs.

"Are you all right, Fuka-san?" Kiyomi touched Fuka on her forearm. "Do you need to rest?"

Fuka coughed before straightening. "Must be close to noon, *neh*? We should press on."

The landscape became an emerald forest, green grass lush upon the hills, *Ibota* growing beneath bamboo and pine trees. The waxy cocoons of the *Ibota* insect glistened on the branches. Kiyomi sought relief in the shade. Ai and Fuka joined her. On the opposite side of the pass, a stream bubbled around stones. Willow trees crowded the water's edge. Secretive bush warblers shouted, "Hooo-hokekyo-hoo-hokekyo," from the trees.

"We should eat our lunch," Kiyomi said, rummaging inside their basket until finding two rice balls. She handed one to Ai, then noticed Fuka had turned away, her head hung. "Fuka-san, do you not have anything to eat?"

"I will be all right," Fuka answered. "Please. Enjoy your lunch. Do not worry about me."

Ai looked at the rice ball in her hand, then up at Kiyomi. "Mama?"

"I know," Kiyomi said. She stepped over to Fuka and held out her rice ball. "I'm not hungry and my rice ball will spoil unless eaten. Please take it."

Fuka shook her head. "You need to eat."

"Then at least take half of the rice ball. I insist."

"I cannot repay such a debt."

"This has nothing to do with debt," Kiyomi said.

"All right," Fuka said. "I must have energy to gather food for Ko."

Kiyomi broke apart the rice ball and handed half to Fuka, who accepted it with a bow. "*Arigatō*, Kiyomi-san."

Fuka retreated to an oak tree and eased onto the grass. She leaned against the tree trunk with a contented smile and closed her eyes, the broken rice ball resting in her hands. Kiyomi joined Ai at the stream. They sat together under a willow, the nodding branches enveloping them. Gnats flickered above snails crawling on the muddy bank. A blackfish rested near the surface of the water. The air smelled fresh and pure, unlike the polluted sky of Hiroshima that carried the stench of destruction and ruin. Sunlight filtered through the sheltering leaves. Kiyomi took a bite of her lunch, knowing it wasn't enough to sustain her.

Ai glanced over her shoulder toward Fuka. "Will she eat, Mama?"

"*Hai.* She is resting first."

"Sleep sounds wonderful. I would love to slip into a dream." Ai sat up. "May I tell you about my dream from last night?"

"All right."

"I dreamed I awakened and went outside. I found you in the garden talking to Micah-san."

Kiyomi gazed past Ai to the stream. She remembered talking to Micah-san in the garden, but the memory remained an enigma, for although she knew Micah to be real, her experiences with him were like meandering through heavy fog. He had entered their lives for some purpose, but she had no idea what that purpose might be. "What happened next?"

Ai finished her rice ball and licked a morsel from her upper lip. She brushed off her hands. "I watched you talking and don't remember anything else. Strange, *neh*?" Ai considered the willow branches. "Do you think Micah-san is here with us?"

"I would not be surprised."

Ai tapped her lips while gazing past the water.

"What's on your mind?"

"Mama, you know the story of the red string?"

"The one tied by the gods to the pinky fingers of two people who will find each other in life?"

"*Hai.*"

"What about it?"

"Do you believe it's possible to see this string?"

"I've never heard of anyone seeing the string, but I suppose it's possible. Why do you ask?"

"No reason." Ai grinned and stretched out on the grass, fingers laced over her chest. "This spot is peaceful. I wish we could stay here."

Kiyomi thought the same thing, but would never tell Ai, not when there were obligations waiting back in Hiroshima. "We better get moving. There is much to be done before the sun sets."

They emerged from their temporary sanctuary and returned to the trail. Fuka remained seated beneath the oak.

"She is most tired," Ai said. "Must we wake her?"

"I'm afraid so," Kiyomi answered. "Fuka-san can sleep tonight after we have gathered food." Kiyomi stepped toward Fuka and stopped. Flies speckled her face and buzzed around her head. Kiyomi lurched, pieces of rice ball exploding into her mouth. She leaned over her knees and spat.

"What's wrong, Mama?" Ai moved alongside her. "Oh no."

Kiyomi straightened and wiped spittle from her lips onto the back of her hand. "We could do nothing."

"What will happen to her son?"

"I don't know." Kiyomi walked to Fuka's basket and picked it up. "We will gather food for Fuka-san and take it to her son in Hiroshima."

"*Hai.* I like that plan. What will we do with Fuka-san?"

Despondency anchored Kiyomi to the moment as she watched the flies swarming over Fuka's body. Even if they possessed a shovel, she lacked the strength to bury the body. "We must leave her."

"So sad," Ai said.

"*Hai.* But at least she died in a tranquil place, *neh*? It's lovely here."

"Can we go now?"

"Of course," Kiyomi said.

They resumed their journey. The loss of Fuka aggrandized their torment. The sun lashed their backs with a fiery whip, hunger plunged a dagger into their stomachs, and fatigue added heavy stones to their shoulders. Skin turned raw where the *geta* straps dug into the tops of their feet. Kiyomi attempted to lock her suffering deep within herself, but when she managed to clear her mind, an image of Fuka covered in flies returned. The thought of Fuka's son losing his mother filled Kiyomi with profound grief. How would Ai survive if something happened to her?

The forest grew thick all around them. Trees fought for sunlight, their branches tangled above the earth. The approaching dusk painted the grass a dull grey. "There," Kiyomi said, pointing at the underbrush. "We can collect *kōgōmi* to eat."

Kiyomi steered Ai into the cool shelter of the woods. Bright green grasshoppers leaped through the knee-high grass. A lizard scurried beneath the trunk of a fallen tree. Kiyomi knelt before a fiddlehead fern. "Pluck the curly fern buds," she said to Ai, then demonstrated by breaking off a bud and putting it in Fuka's basket. "We must be wary of hornets," Kiyomi said. "And watch for *mukade*. If one of the giant centipedes bites you, the only way to get it off is to burn it."

After they filled the bottom of the baskets with the buds, Kiyomi spotted a nearby *zenimaki*. She inspected the leaves of the royal fern. "Good. Good," she said. "This is a female plant. The leaves of the male zenimaki are too tough to eat."

"Where did you learn about plants, Mama?"

"My aunt used to take me to gather mushrooms."

Ai stuck out her tongue. "I don't like mushrooms, but Ojiisan insists I eat them."

"Your grandmother makes unreasonable requests."

"Like you getting married."

Kiyomi snapped off a leaf and handed it to Ai. "It will be good to have something in our stomachs, even if it's ferns, *neh*?"

Ai accepted the leaf with a scowl. "You don't have to answer, Mama. I know what you're thinking."

You know more than you should, Kiyomi thought as she broke off another leaf.

When they finished with the ferns, Kiyomi stood with a groan, her spine cracking like a squeezed ginko nutshell. "Come. With any luck, we will find more food before it gets dark."

The sun jumped ahead of them, burning over the distant mountains. Their throats filled with dust. They drank greedily from a stream, lapping up cold water like wild dogs. Returning to the trail, Kiyomi examined Ai and debated if they should stop. How much farther could Ai travel? Did she have the strength to continue?

"How soon before we come to a village?"

Kiyomi had no idea where they were, but instead of troubling Ai with the truth she said, "Not much longer."

After another hour of walking, the landscape changed once again. The forest ended at the edge of rolling hills cultivated into layered squares, each section harboring a meager crop of green rice. A large number of people worked near an iron cauldron that rumbled and spit out grey smoke. Some used shovels and mattocks to pry exposed pine roots from the ground, while others chopped the roots with axes until they were small enough to feed into the cauldron. The chop, chop of the axes and throaty growl of the cauldron rose over the placid afternoon.

They pushed on until daylight began to wane, the muted shades of evening settling all around them, deepening the green of the hills. Kiyomi led Ai onto a path cut between rice fields. A centipede scurried for cover at their approach. Frogs croaked inside the flooded fields. The odor of manure made Ai hold her nose. Kiyomi laughed and pointed to plants with long slender leaves growing at the edge of a field that was more mud than rice. "We are fortunate to find *yabu-kanzō*." She plucked off leaves.

"Is it good, Mama?"

"I can cook it in soup."

After stacking the leaves inside their baskets, Kiyomi leaned onto her thighs. "We have made a good start. Tomorrow we can look for bamboo sprouts and lotus root."

"Are you going to trade with a farmer for vegetables?"

"*Hai*. I will try." Kiyomi motioned toward a copse of oaks growing atop a nearby hill. "We should rest and eat."

"What will we eat?"

"We can eat bamboo grass."

Ai stuck out her tongue.

"You must be turning into a snake, Ai-chan, as much as you are sticking out your tongue."

"You're silly, Mama."

They rested beneath a sheltering oak and nibbled fern buds. As she watched Ai eating, Kiyomi couldn't stop thinking about Fuka. It would take more than a basketful of wild vegetables to keep them alive back in Hiroshima.

Darkness spilled over the hills and rice fields, accompanied by a refreshing mountain breeze. Kiyomi sat with her back against the trunk of the oak. Ai settled against her, head on her chest. Across the rolling landscape, the yellow glow of fireflies weaved through the air. "Look at all the *Hotaru*. We never have so many in the city, *neh*?"

"I wish I could catch one."

"Some people believe the spirit of a living person, or the ghost of someone who has died, assumes the shape of the Hotaru."

Ai sat up with an expression of discovery on her face as if she had figured out a difficult problem at school. "If that's true, Micah-san could be one of the Hotaru."

Kiyomi stared past her at the tiny lights sweeping the somnolent fields. "He is more than a firefly."

"*Hai*, Mama."

Kiyomi kissed the top of Ai's head. "We should sleep. Tomorrow there is much to do."

Chapter Twenty Three

Micah stood beneath an oak tree watching Kiyomi and Ai as they slept. He recalled their long journey into the mountains, and the food they gathered, fern buds and leaves. How could anyone survive on that? But they had to survive. He'd lost so much due to the war, he refused to allow the conflict to add Kiyomi and Ai to its growing list of victims.

Ai's spirit escaped her body like mist ascending over a meadow. She smiled upon spotting him. "I knew you'd be here, Micah-san."

"Where else would I be?"

"You like us."

"I do."

"Especially, Mama."

Ai was a clever girl. Too clever. Micah didn't recall being this intuitive as a child. He was all about baseball and worshiping Levi, who could do no wrong in his eyes. The war forced Ai to grow up too fast. She should be hugging a doll instead of gathering weeds to eat.

"I like you both," he said, but from Ai's expression, he knew she saw through his deception.

"You and Mama are attached."

He ran a hand over his jawline. "Attached? How so?"

Her gaze traveled past him to a wave of golden light spreading over the fields. "Can we go and see the fireflies?"

Although intrigued by her comment, he knew not to press her. Micah held out his hand. "All right. Let's go look at those fireflies."

A sensuous moon painted creamy light onto the murky canvas. Hidden within the rice, frogs croaked without end. The air was crisp and carried a variety of smells; the richness of the soil, the pungency of the grass, and the acrid stench of manure. They paused at the edge of the rice paddy. The glow of the fireflies reflected across Micah's eyes. He couldn't begin to estimate their number, thousands, maybe tens of thousands.

"Beautiful, *neh?*"

"Yes, they are."

"We should join them."

He studied Ai's face. "They might fly away."

"Only to return."

"You should be a teacher when you grow up."

"That is a nice dream, Micah-san … but … the war."

"Must end soon."

She forced a smile as if to placate him. "We shouldn't talk about the war. The war is ugly."

"The fireflies?"

"*Hai.*"

Looking at Ai, Micah wondered what it would have been like to have been a father. He pictured himself teaching his son to ride a bike or playing a game of catch—the slap of the ball against leather vivid in his mind. He imagined a daughter snuggling against him as he read her a bedtime story. A daughter like Ai.

They strolled into the rice field, cool water rising past their ankles. The frogs stopped croaking and the world turned serene, oak leaves rustling as a breeze brushed past, crickets chirping somewhere in the surrounding grass. There were so many fireflies, their incandescence swept the paddy, but as Micah and Ai ventured farther into the field, the fireflies drew back as if golden doors yawning open to welcome them into a new realm where anything was possible.

"I told you they'd leave," Micah said.

"They'll return."

"Why should they return?"

"Because they like me."

"I can believe that, but they might not like me."

"I like you, so they will like you." Ai raised her hands, palms up. "I will sing them a welcoming song." She took a deep breath and began to sing;

"Come, fireflies,

The water on that side is bitter.

The water on this side is sweeter.

Come, fireflies."

The fireflies kept their distance at first, but returned as Ai had predicted, closer, closer, until crashing against them like waves of a luminous sea. Micah's eyes widened as he took in the spectacle, and he wished Levi was there to share this moment with him. Around him, the radiance of the fireflies intensified, brighter and brighter, until a stinging pain stabbed at his eyes. The light flashed into a fiery bloom, so hot, it felt as if his eyes were melting. Ai screamed as the flame consumed her. Micah sank to his knees. "No, no, no! Not this."

"Micah-san, what's wrong?"

The world came slowly into focus. Ai and Kiyomi stood nearby. Ai was biting her lip. Kiyomi's brow furrowed. "I'm fine," he said and rose from the water flooding the rice plants.

"What happened?" Kiyomi asked.

"You scared us," Ai added.

I'm dead, but the pain of the world remains with me. Micah remembered the terror of his vision. What did it mean? I won't share it with Kiyomi and Ai, he decided. What good could come from bringing them additional stress?

"I'm sorry."

Kiyomi's eyes narrowed on his face. "Did you see something?"

He lowered his gaze. "No."

"I was hoping you followed us."

Still shaken by his vision, Micah concentrated on Kiyomi's eyes to clear his head. He loved looking into her eyes for they held the promise of something exotic, yet lasting, wild, but pure. She turned away, as she always did, a subtle reminder that she didn't see him in the same light he saw her. "That was some hike you made. I was dead tired just watching you."

"But you are dead."

"You know what I mean." He grimaced. "I'm sorry about the woman."

"Her name was Fuka. She has a son waiting back in Hiroshima."

"Are you gathering food to bring back to him?"

"*Hai*. It is the proper thing to do."

"Look at all the Hotaru, Mama!" Ai's face shined with contentment in the glow cast by the fireflies.

"Beautiful, *neh*?"

"Maybe I can hold one."

"You can try," Kiyomi answered.

Ai ran out amongst the fireflies, arms outstretched, prepared to snare an unlucky slow one. The fireflies scattered as she tore into them, flashing through the night in an explosion of twinkling gold.

"She just might catch one," Micah said.

"She might," Kiyomi agreed. She turned toward Micah, but would not look him in the eye. "I never asked you why you wanted to be a teacher."

"I loved to read and wanted to share my passion with kids."

Kiyomi smiled as if amused.

"What's so funny?"

"No. Not funny. It's just … I too love to read."

Ai stopped running and held her arms out to the side. Fireflies frolicked all around her, golden sparks flashing through the darkness. It wasn't long until a brave firefly settled on her arm, followed by another. Soon, hundreds of fireflies had landed, making Ai glow like a candle. She smiled at their intrusion and her reaction caused Micah to smile as well.

"What books did you enjoy reading?"

Kiyomi blinked. "Excuse me?"

"You said you loved to read."

"Oh yes," she said, her face animated. "When I was young, I read fairy tales. As I matured, I graduated to novels. Books offered sanctuary."

"I suppose they do," he agreed.

Kiyomi looked straight into his eyes before turning away. "Tell me more about your life. What was your family like?"

"My father owned a boat repair business. My mother was big and brash, quick with an opinion, and quick to argue. But she loved her family with unbridled devotion."

"Your parents must have been proud of you and your brother when you enlisted in the military."

"Proud and scared. My father hated war. He saw no glory in it."

"Your father is a wise man." She continued to keep her gaze low. "You were close to your brother."

"As close as brothers could be. We used to talk for hours inside our bedroom after the lights went out. We had such big plans. I dreamed of being the Yankees' shortstop. Levi wanted to be a businessman like our father."

"I like baseball," Kiyomi said. "My uncle kept up with American baseball. Each week he would buy a copy of the *Los Angeles Times* to read the sports section. He discussed baseball news with me. My favorite team was the Cubs."

Micah groaned. "You have a lot to learn about baseball."

Kiyomi's expression turned serious. "Do you wish you had gotten married?"

"I used to think about getting married, but I'm glad I never did."

"Why are you glad?"

"If I had gotten married, my wife would be a widow."

Kiyomi's attention shifted to Ai standing amongst the fireflies. To the east, dawn awakened on the horizon. She opened her mouth to speak, but nothing came out.

"I would have liked to have known you before the war," Micah said.

She faced him, her expression somber. "Why do you say this?"

"Isn't it obvious?"

"Micah-san, what you say is—" Her attention shifted to the oak tree where she slept with Ai. "Something is wrong. We must go." She cupped a hand over her mouth and shouted, "Ai, come quickly!"

"What's wrong?"

Kiyomi held out a hand to Ai. "We must return to our bodies. We must do it now."

Chapter Twenty Four

"Wake up, thieves!" An old woman stood in front of them holding a rifle. She wore a grey long-sleeve shirt and black *monpe*. A conical bamboo hat shaded her face. Kiyomi sat up and Ai groaned at the loss of her pillow.

"What have you stolen?" the woman demanded.

"We're not here to steal," Kiyomi said. "We're here to gather food, and if possible, trade for vegetables."

"Where are you from?"

"Hiroshima."

"Liar! You have not hiked here from the city."

Ai yawned as she opened her eyes. Her focus traveled from Kiyomi to the old woman. "Mama, what's wrong?"

Kiyomi drew her close while never taking her eyes off the rifle. "There has been a misunderstanding. She believes we're here to steal."

"But Mama we—"

"Shh," Kiyomi said, touching a finger to Ai's lips. "I will talk for the both of us, *neh*?" When she was certain her face held no emotion, Kiyomi brought her attention back to the old woman. "My name is Kiyomi Oshiro. This is my daughter, Ai. We traveled far into the country hoping to find a place where others from the city had not gone. We're not thieves. Check our baskets if you do not believe me."

"Why are there two baskets?"

"A companion died on the pass. We're gathering food for her son."

The old woman thrust out her chin. "Have the girl bring the baskets."

"Mama, I'm scared."

"Don't be frightened," Kiyomi said, looking into her daughter's eyes. "We've done nothing wrong."

Ai pushed off the ground, her shirt and *monpe* damp from dew. She gathered the baskets and brought them to the old woman.

"You're a young one."

"I'm eight."

"Show me what you have inside."

Ai rummaged through both baskets, allowing the woman to inspect their contents. When Ai held up Kiyomi's white kimono, the woman lowered the rifle.

"This is a wedding kimono," the old woman said, reaching out to stroke the fabric. "An expensive one. This is what you've brought to trade?"

"*Hai,*" Kiyomi said, standing. "It's all I have of value."

"What would I do with a wedding kimono?"

"You could sell it on the black market."

"The kimono means nothing to you?"

"Nothing," Ai said.

Kiyomi and the old woman both stared at Ai with raised eyebrows.

"I cannot use a wedding kimono," the woman said, "but you might be of some value since you are not thieves. Bring your things and follow me."

Kiyomi picked up the baskets. "What's your name?"

The old woman pushed her hat onto the back of her neck. She had inquisitive eyes and skin the hue of a *satoimo*. "I'm Emi. This land belongs to me." She pointed at a path through the rice fields. "My house is over the hill."

They climbed a dirt trail between rice fields. Sunlight spread over the land in gentle waves. Birdsong carried from maple and oak trees. A breeze stirred pollen from wildflowers, creating a wavering golden blanket that sparkled in the air. Grasshoppers leaped out of the sparse rice plants.

Emi sighed. "We pray to *Ta-no-kami* for an abundant harvest. Our prayers go unanswered."

Kiyomi stopped at the crest of the hill. Below, a solitary house with a reed-thatched roof sat near a winding stream. Ai doubled over, hands on her knees. Her chest heaved with each breath. "Are you all right?"

"I should not be tired," Ai said.

Emi came alongside Kiyomi. "She needs to eat." Emi slid a finger under Ai's chin and raised it. "Not much farther, little one. Then you can eat and rest. I have hot soup in my kettle. You would enjoy some, *neh*?"

"*Hai*," Ai said. "Soup would be most welcome."

Emi set off down the slope. Kiyomi moved in front of Ai. She clutched her shoulders. "You must tell me if you feel ill. Do not push yourself beyond your capability."

"I'm sorry for troubling you, Mama."

Kiyomi took the basket from Ai. "I can taste that soup in my mind. How about you?"

"Will it be made from a dog?"

"If it is," Kiyomi said, "it will be a tasty dog."

Emi's farmhouse was a one-story structure constructed of wood and mud with a detached barn. The surrounding hills cocooned the house against the wind. Overhead, color bled from the sky leaving it translucent. Heat poured from the sun as if an oven door had been opened. The rising temperature brought out the sweet odor of cut hay, the sharp aroma of burning wood, and the repellent stench of manure. Chickens scurried from behind the house, clucking like gossiping wives. The chickens gathered near Emi's feet.

In her mind, Kiyomi pictured a chicken boiling in a pot. She unconsciously ran her tongue over her top lip, drawing the attention of Emi who grunted and said, "The chickens are for eggs, not eating."

Four black—and—white baby goats raced from the barn, bleating as they neared Emi. The goats stopped when they reached Ai. They surrounded her, bumping up against her legs. Ai giggled, which made Kiyomi smile.

"I use goats for milk. Some are eaten."

Ai's brow furrowed. "You eat these goats?"

Emi reached in a pocket of her *monpe*. She brought out a handful of grain and tossed it down. The chickens dove onto the grain. "We all have a purpose in this life. The goats' purpose is to provide milk and food for us. I've walked this land for more than seventy years and I still don't know my purpose. Feed the chickens and goats, I suppose. That is something, *neh*?"

Ai stroked the back of a curious goat. Her eyebrows twitched as she thought. When her eyebrows stopped moving she said, "I'm glad I'm not a goat."

Emi let out a hearty chuckle. "You are a wise one, child." Emi continued toward the house, waving for them to follow.

After removing their *geta* at the *doma*, Kiyomi led Ai inside the building. Both the outer *Amado* and *shōji* screen doors remained closed as if it were winter. With little natural light filtering inside, darkness filled the corners. Emi went to a square fireplace cut into the floor. A bed of coals glowed red within the pit, where an iron kettle was suspended on a braided rope. Emi stirred the coals with a poker. "Please, sit," she said, gesturing to the tatami mats near the fire pit.

Kiyomi lowered onto her knees and glanced around the house. The supporting beams were painted black. Paper covering the *fusuma* had withered like Emi's skin. Kiyomi perceived age and history inside the house; heard laughter from days long passed, and cries of anguish locked within the walls. She sensed the love shared by the inhabitants, the hopes, and dreams that carried them forward, and drove them to awaken for work while the moon shone upon their fields.

Emi held up a finger. "Please excuse me. I will return." She padded off toward the kitchen.

Ai leaned close and whispered, "Why is the house so dark?"

"I don't know," Kiyomi said.

Emi returned carrying a tray containing three wooden bowls. She ladled soup into each of the bowls. "Eat," she commanded.

Steam curled from the bowls, bringing a peculiar scent Kiyomi couldn't place. Thick yellow broth contained diced potatoes, chopped parsley, and meat she assumed was goat. "Smells wonderful," Kiyomi said. Emi smiled at the compliment. Ai frowned. Kiyomi brought the spoon to her lips. Compared to the wild vegetables in her basket, goat meat would be a delicacy. The hot soup flooded her palate with a delightful taste, like biting into a piece of warm milk bread. Ai dipped her spoon into her bowl and examined the contents. Her jaw popped as she chewed the meat, which she swallowed with a gulp. Ai's face remained expressionless for a moment, then she grinned.

"The soup is very good, Emi-san."

"I'm glad you enjoy it, little one."

"You have been an excellent host," Kiyomi said. "I wish I had a gift to offer you."

Emi waved her off. "Having someone to talk with is a gift."

Kiyomi spotted a lightbulb hanging on a wire. "You have electricity?"

"We did. But not for some time. Now the *tankui* come down from the mountains on moonless nights. The badgers carry lanterns. At first, you'll see one, then others join it until a string of bobbing lights appear. If you're outside in the fields at night, you can hear the badger's drumming."

"I would like to see the badgers," Ai said.

"I don't think so," Emi answered. "Badgers can assume a variety of forms. In *Takabatake-buraku*, a *tankui* appeared to a farmer as the ghost of his dead relative. Turned his hair white."

They ate the rest of the meal in silence. Emi tossed sticks onto the coals, the wood crackling and hissing. Ai clutched her stomach. "My stomach hurts, Mama."

"When's the last time she ate meat?"

"It's been a while." Kiyomi pushed her empty bowl aside and placed a hand on Ai's shoulder. "Do you need to rest?"

Ai nodded and Kiyomi eased her onto the mat, Ai's head resting on her lap. Kiyomi stroked her daughter's hair and within a few minutes, Ai had fallen asleep.

"Poor child," Emi said. "When I noticed you sleeping under the tree, I thought I'd come upon a pair of skeletons."

To hear herself and Ai described as skeletons proved unsettling. Kiyomi hoped her distress wasn't evident to Emi. "There's little food in Hiroshima."

"The government forces farmers to surrender our crops for the war effort. Ha. Some effort. Villagers dig up pine roots and boil out their oil. And this is what our planes are supposed to fly on?"

Kiyomi remembered the villagers working at the edge of the woods.

Emi stirred the coals. "I don't imagine the Emperor shares in our suffering."

It shocked Kiyomi to hear Emi speak this way about the Emperor. Emi removed their bowls to the kitchen. She returned with three cups. "Tea," she said, handing one to Kiyomi. "Ai can have her tea when she awakens."

Kiyomi bowed. "*Arigatō*, Emi-san." She sipped the warm green tea, which smelled of jasmine. "I hope you don't think I'm rude for asking, but why do you keep your house closed in the summer?"

Emi stared into her cup. "I closed the screens when my sons joined the army. I vowed to keep them closed until my sons returned." Her chin sank toward her chest. "The darkness will never leave me." Emi sighed. "Sometimes, when I'm walking in the fields, I can hear their voices singing planting songs. But it's the wind. *Hai*. It must be the wind."

Kiyomi followed Emi's gaze to a simple Buddhist altar.

"After my sons received their red cards, we traveled to Hiroshima to have their photographs taken. We went shopping on Hondori Street. I remember the beautiful lanterns."

"Lily of the valley lanterns."

"*Hai*. Most beautiful."

"They were removed and melted for the war effort."

Emi's face screwed up at the news. "Is there nothing of permanence in Japan anymore?" She pinched the bridge of her nose. "We should drink sake until we pass out. When we recover, we should drink more sake. With any luck, we will be drunk the remainder of this awful war. Tell me," Emi said, tossing another stick onto the fire, "is it true Tokyo has been destroyed?"

"*Hai*. Many cities have been reduced to ashes."

"And what of Hiroshima?"

"The Americans have not launched a major attack on the city."

Emi massaged her eyes. "Strange, *neh?*"

"Their planes fly over Hiroshima night and day. Our air raid sirens go off constantly. Hard to sleep with that noise."

"Fortunately, we do not have that problem here." Emi's gaze focused on Ai. "And there is no food?"

"Not for civilians."

"Why not leave?"

"People who have relatives outside the city are leaving. The rest of us remain."

"And that's why you stay?"

Kiyomi lifted a strand of Ai's hair and let it slip through her fingers. "I have a job at the Tōyō Kōgyō factory making rifles. And my in-laws need me."

Emi replaced the lid on the kettle. "What are your plans after the war?"

"Well … I—"

"Baa-baa and Ojiisan are finding Mama a husband." Ai sat up and yawned.

Kiyomi glared at Ai. "If you're going to speak of things you don't understand, then maybe you should remain asleep."

Ai picked up her cup and traced a finger around the lip. "Please excuse me. I did not mean to upset you."

Emi shivered. "Do you feel a cold draft?"

The temperature dropped as if winter had arrived early. Ai smirked behind her teacup, and Kiyomi knew they shared the same thought: *Micah was with them.*

Emi pushed off the floor with a groan. Kiyomi couldn't help but admire Emi's strength and resolve. How could a woman her age live alone and maintain a farm?

Emi turned to Ai. "Would you help me in my garden, little one?"

"Is it all right, Mama?"

"If you believe yourself capable."

"Emi's soup has given me strength."

Emi snorted. "Most people say it gives them gas." She shuffled toward the door, the wooden floor creaking with each step. "Come along."

They followed Emi to a patch of tilled earth planted with rows of potatoes, radishes, peas, beans, and pumpkins with vines stretching past the garden boundary. A small grey rabbit edged out from one of the vines, nostrils twitching as it tested the air.

"Look at the bunny," Ai said, her voice rising.

"Those rabbits are only good for . . . "

"What?" Ai asked. "What are they good for?"

Emi turned to Kiyomi, her eyes half-closed, and a secret knowledge passed between them. Her attention then shifted to the rabbit and Emi said, "The rabbits are good companions, *neh?*"

Ai smiled.

"If you help me pull weeds, I'll let you sleep near the fire, little one. Here in the mountains, it still gets chilly at night."

"Being warm is nice."

"My old bones take a long time to get warm." Emi examined Ai like a parent preparing their child for school. "I shouldn't complain, there are worse things than being cold."

Emi put them to work pulling weeds. Kiyomi groaned as she battled stubborn weeds with roots sunk deep into the earth. The sun perched high overhead. A breeze rustled leaves and brushed across the grass, blades transforming from green to silver depending on the direction of the wind. Emi's chickens crept to the edge of the garden, clucking and pecking at the dirt. Emi worked alongside Ai, entertaining her with stories. "No," Emi said with a chuckle, "we've never had a dragon in these parts. Yes, little one, there is a hare on the moon pounding rice. I saw him leap up there myself." Ai grinned as she listened, her eyebrows rising whenever Emi shared a detail so outlandish, even Kiyomi smiled.

After they had worked for some time, dirt turned their hands a rich brown, and tiny rocks wedged painfully under their fingernails. Kiyomi wiped sweat off her brow onto her forearm. She clutched a large weed and yanked hard, but the weed held fast. Kiyomi released the weed and stared at her hands, which tingled from the effort. Ai and Emi labored together to rip out a troublesome weed near the pumpkins. They cheered when the weed emerged showering them with dirt. Emi pushed off the ground and stood. Dust powdered her *monpe* pants. "We have done enough this day."

They returned to the house where Emi served them more soup, cautioning Ai to eat small portions of the meat. Ai did as instructed. When she finished eating, Ai asked for a second bowl.

"Eat slowly, little one," Emi said. "Your stomach is not used to digesting food." Ai took her time with the soup, but soon after finishing, clutched her stomach and vomited into the fire pit.

"So sorry," Ai said, her face ashen. "I enjoyed your soup." She stretched out on the floor, yawned several times, and then drifted off to sleep.

Kiyomi helped Emi clean the dishes. Afterward, Emi invited her to take a walk. She led—Kiyomi to the stream. Green water bubbled through the shadows of trees. Dragonflies fluttered near a fallen tree branch. Kiyomi remembered the Ota River in Hiroshima, filled with laughing children. Would she ever hear their laughter again?

"I believe Ai enjoyed herself today," Emi said, kneeling in a patch of grass. She plucked several blades and examined them.

"The war seems distant here."

"*Hai.* I can't imagine the strain you both are under." Emi dropped the grass, stood, and brushed off her hands. "Ai's father died in the war?"

Kiyomi stared at her *geta.* "He wasn't Ai's father."

"I see."

"And now your in-laws expect you to remarry?"

"So they will have an heir."

"And you will have more heartache. What life can a woman enjoy when she is a slave to obligations?"

Kiyomi had wondered this same thing. "They have been kind to me and Ai."

"I'm sure they have been," Emi said. "But at what price?"

Kiyomi could not meet her gaze.

A long silence moved between them. The birds continued singing, joined by screeching cicadas and buzzing bees. Emi picked up a stick and held it before Kiyomi. "This is you," she said, gesturing to the stick. Emi snapped the wood in half. "And that is what they'll do to you."

Emi spoke the truth, but Kiyomi could see no way around her obligation to Banri and Sayoka.

Emi tossed the stick aside. "If you weren't in Hiroshima, you wouldn't need to remarry."

"Yes, but—"

"You and Ai could live with me. There's enough food and no bombs will find you here."

Blood pulled down from Kiyomi's head and the ground trembled beneath her as if an earthquake rolled past. She leaned against the trunk of a nearby tree. *How can we stay with Emi? I have made promises to my family. I have an important job making rifles for the Emperor.* Still, the thought of Ai being safe from the war charged her blood with anticipation.

"There are people back in Hiroshima who are counting on me."

Emi's lips pressed flat. "You must decide, Kiyomi-san, what is most important to you—your obligations, or your daughter's life. Ai is sick. She needs more food than you can provide. What happens to you if she dies? Will you be able to live with your regrets?"

Chapter Twenty Five

In the shimmering moonlight, Micah trooped up and down slopes surveying the countryside: the meticulously cut rice fields, the web of trails dividing the crops, thickets marking locations of water sources, and faraway mountains rising as jagged silhouettes. Gnats swam through the wavering glow. An owl launched from an oak tree and circled overhead. When he returned to the farm, Micah discovered Kiyomi waiting near the stream. She kept her gaze low as he approached. "I'm surprised to find you here," he said.

"I have no control over my appearances," she answered, and then added, "but I'm glad to see you. Where have you been?"

"I went on a walk. The landscape here reminds me of my uncle's farm outside Bellingham. How's Ai feeling?"

"You saw her bring up the soup?"

"Poor kid."

"*Hai,*" she whispered, "poor kid." Mosquitoes flitted through the air with incessant buzzing. "I want to save Ai from this war, but what more can I do?" She turned her face away. "Emi has offered to let us stay with her."

"You should accept Emi's offer and remain on the farm."

"That's not possible. Banri would never agree. He wants to adopt a man for me to marry. This is the way of things."

"If that's what you want."

"This is not America, Micah-san. I cannot love whom I choose to love."

Micah went to her and took hold of her hand. She stared at her hand in his but made no attempt to pull away. He wanted to ask her if she could love him but knew she would accuse him of making impossible inquiries. "I wish you could look past the country of my birth and the color of my skin. Maybe you could find some quality in me."

"You've changed, Micah-san."

"I suppose I have."

Kiyomi squeezed his hand. "So many unfulfilled desires. Karma, *neh?*"

"You believe I deserve to suffer because of the war?"

Her eyes betrayed sadness. "According to The First Truth, all life is suffering."

Kiyomi had always been guarded when it came to showing emotion. To see the anguish in her face surprised him. "The First Truth? What's that?"

"A Buddhist belief."

"You don't have to suffer. You and Ai can survive the war."

Kiyomi looked to the stars. "The night is beautiful."

"I never meant to hurt you, Kiyomi-san."

"You could never hurt me." Kiyomi pulled her hand away slowly, her soft fingers gliding over his palm. "I must return to my body. We have a long journey tomorrow."

As she walked away, a feeling of hopelessness grew inside him, as if he were lost in a forest engulfed by fire. Kiyomi and Ai had to survive the war, but how could he convince her that leaving the city was their best option when she remained a slave to tradition? Micah sat at the water's edge. Before him, the slow-moving stream coursed toward a river leading to Hiroshima.

Chapter Twenty Six

They said their goodbyes before sunrise. Emi made a final push for them to stay, offering to open up the house if they remained, and letting Banri and Sayoka come and live with her. Kiyomi promised to give the matter some thought.

Emi supplemented the *yabu-kanzō* and *kogomi* inside their baskets with vegetables from her garden. Ai's arm sagged under the heavy load and Kiyomi knew it wouldn't be long until she carried both baskets. Kiyomi's focus drifted to the stream, where she had stood with Micah only hours earlier. Why did she recall this moment with such clarity as if it were a part of her normal existence? Warmth spread in her cheeks at the memory of holding Micah's hand. If he were alive, could she give her heart to him? He asked her if she could look past his nationality and the color of his skin. At one time, such a request would have been unimaginable, but if she were to be honest with herself, she had stopped thinking of Micah as an American. Now she considered him a man with an honorable heart who wanted to keep her and Ai safe.

The journey back to Hiroshima seemed to go by faster, perhaps because they traveled downhill most of the way. A cool breeze brushing the back of her neck reminded Kiyomi that Micah accompanied them. When they reached the spot where Fuka died, Kiyomi was relieved to see that someone had removed her body. After stopping for lunch, they took a nap under a shady oak. Kiyomi dreamed of being with Micah at a house by the sea. When she awakened, she found herself wanting to return to the dream. Something had changed inside her and she no longer understood her own mind.

They arrived at Hiroshima in late afternoon. As they stood on a hillside staring down at the city, Ai whispered, "We should have stayed with Emi."

In the past, Kiyomi would have reprimanded her and explained the importance of obligation. Now she held her tongue, unable to think of a counterargument to Ai's opinion. "Let's find Ko and deliver his food."

"*Hai*. We should do this for Fuka-san."

Kiyomi watched for *Kempeitai* as they traveled along the crowded sidewalk. If the military police stopped them, they'd search their baskets and confiscate the vegetables. Ai pressed close and whispered, "The city has changed since we left."

Kiyomi absorbed every detail of their surroundings: the buildings, evacuees trudging along the road with weary faces, soldiers milling about, and bridges over rivers that divided districts. All was as she remembered, and yet, Ai was right, the city felt different. The atmosphere seemed oppressive, the air hotter as if the sun had drawn closer, the yellow dust from demolished buildings thicker, leaving a bitter taste on her lips. The nearer they drew to their home, the stronger her sense of emptiness, until at last, it seemed her flesh, muscles, and bones had been torn away. There was nothing left of her except memories of moments shared with Ai. The future was a night sky without stars, impenetrable darkness stealing what light remained.

A long line of people stretched out from the food distribution center. The basket Kiyomi carried became heavier as she struggled with guilt. *I should not feel this way. We earned these vegetables through sweat and toil.* Still, if she could, Kiyomi would find a way to bring food to everyone who hungered. *God, please end this war soon. Please end the suffering in Hiroshima.*

They turned off Aioi-Dori Street and passed the Industrial Promotion Hall. Government men hustled in and out of the building. Kiyomi looked away, afraid she might spot Mitsuyo.

Sunlight glistened upon the Motoyasu River and she had the sudden urge to walk onto the riverbed and lie down. "There is the electric substation. Fuka said she lived nearby."

"How will we find her home?"

"We will ask if anyone knows her."

Kiyomi spotted an old man with a pipe clenched between his teeth. She moved before him and bowed. When she inquired if he knew a woman named Fuka with a son, Ko, the man shook his head. The scene repeated itself dozens of times, no one claiming knowledge of Fuka. Kiyomi was starting to believe Fuka-san had been a ghost until a woman carrying a baby on her back recognized the name and pointed at a single-story home near the end of an alley. Kiyomi led Ai through the narrow passage where shadows took up permanent residence. The wailing of a child reached into the darkness. A sense of unease quickened Kiyomi's pace. When they arrived at the house, weathered and battered with broken window coverings, Kiyomi unlatched a side gate and steered Ai inside a tiny yard. There was a garden with a yellowed pine, a pond covered in grey film, and a cracked pagoda. Kiyomi stepped onto the veranda and paused at the door. "I hate that Fuka-san came from such a place. So much sadness, *neh*?"

"*Hai*. I don't like it here."

Kiyomi knocked on the door and stepped back. The door creaked open and a bent old man joined them. He dressed in the manner of a coolie, khaki shirt and trousers drooping on his slender frame. "What do you want?" he asked.

Kiyomi bowed. "Please excuse. We were wondering if you know a woman named Fuka-san?"

"*Hai*. She is my daughter-in-law."

This was the part Kiyomi dreaded. She bowed again. "We met her in the countryside outside Hiroshima. I'm sorry to inform you Fuka-san has died."

He reached up to scratch stubble on his chin. "She was ill."

Kiyomi took the basket of vegetables from Ai and held it out. "We have brought food for her son."

The old man stared at the basket through narrowed eyes. "For Ko?"

"*Hai*."

"Ko died three months ago."

"But, Fuka said ..." A sharp pain radiated across her chest. Kiyomi bowed again. "Please excuse our intrusion." She pressed the basket closer to the old man. "Here, this food is for you."

"I'm old and will die soon. Why do I need extra food? Please, take this for yourself." He turned and shuffled back into his house.

"Why did Fuka believe Ko was alive?" Ai asked.

"She could not accept his death."

Back inside the alley, shadows deepened. Kiyomi thought of what she would do if Ai died. How could she go on? How could she face the rising sun without a reason for living? She remembered Ai standing in the rice field, surrounded by fireflies, her body aglow. The moment had been surreal, but the serenity she experienced at that instant was within reach. Their fates balanced on a delicate scale, and her decisions would either maintain the balance or bring them crashing down.

Chapter Twenty Seven

Frank smiled as Micah approached the boat. Oda slept on the deck, his shirt raised, exposing a bloated, hairy belly. Frank followed Micah's gaze to Oda. "Even a dead man can have one too many, it seems."

Micah pressed against the gunwale. The morning sun beamed across the copper dome of the Industrial Promotion Hall, casting greenish sparks. On the riverbed, four men hunched over fishing poles.

"Where have you been?" Frank asked. "You haven't visited us in a week."

"I went away for a few days."

"You left the city?"

"Kiyomi and Ai went out into the country looking for food."

Oda sat up and groaned. "What did I miss?"

"Micah was explaining how he followed Kiyomi into the country."

Oda dropped onto a barrel. "Bad idea, Micah-san."

"I worry about them. They're starving."

"Most of the people in Hiroshima are starving," Frank said. "This damn war needs to end soon." He reached under his shirt to scratch. "You've been visiting her spirit while she sleeps."

"I have."

"Another bad idea, Micah-san," Oda said.

"They met an old woman who lives alone on a farm. She offered to let Kiyomi and Ai stay with her. They would have plenty to eat and be safe from the war."

"And Kiyomi refused the offer," Frank said.

"Yes, she—"

"Has obligations?"

"Her in-laws are trying to find a man for her to marry."

"*Hai*, I remember. Have they found someone?"

"He comes tonight for dinner."

Frank struggled to suppress a smile. "And this is what upsets you? The idea of Kiyomi marrying this man."

"She doesn't want to marry him."

"Kiyomi told you this?"

"She will marry because this is what her in-laws expect her to do."

"Welcome to Japan," Oda said.

Micah watched the men fishing for a moment before bringing his attention back to Frank. "I realize we can't be together. But if circumstances were different, and there wasn't a war, and—"

"You weren't dead," Frank said.

For some reason, Micah found this funny and grinned. "Yeah. That too." He let out a breath. "I care about them. They've become like family to me. I know how that must sound."

"How does that sound to you, Oda?" Frank asked.

"Crazy. But I was never much of a family man."

Micah turned to Frank with a look of desperation. "How can I convince Kiyomi to evacuate into the country?"

"You think something is going to happen to them?"

"Yes." Micah gripped the gunwale. "While I was in the country, I had a vision. A bright flash of light accompanied by intense heat."

Frank joined him at the railing. "If Kiyomi is determined to fulfill her obligations, there's nothing you can do."

"She won't marry right away," Oda said. "What is today? August fourth?"

"The fifth," Frank responded.

"There you go," Oda continued. "*Obon* starts on the fifteenth. They will want to wait until after the festival of the dead. Very bad luck to marry near *Obon*."

"Is this true?"

Frank shrugged. "Maybe. Weddings take time to plan unless they're going to have a simple ceremony."

"Kiyomi has been married before," Oda said. "Her in-laws will keep it simple."

"I need to talk to her again," Micah said. "I have to convince her to postpone the wedding and evacuate."

"Her in-laws would never agree to that," Frank said.

"It doesn't matter if they agree or not."

"You're suggesting Kiyomi and Ai flee their home?"

"Yes, Frank. That's exactly what I'm suggesting."

Oda held out the sake bottle. "You need this more than I do, Micah-san."

"I need more than that. I need a goddamn miracle."

Oda brought down the bottle. "God does not grant miracles to people who use his name in vain. Trust me. I know these things."

"Kiyomi has to leave Hiroshima." Micah ran a hand through his hair. "There's something I've been meaning to ask you, Frank. Whenever I talk with Kiyomi, she won't look me in the eye. Why is that?"

Frank smirked. "A Japanese woman won't look a man in the eye when she is attracted to him."

"Kiyomi's not attracted to me. There must be another reason."

"She is attracted to you," Oda said.

Frank nodded. "We both noticed it the day she stormed onto the boat looking for her daughter."

Micah knew he should be elated, but a feeling of sadness seized him. "I have no future with Kiyomi," he whispered. *I have no future with anyone.*

Chapter Twenty Eight

Kiyomi shuffled around the kitchen like an old woman. Mitsuyo would soon arrive to carve his name into the wheel of time that defined her life. Her future set as an obedient wife, she would surrender whatever dreams remained inside her heart. She knew this was in her best interest, and in the best interest of Ai, but dark thoughts followed her throughout the day. She struggled to concentrate at work, drawing the wrath of Mr. Akita, who barked at her in a gruff voice, accusing her of trying to help the Americans win the war. As she listened, Kiyomi knew she no longer cared who won the war. Only fools went to war when a chance at peace remained.

On the streetcar ride home, she kept her head down. The city and its people no longer felt like a part of her. Her mind traveled to Emi's farm and the memory of Ai's smile as she dug in the dirt. Kiyomi recalled the kettle warming over simmering coals. Steam rising from soup to tickle her nose. The taste of hot food pleasing her tongue.

When she arrived at Ai's school, Kiyomi found her pouting on the playground. "I don't need a father. I don't want a father," Ai said. Kiyomi led Ai from the schoolyard without a word. What could she say to placate her daughter's troubled mind?

The brooding silence continued at home. Only Sayoka demonstrated exuberance as she bustled from room to room giving Kiyomi instructions on how to prepare for Mitsuyo. She must wear her hair just so and dress in a manner that showed her feminine qualities without revealing too much. "You don't want Mitsuyo to notice your body has wilted under the strain of war," Sayoka told her. "He must believe you are a prize worth capturing, *neh*?"

Why did it matter if she no longer possessed the seductive body of a younger woman? Mitsuyo was a cripple. She was a plum tree stripped of its blossoms. Together, they would produce children with plain faces, and dull eyes. But Banri and Sayoka would have their heir. An ugly heir, *Hai*, but someone to carry on the Oshiro name.

As she stirred the potato soup, Kiyomi recalled Emi's question. "Will you be able to live with your regrets?" *I have made so many wrong choices.* Kiyomi closed her eyes against the despair that crawled through her brain like poisonous spiders. No tears. Not tonight. She would steel herself against her doubts while looking toward the future. What kind of life would Ai have without a father? Ridicule from more fortunate peers? Shame at having a stupid mother who failed to use reason when choosing what path to take?

Sayoka made Ai dress in her best kimono. She took her into the bathroom and insisted on styling her hair into a *chocho mage,* which resembled a butterfly. Sayoka raked the brush through Ai's hair over and over, the bristles scraping Ai's scalp and yanking her head back. Kiyomi spied on Sayoka from the hallway, her stomach clenching each time Ai grimaced. *I should be the one brushing Ai's hair,* she thought, but kept her distance out of respect for her mother-in-law.

When Mitsuyo arrived with a timid knock, Ai faced Kiyomi with a look of sadness. Guilt forced Kiyomi to turn away. Banri led Mitsuyo into the house, Mitsuyo's steps awkward and unbalanced. He hunched to the left, his shoulders rolled forward the way a bird positioned its wings against the rain. Kiyomi had seen him using a cane as he traveled to his job. Tonight, he stood unassisted, with three small packages tucked under his right arm. Sayoka walked over to greet Mitsuyo. She bowed. *"Konbanwa,* Mitsuyo-san. Welcome to our home."

He bowed while looking past her at Kiyomi. "*Konbanwa,* Sayoka-san. Thank you for inviting me into your home." Mitsuyo held out a package. "For you and Banri."

Sayoka received the present with another bow. "You are too kind."

Mitsuyo smiled. "And I have presents for Kiyomi and Ai."

Ai glanced over at Kiyomi, who nodded. Sayoka encouraged her with a pretentious smile. "Don't be shy, child." Blood rushed into Ai's cheeks.

"I hope you like this, Ai-chan," Mitsuyo said, holding out a small package.

Ai took the package and bowed. "*Arigatō,* Mitsuyo-san."

Mitsuyo appeared pleased with himself, a smile flashing over his mouth. "For you, Kiyomi-san," he said, offering the last present.

Kiyomi hesitated. This should be a joyful occasion, the merger of two souls, but she experienced no joy, no sense of anticipation or longing. Instead, she pitied Mitsuyo, an honorable man who now suffered because of the war. She caught Sayoka glaring at her. Kiyomi took a clumsy step forward and stumbled. Mitsuyo stopped her fall with his free hand.

"Are you all right, Kiyomi-san?"

No, I'm not all right. "So sorry. I'm fine." Kiyomi accepted his gift with a bow and waved for Mitsuyo to enter the living room. "Please, sit and make yourself comfortable."

Mitsuyo eased onto a pillow, his body swaying. Banri and Sayoka exchanged worried glances before lowering onto their own pillows. Kiyomi directed a scowling Ai toward her pillow. When everyone was seated, Kiyomi offered Mitsuyo tea, which he accepted with a formal air, nose elevated as if he were being served by a geisha. Kiyomi hurried into the kitchen, anger coursing through her veins. *He's been in the house less than five minutes and already acts as if he's my master.* A cold draft slipped across her neck. *Oh, Micah-san, why am I confused at a time when clarity is needed?*

Sayoka burst into the kitchen. "What are you trying to do?"

"I'm preparing tea," Kiyomi responded.

"You know how important this evening is to us. Are you intent on ruining it?"

Kiyomi faced her mother-in-law. "I know how important this evening is to you."

"Then try and show a little more enthusiasm toward our guest."

Sayoka whirled about and hurried from the room. Kiyomi gnashed her teeth while lifting the tray that contained the teapot and cups. "I'm living a nightmare."

Mitsuyo behaved as a proper guest, focusing his attention on Banri and Sayoka. The men drank tea and smoked pipes, laughed at bad jokes, and discussed the current state of the war. Banri struggled not to cough, his face turning red from the effort. Kiyomi kept her gaze on the floor, looking up only when spoken to directly. From time to time, she stole a sideways glance at Ai, who rudely stared straight at Mitsuyo as if examining a praying mantis that had wandered inside the house. When they finished eating, Mitsuyo complimented Kiyomi on her cooking. Sayoka cleared her throat and added, "Kiyomi learned how to cook from me." Upon hearing this, Kiyomi decided that if Mitsuyo ever returned, she would make a dish that tasted like dung.

Kiyomi rose from her pillow to gather the dishes, only to have Banri wave for her to sit. "We have business to discuss, neh?" Banri smiled, oblivious to the discomfort on Kiyomi's face. Banri pointed a finger into the air to stress the point he was about to make. "We all know the purpose of Mitsuyo's visit. Under normal circumstances, we would allow Mitsuyo and Kiyomi to become better acquainted before important decisions are made, but with the war going on, we don't have that luxury."

Mitsuyo bowed. "I understand, Banri-san. I'm most honored to be invited into your home to discuss these matters."

Sayoka leaned forward. "With both of our sons lost to the war, we have no one to carry on the family line. We need a son. Kiyomi needs a husband who will help her have a son. You come from an honorable family. You have represented your family and the Emperor with honor while serving your country. The match makes sense."

Mitsuyo produced a handkerchief from his coat and used it to clean the lenses on his glasses. After returning the handkerchief, he smiled at Sayoka. "I agree with what you have said. To be your son and have Kiyomi as my wife would please me. What does Kiyomi think of this plan?"

Everyone turned toward her and Kiyomi trembled under the weight of expectation. She glanced at Ai, and the anguish in her eyes caught Kiyomi unprepared. Ai's sense of betrayal was absolute. If Kiyomi accepted this marriage, her relationship with Ai would never be the same.

Kiyomi looked straight at Mitsuyo to stress the finality of what she had to say. "I'm honored Mitsuyo would want to marry me, but I'm not worthy of him."

Sayoka sat up straight. Her eyes flew open as her attention shifted between Banri and Mitsuyo before coming back to Kiyomi. "Of course you're worthy," she said.

"I can't agree to this arrangement," Kiyomi went on, "not at this time. Not with our lives surrounded by uncertainty because of the war. We all could die soon."

Banri huffed. "If the Americans wanted to destroy Hiroshima, they would have done so by now."

"And if they invade the mainland, we'll drive them back into the sea," Mitsuyo said.

Kiyomi plucked at the fabric of her kimono. "The way we did on Iwo Jima and Okinawa?"

Sayoka sprang off her pillow. "Enough of this defeatist talk! You forget our sons died with honor fighting in this war."

Kiyomi stared at the floor. Her words had produced the desired effect. There would be no marriage between her and Mitsuyo. Now she must be careful and not reveal her innermost thoughts. "So sorry. It is easy to lose hope when your stomach aches for food and American bombers fill the sky."

Sayoka returned to her knees. "Mitsuyo-san, I'm certain Kiyomi meant nothing by her stupid comments."

An unsettling silence filled the room. The swallows stirred inside their nest. The butane lamps hissed and flickered. Mitsuyo shifted on his pillow with a muted groan. He attempted to straighten, only to sag toward the floor. "The Emperor will not allow us to lose this war. Japan is united as never before."

Kiyomi wanted to get up and slap his face. Clearly, Mitsuyo had learned nothing during his time in the army. Instead, she sought to appease him, for the best conspiracies often started with misdirection. "Of course, you're right, Mitsuyo-san. I'm a foolish woman. What do I know of such matters?"

Sayoka nodded. "Now may we return to the subject of adoption and marriage?"

Mitsuyo struggled to stand. His face held a strange look of contentment as if the prospect of marriage and family had never been important to him. "Kiyomi is right," he said. "We should wait until the proper time." He bowed to each person in the room, wished them goodnight, and turned to leave before Sayoka could intervene.

When the door closed behind Mitsuyo, Sayoka turned on Kiyomi. "Are you trying to sabotage this arrangement? What were you thinking, talking to Mitsuyo like that?"

"I need time," Kiyomi said in a quiet voice.

"Time for what? It's a good match."

Banri pointed at Kiyomi. "This is our decision. Mitsuyo will make a fine husband."

Kiyomi stood and bowed. "I will take the dishes now."

Inside the kitchen, she smiled while remembering the night's events. Absorbed in the details of Sayoka's anguish, Kiyomi failed to notice her entering the room. When she saw Sayoka standing at her shoulder, Kiyomi jumped and held a hand to her chest. "So sorry. You startled me."

Sayoka pressed closer, her face void of anger. "You dream of love. Japanese women do not have that luxury. But perhaps in time, you can learn to love Mitsuyo. Then you will be happy, *neh*?"

"Is my happiness important?"

"Sometimes we must accept what we are given and find what happiness we may."

And sometimes we must find happiness for ourselves. Kiyomi faced Sayoka and bowed. "Thank you for sharing your wisdom. I'll try to remember what you have said."

When she returned to the living room, Kiyomi found Banri reading and Ai on the floor drawing a picture of a girl chasing fireflies. Kiyomi went to work polishing the beams, careful not to draw attention to herself. The evening passed slowly until Banri stretched with a yawn and announced it was time to sleep. "Maybe the Americans will leave us alone for once," he said.

After Ai helped with their futons, she snuggled down facing Kiyomi. "Does this mean you won't be marrying Mitsuyo?"

Kiyomi leaned close to whisper. "Remember when you said we should move in with Emi?"

"*Hai*. I remember."

"Would you still like to do that? Just the two of us."

Ai massaged the silver moon at the end of her necklace. "We would run away?"

"No one must know where we're going."

"Like playing hide-and-seek?"

"*Hai*," Kiyomi said.

"Can we leave tonight?"

"No. We must act normally to not arouse suspicion. I will go to work in the morning. You will go to school. When we come home, I'll prepare what supplies we'll need, then we will sneak away while Baa-baa and Ojiisan are asleep."

Ai released the necklace and frowned. "Why can't we go tonight? I want to leave now."

"There is something I must do tomorrow." Kiyomi brushed the back of her hand across Ai's warm cheek. "Only one more day, my love. We can endure that, *neh*?"

"You promise we will leave tomorrow?"

"*Hai*. I promise."

Chapter Twenty Nine

Micah stood on the Aioi Bridge staring out over the Motoyasu River. Hiroshima reposed under the August moon, gaining strength for the coming day. Inside clustered houses, weary people escaped into dreams of a better future, while on the river, moonlight captured every ripple of water. The city had come to feel like a second home to him. The neighborhoods, the quiet temples and alleys of Nakajima-Hommachi, the streetcars clacking past businesses in Ebisucho, the tranquil view of the Inland Sea from Mukainada. One day, the war would end, leaving Hiroshima at peace, and the sound of children laughing as they jumped from bridges, swam in the rivers, or smacked a baseball into the summer sky would return.

He breathed in the smell of the sea, carried on a gentle southern breeze, and pictured his father standing alone at the edge of Bellingham Bay. Micah wished he could go to him and offer some assurance. He could picture the expression on his father's face upon hearing that Micah had found peace in the last place he would have expected.

Micah revisited the scene from earlier in the evening. Did Kiyomi change her mind regarding an arranged marriage?

"Micah-san."

Micah turned to see Kiyomi standing nearby, a vision in her green kimono.

"I wasn't sure I would see you tonight," Kiyomi said, moving beside him.

"What happened at dinner? Did you accept the arranged marriage?"

"I told them I wasn't ready."

He nodded. "That's good."

She smiled at his reaction. "And I've decided to take Ai to Emi's farm. We leave tomorrow night. The right decisions are the easiest to make, *neh*?"

Micah leaned onto the railing beside Kiyomi, his nerves on fire when their arms touched. He reveled at the softness of her skin. What did she feel when touching him? The spirit world was a place of illusion where the brain created what was needed, and at that moment, everything he needed was standing within reach.

"When I was a boy, we'd sometimes picnic near Deception Pass. There's a tall bridge over the pass. I liked to stand at the railing and drop stones in the water. Of course, at that height, I never saw the stones impact. The clouds must've captured 'em on the way down."

"I used to do the same thing when I was a girl, but the bridge I stood on wasn't tall, and I could see the stones splashing and the ripples they created. Maybe one of your disappearing stones found its way to Japan. Carried on a cloud and dropped into my hands."

Ayu flashed near the surface of the river. He turned to face her. "Why wait? Why not leave tonight?"

"You will think I'm foolish."

"Try me."

"Tomorrow, I'll write a letter to Banri and Sayoka explaining my actions."

"In case you need to return to their house after the war ends."

"*Hai.*"

"If you return to Hiroshima, you'll be forced to marry Mitsuyo."

"Micah-san, if you haven't noticed, I'm not easily forced into anything."

He suppressed a grin. "I've noticed."

A sliver of light appeared on the horizon, announcing the coming day. And what a day it would be with Kiyomi and Ai leaving to start a new life. A *better* life.

Kiyomi straightened to face him. "Will you be following us to Emi's farm?"

Micah hesitated to respond, worried she might want him to stay behind. And if this was the case, he would have no recourse but to remain in Hiroshima. "Would you like me to follow?"

"It seems I'm living two lives. A waking life and a life in dreams. Somehow you've become part of both worlds." She took hold of his hand. "Did I ever mention I danced with Americans before the war?"

"I believe you said something about sailors."

"Those men were nothing like you."

"Is that a good thing or a bad thing?"

"A good thing."

Micah stared at his shoes, overcome by sudden shyness. "If I had known you then, would you have danced with me?"

"I'll dance with you now," she whispered.

He looked up and glanced around. "Here? On the bridge?"

"Why not?" Kiyomi patted her hip. "Put your arm around me."

Micah slipped an arm around her slender waist. The moment felt so right, so perfect, that his doubts and fears, accumulated through years of rejection disappeared. "I must warn you, I haven't done this since my fourth-grade teacher made me dance with Molly Perkins."

"And how did that go?"

"As I recall, Molly screamed every time I stepped on her toes."

"So, you've never danced with a woman?"

His face tingled. "Never."

"Then I'm honored to be the first one."

He'd never had a woman instill confidence in him the way Kiyomi did. With her, anything seemed possible. "What dance will we be doing?"

"We could try the jitterbug, or maybe a waltz. The swing is fun."

"As long as you don't swing me off the bridge."

"You're funny, Micah-san. I'll tell you what . . . How about a nice slow dance? Side to side, like grass swaying in the wind?"

"I should be able to handle that."

Kiyomi stepped sideways and he followed her lead. Their bodies drew closer until her warm breath tickled his neck. She rested her head against his chest. "Your heart beats strong for a dead man."

"That's because you make it so."

"I will always remember this moment," she said.

Micah's gaze moved over the tranquil city, the ageless river, and the stars glowing against the black canvas like the fireflies they would be joining in the countryside. He rested his cheek against the top of her head and closed his eyes.

Chapter Thirty

Kiyomi stepped onto the veranda and breathed in the morning. A brilliant blue sky covered the city, with no clouds and a blazing August sun. She closed her eyes. A breeze stirred the *furin*, its fragile glass tinkling. As she listened, Kiyomi recalled her dance with Micah. The memory filled her with hope. In a few hours, they would leave Hiroshima and travel the mountain pass to Emi's farm. No more hunger. No more sleepless nights worrying about American bombs.

She opened her eyes at the sound of Ai coming outside. Ai shouted goodbye to her grandparents, and then faced Kiyomi with the quiet confidence that came from holding a great secret. Her eyes shined in the bright light. Her lips held a conspirator's smile.

"Are you ready?"

Ai patted the emergency supply bag at her side. "*Hai*. I have everything, including my padded hood. But Mr. B will not return this morning."

"How can you be certain?"

"The air raid has ended. This will be a quiet day."

A flight of three B-29s circled over Hiroshima earlier producing an air raid alarm that had recently ended. The appearance of reconnaissance aircraft was so frequent, no one gave them much thought anymore.

Kiyomi held out her hand. "Come along. We don't want you late for school."

Cicadas screeched from the willow tree in the garden. "There are a lot of insects in the country," Ai said. "My favorite are the fireflies. Will you let me stay up to see them?"

Kiyomi unlatched the gate leading to the street. "You'll be too tired after Emi has worked you all day."

"*Ha*i. But at least we won't be sleeping in a hole."

Kiyomi closed the gate behind them. She stopped, her gaze traveling to the rooftops of neighboring houses. Hundreds of crows perched on the tiles staring down at her. A sudden chill stole the warmth from her face.

"What's wrong, Mama?"

The black eyes of the birds bored into her. *I won't let them intimidate me. Not on this day.* She squeezed Ai's hand. "Nothing's wrong. We should hurry or you'll be late and Sensei-Kondo will be angry."

"Sensei-Kondo never gets mad at me. I'm his favorite student."

To take her mind off the crows, Kiyomi decided to talk about their move. "Are you anxious for our trip?"

"*Hai.* I wish we had gone last night."

"Only a few more hours, my love."

"Emi says she will teach me how to knit."

"Is that so?"

"And how to make fried rice with eggs."

"Living in the country will be great fun for you." The crows lifted from the rooftops with raucous cawing, the grating sound echoing through the narrow streets below. When the crows were no longer in sight, the tension left Kiyomi's shoulders.

"Crows give me a headache," Ai said.

"*Hai,*" Kiyomi agreed. "They remind me of Sayoka."

"We should not say bad things about her, even if they are true."

"Your grandparents will miss you."

"And they will miss having you cook and clean."

"Dust everywhere," Kiyomi said.

"And burnt food for dinner."

Mr. Hamai glanced up from his sweeping as they approached. He faced them and bowed. "Good morning, Kiyomi-san. Good morning, Ai-chan. How are you on this fine morning?"

Kiyomi bowed. "Good morning, Mr. Hamai-san. We are well. How is business?"

"Things have been slow. Too many soldiers in town. Soldiers don't need haircuts. But business will pick up when the war ends."

"Do you think it will end soon?" Ai asked.

"The war cannot go on forever, Ai-chan." He glanced around him. "I look forward to peace. Maybe the government will restore our beautiful streetlights."

When they were past Mr. Hamai's barbershop, Ai leaned close and whispered, "Is Mr. Hamai right?"

"Right about what?"

"The war ending soon."

Kiyomi eyed the boarded-up shops lining the street. "We can only hope."

"Will you miss living in the city?" Ai asked.

"I will miss the rivers. How about you?"

"I'm ready to leave."

Children played outside the Nakajima National School, floating like butterflies over a field of wildflowers. Kiyomi stopped at the edge of the playground. As she surveyed the scene before her, the wrestling boys and giggling girls, she tried to imagine them in a few years as adults. Hopefully, they would do a better job of shaping the world than their elders.

"I miss Jun," Ai said with sadness in her voice. "I look forward to her return."

"It shouldn't be much longer." Kiyomi noticed Ai's necklace had slipped out of her shirt. She took the tiny silver moon in her palm. "You must keep this close to your heart, *neh*?" Kiyomi dropped the chain beneath Ai's shirt.

Ai's expression turned serious, her dark eyes filled with tenderness. "I love you, Mama. I love you so much."

"And I love you too."

Ai glanced toward the school, then back at her. "This will be a great day for us, *neh*?"

"*Hai.* A great day."

Ai leaned close and kissed her on the cheek. She pulled back with a smile. "Sayōnara, Mama."

"Sayōnara, Ai-chan." Kiyomi watched Ai run over to greet her classmates. When she knew Ai wasn't watching, Kiyomi brushed tears from her face.

Kiyomi continued on to the Aioi Bridge tram stop. She sensed tension in the hardened expressions of the commuters crowding the platform. With Okinawa lost, an Allied invasion of the Japanese mainland couldn't be far off. What did this mean for Hiroshima? Some people continued to insist the Americans would spare the city from the destruction of firebombing. Kiyomi would take no chances. A streetcar arrived from Falconer Town with metallic clanking and rattles. Kiyomi joined the line of people inching toward the open door. She stepped inside and was prepared to take an empty seat when someone called her name. Umi waved from a seat toward the back. "I'm happy to see you, Kiyomi-san."

Kiyomi eased onto the seat. "Good morning, Umi-san. I didn't expect to see you."

The streetcar jerked ahead, a strong vibration moving up from the tracks and into Kiyomi's back. As they crossed the bridge, she gazed through the dusty window at the passing river. Two men poled an oyster boat through the shallow draft. Gulls hovered near the mast. On the riverbed, an old man stood beside a young boy. They both held bamboo fishing poles with lines cast into the sleepy current. Bright sunlight glistened on the dome of the Industrial Promotion Hall. Evacuees crowded the road ahead. Workers hurried along the sidewalks. A young woman wearing a kimono in violation of the dress code sauntered among the workers, a baby strapped to her back. Kiyomi couldn't wait to leave the strain of city life behind.

"Kiyomi-san, I must show you something."

Umi held out her left hand. A gold band adorned with a small diamond sat on her ring finger. "Yoshio has asked me to marry him. Isn't it wonderful?"

Memories of her own disappointments flashed through Kiyomi's mind. Love had never shown her respect or kindness, but she wouldn't let this steal Umi's happiness from her. Not on a day when the future appeared as bright as the morning sun pouring through the streetcar windows.

"I'm happy for you, Umi-san. When will you be married?"

Umi admired her ring. "We have not set a date. Yoshio wants to wait until fall."

"You can have an outdoor ceremony when the weather cools."

"That's a good plan, Kiyomi-san. Will you attend? You can bring Ai-chan."

It would be impossible to attend Umi's wedding while they lived in the country but she couldn't tell this to Umi. "We would be honored to come."

"Excellent," Umi said. She pulled off the ring and held it out. "Here, Kiyomi-san, try it on."

"No, I couldn't."

"Please? I want to see how it looks on you."

Kiyomi sighed before taking the ring. To her surprise, the ring slipped on easily.

"See how it shines on you, Kiyomi-san? You deserve a good husband."

Kiyomi admired the glistening diamond and the rings' weight. "Marriage is for young people. I'm much too old."

Umi leaned away her from. "Twenty-eight is not old."

"In Japan, twenty-eight is old." Kiyomi removed the ring and held it out.

The streetcar jolted over rough track, causing the ring to slip from Kiyomi's grasp, and fall to the floor under the seat in front of them. "So sorry," Kiyomi said. She went onto her knees to retrieve the ring and a brilliant white flash poured through the streetcar, accompanied by a wave of searing heat. Kiyomi flew off the floor, levitating briefly, before slamming against something hard.

Grey smoke floated in front of her, accompanied by a hissing sound. She groaned as fiery needles pricked the skin on her back and neck. *What happened? Did a bomb hit the streetcar?* Kiyomi pushed off the floor. Her body tingled and a fire raged inside her belly. The interior of the streetcar was scorched black with smoke rising from the floor. The passengers sat upright, their blackened bodies smoldering. She turned toward Umi and vomited at the sight of her friend. Kiyomi stumbled toward the exit. A smell like burnt squid filled the air. The driver had died standing, her hand still clutching the steering rod.

Kiyomi staggered outside into swirling black and grey clouds. The air rumbled overhead as if hundreds of cannons were being fired simultaneously. Furious wind pelted her. Tongues of flame broke through the surrounding gloom. Kiyomi panted. Her lungs ached each time she inhaled, and a burning pain crawled along her throat as if she had swallowed shards of glass. *Where am I? Am I near the factory? No. We didn't travel that far.* The sky overhead flashed scarlet, purple, green, and blue.

The enveloping clouds lightened near the ground. Kiyomi gasped as the city was revealed to her. Shops and houses were flattened into flaming heaps of rubble. Only a few of the concrete buildings remained. Corpses lay scattered on the road and sidewalk. *No, no, no, this isn't possible.* There had been no warning. No air raid sirens directing them to safety. Her insides turned to sand as insatiable thirst set in. But as strong as her thirst was, a single idea pushed her to take a step forward. She must find Ai.

Small fires raged all around her. People emerged from the swirling cloud of yellow dust that swept through the air. They trudged across the ravaged landscape, stepping over the dead, their arms held away from their injured bodies, skin hanging in loose strips from their limbs. Many wore tattered rags. A few staggered about in the nude. Cries of *"Mizu, mizu,"* went out, but no one brought them water. The surrounding fires merged into a wall of howling flames, heat slashing at Kiyomi's back.

A man with glass shards protruding from his bloody face said, "We must get to the river."

Kiyomi fell in with a group of survivors moving away from the fires. The road beneath her burned through the bottom of her *geta*. She grimaced against the pain and kept going. Behind them, the conflagration roared, flames taller than the surviving concrete buildings. Faces and arms protruded from collapsed houses. Trapped residents called out, "Help if you please!" Here and there, someone responded and attempted to free them. For most of those trapped, there would be no assistance as the flames raced closer, devouring everything in their path.

More and more people stumbled out of the darkness. The number of survivors swelled into the thousands. They shuffled along in silence, an occasional plea for water rising over the shrieking fire. Bodies lay in the streets, atop the rubble, and boiling inside cisterns. Corpses without heads, arms, or legs. Corpses burned beyond recognition, filling the air with the same terrible stench Kiyomi first encountered on the streetcar.

"Where are we?" a woman asked. "Without landmarks, how can we tell if we are going in the right direction?"

A man pointed back at the advancing flames. "That is the wrong direction." He then pointed to a spot on the horizon that wasn't on fire. "That is the right direction."

Kiyomi was forced to step over bodies. "So sorry," she whispered whenever her foot struck a corpse.

Her stomach and intestines ached. Each breath felt as if she had swallowed a nest of stinging hornets. A buzzing developed in her ears. Black spots danced before her eyes. Her bones vibrated. The skin on her shoulders had roasted a brownish-black, and she was certain her back looked worse. Intense heat seized her burnt flesh like the talons of an eagle. Struck by a wave of nausea, Kiyomi doubled over and vomited thick yellow bile tinged with ashes. When she straightened, the taste of ashes remained in her mouth.

Fireworms rose from the burning city, warping and crackling as they tore across destroyed houses, igniting paper screens and wooden beams. The worms merged into larger fire tornados. Red-hot embers whipped through the air, accompanied by pieces of burning paper and strips of cloth. A searing pain moved over her scalp. Kiyomi leaned forward as far as she could and shook her head. A glowing ember fell out of her hair.

She staggered onward, putting her trust in the strangers at the front of the group. They had to find the river. She could drink from the river and regain her strength before crossing the bridge into Nakajima-Honmachi. *Maybe our neighborhood has been spared from the worst of the destruction*, she told herself. The shell of a shattered building appeared through the brown haze. A feeling of hope rose within her as she recognized the familiar dome of the Industrial Promotion Hall. The river was close. *Thank God.* She would drink and extinguish the fire inside her.

As they neared the embankment, Kiyomi's heart shattered into a thousand splinters of glass. Across the river, Nakajima-Honmachi lay in ruins, every shop, tea room, theater, temple, and home flattened. Grey smoke rose from the rubble. Her eyes stung as they tried to produce tears. "Ai, where are you?"

I will drink from the river and rest a few minutes before I look for Ai. She is safe. She was taken into the hills with the rest of the children. The buildings collapsed after they were evacuated. Ai is all right. She has to be all right.

Kiyomi paused at the top of the steps leading to the riverbed. She blinked, her ash-covered lips trembling as she surveyed the scene. Hundreds of blackened bodies obscured the surface of the river. Wounded and dead people stretched along the riverbed as far as she could see. Someone bumped into her, sending a sharp pain racing down her spine. Dozens of injured survivors waited behind her. Kiyomi eased down the steps, each footfall sending spasms of agony along her nerves. She staggered past bodies on the riverbank.

Kiyomi splashed into the water, shoving aside corpses. The warm river lapped against her waist as she cupped a hand to scoop the purple water. Bobbing corpses slammed into her. She ignored their clouded eyes and frozen grimaces while greedily swallowing. Dozens of injured survivors piled into the river. Kiyomi braced herself but her feet slipped out from under her and she plunged beneath the surface. Bodies closed in above her, stealing the light. *I won't die in the river. No. I must look for Ai.* Kiyomi pushed toward the surface. Her head slammed into a corpse and she sank. The body of a young boy caught in the current glided past, his innocence frozen in time. Kiyomi gnashed her teeth and tried again. She emerged beside a woman whose nose, eyebrows, and hair were burnt away. The woman shoveled water into her swollen lips with a series of grunts. Kiyomi struggled to the riverbed, muscling corpses out of her way. She reached the sand and collapsed, her lungs screaming for clean air. Too weak to stand, Kiyomi crawled toward the embankment through pools of blood, vomit, and feces. At the wall, she wedged between the body of an old man and an injured woman whose face was swollen to twice its normal size. To her left, several schoolgirls lay in a row, nude from the waist down, burnt skin gathered around their ankles like fallen stockings. Some of the girls cried for their mothers.

Kiyomi closed her eyes. The water failed to quench her thirst and she believed her blood was evaporating. The buzzing continued inside her head. Her bones were twigs ready to snap. All along the riverbed, people vomited while others cried for water. Behind them, the fire growled like a hungry beast as it burned through central Hiroshima. *I must rest a few minutes before crossing into Nakajima-Honmachi,* she thought. *Maybe I'll find Banri and Sayoka. They can help me search for Ai. Hai. This is what I will do.*

A drop of cold rain snapped her eyes open. Fat slimy raindrops, the color of coal, poured out of the clouds.

"The Americans are dropping oil on us!" someone shouted. "They are going to burn us."

Kiyomi shivered. Her strength gone, all she could do was lie still and let the rain pummel her.

"Excuse me."

The woman next to her sat up. "I must feed my baby. He is hungry." She held the charred body of an infant to her breast. Kiyomi closed her eyes again, unable to bear the woman's suffering.

Time slipped past, minutes like hours in the living hell surrounding her. The black rain chilled her to the bone, while heat rolled in from the fires. Partially destroyed houses crashed down from the embankment, beams cracking, people on the riverbed screaming as debris buried them. After a while, an eerie stillness settled over the scene as more of the injured succumbed to their wounds. The pleas for water went on, accompanied by vomiting and quiet moaning.

"Do not give water to the injured," a man said. "It will kill them."

Hearing this frightened Kiyomi more than the firestorm raging all around her. She couldn't die, not until she found Ai.

The rain ended and a faint rainbow appeared within the swirling grey clouds. Without the rain, the heat intensified, settling over her like a blanket soaked in gasoline and ignited. Kiyomi writhed against the pain, flesh peeling off her back in long strips. *I must go now,* she decided. *I must find Ai before it gets dark.* She raised her head, her body shaking. Kiyomi collapsed back onto the sand. *Forgive me, Ai. I cannot come now. But I will find you, I swear it.*

Chapter Thirty One

After Kiyomi and Ai left the house, Micah headed off to visit Frank and Oda. He would tell them goodbye before following Kiyomi to Emi's farm. As he journeyed along Tenjin-machi Road, Micah examined the houses and shops like a man on a vacation in an exotic land. He needed to memorize every detail of their appearance: the pitched roofs covered in tile, the latticed window coverings, and the side gates which led to tranquil gardens. In addition to the structures, he studied the people he passed on the street: mothers accompanied by children too young for evacuation; idle men who stood in front of closed businesses; and old folks who viewed the world through cynical eyes. He had no idea when or if he would return to Hiroshima and he wanted to take the scenes from this fine August day with him. Across the city, shadows retreated into corners and narrow alleyways. Doors opened. *Geta* tapped over concrete. Streetcars rattled and banged as they transported people to jobs.

Micah paused at the top of the steps leading to the Motoyasu River. On the far embankment, sunlight beamed onto the copper dome of the Industrial Promotion Hall. An old man fished with a boy on the opposite side the river, reminding him of Levi and his son. Two men poled an oyster boat toward open water. Gulls trailed with their familiar "Ha-ha-ha-ha."

"Hey there, Micah-san," Oda said, looking up from the bowl of rice on his lap.

Micah climbed aboard the oyster boat, dodging the boat's captain, Ryō, as he made his way to the stern and peered over the side. A teenaged boy was busy checking the furled sail. "Is Ryō taking the boat out?"

"It would appear so," Frank answered.

"Fool," Oda mumbled. "Ryō's going to get sunk by an American submarine. They patrol the Inland Sea now."

"Will you be going out with Ryo?"

Frank set his empty bowl on the deck, where it vanished. "I have business in town. Oda might go."

"Frank has Geisha business."

Frank dismissed Oda with a wave. "So, Micah-san, how are things with you? Will Kiyomi marry soon? You should come and live with us when she does."

"Unless you want to watch her making love with her new husband," Oda added.

"That's why I've come to see you. I'll be leaving tonight."

The muscles in Frank's face tensed. "Leaving? Where to?"

"Into the countryside with Kiyomi and Ai."

Frank and Oda exchanged amused glances before Frank said, "So, Kiyomi isn't getting married. How did you manage that?"

"I had nothing to do with her decision."

"Does she know you'll be following them?"

"We've discussed it."

"Then we're happy for you, aren't we, Oda-san?"

"Frank is happy for you, I'm not. You should stay with us."

"Oda hasn't been happy for a long time."

"This is true," Oda said.

"But you must feel contented, eh, Micah-san?" Frank said.

"Don't worry," Micah responded, "I know my place in this world."

"Your feelings for Kiyomi run deep."

"Yes."

"In that case, you must—" Frank slid off the barrel and stood, grasping the gunwale as he gazed across the river.

"What is it?" Micah asked.

"I'm not sure. I felt something."

"I felt it too," Oda said. "Like static electricity in the air before a storm."

Ryō and the boy stopped working and stared at the sky as if they too had experienced whatever Frank and Oda had sensed.

Micah opened his mouth to speak and—

A blinding flash burst overhead as if the sun ruptured into a billion pieces. Stabbing white light descended onto the waiting city, sweeping crowded streets. Buildings blew apart. Tiles, beams, and paper screens sailed through the air. When the flash reached the river, it burst out the windows of the Industrial Promotion Hall and melted the dome. Houses and businesses lining the embankment imploded. Trees ripped out of the ground and flew away. The explosion swept over the river, pulling the water skyward in great sheets taller than the embankment, then hit the oyster boat with unimaginable heat. The boat erupted into fragments of wood that caught fire and burned to ash. Light shot through Ryō and the boy, and bit by bit, their bodies tore apart, flesh from muscle, muscle from bone, and blood evaporating into the churning dust. A shock wave punched through Micah producing pain so pronounced, he believed he was somehow dying again. He flew off the disintegrating boat and slammed into the ground, angry flames racing overhead. Micah covered his head and closed his eyes against the horror. His insides tingled as if an electric current pulsed along his veins. The searing heat of the flash gradually diminished inside him. When the pain dissipated, he pushed into a sitting position. "What the hell," he whispered. *Hitodama* burst upward all around him; so many they painted the sky in streaks of blue. *This can't be happening.*

He had been blown away from the river and onto a pile of smoldering timbers and roof tiles. Micah rubbed his eyes. Every building around him was flattened. *A thousand bombers couldn't produce this level of damage.* Then it hit him. A new weapon. An atomic bomb. Yes, that had to be it. He'd read about the destructive power of such a weapon in science journals but never imagined one being used against people. *My God, what have we done?* Micah stood. Yellow dust swirled around him, accompanied by flakes of ash.

"Micah, are you all right?"

Frank shambled toward him.

"The city is—"

"Destroyed." Frank stopped nearby and clutched his knees. "How is this possible?"

Micah's guilt kept him quiet, rather than share what he knew about the atomic bomb. "Where are we?"

"Looking at the Industrial Promotion Hall, I'd say we're standing in Nakajima-Honmachi, or what's left of it."

Nakajima-Honmachi, the place he'd called home for the past three months. It couldn't be gone. A sudden panic seized Micah. "I have to find Kiyomi."

Hitodama continued to flood the skies over Hiroshima. Frank shook his head. "Just look at them. How could anyone have survived this?"

"I don't know," Micah said, "but I've got to try." He stared across the river in the direction of the Tōyō Kōgyō factory. Grey smoke boiled up from the city, filled with tongues of flame. The yellow dust obscured visibility, but Micah could see enough to comprehend what he was up against. "She was on her way to work. With any luck, she managed to get there prior to the explosion. The factory is shielded by a hill."

Frank removed his glasses. Eyes closed, he pinched the bridge of his nose. "What about Ai?"

Micah glanced around at the burning piles of rubble. A dull ache settled in the pit of his stomach as despair overwhelmed him. The last time he had felt this way, he was standing in a cold rain at the Bellingham cemetery, watching his mother's coffin being lowered into a hole. Nakajima-Honmachi appeared to have taken the brunt of the blast. How could Ai survive such devastation? He went to Frank and laid a hand on his shoulder. "I will search for Ai after I find Kiyomi. We can only hope she made it."

"Hope has deserted me," Frank said, putting on his glasses. "I must go check on my family in Hakushima Kuken-cho. I pray they're well."

Oda staggered up from the river, sake bottle in hand. His wide eyes surveyed the scene. His trembling lips betrayed shock and anguish. "Our boat disappeared."

"Everything is destroyed," Frank said.

Behind Oda, injured people careened toward the steps that led to the riverbed. Their jerky movements suggested they suffered agonizing pain. Oda sank to his knees and wailed. "I can do nothing to help them. I have no honor." He heaved the sake bottle aside. Hands pressed to his face, Oda sobbed, his massive body shaking.

Frank went to Oda and gripped his shoulder. "You can help. Go out among them. If you see anyone heading toward danger, whisper a warning. They might hear."

Oda sniffled and stared at Frank with wet glassy eyes. "You think so?"

"You should try."

Oda pushed off the ground. "I'll do what I can." He set out in the direction of the bay.

"Do you believe he can help?" Micah asked.

"Against this? No. But it will give him something to do, otherwise, he'll drink sake and feel sorry for himself."

Micah trekked with Frank to the Aioi Bridge, passing through the ruins of Nakajima-Honmachi. Blackened bodies and skeletons lay everywhere. Micah remembered Ryō's body disintegrating in the blast. How many others shared his fate? How many people vanished as if they had never been a part of this world?

Frank waved a hand in front of his face. "This smell ... like burnt squid. Awful."

Micah tried to ignore the terrible stench of burnt bodies, but there was no escaping the constant reminders of death and suffering that surrounded them.

A churning cloud expanded over most of Hiroshima, crackling as it sucked up dust and debris. The cloud billowed upward, changing color from bright red to brown, and finally to black. *Hitodama* continued to streak into the sky nonstop. The souls of the dead escaping the horror of life. On the ground, the wind picked up speed. Glowing red sparks flashed past. His stomach clenched upon realizing the sparks were burning scraps of wood and ragged strips of cloth torn off victims. At the Aioi Bridge, Frank pointed toward the hills.

"I'm heading to Kio first." He stared down Aioi-Dori Street. "Are you certain you want to do this?"

Across the bridge, smoke filled the air from small fires raging throughout what had been, Otemachi, Onomichicho, and Sarugakucho.

"If Kiyomi survived, I'll find her."

"Then I wish you luck," Frank said. "But if you fail, yours won't be the first heart broken in Hiroshima today."

The concrete walkway of the bridge had buckled and the steel railings folded outward. Smoke rose from the blackened body of a person welded to their bicycle. Micah paused in the center of the span. Below, survivors stumbled onto the riverbed, most with flesh like charred meat or painted in blood. Bodies floated on the water like logs. Except for an occasional cry, the scene was orderly. No one pushed or fought. Up and down the riverbed, the injured stretched out on whatever ground was available.

Micah continued across the bridge, heat rising into the soles of his shoes. Power lines, telephone poles, and steel supports used to suspend cables over the streetcar lines lay twisted and broken, all pointing eastward. Ash fell like snow, settling over the dead. Micah leaned onto his knees and took a deep breath. A pile of simmering meat lay near his feet. A tiny hand poked out of the mass. "Jesus Christ," he whispered.

Survivors staggered out of the darkness, alone and in small groups. Some had swollen, deformed faces. Even knowing they didn't see him, Micah could not meet their gaze. What had been done to these people went beyond cruel.

He pressed onward against extreme heat blowing in from fires bellowing all around him. The blackened shell of a streetcar appeared through the blowing smoke and ash. Micah stepped over smoldering corpses to peer inside. The passengers had died where they sat, their bodies transformed into lumps of charcoal. On the street, a long line of survivors trudged in the direction of the hills. Could Kiyomi have survived and sought refuge outside the city? No. She would never leave Ai behind.

The wind intensified. Tendrils of fire, like glowing red worms, shot up from the ground. The fireworms weaved back and forth through the thickening black smoke. *I must turn around,* Micah told himself. *If Kiyomi traveled beyond these flames, she's probably dead.* His eyes squeezed shut as the thought of Kiyomi dying made him wish he had never known her. This feeling passed as he remembered dancing with her. Micah stared in the direction of Nakajima-Honmachi. *If she's alive, I'll find her.*

He happened upon a burning corpse that bubbled and sizzled. Farther down the road, a slight man dragged the body of a woman. Thousands of grass blades had driven into the man's back, turning the flesh green. An odd clicking sound approached from behind. A man ran toward Micah flapping his arms. The man had no right foot and his shinbone chipped and fractured each time it hit the asphalt. His eyes bulged with fear as he passed moaning, "Uh-uh-uh," and vanished into a wall of smoke.

Fire worms whipped through the air, twisting and snapping as they fed. Soon, the worms merged into fiery tornados. A cry caught Micah's attention. He left the road and picked his way over the smoking rubble. The cry grew stronger. Micah gasped when he found the source—a woman and child were trapped beneath the fallen timbers of their home. The woman reached out an arm, hoping someone would rescue them. Micah squatted in front of the woman. The child was a little girl no more than two or three years old. Rivulets of sweat cut grey rivers in their ash-covered faces. The fire closed in on their house. The woman continued to call for help in a calm voice. Micah worked his arm under a timber. With a strained groan, he tried to move the heavy wood, but it held fast. The flames drew closer. Micah tried once more to move the timber without success. He dropped to his knees and thrust out an arm. The woman retreated into the shadows with her child until all he could see were the whites of their eyes. Flames leaped onto the house and the woman screamed. He took off running, unable to bear their agony.

Micah made his way back to Aioi-Dori Street. He planned to look for Kiyomi along the riverbed, starting at the Aioi Bridge. He fell in with a group of survivors. They shuffled forward as if sleep-walking, seemingly oblivious to the fires that threatened to engulf them. The shattered Industrial Promotion Hall appeared in the distance, a solitary reminder of a Hiroshima that once existed.

Cold rain fell in large black drops. A man tilted his head to capture rain in his mouth. Others followed his lead. The dark water speckled their faces and washed ash from their hair.

Micah descended steps to the riverbed. He paused near the bottom. Injured survivors crowded the sand. They laid together in silence—an occasional moan or someone vomiting the only sounds. *Hitodama* exploded upward through the rain, leaving a bright blue tail in their wake. He stepped onto the sand and picked his way around the wounded and dying. Whenever he spotted a burned woman about Kiyomi's age, Micah knelt beside her to examine her face. This was the only way he could be certain of her identity. Some of the women turned toward him, their eyes opening wide as if they sensed his presence. Thousands of women lay burnt and broken along the riverbed.

The black rain ended. He'd been searching for hours, the western sky taking on a deeper hue over the mountains. *How can I find Kiyomi in the dark?* In desperation, Micah shouted her name as he neared the Motoyasu Bridge. He knew Kiyomi couldn't hear him and yet, he held out hope that somehow she could respond.

Micah sank to his knees beside countless women as if a priest hearing their confessions, only, they had no sins to account for. He was the one who needed absolution, because he had come to kill them all and now his wish was coming true. He deserved to rot in this man-made hell; they did not. People stirred around him. Voices raised. Eyes opened and contemplated the vermillion sky where three B-29s circled overhead. People pointed to the bombers, their faces filled with dread. It took Micah a moment to understand that the survivors believed the Americans had returned to drop more bombs. Micah shook a fist at the planes and shouted, "Go away. Haven't you done enough?" Micah sank to his knees and doubled over. Forehead pressed against the warm sand, he wept.

After passing beneath the Motoyasu Bridge, he paused to stare across the river. Fewer people crowded the opposite riverbed and this meant one thing—essentially every person in Nakajima-Honmachi died in the attack. Taking in the agony of Hiroshima, Micah could imagine the hatred the people must feel toward Americans. As he stumbled through the gathering darkness, weaving around the dead and dying, *Hitodama* launched skyward in an endless procession. As he watched the fiery balls take flight Micah thought, how many more must die?

His feet felt heavy as if encased in cement. An invisible weight pushed down on his shoulders. Fatigue set in, and he yawned while searching for a space to sit. Micah spotted an opening between the bodies of two children. Looking at their faces, he remembered Ai with the fireflies. Would he ever see her again? Micah buried his face in his hands and groaned. *I'll never find Kiyomi,* he told himself. *Never.* For the first time he believed she was dead and hoped she had died instantly, without suffering. He drew his knees up and leaned forward to rest his head on his arms. A woman's frail voice carried across the quiet dusk.

"Ai … Ai … Ai."

Micah scrambled to his feet and set off in the direction of the sound. After traveling a few yards, he found a woman lying on her back, her head tossing from side to side as she murmured the name, "Ai."

"Sweet Jesus," he whispered, dropping beside her. Could this be Kiyomi? The flesh on the sides of her face, neck, and shoulders was burnt black. Ash powdered her hair and lips. Her head stopped moving and she stared straight into his eyes as if she could see him. Micah's face screwed up into a series of fine wrinkles and his lips trembled. "No. No. I didn't want this for you." He touched her face. "You should have died, Kiyomi. You should have died without suffering. I'm so sorry."

"Ai … Ai … Ai," she whispered, her attention shifting skyward as if she would find her daughter hidden amongst the stars.

"I don't know what happened to Ai. Maybe she …" Micah shook his head. "I would pray for you, Kiyomi, except, in my heart, I'm not certain there's a God anymore. How can I believe in a God who would allow this to happen?"

Darkness closed in over the city. Smoldering fires cast a yellowish glow above the ruins while shooting stars streaked across the night sky. He had never seen so many shooting stars and wondered what they meant, if anything. Kiyomi lay still. She stopped calling Ai's name, her gaze fixed on the heavens. Kiyomi closed her eyes after a shooting star passed and died soon after.

Chapter Thirty Two

Kiyomi sat up and blinked as the world came into view. "Micah-san, why are you here? Am I dreaming?"

Micah's tired eyes revealed his distress.

"What's wrong?"

"I'm afraid you're not dreaming."

Why did he say afraid?

Micah rested a hand on her shoulder. "What do you last remember?"

"I ... I ... was riding on the streetcar to work. Talking to Umi. She's getting married. She showed me her ring and then ..."

"What?"

"A bright flash. I blacked out. When I came to—" She covered her eyes to hide her tears. "I was in pain. Umi was dead. Everyone on the bus had died. I went outside. Smoke and fires. Buildings gone. Bodies everywhere." Kiyomi sniffled and brushed away tears.

"What happened next?"

"I remember being thirsty. I joined with some people and we headed toward the river." It was then she noticed bodies bobbing on the surface of the water, and burnt and bleeding people lying on the riverbed as far as she could see. Her focus returned to Micah. "You were right. It was no dream. What happened?"

He hung his head. "Hiroshima has been destroyed by a new bomb."

"What? Destroyed? Impossible."

"I'm afraid it's true. Everything has been wiped out; all the houses and businesses, the college ... even the castle ... gone."

"Hiroshima Castle?"

"Yes."

"Have you been to Nakajima-Honmachi?"

"There's nothing left."

Her fingers feathered over her parted lips. "Have you seen Ai?"

"No."

"Her school?"

"It's not there anymore."

Kiyomi remembered saying goodbye to Ai at her school and Ai telling her she loved her. "I must find her. Ai can't be dead. No."

The expression on his face surprised her, for it contained both sadness and pity.

"What aren't you telling me?"

He stood and held out a hand.

She accepted his hand and he helped her stand. He then reached out to embrace her. "Why are you holding me?"

"I must tell you something. It will come as a shock."

What could be more shocking than waking up to find your home destroyed and daughter missing? "All right, Micah-san. What do you want to tell me?"

"You were injured when the bomb went off. Badly injured. Your back, shoulders, and face suffered deep burns."

"I don't understand. I'm not injured. Look at me."

"Kiyomi, this isn't easy to tell you but ..." He shook his head.

She encouraged him in a quiet voice. "Tell me."

"You died from your wounds."

His words sent a shock through her. *Why would he tell me this?*

"Look behind you."

He released his hold and she turned around. The body of a woman lay on the sand looking up at the night sky. Kiyomi concentrated on the face, then gasped and covered her mouth. "It's true. I died."

"I was with you when you passed. I thought you might leave me, but no *Hitodama* appeared."

Along the riverbed, countless bodies lay on the sand, which glowed red in the light cast by fires atop the embankment. Anguished cries of "*Mizu, mizu,*" "*sore wa itai,*" and "*tasukete kure,*" filled the night, but no one would bring them water, care about their pain, or come to their aid, no matter how politely they asked. A raw wind carried the stench of burnt flesh. "My heart is beating. I have all my senses. Why?"

"I don't know. Frank told me our minds continue to believe our bodies are alive. Something about easing our transition into the afterlife."

"*Hai.* That makes sense. My uncle taught me the dead experience the afterlife as if they were still alive."

"I've been watching *Hitodama* rising out of bodies all day. I'm assuming they're going to the Pure Land that Frank talked about. Why did you get stuck here like me?"

"I don't know. I don't care. Nothing matters except Ai. I must find her."

"Then we will find her."

"We should go to my in-law's house. It's on the way to Ai's school."

"All right."

She followed him across the riverbed, stepping over bodies with care, then up the steps to the embankment. At the top, she stood mouth agape, eyes taking in the devastation. Small fires flickered across the darkness, smoke rising toward ominous red clouds. Kiyomi's attention shifted to the opposite side of the river. She squinted while trying to recognize any of the surviving buildings. The Füji Trading Company remained, as did the fire insurance company building. Across the river near Falconer Town, the gutted remains of the Honkawa Elementary School stood tall, as did the nearby Kodō Elementary school. The sight of the schools lifted her spirits momentarily, until she remembered that Ai's school was constructed of wood. When they reached the Motoyasu Bridge, Kiyomi hesitated to cross.

"What's wrong?"

"I'm afraid what I will find on the other side."

His gaze fell to the road. "I'm scared too. But what choice do we have?"

She found strength in his response. "I'm glad you are here. To face this task alone would have been too much for my heart."

They walked onto the bridge. Kiyomi's attention shifted to the water, where corpses bobbed and slammed together. As she took in the scene, a thought played through her mind: *So this is what victory looks like.* At that moment, she hated the men who steered Japan into war. Another idea came to her as she passed a blackened body: *What men created a weapon that could wipe out an entire city and kill so many people?* She wished they were in Hiroshima to see the results of their achievement.

Kiyomi stopped at the far side of the bridge. Even in the darkness, she noticed how once distant hills now crowded the ruins. She felt disoriented without the familiar buildings surrounding her. Kiyomi remembered the people who had walked these streets and operated shops, businessmen like Mr. Hamai. She imagined him outside his barbershop sweeping the sidewalk when the bomb went off. He wouldn't need to worry about sweeping anymore.

Charred bodies lay scattered across the debris. Her stomach clenched at the sight of a tiny blackened corpse fused against the back of an adult. She glanced at Micah, who shook his head.

"When you're dropping bombs at eight thousand feet, you can't imagine the conditions on the ground. You see the fire, but not the people who get caught up in it. Seeing this makes me ..." He flattened his hands on his hips and gazed at the sky. When he looked back at her, Kiyomi saw shame in his eyes.

"You were dropping leaflets on Hiroshima," she reminded him. "Leaflets that warned us to evacuate."

"That doesn't matter," he said. "I wanted to kill all of you for starting this war that took my brother from me. Why is it the people least invested in the cause of war suffer the most from its outcome?" He gestured toward the bodies of the adult and infant. "They didn't deserve to die. They weren't a threat to anyone. And you ..." Micah closed his eyes for a moment. "You've lost everything. The war needed to end, but not like this. Never like this."

She stepped closer and rested a hand on his forearm. "You and I have suffered, and will continue to suffer. But now, we must push aside the pain, *neh?* We must find Ai."

"You're so strong. My grandfather would have liked you."

Kiyomi found this idea amusing, but wouldn't allow herself to smile, not while standing on smoldering rubble, surrounded by bodies. "I believe this is Tenjin-machi Road."

"Are you certain?"

"I'm not certain of anything." Kiyomi scanned the horizon, noting the position of the Industrial Promotion Hall and the Honkawa school building. "We're not far from the Oshiro's house."

When they arrived where the house should be, Kiyomi's chin sank toward her chest. She had known what to expect, but seeing the flattened pile of rubble still came as a shock. The leaves on the garden willow had turned rusty brown, and dead fish floated in the pond. She stepped across smoldering piles of wood and tiles.

"Over here," Micah called.

Kiyomi made her way to where Micah stood staring down at something. Two skeletons lay side by side beneath a beam, their arms extended as if they had been trying to escape. The whiteness of their bones contrasted against the burnt wood. Kiyomi pictured Sayoka standing before her, so proud and full of vile. She had hated her mother-in-law in life. She could not hate her in death.

"We should find the school."

Kiyomi stood. "There's no school left to find."

They advanced in the direction of Nakajima-Hondori Street. The once thriving roadway was now a morgue. In the distance, yellow lights floated through the ash-choked air.

"Are we getting close?"

Kiyomi spotted the toppled headstones of the cemetery located near the school. "*Hai.*"

They entered an area of open ground. Here, people carrying lanterns went up and down rows of small blackened bodies, moving from corpse to corpse, pausing to kneel and shine light on what remained of their faces. A man cupped his hands around his mouth and shouted out a name, only to be answered with silence. Hundreds of bodies lay scattered over the schoolyard. As despondent people searched for a lost child, others added bodies to the growing lines. Kiyomi's throat tightened. She turned to Micah, who stared at the scene with grim resolve. "I knew it would be bad. I didn't expect this."

"They must have been outside when the bomb went off."

"I have to find her."

Micah held out a hand. She accepted it without comment and allowed him to steer her onto the schoolyard. "We should start where the bodies have been lined up."

Kiyomi couldn't find the words, so instead, she squeezed his hand to signal her agreement. They stepped around and over bodies until arriving at the farthest row.

"Are you ready?" Micah asked.

How could she be ready for such a task? In a small voice that seemed to rise out of a deep well, she said, "We should start."

They knelt beside a waxy corpse. "This child isn't burned like the others."

"Maybe they weren't caught out in the open," Micah said.

"This isn't Ai."

"I agree," he said, standing.

They worked their way down each row, stopping to kneel over dead children. The sky lightened. Grey replaced black. A scarlet haze replaced grey. Long shadows pulled back revealing more of the destruction. Yellow and red ash buried the flattened city. Small fires flickered across the horizon. On the playground, more people arrived to join in the desperate search. A spark of hope grew inside Kiyomi when they finished examining the bodies laid out in rows without finding Ai. "Do you think she survived? Is it possible she was protected from the blast?"

The muscles in Micah's face pulled tight. "We still have bodies to examine."

"But there's a chance she survived."

He held her in his gaze for several seconds. "Let's keep looking."

She followed Micah as he stepped around bodies and knelt beside him as they examined scorched faces. She saw in his eyes the question that lingered inside her own mind. How will she be able to recognize Ai? *I will know. I am her mother. A mother will know her own child.*

As their search dragged on, the rising sun hot on her shoulders, the possibility of Ai surviving grew stronger within Kiyomi. Her mounting exhilaration turned to panic. What would happen to Ai if she had survived? Who would take care of her? As she grappled with this dilemma, trying to think of a way she could help Ai from beyond the grave, Kiyomi discovered the bodies of an adult and child near the torched remains of a pine tree. She stopped beside the child and started to kneel when something caught her eye—a blackened necklace around the child's neck. When her gaze traveled to the dark orb attached to the bottom of the chain, the sky tilted, and the ground trembled beneath her. "No! No! No!" Kiyomi sank to her knees. She reached for the orb and frantically rubbed at the scorched surface. When the first hint of silver appeared beneath the black, she looked over at Micah. "It's her. My daughter is dead. Ai is dead." He brought her against his chest and Kiyomi's tears spilled onto his shirt. "I can't believe she's gone. Not my Ai."

"I'm so sorry," he said, massaging her back.

"It's my fault. She wanted us to leave during the night. If I'd listened, we'd be safe at Emi's farm. Ai would be alive this morning."

"You can't blame yourself," Micah whispered. "You had no way of knowing this would happen."

She felt suddenly exhausted, her body ready to melt into the waiting earth. Down into whatever Hell awaited her. "Did she suffer?"

"No. She died instantly."

Kiyomi pulled back, her eyes wide and filled with fear. "She died before me."

After a pause, he said, "Yes, she must have."

"This isn't right."

"What's not right?"

"Ai is …" Kiyomi brushed tears from her eyes.

"Ai is what?"

"She's lost. Her soul is lost."

Micah blinked, confusion washing over his face. "What do you mean by lost?"

"The *Hitodama*, the souls of the dead, they travel north to Sai no Kawara, the river they must cross on their way to Mount Osore."

"And they descend into the mountain to gain access to the Pure Land. Frank told me about this."

"Because she died before me, Ai has no one to guide her to Sai no Kawara. And even if she managed to get there, *Datsueba*, the old hag who guards the river, keeps the souls of the children trapped on the other side."

"If Ai can't find her way to Sai no Kawara, where would she go?"

Kiyomi pictured Ai stumbling along Akudo, one of the worst paths a soul could take. She imagined her falling into Jigoku, the dark pit of hell. No. This would not be Ai's fate. Not with so many children dying together. She took hold of Micah's hand. "Ai's soul will have traveled to Kyu-Kudedo, the cave of lost children."

"The cave of lost children?"

"*Hai*. There they wait for *Jizō*, the protector of children, to come guide them to Sai no Kawara." Kiyomi stared past him to the hills surrounding the city on three sides. Grey smoke covered the tops of the hills like low-lying fog. "I must go to Kyu-Kudedo and find Ai. I must lead her to the Pure Land. If she hasn't entered Mount Osore within forty-nine days, she will be doomed to an eternity in hell."

"Where is this cave?"

"On the west coast of Honshū, not far from Matsue."

"And how are you going to get there?"

"I'll take a pass over the mountains. There's no other way."

Micah looked at Ai's body, then back at her. "I'll come with you."

"I can do this on my own."

He appeared hurt, but recovered and said, "My grandmother told me two people shorten the road."

"Micah, I don't—"

"Please," he implored. "I want to do this. For you, and for Ai."

"All right."

Kiyomi's attention returned to Ai's charred body. She remembered lying beside her, Ai nestled in the crook of her arm. "I would like to hold her again."

"You want to hold her now?"

She nodded. Kiyomi sat with her legs tucked beneath her.

"You must help me," he said.

"I'll try." Kiyomi wiggled her arms under Ai's body.

"This might not work."

"It will work. We will make it work."

Micah cleared his throat. "All right then. On the count of three, lift. One, two, three."

Kiyomi strained against the weight of Ai's body, grunting as she pulled Ai toward her while Micah pushed from the other side. At first, Ai remained fixed to the ground before slowly lifting. "We're doing it!"

"Keep pulling," Micah groaned.

When Ai's body reached Kiyomi's thighs, it felt somehow lighter. Kiyomi brought the blackened corpse against her chest. She rested a cheek on Ai's head and rocked back and forth, tears streaming down her face. "I'm so sorry, my love. I should have listened to you. Look what my ignorance has brought us. Please forgive me." She pulled Ai closer. "I will come for you. I will not leave you in darkness."

The wind intensified and Ai's body crumbled, bits of flesh flaking off as ash. Kiyomi held on tighter as if this would stop Ai's remains from deteriorating, but the harder she squeezed, the more ash appeared. Little by little, the wind whittled away the burnt flesh, until all that remained were bones and a black lump inside the ribcage. *Ai's heart.* Kiyomi worked the moon necklace over Ai's skull, then kissed the top of her head. "You have always been a good girl."

Micah helped Kiyomi to her feet. "Should we try to bury her?"

She shook her head. "Her bones should rest with the others who died here."

Chapter Thirty Three

Morning belonged to the flies. They buzzed through the dusky air in black swarms, settling over the dead and wounded. Micah stood on the Aioi Bridge next to Kiyomi, surveying the remains of Hiroshima. With smoke rising from ruins buried in reddish-brown ash, the flattened city resembled the crater of a volcano. Less than twenty-four hours earlier, the city was vibrant, alive. Streetcars rattled along roads crowded with people pushing carts and riding bicycles; children shouted and laughed on playgrounds; fishermen unfurled sails to capture the wind. Now, Hiroshima was a tomb. A powerboat crept along the river, its engine sputtering and belching black smoke. Two men stood at the bow, using long poles with hooks to snag corpses. Dead crabs and split open fish littered the riverbed.

"All the temples in Tera-machi are destroyed," Kiyomi said.

"Yes."

"The priests should have prayed harder for peace."

They set out across the bridge, the sidewalks broken and pushed into the shape of a W, reinforced iron rods exposed like ribs. Strange shadows on the road resembled people. Did heat from the blast burn the shadows onto the pavement? Asphalt beneath their shoes felt warm and gooey. An old man stood on the embankment looking down at the dead and dying, his hands raised. He chanted, his voice charged with emotion.

"He's performing a Buddhist incantation for the dead," Kiyomi explained.

The old man would have a long day, Micah thought. The dead covered the road and surrounding rubble, blackened and broken bodies, some missing eyes or limbs, others bleached skeletons. A middle-aged man sat beside the body of a young woman. She was covered with a white cloth, her head resting on a small pillow. A bowl of rice sat nearby. The man ran a brush through her hair, murmuring something with each stroke. Long lines of survivors trudged up the hills, while others moved into the city.

"Must be people from the country searching for relatives. They will only find sorrow. Hiroshima is dead. What is done is done."

Micah worked her words over in his mind. How could she accept this tragedy so easily? If this happened in Bellingham, he would want to go and kill someone. An idea weighed on him. He had wanted revenge after Levi was killed and nothing good came from it. Maybe Kiyomi was right. What could be gained from continuing to hate?

Soldiers wearing medical masks labored to gather corpses. They stood bare-chested, sweat glistening on their shoulders. Flies buzzed around their heads. A pair of soldiers rifled through the pockets of the dead, lifting wristwatches, fountain pens, and whatever valuables they could find.

Kiyomi's face darkened. "What's happened to the world?"

Black smoke and flames billowed from two stacks of bodies. Trails of silvery phosphorous weaved between the pyres. Similar fires could be seen across the city. Smoke merged with blowing dust to tint the air a golden hue.

They fell in with a group of evacuees heading north out of the city; old people who struggled on wobbling legs, men and women with emotionless faces, wide-eyed children struggling to comprehend their new reality. Many of the displaced bore the scars of serious injury—blackened and broiled skin, gashes and cuts. Mixed in amongst the wounded were those who had escaped physical trauma. They kept their heads bowed as if ashamed to be with people who suffered. No one wailed. No one cried. They remained calm and disciplined, despite their pain and overwhelming grief. How could they accept this cruel turn of fate? Did they all believe what Kiyomi believed; *what is done is done?*

Kiyomi's expression remained resolute, her eyes free of tears. He wanted her to damn him and America for destroying everything good in her life.

"This isn't the road you took to Emi's farm."

Her eyebrows went up. "No. We're heading toward Mukaihara Town, but will leave the road and take a pass over the mountains."

"And you've gone this way before?"

"No."

"Then how do you know which way to go?"

"I will know."

Her cryptic response troubled him, but he decided not to press the matter, assuming there must be a supernatural element behind her confidence.

The sun emerged above the opaque air that settled over Hiroshima. Fierce rays sliced through the haze like flaming swords making the back of Micah's neck ache. He thought about the burn victims and how they must suffer in the heat. As they climbed away from the city, the spoiled meat fetor from dead bodies dissipated. A small mercy.

An older man toddling beside a woman and girl turned toward Micah. "You're an American?"

Micah looked down. "That's right."

"Pilot?"

"Bombardier."

"You must have been part of the crew that went down over Hiroshima back in May."

"Yes."

"War is a terrible thing."

"I agree."

"I'm Eito from Otemachi. I owned a bike shop."

"I'm Micah from Bellingham, Washington."

"A pleasure to meet you, Micah-san." He gestured toward the woman and child. "My daughter-in-law and granddaughter. They were fortunate to be in Fuchu Town when the bomb went off. I was not so fortunate. Now they are going to my brother's home in Tottori Prefecture. The army drafted my son. He died of fever in New Guinea. Tōjō should be shot."

Eito stepped over to his family and rested a hand on his granddaughter's shoulder.

"How can he see you?" Kiyomi asked.

"He's dead like us. Don't you notice how he glows? There are a number of spirits among us, but I suspect the majority of those killed traveled to the Pure Land."

She stared at her *geta*. "I could not."

"What?"

"Travel to the Pure Land. I didn't call to Amida before I died. I must have known that I needed to stay behind for Ai."

The road ascended through the hills, higher and higher until at last they could no longer see Hiroshima behind them. Overhead, the sun followed their progress with a torturous glee. Kiyomi panted and waved a hand in front of her face. "I'm hot and thirsty. Why do I thirst when I'm dead?"

"Your brain believes you need to drink. This will pass in time. However, if you want something to drink, all you have to do is picture what you want and it will appear."

Her left eyebrow arched. "This is true?"

"Put out your hands and imagine you're holding a cup of water."

She extended her arms. "Like this?"

"Yes. Now picture yourself with the water."

Her eyes narrowed in concentration and a porcelain cup appeared. "It worked," she said.

"How do you think Oda always managed to have a bottle of sake?"

Kiyomi brought the cup to her lips. "The water tastes cold. Would you like a sip?"

Before he could respond, she dumped out the water. "I cannot drink when so many here are thirsty." The cup vanished from her hands and she slowed. "What's happening up ahead?"

Dozens of men holding axes and pitchforks blocked the road. One of the men stepped forward. "You must turn around. We have no way to help you and not enough food. Go back to Hiroshima."

"We must get through," a woman wailed. "I have a sister in Tojo Town."

"And I have family in Shobara," a man added.

"Turn back! You can't get through on this road."

The evacuees exchanged bewildered glances before silently retreating. Eito grunted. "I never thought I'd see the day when Japanese people turned against each other." He continued to shake his head as he headed down the hill beside his family.

"How awful," Kiyomi said.

"War brings out the worst in people."

"These men should be punished," Kiyomi said as they passed the group. "What gives them the right to treat others this way?"

"Hunger," he whispered.

After they had traveled some distance, Kiyomi pointed at a dirt trail. "That's the pass we want. It leads to Matsue."

The rocky pass climbed deep into the mountains, past green meadows overrun with yellow, red, and purple wildflowers. Clear streams burbled around grey stones. Lonely waterfalls poured into mirrored pools. Larks, sparrows, and robins serenaded with chirps and whistles. Maple and oak trees growing beside the path greeted them with pockets of welcoming shadow. Kiyomi walked in silence, her focus on the trail. Micah longed to talk with her. Anguish and elation collided within him and he needed to remind himself that just because she was now a part of the spirit realm, things wouldn't stay this way forever. After finding Ai, Kiyomi would lead her to the Pure Land, but he would be left behind.

Kiyomi stopped. "I'm tired. Why should the dead feel this way?"

"I don't know. There are times I still need to sleep."

"And dream?"

"Yes."

Daylight faded over distant mountains. Insects and birds fell silent. A cool breeze brought relief. They arrived at a mountain lake, the smooth surface capturing the last of the sunlight in flashes of scarlet, orange, blue, and violet.

"We should rest," Kiyomi said, pointing at a tree near the water.

Micah slumped against the trunk and stretched out his legs. Kiyomi eased onto the ground with measured grace, close enough to reach, but a million miles from his touch. He closed his eyes and slipped into a memory of hiking the backwoods with Levi, morning fog damp on their faces. The scent of pine heavy in the air. He recalled the day they happened upon a twelve-point buck. They locked eyes as the buck contemplated their intent. After several tense seconds, the buck nodded its understanding, and they continued on their way, mortals in the land of woodland gods.

He opened his eyes to discover Kiyomi missing. Micah leaped to his feet and searched up and down the shore without spotting her. Where would she have gone?

Micah set off to find her. Wind whistled through tree branches. An unseen owl hooted. *Where could she be?* The longer he searched without finding her, the stronger his despair. Micah forced his way through trees and heavy underbrush. He spotted light ahead and broke through onto a clearing.

Kiyomi sat near the water's edge, legs pulled under her, upper body slumped over her thighs, hands covering her face. Her body quaked as she moaned. Micah wanted to go to her. He longed to take her into his arms, but knew this wasn't what she needed. Instead, he retreated without a sound, leaving her to face a long and torturous night.

Chapter Thirty Four

Morning arrived with a kiss of sunlight that sparkled across the surface of the lake. Kiyomi stood over Micah, watching him sleep. She had always found him attractive, even when she considered him an enemy. *Strange how I can find beauty where I've been told none exists.* Her aunt warned her to stay clear of foreign men. "You want a nice Japanese man. Japanese men have shiny black hair and perfect skin. They do not mar their faces with ugly red beards. Japanese men have dark, mysterious eyes. A *Gaijin's* eyes resemble paint spilled from a palette." Micah's eyes matched the color of a summer sky; even her aunt would have recognized that quality.

Micah awakened with a yawn. "How are you feeling?"

"How am I supposed to feel?" she asked.

He pushed off the ground and stood. "I don't know," he said, brushing off his pants. "I can't imagine the pain you must be experiencing."

"I had a vision last night. A little girl all alone. Crying. Waiting for family to come get her."

"Ai?"

"It was Jun, Ai's friend from school."

"I remember her. They used to lie on the floor drawing pictures. Wasn't she evacuated?"

"*Hai.* She went to the temple. In my vision, that's where I saw her." Kiyomi focused on the ground. "Ai must be so scared."

Micah rested a hand on her shoulder. "We'll find her."

Having him touch her felt comforting, as if she were meant to accept this small mercy without regarding the ramifications. "Thank you, Micah-san. I apologize for my behavior yesterday. You're doing me a great favor and I—"

"No need to apologize." He pulled back his hand.

"We should get going, *neh?*"

"*Hai.*"

"Are you turning Japanese?"

"No. But I'm starting to understand your culture. A little bit. I have much to learn."

"We must seem odd to you?"

"No more than Americans would seem to you."

"*Hai.* You are most odd, Micah-san."

"My mother always said I was the oddball in the family."

"What is an oddball?"

"It means, the crazy one."

"If we start now, we might reach Matsue tomorrow."

"I will follow you, my lady." He bowed and held his right arm out to the side as if greeting royalty.

"Micah-san, the crazy one. I must remember this."

They returned to the pass. The red clay trail wound upward through the mountains, higher and higher toward a collision with the sun. Kiyomi waited for Micah to begin walking. When he drew ahead, she fell in behind him. He stopped after going a short distance.

"Why aren't you walking beside me?"

"Well ... you see ... I must ..."

"Must what? Walk behind me because I'm a man?"

"Please excuse. This is the way I've been taught."

"All right, but you're dead now. No one's going to care if you walk next to me."

What if they ran into another spirit? Would she be judged harshly for disregarding this rule of etiquette?

"I refuse to move until you walk next to me."

Kiyomi scanned the surrounding forest before drawing alongside him. "You're a stubborn man."

"Stubborn and crazy." He smiled, the sun gleaming on his white teeth. "I'm glad you've decided to talk to me today."

"I can't promise you many words. My tongue will remain silent before I say foolish things."

"And I would have you feel comfortable enough to say whatever is on your mind, foolish or not."

Kiyomi advanced with her head bowed, stealing glances at Micah. She told herself to relax, but tension continued to weigh upon her. Her stress wasn't from being with Micah. No. Having him with her was like snuggling into a warm futon on a cold night. The hands of an invisible clock moved inside her mind. Time was an enemy she must overcome.

The trail led through shadowed ravines, over rolling hills carpeted with bamboo grass, and past rice fields cut square into the earth. They entered a grove of bamboo, the long stalks creaking while the leaves rustled like the bells of a *kagura suzu*. Interwoven among the bamboo and grass, white morning glory blossoms begged for sunlight. A mountain stream burbled against its muddy banks. Green fish flashed near the surface of the water.

Orange and yellow butterflies fluttered through a shaft of sunlight. Kiyomi recalled how Ai had noticed butterflies on their trip to the countryside. What would Ai say if they were together now? Would she point at the butterflies and laugh?

"What's wrong?"

She took a moment to gather herself. "I was thinking about Ai."

Micah stared at the butterflies, then back at her. "I see."

"I'm afraid I'll forget her before we arrive at the cave. The way she smiled and laughed. The way she looked at me before she fell asleep."

"You won't forget her. My memories of Levi remain fresh in my mind. No one can take that away from me."

"I want more than memories, Micah-san. I want Ai."

They stopped at a fork in the road. To the right, the trail climbed. The left fork descended into darkness.

"Which way?"

"I say we continue west-north."

His eyebrows went up. "You mean northwest?"

"No. West-north."

He chuckled. "All right, if you say so."

His incorrect use of the term west-north amused her. Americans had things mixed up inside their heads. She would need to show him the proper way of things if he was to remain in Japan.

They came upon a forest of maple, *Bodhi*, and cherry trees. The dense foliage suppressed sound and the world turned quiet. Kiyomi remembered the eerie silence that settled across Hiroshima on the morning after the bombing. She pictured bodies scattered throughout the ruins and smelled burning flesh on funeral pyres. These memories stabbed at her brain, over and over until she wanted to scream.

Something stirred the underbrush. A fox broke free of the shadows, pacing them from the woods. What could the fox want?

"I used to go hiking with Levi," Micah said. "We tromped all over the Cascades, just a couple of fools who wanted to get away from civilization." A smile twitched at the corners of his mouth. "He used to drag me into the drugstore on Saturday mornings to sit at the counter and watch the girls."

"Did you know any Japanese girls in Bellingham?"

"A few. I went to school with Rachel Kudo. Her father grew apples."

"You never talked to her."

"Rachel sat by herself, drawing."

"Like Ai."

"Yes, like Ai. Rachel was quiet."

"You were quiet."

"I suppose."

"Was Rachel pretty?"

"Not like you."

She felt lightheaded. "I am talking about Rachel."

Micah shrugged. "She had nice teeth and wore a bow in her hair."

Kiyomi fought back a smile. Undoubtedly, Micah had noticed her more than he let on. "Did girls scare you?"

He stopped. "I wasn't scared of girls. Why would you ask that?"

"I meant no offense. Most boys are afraid of girls."

"Well, I wasn't like most boys."

Kiyomi knew he was lying to impress her, but decided to change the subject to get him moving. "I wonder how far we are from Matsue."

"Hard to say," he answered. "It seems as if we've been walking for years."

Kiyomi seized his wrist. "Don't say that! We only have forty-nine days to find Ai."

Micah's face flushed. "I'm sorry. I didn't mean to frighten you."

"I know. I shouldn't be sensitive, but I—"

"Pardon me." A woman stood in the middle of the trail, hands on her hips. A grin creased her round face. Her eyes were bright and focused.

Kiyomi leaned toward Micah and whispered, "How can she see us?"

"I don't know."

She bowed as they drew closer. "I'm Chiyo Takagi from the village of Fukiya."

"Fukiya?" Kiyomi repeated. "We're far from Fukiya."

"Not so far," she said. "Are you traveling to Kyōtō?"

"We're going to Matsue."

Micah put an arm in front of her as if she needed protection and said, "We're dead."

"*Hai*, so am I. A wagon crushed me. I'm traveling to see my daughter in Masuda. I have spent many years on these trails."

"Then you must know the way to Matsue?" Kiyomi said.

"You're on the wrong path. You should have taken the road to the west-south."

"Where the pass forked?"

"*Hai*. It's a common mistake. People believe they should continue to the west-north if they want to get to Matsue, but this trail leads to Kyōtō. The other path starts west-south before turning toward the coast."

"We are grateful for your assistance," Kiyomi said.

"My pleasure."

"We should go back," she said.

Micah stared at Chiyo through narrowed eyes. "If you believe that's the right way."

They circled around and went back down the trail. Kiyomi glanced over her shoulder and noticed Chiyo was gone. *How odd?*

At the fork, they turned onto the trail recommended by Chiyo. The branches of maple and oak trees stretched across the path, forming a canopy. Sunlight filtered through the leaves, painting delicate shadows on the ground. Micah kept glancing over his shoulder.

"What's wrong?" she asked.

"I don't know. Something about that gal is off."

"Off what?"

"You know ... strange. For one thing, she doesn't glow like a normal spirit."

"We could go back," Kiyomi said, "but if we ended up in Kyōtō, we would—"

"Be way behind schedule. No. We should stay on this road to see where it leads."

The trail twisted through ravines, climbed hills, and descended into grassy hollows. Late afternoon, black clouds swept in. She pointed at the sky and Micah nodded. A "po-po-po-po-po" rose from the trees and carried onto the pass. Kiyomi shuddered at the sound.

"Are you all right?"

"Do you hear that? It's the call of a cuckoo. My aunt told me it's the cry of dead souls longing to return to life. We shouldn't travel by night. Not with goblins about."

"Goblins?"

"You don't believe me."

"Levi and I spent two nights at the Bayview Cemetery trying to spot a ghost. We never saw one, but we did see balls of light floating around the gravestones. If you say there are goblins in these hills, who am I to disagree?"

Kiyomi's eyebrows went up. She had never heard of anyone who went looking for ghosts. *I have much to learn about Micah,* she decided.

Granite walls closed in on both sides, forcing them to advance single-file. She allowed Micah to take the lead, for, despite his American ideas on equality, this was the proper thing to do. The storm advanced, stealing what light remained. When the trail opened up, Kiyomi returned to Micah's side. Thunder rumbled overhead. She searched the clouds for *Raijin* and his twelve drums. Would he come to earth this night in search of navels to eat? Lightning splintered the sky with a crack.

"Come on," Micah said, taking hold of her hand.

He guided her off the pass and under the sheltering limbs of a *yanagi* tree. Micah sat against the trunk of the willow and patted the ground next to him. Kiyomi reluctantly joined him, while debating if she should tell Micah the *yanagi* tree was a goblin tree? The sky opened and rain came down in ghostly tendrils.

Lightning exploded overhead. Kiyomi imagined what creatures traveled along the pass in the darkness. Something rattled in the wind. Could it be the bones of *Gashadokuro*? The giant skeleton roamed about at night. Surely he would crush them and bite off their heads if they were discovered. Or maybe *Joro-gumo,* the giant spider, would appear as a beautiful woman to seduce Micah and wrap him up in her web before devouring him. What if Sayoka returned as a vengeful *Onryo*? Did anger fill Sayoka's heart while the fires of the atomic bomb consumed her? Kiyomi sighed. *I'm dead. Why must I fear these things?* She lifted Micah's arm across her shoulders, which made him smile. *This feels right,* she thought. With the sound of Micah's heart in her ears, Kiyomi closed her eyes against the storm.

Chapter Thirty Five

Micah awakened to raindrops glistening like diamonds on the willow leaves, and Kiyomi sleeping with her head on his chest. He had envisioned being this close to her but stopped believing it could happen. Now that she was here, he didn't want to let her go. Kiyomi stirred, her eyes opening wide to look up at him. Outside their shelter, birds announced the new day with throaty chirps and whistles. Somewhere in the distance, water rumbled over a crest.

"How did you sleep?" he asked.

"Better than expected. Thank you."

"I didn't do anything."

"You made me feel safe. I haven't felt safe in a long time."

His arms ached, the desire to hold her overwhelming reason. He hoped she couldn't see the yearning in his face.

"We should get started," she said.

He pushed aside branches and they stepped into bright sunlight. A fox scurried past in the undergrowth, its black eyes watching them as it went by.

The storm had left the ground sodden. Kiyomi walked beside him without protest and Micah was pleased to see her in a better mood. They had been traveling a while when she stopped and shielded her eyes from the sun.

"What is it?"

"We're lost. Chiyo promised this path would turn west-north, but it leads west-south."

"We've come too far to turn back."

"I should have let you lead us."

"I'm not from Japan. Why would you trust me to get us to Matsue?"

"You studied maps of the country for your missions, *neh*? You helped guide the pilot."

"No, the navigator did that. My job was to ..." He stared at his dusty boots.

"Drop bombs. *Hai*. That's not important now. Finding our way to Matsue is important."

"What do you suggest?"

"I think we should ..." Kiyomi's eyes grew wide. Her lips parted. "Do you feel that?"

"Are you all right?"

Kiyomi held her arms out as if balancing on a high wire. "The earth trembles."

"Earthquake?"

"No. Not an earthquake." She looked to the south. "That sound. So loud, like last night's thunder."

"I don't hear anything."

Kiyomi dropped to the ground and curled into a ball. "Oh, God. It hurts. It hurts."

Micah knelt beside her and grabbed her by the shoulders. "What's wrong? Where does it hurt?"

"My back! My back! I'm burning. Help me."

Micah rolled her onto her side. "Kiyomi I don't—"

"Hold me, Micah-san."

He brought her against his chest. "What can I do?"

"My bones are rattling. Can you hear them? Oh. It hurts."

Micah rocked her and whispered, "I have you. I'm not going anywhere."

Kiyomi trembled in his arms before relaxing. "So sorry. Please excuse me. I don't know what happened."

"Are you still in pain?"

"No. Not anymore." She pulled back. "It felt like ..."

"What? What did it feel like?"

She focused on his face and in her eyes, he observed the same agony he saw when they discovered Ai's body. "The way it felt when the bomb went off in Hiroshima."

"Come on," he said, pushing off the ground. "Let's get you on your feet."

Kiyomi stood and brushed dirt from her clothes. "Am I cursed to experience the event over and over?"

"I don't believe that."

"We should continue then."

They advanced deeper into the mountains. In time, Kiyomi regained her composure and walked with her head up. Still, he couldn't help but wonder if she was indeed cursed. The sun lashed at his neck and shoulders. He wanted nothing more than to stretch out on the dirt and sleep. His boots dragged along the trail kicking up dust. *What's wrong with me?*

"Are you all right, Micah-san? You look ill."

"How can I be ill without a body?"

"You have your spirit body."

"That I do."

They continued their journey, but with each step, his body turned to lead, and the road stretched onto a distant plain where a hazy glow awaited. He stumbled and she caught him by the arm.

"We should rest," Kiyomi said.

"Yes."

"It's been an odd morning," she said. Kiyomi gestured toward an oak tree. "Some shade."

"Shade would be nice."

Micah staggered toward the tree, sinking to his knees when he reached the trunk and collapsed in the dirt. He found himself floating on a river of stars, the sparkling band bearing him farther and farther from the earth toward a pinprick of light.

Chapter Thirty Six

The ground rolled beneath him as Micah breathed in the pungency of salt water. Where they close to the Sea of Japan? He groaned and lifted his head. When the fuzzy surroundings came into focus, Micah gasped. He was sitting at the table inside his grandfather's troller. Levi sat across from him fingering a shot glass. His Grandfather Finn, stood in the galley sipping out of a mug, steam frosting his beard. Outside the window, black water lapped against the hull. *What happened to Japan? Where's Kiyomi?*

Sweat and blood soiled Levi's uniform. His skin had tanned the color of a worn penny, and crow's feet splintered from the corners of his eyes. Levi glanced over his shoulder. "Mind fetching my brother a glass? Micah looks as if he could use a stiff drink."

Finn banged a shot glass onto the table. "*Skjerp deg.* You ain't much good to me if you're gonna get drunk. You've got lines to set before dawn."

"Now, *Farfar*, you know that's not going to happen." Levi winked at Micah.

Finn grumbled as he returned to the galley. "The fish won't wait on a couple of lushes."

Levi filled the glass and pushed it toward Micah. He raised his own glass in a toast. "Here's to us, little brother. We went to war and came back ... dead." Levi threw back his drink and refilled his glass. He jerked his head toward their grandfather. "Least we didn't go down in a squall, chasing salmon." His eyes narrowed on Micah's untouched glass. "Come on, Micah. Don't tell me you've gone soft in your afterlife."

Was this all a dream? It had to be a dream. Micah picked up the glass. It felt real in his hand. He drank the whiskey and suffered its burn.

Finn shuffled over to the table and motioned for Levi to scoot over. "Make room."

A swell rocked the boat and coffee mugs hanging on hooks over the sink clattered together. Finn settled in and took a long slug from the bottle, then wiped his mouth on the back of his hand. "You look troubled, boy."

"Micah's confused about why he's here."

"That so? Well, it's time he got used to being dead. Things ain't gonna change."

"Things changed for Micah."

"How's that?"

"This is his first time with us."

Finn raised the bottle. "We should celebrate. The family coming back together, imagine that, and on my troller. We're going to catch us some fish tomorrow. Yes, sir."

Finn and Levi finished off the bottle. While excited to see them again, Micah struggled to comprehend why he was there and what it meant for him moving forward. How long had he been back home? Would he be staying here forever?

Finn slid off the bench and stood. "That's enough drinking. Dawn comes early." He placed a hand on Micah's shoulder. "Good to see you again, boy." A belch accompanied him as he staggered toward his cabin.

Levi smirked. "And he calls us lushes. Geez."

Micah laughed and Levi's expression softened. "That's what I want to see. Why let a little thing like death put you in a foul mood?"

"Did you ever imagine we'd end up like this?"

"Stuck on a troller with our stinky old *Farfar*?"

"No. Not that. I meant that we'd both die in the war."

"People die in wars."

"Have you seen Mom?"

"Yeah, I see her from time to time. She's fine. Misses you for some dumb reason."

"I always was her favorite."

Levi reached over to give Micah's arm a shove. "Like hell you were. The first born is always their mama's favorite."

"I heard it got rough on Guadalcanal."

"Those Japs put up a helluva fight." Levi rolled the shot glass between his palms. "You must have been scared when your plane went down. Falling out of the sky and all."

"You saw that?"

"Yeah. It was a hard thing to watch."

"How's that's possible?"

Levi shrugged. "I don't know and I don't worry about it since there's no one here to ask."

"I thought there were guardian angels in Heaven."

"Is that what this is?" Levi whispered.

Micah sensed a touch of sadness in Levi's tone. "Tough what happened to Mom."

"She's all right now. Dad's the one suffering. Ruth goes to see him when she can. Kind of depressing though. They sit in a room listening to the radio and don't talk." Levi scooted to the end of the bench and stood. "Let's go for a swim. We can race."

"Are you crazy?"

"You're saying that because you know I'll kick your ass."

"Fat chance."

"I always whipped you, little brother. If you recall, I was on the high school swim team."

"Why? You never won anything."

A devilish smile played on Levi's mouth. "Honest truth? I did it to be near the girls' swim team." Levi tugged on his sleeve. "Come on, Micah. A little swim won't hurt you. Might help clear your head."

"I'm not the one who's been downing the shots."

"Then for old time sake? What do you say?"

"I say you're out of your mind."

Levi continued to grin. "I knew you'd agree to it."

He followed Levi outside to the hold. A numbing wind at their backs shook the taglines and made them clash with a metallic pop. Levi pressed against the bulwark. He looked down at the water, then back at Micah. "Perfect night for it."

Micah moved alongside him. He shook his head as he stared out over the dark water. "We're going to jump in wearing our uniforms?"

"Hell yeah. Boots and all."

"That's the dumbest idea I've ever heard, and you've come up with a ton of dumb ideas."

"Why, thank you." Levi grabbed the rail and hurled himself overboard. He hit the water with a splash, disappearing briefly before his head surfaced. "Come on, Micah. Don't be scared."

"This is so stupid," Micah said, climbing onto the gunwale.

Frigid water smashed into his face. The world turned dark, the surface of the sea fading as he sank. A rush of panic gripped him. He pushed upward, surrounded by memories that appeared in the murky water like scenes from a movie. Watching Kiyomi as she bathed. Playing with Ai in the garden. The fireflies in the countryside. Every recollection took him back to Japan. Every memory made his heart long for what he'd left behind. His head broke the surface. Levi treaded water nearby, a smile on his face. "Thought you were going to drown, little brother, until I remembered that wasn't possible. You ready for a swim?"

"No, but what choice do I have?"

"That's the spirit." Levi lunged forward, his body slicing through the water.

"Where are we going?" Micah asked, drawing alongside.

"Does it matter, as long as it's not hell?"

With his limbs stiff and frozen, it took Micah a while to feel comfortable, but then he relaxed and fell into a rhythm. He recalled swimming with Ai in the river. Where could she be? *The cave.* Yes. Kiyomi said Ai was in the cave of lost children. They must find her.

They swam in the direction of the distant mountains. From time to time, Micah looked over at his brother. He couldn't believe they were together again. What twist of fate made this possible? As much as he loved Levi, something felt off, as if Micah's presence here was a mistake.

After swimming for what seemed like hours, they moved into shallow water. People crowded the shoreline. Children ran with burning sparklers. Adults gazed skyward where fireworks exploded in flashes of red, blue, green, and gold. Levi placed a hand on his back when they reached knee-deep water. "Apparently we arrived in time for the Fourth of July celebration."

If this was the Fourth of July, how many months or years had passed since he was in Japan?

The spectators paid no attention to them as they strolled onto the beach. Micah noticed for the first time what the people wore. The men dressed in suits with top hats and bowlers, while the women wore long white dresses with lace. He turned to Levi, who watched the show overhead. "What's with their clothes?"

Levi leaned close with a hand cupped around his mouth. "What'd you say?"

Micah raised his voice. "Why are these people dressed in old-fashioned clothes?"

"That's what they wore when they were alive."

"We've gone back in time?"

"It doesn't happen a lot, but it does happen," Levi said.

Fog blew in from the bay, pouring over the beach like spilled cream. Levi tugged on Micah's sleeve. "Let's go."

"Where are we going?"

"Somewhere else."

"That tells me a lot," Micah grumbled.

The fog thickened until the entire world lay hidden in white. "Stay with me," Levi said, glancing over his shoulder. The dark shapes of buildings emerged around them. Powerlines crisscrossed overhead.

"Are we in Bellingham?"

"Looks like it," Levi said.

"But what year?"

"Does it matter?"

When the fog lifted they were tramping through an apple orchard, the waking sun filtering through branches. Dew covered apples that glistened like rubies. Beyond the orchard, veiled woods promised mystery. Dry needles and pinecones cracked beneath their boots. The forest swallowed up most of the sunlight, patches of golden color slanting through an occasional glade. Levi stopped. "Close your eyes," he said.

"What? Why?"

"Must you question everything?"

"Usually."

"Well, just this once, trust your brother."

Micah closed his eyes. "Now what?"

"Open them."

Micah opened his eyes. They were sitting in a forest on tree stumps. Before them, a campfire hissed and popped. "How'd we get here?"

Levi shrugged. "Who knows? I was tired of being cold and this seemed like a good idea. You and I had a lot of interesting conversations beside campfires."

Micah smiled. "We did indeed."

Levi tossed a stick into the flames. "I'm sorry you're in such a mess."

"Forget it. Besides, you're the one who left a wife and son behind."

"They'll get along all right. Maybe they'll remember me on Decoration Day. Too bad there wasn't enough left of my body to send back home. Would've been nice to have been buried in Bellingham."

"I don't know what happened to my body," Micah said. "The Japanese probably used it for target practice."

"You meant to say Japs, right?"

Micah stared at the ground, not sure how to respond.

"It's all right, little brother. Things happen. People change. We can't go on hating forever."

Red hot embers floated toward the treetops. "I hated the Japanese after you and Mom died."

"I'm glad you put that behind you." Levi's gaze traveled to the open space overhead. "Look at those stars. Man, oh, man. We used to make a lot of wishes on those babies."

"Yeah, we did," Micah agreed.

Levi stared at his boots. "You're not going to stay, are you?"

"I can't."

"Because of Kiyomi?"

"You know about her?"

Levi grinned. "I never thought my little brother would fall for a Jap gal."

"It's not like that."

Levi's expression turned serious. "Then make it like that."

"She needs my help."

"Then why are you still here? Go and help her." Levi snapped a twig. "I'm going to miss you, little brother. Damn, but I'm really going to miss you."

Chapter Thirty Seven

Kiyomi closed her eyes and thanked the gods as Micah awakened. He groaned as if in pain, and struggled to sit up. "Let me help you," she said working an arm behind his back.

"How long was I asleep?"

"Nine days."

His body went rigid. "Nine days? Are you sure?"

"I counted each one." She avoided his gaze. "I became scared. At first, I feared *Onryo* and *Gashadokuro*, but then something remarkable happened. Fireflies appeared. Hundreds of them. They hovered around me, bathing me in their warm glow. The fireflies returned each night and I was no longer afraid of ghosts and monsters. Then a new fear grew within me."

"You were afraid you wouldn't see Ai again?"

"I was afraid you wouldn't wake up." Kiyomi plucked a blade of grass and rolled it between her fingers. "Where did you go, Micah-san?"

He hesitated before saying, "I was with my brother. At first, we were with my grandfather on his troller. Then we swam ashore. I think we were in Bellingham. We ended up beside a campfire in the woods."

"Was it Heaven?"

He shrugged. "I suppose. One type of heaven."

Now it was her turn to hesitate. Kiyomi knew what she had to ask, but this didn't make the question any easier. "Why didn't you stay with him?"

"Why didn't you go on to Matsue without me?"

The right thing to do would have been to leave him, but she never considered that option. Ai believed Micah had come into their lives for a purpose. Why should she question her daughter's wisdom? "I have no idea where we are."

"If I can find my way back to you, we can find our way to Matsue."

"All right. What do you suggest?"

He stood and stretched. "We might as well hold course. We're likely to come upon a village."

"And how's that going to help? There will be no one there we can talk with."

"There's bound to be a spirit that can help us."

She lifted off her knees. "We should go."

They set off down the trail, walking side by side. Kiyomi felt happier than she had in a long time. Her anxiety over the prospect of losing Micah had been genuine, as was her anxiety over why she was worried in the first place. She found herself curious about him. *Why was this?* Answers came to her but she dismissed them as childish, schoolgirl thoughts.

Beside the dirt path, the bamboo grass and maple trees stood still. *Fūjin*, god of the wind, had not opened his bag to release the wind on this day. Flies buzzed around their heads. A black snake slept on a boulder, absorbing heat. Sparrows and blue flycatchers flittered in and out of the trees. After they had journeyed an hour or so, she noticed Micah had become withdrawn, like an old turtle content to hide in its shell. His sullenness made her unhappy. While there was value in silence, she found none in Micah's silence. "Did you enjoy visiting your brother?"

"It was good to see him again." Micah shoved his hands into his pockets. "He knows about you."

"He can watch us?"

"Apparently so."

"If your brother can watch us, then others can as well. Maybe my ancestors or Banri and Sayoka."

"Or maybe Ai is watching."

Kiyomi smiled at this idea. "I hope she sees us, then she will know I haven't abandoned her."

"She knows."

The pass entered a grove of bamboo trees, before opening onto a flat plain where the earth was terraced into rice fields. Beyond the fields, a dozen wooden houses with thatched roofs lined both sides of the road. Shirtless men wearing straw hats and loin-cloths worked in a field, using hoes to chop the earth, their skin the color of cedar bark. Three men repaired the roof on a house. Two women threshed barley through an old-style machine.

"I don't think we'll find anyone here to help us," Kiyomi said.

A man and woman approached on the road. She leaned onto his arm, turning her head from side to side as she sniffed the air. As they drew closer, Kiyomi noticed the woman's eyes were milky orbs, which saw only darkness.

"Stop here," the woman commanded, when they had come to within a few feet of Kiyomi and Micah.

The man grimaced as if he had stepped on a thorn. He was middle-aged with a broad, serious face and cynical eyes. "Why are we stopping?

The woman bowed. "I'm Mio Fumi. This is my son, Doi."

"Can you see us?" Kiyomi asked.

"*Hai*. I can see you, Kiyomi Oshiro, and your American friend, Micah Lund. You have come from Hiroshima, *neh*? You were killed in the bombing. Micah died earlier."

"You know about the bombing?"

"Bad news has wings."

Micah leaned close to whisper. "She's blind."

"Mio is an *Itako*. A blind medium who can see and talk with spirits."

"Mother, you're embarrassing me again," Doi said, while scanning the village to see if anyone watched them.

"You must excuse my son, he does not believe in my gift." Mio waved for them to follow. "We will talk inside my house."

"Wait!" Kiyomi said, causing Mio to stop. Kiyomi lowered her gaze. "Please excuse, but can you tell me if we are near Matsue?"

"Matsue? Oh no. You're in Onomchi, near Hamada."

"Near Hamada? That cannot be."

"How did you end up here?"

"We met a woman on the pass," Micah said. "She gave us directions."

"What was her name?"

"Chiyo," Kiyomi answered.

Mio nodded. "Chiyo is a fox. Foxes love to play tricks on travelers, both the living and the dead. Oh well. What is done is done. Come along."

Kiyomi started after Mio, but stopped when Micah put out an arm. He waited until Mio and her son were farther ahead then said, "What does she mean Chiyo is a fox? Is she suggesting Chiyo is an actual fox, like the animal?"

"In Japan, foxes are known to have supernatural abilities, including the power to turn themselves into humans. I should have recognized what was happening. I spotted a fox trailing us shortly before Chiyo appeared. We're lucky to have found Mio-san, *neh*?"

"I'll reserve judgment until we hear what she has to say."

Mio led them to a farmhouse built on a hill overlooking the main village. An old *ginnan* tree grew near the property, its trunk as wide as an oxen. Sparrows chattered among the leaves. Chickens clucked near the front door. A *fūrin* tinkled in the breeze, and an invisible hand squeezed Kiyomi's heart as she remembered putting up their *fūrin* with Ai. Mio paused to remove her *geta*, then glanced back at them. "Don't worry about removing your shoes."

The *shōji* stood open, allowing in plenty of sunlight. Coals glowed red inside the *irori*. Mio motioned at the pillows near the fire pit. "Please, make yourself comfortable."

Doi grunted. "This is madness." He tromped to a far corner where he sat and filled a pipe with tobacco.

Kiyomi smiled at the sight of a *Fukusuke* on a shelf. Her aunt had kept one of the good fortune dolls back in Tokyo. She recalled her aunt saying the doll brought good luck and made one generous in helping others in need. The presence of the *Fukusuke* eased her suspicions toward Mio. Kiyomi knelt onto her pillow. Micah attempted to follow her lead with the grace of a drunken monkey, which made her giggle behind her hands. When they were all settled, Kiyomi turned to Mio. "Please forgive my rudeness, but have you always been blind?"

"*Hai*. That's why I had an ugly husband, or so I've be told."

"How long have you been able to see and speak with spirits?"

"As far back as I can remember."

"Were you not afraid?"

Mio held her palms toward the burning coals. "Ghosts were my friends as a child."

Micah looked across the room. "Why doesn't your son believe in your powers?"

"Doi is a practical man, like his father. They only see what's in front of them." Mio lowered her arms. "Now, Kiyomi-san, tell me all about yourself. I know a little from my visions, but I must learn more before agreeing to help you. Hold back nothing. Start from your childhood. What you tell me will not travel beyond my ears."

The coals in the *irori* burned to ashes by the time Kiyomi finished telling her story. Mio said nothing, only nodded. "I smeared mud on the faces of my family," Kiyomi whispered.

"We're all guilty of that offense at some point," Mio said. "But it's good you accept accountability for the rust of your body." She raised her milky orbs toward Micah. "Now, Micah-san, it's your turn."

Micah squirmed on his pillow. "There's not much to tell."

"You know that's not true. Tell me everything or I will turn you into a chicken and we love to eat chicken around here."

Micah flushed and Kiyomi was amused to see that Mio's threat frightened him. An *Itako* had no such power.

"Kiyomi's story is more interesting than mine," he said.

"I have the perfect pot in which to roast you," Mio responded.

He proceeded to tell her his life story, from his days as a Boy Scout, through his high school years when playing baseball was his first love, all the way to the day he died in Hiroshima.

Mio leaned back and pulled on her lower lip. "You have been living with Kiyomi since your death?"

"Yes."

"Watching over her, even while she bathed?"

Kiyomi's eyebrows raised. "Is that why I felt a rush of cold air inside the bathing room?"

Micah kept his head down. "I did it once. For research purposes."

"Research purposes?"

"Please don't ask me to explain myself. I'm sorry if I offended you."

Mio cackled. "What makes you think you offended Kiyomi? You're a man. She's an attractive woman. Of course, you would be curious about her body. Tell me, why did you decide to stay with Kiyomi?"

"She was the first person I saw after I died."

"This is true," Kiyomi said. "I watched him fall from the sky."

"You were meant to see this," Mio said.

"I don't understand."

"It was your destiny to be there when Micah died. However, Micah is not being truthful about why he decided to stay with you. I assume he has his reasons for doing this, but sometimes the truth is so obvious it's better not to lie than make a fool of oneself, *neh*?"

Micah stared into the ashes, refusing to meet Kiyomi's gaze. What Mio implied was true, but Kiyomi knew Micah would never ask more of her than she was willing to give.

"The Four Noble Truths teach that desire causes suffering, and suffering can be ended by ending desire. Whoever came up with that obviously had never been in love." Mio smiled as if taking pleasure in some internal thought. "So, you're on your way to Kyu Kudedo to find Ai. And you have been on the road how long?"

"Twelve days."

Mio blinked. "Twelve days and you have only made it this far?"

Kiyomi stared at her lap. "We had a delay."

"*Hai*. A big delay."

"According to *Bushidō*, a soldier's death is lighter than a feather. This might be true," Kiyomi said, "but a child's death carries the weight of a mountain." She closed her eyes, an image of her final goodbye to Ai on the schoolyard still fresh in her mind. *A rosy face in the morning, white bones in the evening.*

"You're burdened with regret. You worry about your *Guri* to Ai."

"I wasn't able to perform the proper rituals for the dead. I read no sutras on her behalf. If I cannot find her before the forty-ninth day …"

"The final verdict will be handed down."

"*Hai*," Kiyomi said, "and the decision will be made to which world Ai must enter. She could go to Jigoku, or come back as a *Yūrei*."

Mio wrung her hands over her lap. "I don't believe Ai will go to hell. Not with so many children dying in Hiroshima and Nagasaki."

Micah's jaw dropped. "What are you talking about?"

Mio stopped moving her hands. "You haven't heard?"

"Heard what?" Kiyomi asked.

"The same weapon used in Hiroshima was also dropped on Nagasaki."

The news jolted Kiyomi like an electrical shock. "I experienced something in the mountains. Tremendous pain. Like on the day Hiroshima was bombed. That must have been when the bomb went off in Nagasaki. Did as many people die as in Hiroshima?"

"Thousands." Mio gestured toward Doi with a sideways nod. "A rumor spread that Japan dropped a similar bomb on Los Angeles and San Francisco. My son cheered the news. Damn fool."

"I wouldn't want an American mother to suffer as I have," Kiyomi whispered.

"And they won't now that the war has ended."

Micah sat up straighter. "What do you mean?"

"The Emperor spoke on the radio. He said we must endure the unendurable and suffer what is insufferable."

"It's dishonorable to surrender," Doi called out from across the room.

"What does my son know of honor?" Mio said. "He could not serve in the army because a horse once kicked him in the back, but he's not paralyzed. He can work the fields, but not serve his country."

"Do you wish I had gone off to war, Mother?"

Mio closed her eyes and pinched the bridge of her nose. "No. I would never wish that."

Kiyomi shifted on her pillow. "Are the Americans coming to Japan?"

"*Hai*. They will occupy Japan soon. Let us hope these men are of good character like Micah."

Kiyomi looked at Micah and nodded. "*Hai*. We can hope."

Mio pushed up from her pillow and stood. "I will have Doi take you to Matsue, then on to Mihonoseki. There you will take a boat to Kyu Kudedo."

"We can't go overland to the cave?"

"Only the living can go overland. Spirits must take a boat."

"I see," Kiyomi answered.

Mio gestured for Doi to stand. "You will escort Kiyomi and Micah to Mihonoseki. Pack what you need; you leave immediately. And remember, I'll be watching you in my mind, so treat our guests with respect."

Chapter Thirty Eight

After Doi finished preparing for the journey, he led Mio outside, then strolled to the middle of the road where he stood, arms folded over his chest. "I won't return until tomorrow," he shouted.

Mio sighed. "This means he will find a prostitute in Matsue. My son is easily satisfied."

"Isn't that true for most men?" Kiyomi said.

"*Hai*. Their minds are simple when it comes to physical pleasure. Give them enough to satisfy their craving, but not enough to make them take you for granted."

Heat rose into Micah's face and he turned away to hide his discomfort.

Mio touched him on the sleeve. "Please excuse us, Kiyomi-san. I must talk to Micah-san in private."

"Of course. Take your time."

"Let us talk beside the well," Mio said.

When they reached the well, Mio ran a hand over the lip of the stone enclosure. "My husband dug this well, back when he would put in a full day's work."

"What did you want to tell me?"

"Is the afterlife what you expected, Micah-san?"

"No. Not exactly. I never imagined I'd be in Japan."

"You grew up a Christian?"

"Yes."

"Heaven is all around us, Micah-san. Buddhist or Christian, it doesn't matter."

"Are you saying the Pure Land isn't a real place?"

"No. I'm saying there's one God with many servants."

"None of it makes sense to me," he said.

"The mind is a powerful thing, Micah-san. It allows you to experience the afterlife in a manner you're accustomed to, even though your body no longer requires blood or air. It allows me to see you when I'm otherwise blind."

"What do you see?"

"I can see you and Kiyomi. Everything else is a blur." Her expression turned serious. "You are playing a dangerous game, Micah-san."

"Game? What game?"

She pointed a finger at his face. "Don't offend me by feigning ignorance. Is what you seek worth the risk? Your chance for success is poor."

"Whatever hope I once had is gone."

"Now you're lying to yourself. Very well. Cling to your hope, Micah-san, for even a dying flame continues to light the darkness." She turned away and walked over to Kiyomi.

Micah stared past the houses to a spot where sunlight beamed down through a grove of bamboo trees. He breathed in the smell of the manure spread over the rice fields, and the wild grasses sprouting alongside the road, all the while remembering what Mio had said. He knew he must bury his desire deep within his heart. Bury it and never let it surface again.

Doi waved for them to follow before setting off.

"You'd better get going," Mio said. "He won't wait."

Kiyomi bowed. "Thank you for your assistance, Mio-san. I would repay you, if possible."

"Repay me by finding your daughter." Mio turned toward Micah. "I will pray for you, Micah-san."

Kiyomi joined him and together they set off after Doi, who marched along at a quick pace. She kept her head down as they left the village, but from the corner of his eye, he caught her glancing his direction. Outside the village, she looked up and said, "What did Mio-san want to discuss with you?"

"She was curious about Americans."

"You're lying."

His back stiffened. "Why would you think that?"

"Western men don't know how to lie with their eyes. We're taught from an early age to mask our true feelings."

"So I've noticed."

"What does that mean?"

"It means I should hold my tongue before saying something I'll regret."

She smiled. "I thought I understood you. I was wrong. You're more of a mystery than expected."

"Is that a bad thing?"

"No. It makes you more interesting."

Micah remained quiet.

Doi waited ahead, hands on his hips. He spit out a flurry of words while shaking his head.

"Doi says we must hurry along if we want his assistance. He added that he is a fool, talking to the wind."

They fell in behind Doi who grumbled as he trudged along the pass. From time to time, he offered insults such as, "If you are real, you must be dumb ghosts, getting lost in the mountains. *Hai.* Most stupid," or "What Japanese woman would travel with the enemy? Kiyomi-san is a traitor."

Kiyomi's jaw flexed after the last insult. "How can I be a traitor to a cause that is over? Why does Doi believe he can define my character?"

"He's the village idiot," Micah answered. "Action establishes our character, not words. I've never known a mother more devoted to their child than you, Kiyomi-san."

Kiyomi focused on the road, a blush in her cheeks. "Thank you, Micah-san. Your words are most kind."

The trail became rocky as it wound deeper into green mountains. Doi led them toward wisps of clouds crowning the peaks. Shadows settled over the path as it passed through a copse of oaks.

Doi ranted over his shoulder, then burst out laughing.

"He says he serves his mother's whims because one day he will inherit her farm," Kiyomi explained. "He called her a crazy woman who invents invisible people because she has no friends. But he says he will do what she has asked of him. After that, we can return to his mother's imagination. Doi is the crazy one," Kiyomi said.

"True. But if I were in his shoes, I might think the same way."

"Your feet are too big for his shoes."

Micah smiled. "You know what I mean."

"It's good to see you smile."

"You as well."

"I have a reason to smile. I will be reunited with Ai soon. Wings lift my heart."

"I'm happy for you," Micah said, but deep inside, he was anything but happy, sensing his time with Kiyomi was coming to an end.

The evening sky turned a rich azure. Gathering shadows transformed the hue of the mountains from green to grey, and the grassland from yellow to brown. Rice tassels turned silvery at the first touch of moonlight. The pass steepened. Kiyomi gasped beside him and grabbed his arm. "Why am I winded?"

"Ask me in a hundred years and I might have an answer."

"I will do that."

Doi waited at the top of a rise. He pointed to something on the other side.

"What is it?" Micah asked.

"Matsue."

The trail descended sharply, winding to a flat plain where the city was built around two lakes. To the west, the sinking sun cast an orange glow over the Sea of Japan.

Kiyomi squeezed his arm. "We're close now."

He wanted to offer words of encouragement but all he could manage was, "We should keep moving."

As they entered Matsue, Micah marveled at the undamaged buildings. He knew the Air Force hadn't made cities on the San-in Coast a priority in their bombing campaign, but after experiencing the destruction in Hiroshima, he expected to see a few bombed-out structures.

"Matsue is a water town," Kiyomi said. "Banri used to visit an uncle here. He told me the city sits between Lake Shinji and Lake Nakaumi, with the Ohashi River connecting them. Banri said you can travel by canals to any district in the city."

After crossing over a canal on an arched bridge, they came upon a group of boys and girls playing in the street. "It's good to hear children laughing again, *neh?*"

"Yes. There's hope for the world as long as children are laughing."

Doi led them to a cobblestone street that ran alongside a tile-capped wall. Behind the wall, tilted lines of grey-blue temple roofs rose skyward. The lakes came into view. Several junks with billowing white sails glided across the surface, accompanied by a little steamer puffing black smoke. Sunlight turned the water into liquid gold. Outside the city, the pass resumed a steady climb before diving into dark ravines. From time to time, rice fields emerged, brown in the gloaming. To their left, the land plunged. Jagged strips of tree-covered rock reached into the Sea of Japan like probing fingers. Waves crashed against the intruders in thunderous reports. Micah noted a lightness in Kiyomi's step and sensed her growing excitement, which contrasted with his increasing apprehension. Overhead, the clouds opened and a gentle rain shower trickled down, cool in the settling darkness. The rain clouds swept inland leaving behind air sticky with humidity.

Doi maintained a steady pace as he traversed the winding path. He stopped occasionally to look behind him and say something.

"Doi says, 'Are you still with me ghosts? Ha, ha. Big joke. Not much farther now. Keep up.'"

On the mountain side, mist rose over a glade. The mist crept upward, covering the green hills in spiraling white ribbons. An owl hooted from a cedar tree whose roots cracked open the earth and jutted into the pass. The air took on a grey hue. Stars emerged. Doi stopped again, his focus on something ahead. Micah and Kiyomi joined him. The trail descended toward a village fanned out along a crescent-shaped harbor. Yellow light glowed in windows.

Kiyomi squeezed Micah's arm. "Doi says this is Mihonoseki. We've made it."

He forced himself to nod. "So it would seem."

Doi said something and then chuckled.

"He says for us to come along. He will find us a ride to Kyu-Kudedo."

Doi tramped down the trail in the direction of Mihonoseki. Micah and Kiyomi stayed on his heels. Rolling hills covered in pine trees pressed against the village, as if trying to shove its inhabitants into the sea. The compacted buildings followed the curve of the harbor. Junks and sampans had been hauled onto the beach stern first. As they drew closer, Micah spotted a group of men gathered near the boats. The arriving darkness muddied the features of their tanned faces. Tendrils of grey smoke floated skyward from the tips of their cigarettes.

They turned onto a narrow street made of blue stones. Traditional ryokan, restaurants, and shops made of dark wood with latticed fronts and planked roofs lined the route. Squares of light spilled out of windows. The air carried the scent of grilled squid, vinegar, and sesame oil. Two women about Kiyomi's age stepped through a door. They wore bright kimonos, with their hair pulled up. Doi bowed before the women and spoke.

"What's he saying?"

"He's asking if any of the fishermen would take him to Kyu-Kudedo."

"Him?"

"*Hai.* He cannot say the journey is for a couple of ghosts." Kiyomi nodded. "They told him to ask the men on the beach."

"That's promising."

One of the women slapped Doi's face. He staggered backward, rubbing his jaw and laughing.

"Doi asked an inappropriate question," Kiyomi explained.

"What did he ask?"

"He wanted to know how much they charged to sleep with him."

"Apparently he asked the wrong women."

"*Hai.* Apparently so. I wish Doi would return to the serious side of life. There will always be time for what he requires."

The women hurried past, taking short choppy steps. Doi continued to massage his jaw as he talked.

Kiyomi translated what Doi was saying, "You should have seen this town a few years ago, back when the foreign sailors visited. There were saloons and plenty of *geisha*. Now, look at it. Lifeless. Just the place for a couple of ghosts. Ha, ha."

Doi thrust his chin toward the end of the street.

"He wants us to follow the harbor to a stone jetty, where we'll find a *tōrō* lantern and a red bridge. We are to wait there. He'll try to find a fisherman willing to take us to the cave. If he doesn't return right away, it means he found an accommodating woman."

Doi set off in the direction of the beach.

"Will he return?"

"Sure," Micah said. "Unless he finds an accommodating woman."

She threw up her hands. "Is this all men think about?"

"Sometimes," he said and laughed. Micah held out his hand. "We'd better find this place Doi was talking about."

"*Hai.*"

They strolled through the business district, then onto the beach. To the west, the sun dissolved on the water in a thin orange line. Waves creamed over the sand with gentle sighs. A sleepy calm settled across the village, and the moment felt romantic as Micah strolled along the beach holding Kiyomi's hand. In his mind, he imagined them together as a couple. What would that be like? Could they overcome their differences? Micah slipped out of his fantasy when the red bridge appeared ahead. Kiyomi pulled her hand free and, in an instant, the moon and stars dimmed, and the sighing waves roared with frustration as their journey ended.

The *tōrō* sat on a point of land built atop flat grey stones. The small red bridge arched between two embankments. Kiyomi crossed the bridge. When Micah hesitated, she beckoned him to follow. "You must cross if we're to reach Kyu-Kudedo."

Micah couldn't explain why he hesitated to cross, nor did he see the connection between crossing and reaching their destination, but something about the act felt wrong, as if he wasn't meant to join her. *Stop being a fool*, he told himself, and with gnashed teeth, he traveled over the small bridge.

"Are you all right, Micah-san?"

He nodded, hoping she wouldn't notice his distress.

Kiyomi gazed across the harbor, strands of black hair dancing in the cool breeze coming off the water. She appeared regal in the soft light of the stars, and he wanted to wrap his arms around her. But this was impossible. If Kiyomi was right about the cave, Ai's spirit waited nearby. Did she sense the presence of her mother? Did Ai call to her on the whispering wind?

Micah jammed his hands inside his pockets. He pictured Levi back on their grandfather's boat. Should he have stayed with them? He quickly dismissed this idea. Whatever his destiny might be, he was meant to be here with Kiyomi. Mosquitoes buzzed past his head. Moths fluttered through the night air. The grey back of a dolphin breached the water and he remembered riding on Hoshi with Ai in Hiroshima Bay.

Doi came strolling out of the night. He crossed the bridge and said something before turning around and walking off.

Kiyomi sighed. "He couldn't find anyone to take us to the cave. The fishermen said no one traveled to Kyu-Kudedo if the wind moved three hairs."

"That's crazy."

Kiyomi put on a brave face. "It's their way."

"What are we going to do?"

She went onto her knees, hands resting over her lap. "I will pray."

"Pray? What good will that do?"

"Dust amassed will make a mountain. Have you never prayed, Micah-san?"

"Sure, I've prayed. But I never received an answer."

"Perhaps you didn't pray hard enough." She waved toward a spot beside her. "Will you join me? Two voices are more likely to be heard."

He knelt on the hard stones and followed her lead, pressing his hands together and closing his eyes. He doubted his words were worth much but he must try. They had come too far to give up.

Chapter Thirty Nine

Kiyomi prayed to every Buddhist and Shinto God she could think of, all the while imagining her reunion with Ai. She prayed until her head and back ached. She had no idea how long she'd been praying when she glanced over at Micah and found him curled on his side, asleep. He appeared younger, moonlight erasing tension from his face. She scooted closer and stroked his golden-brown hair. They had been through so much together. What would happen to him after she found Ai and entered the Pure Land? How could she leave him behind? *Micah should have stayed with his brother. What can I give him?*

Micah groaned and she pulled back. His eyes opened slowly, and after focusing on her face, he sat up and smiled. "I'm sorry. I didn't mean to fall asleep."

"Thank you for your prayers."

He looked around, then back at her. "They didn't seem to work." He stretched with a yawn. "This cave can be reached overland, right?"

"*Hai*, but Mio said spirits must travel there by boat."

"When I was alive, I could pilot just about any boat. In my present state ... well."

"I know," she said.

A sound reverberated across the darkness. *Thump...thump...thump.* Soft at first, then growing louder. "Do you hear that, Micah-san?"

"If I'm not mistaken, someone is banging a drum."

A bluish-glow advanced their direction from the woods to the east-north. The glowing light intensified as it drew closer, and the strength of the drumming increased. Shapes materialized inside the light, gradually taking on the appearance of men.

"They're priests."

"Dead priests."

"*Hai*. They are dead. Why do you think they're here?"

Micah ran a hand over his jaw. "They must have come to help you."

Six priests marched out of the darkness, with fluttering gnats forming halos around their heads. They wore white ceremonial robes with gold vests. Two priests banging small drums led the group. The remaining priests held their hands pressed together in front of them, chanting words Kiyomi didn't recognize. The priests marched onto the pier. The drummers beat their instruments while the chanting men continued their song.

Fog pushed in from the sea. The bow of a ship broke through the mist, followed by the square sail of a junk.

Kiyomi gripped Micah's arm. "A *shoryobuni*."

"A what?"

"A soul ship. After *Bon*, *shoryobuni* carry ghosts back to the spirit world."

"But we're already in the spirit world."

"*Hai*. But we must travel to a different dimension of that world."

The junk approached without a sound, closer and closer, a vessel from an ominous dream. The drumming and chanting stopped as the priests dissolved in the air like wisps of smoke.

The black junk had three masts. A lone man stood at the stern with a hand on the wheel. The same bluish-glow that surrounded the priests shimmered around the ship's pilot. He wore clothing from an earlier time; a gold kimono with a scarlet *kamishimo* over the kimono and a matching *hakama* split skirt. The center of his scalp was shaved, and the long hair at the back of his head brought forward over the crown of his skull in a topknot. With his set jaw and sharp focus, he appeared ready for battle. His dark eyes stared straight ahead without acknowledging their presence.

"We should board," Kiyomi said.

Micah offered his hand and she took it, grateful to have him by her side at this moment. They made their way to the junk. A plank extended from the boat to the pier. Micah's left eyebrow arched. "I don't recall that being there." He motioned with his chin for her to go in front of him. Kiyomi tiptoed across the narrow plank and stepped onto the deck. Micah followed. "What now?"

"Micah, look," she said, pointing behind him.

The plank had vanished and the junk pulled away from the jetty, following the natural curve of the harbor before turning toward open water.

"That's interesting," Micah said, looking up at the billowing sails.

"What?"

"Our point of sail is in irons, but the sails are acting as if the wind is at our backs."

"What does this mean, in irons?"

"We're sailing into the wind." Micah stepped to the gunwale and spread his hands over the railing.

Kiyomi moved alongside him. Behind them, the pilot steered the junk without expression. She wondered who he had been in life, and how long had he been making this journey.

As Mihonoseki faded to a yellow blur, the junk came to life, sails popping with each wind gust. Micah watched the pilot, a mix of admiration and suspicion in his narrowed eyes. Kiyomi examined the stars, spread like a sparkling blanket over the sleeping earth. Her heartbeat quickened at the thought of seeing Ai again. *Please let her remember me. Please let her forgive me for not protecting her.* She gazed down at the water and gasped. "Micah-san, look!"

"My God," he whispered, his hands gripping the gunwale. "We're flying."

The junk floated through the air, some ten feet above the surface of the sea. A peculiar smile lifted the corners of Micah's mouth. "Are you all right?" she asked.

"Yeah, I'm fine. I just remembered the last time I flew was on that mission over Hiroshima. Hey ... would you take a look at that."

Blue flames danced along the top of the masts.

"Are we burning?"

"No. It's St. Elmo's Fire."

"Fire? A real fire?"

"More like a weather phenomenon. A gap in an electrical charge. We used to have it on the plane. Don't be frightened. It won't hurt you."

The blue flames slithered down the masts and leaped onto the gunwales. "Whoa," Micah said, pulling her away. "I've never seen St. Elmo's Fire behave this way."

The flames raced along the gunwales, then shot off the stern, and gathered into a glowing ball. The ball broke apart, leaving a trail of twinkling blue light in its wake.

"Beautiful," Kiyomi said.

"You are."

She faced him and Micah looked away.

"I'm sorry," he said. "I meant the light is beautiful."

Kiyomi remained quiet, but inside, her heart thundered. She hadn't felt this way since her time in Tokyo with Shigeo, and it confused her.

The junk followed a line of black cliffs towering over the sea like jagged teeth. Projecting rocks took on macabre shapes and it was easy to imagine monsters and goblins watching their passage. The junk flew smoothly, the pilot's hands steady on the wheel, the sails rippling in the wind. A swath of moonlight beamed in front of the ship to guide them. Elongated clouds whisked through the sky as if racing to make a destination before dawn.

"It's like a dream," Micah said.

"*Hai*. A dream within a dream."

He smiled. "That was poetic. Reminds me of something Poe wrote."

She stared at the deck, embarrassed to meet his gaze.

They journeyed westward, moonlight transforming waves into white ribbons. The pilot steered the junk through the opening of a bay. A miniature village clung to the shoreline. Beyond the village, the cliff face turned rugged and primitive. Pressure lifted her stomach toward her throat.

Micah leaned over the gunwale. "We're descending," he said.

The junk eased onto the water with a gentle splash and angled toward the mouth of a cavern. Water flowed through the opening. The pilot brought the junk into the aperture, its arched entrance rising twenty feet or more above the water and nearly as wide.

"Is this the cave of lost children?" Micah asked.

"No. This is Shin-Kukedo, the new cavern, said to be the birthplace of *Sada-no-Okami*, protector of the Shimane Peninsula."

"Oh. I see. Like a god to these people?"

"*Hai*. A Shinto deity." She pointed at the cavern walls. "They're as smooth as glass."

"Waves must have done that."

Water showered down from above. Kiyomi opened her mouth to capture droplets on her tongue. She ran a hand through her damp hair and smiled at Micah. "A freshwater spring. Taste it." Micah brushed water off his face and stared up at the ceiling. His lips parted to allow water inside his mouth. Kiyomi gestured at the cavern roof. "Banri said there is a great stone overhead that will fall on anyone attempting to pass through Shin-Kukedo who has evil in their heart." Micah closed his mouth and faced the gunwale. He gripped the railing, his attention fixed on the water. "Are you all right, Micah-san?"

"I'm fine," he said in a subdued voice.

The junk slipped through the cavern and approached a grotto on the opposite side. Dozens of gulls floated on the wind outside the opening. She had never seen gulls flying at night and the sight puzzled her. Kiyomi stepped over to Micah and pointed at the opening. "That's Kyu-Kudedo."

He straightened. "The cave of lost children?"

"*Hai*."

"How can you be certain?"

She touched him on the arm. "A mother knows these things."

The gulls retreated as the pilot brought the junk alongside the cavern opening. The hull collided with rock, a shudder passing through the ship. The pilot turned to face the cliffs. He stood like an ancient cypress hardened against storms.

"We're on our own," Kiyomi said. "I know a little about Kyu-Kudedo from stories my aunt told me. We should be able to find Ai."

"Or she will find you." Micah held out a hand.

She took hold of his hand and followed him to the opposite gunwale, where a ramp led to the rocks. Kiyomi walked down the ramp. Swells lapped against the cliff, throwing up cold spray. She stepped onto the rocks and waited for Micah to join her. A narrow path climbed to the grotto. Arriving at the entrance, Kiyomi stared at the water below. "Micah-san, the junk is gone."

Micah glanced over his shoulder. "I'll be damned." He turned around. "Looks like we'll be leaving overland."

At the mouth of the cavern, they allowed their eyes to adjust to the dim light. Wind moaned within the darkness, the sound becoming voices inside her mind. Darkness lifted to reveal the smiling face of a stone *Jizō*. Dozens of these statues were scattered about the cave surrounded by little towers of grey rocks. Spinning tops, marbles, dolls, and other toys lay near the towers, accompanied by empty rice bowls and pairs of small straw sandals.

"What's all this?"

"The ghosts of the children pile up the stones at night to gain karma. Their parents bring the children toys, food, and straw sandals so their feet won't be injured."

Micah shook his head as he took it all in. "They come from all over Japan to bring these things?"

"*Hai.* Amazing, *neh?*"

A bat passed overhead and flew out into the night. Micah massaged his jaw while staring deeper into the grotto. "This place goes back a ways."

"We must search the entire cave."

"Why don't we see any children? Do they sleep at night?"

"No. The ghost children work at night because they fear *O-Hi-San*, the Lady-sun. The children must be hiding. They're scared of the big American."

"Gee, thanks."

Kiyomi weaved around the stone towers, careful not to touch anything. Some of the *Jizō* with worn faces and broken lotus bases appeared to have been there for centuries. A tiny pair of footprints cut across the path. "Micah-san, come see this."

"What is it?" He bumped into a tower, the sound of crashing stones echoing throughout the cavern, followed by a shrill scream. Micah froze. "Did you hear that?"

"They say the children scream whenever you knock over their stones."

"Why am I afraid of ghosts? I am a ghost."

"They won't hurt you, Micah-san." Kiyomi pointed at the footprints as he moved alongside her. "See. They have been here."

"I never doubted it."

They ventured farther inside the cave. The air turned moist as cold wind whistled in from the sea. Trails splintered off the main path throughout the grotto, each one winding past piled stones and watchful *Jizō*. She pointed at a white rock projecting from the ceiling. A slow stream dripping from an orifice above the rock appeared as white as milk. "That's the Fountain of *Jizō* from which the dead children drink."

Kiyomi stopped. Hands on her hips, she scanned the cavern. The same measure of hopelessness she endured on the riverbed after the atomic bombing impressed upon her mind. She turned to Micah and could tell from the look in his eyes he sensed her despair. "Where could they be? Where is Ai?"

"You said they might be hiding. If that's true, you might need to draw her out."

"Draw her out?"

"You know … call to her. Ai should respond to your voice."

"*Hai*. She will come when I call her name. Thank you, Micah-san." She cupped a hand around her mouth and shouted, "Ai. Ai. It's Mama. Come here."

Nothing.

Kiyomi glanced back at Micah.

"Don't stop," he said. "She might be farther away than you realize."

Kiyomi advanced deeper into the grotto, all the while shouting, "Ai. Ai. Please come here." They traveled from chamber to chamber, past stone towers, toys, and *Jizō*. Reminders of a love so strong it survived the ravages of time. Her anguish returned at the idea they had failed. *I cannot let Micah see my grief. I must …* Kiyomi sank to her knees and covered her eyes. She felt Micah's arm on her shoulders and turned to bury her face against him. "Ai's not here. If she were here, she would answer me. I have failed her. Now she will rot in hell."

"No. No. You don't know that. Please, don't give up."

Her face burned with shame. She had no right to burden him with her troubles. Kiyomi wiped away her tears. She looked into his eyes and was startled by the compassion she saw. "I'm not sure what to do."

"Call her. Be firm. Make her understand she must come to you."

"I'll try." She cupped her mouth once more and shouted. "Ai Oshiro! This is your Mama. Come to me at once!"

Nothing happened and her chin sank toward her chest.

"Mama."

Kiyomi's head snapped up. "Did you hear that? It was a girl calling for her mama."

"I heard it," Micah said. "But was it Ai?"

She pushed up from the rocky floor. "Ai! Ai! Come to Mama! Mama is here!"

"Mama! Mama! Mama!" Not one voice, but dozens, boys, and girls, growing in number and intensity with each passing second. "Mama! Mama! Mama!"

Glowing ghost children squeezed out of the walls. They enveloped Kiyomi, their tiny arms battling to embrace her. The children kept coming in a rush of a blue light. As they touched her, she saw images of their families, proud fathers and mothers, gentle grandparents, and playful siblings. She heard their laughter. She felt the warmth of arms holding her. There had been so much love, to sense it all overwhelmed her. "Mama! Mama! Mama!" the children continued to shout as more emerged to stake their claim on her heart. "She's not among them!" Kiyomi shouted. "Ai's not here."

"There's so many," Micah said. "Are they all—"

"From Hiroshima and Nagasaki? *Hai.* I believe so." She held out her arms. "There's nothing I can do for them. Help me."

Micah tore Kiyomi from the grasp of the ghost children and pulled her back in the direction they had come. The ghost children pursued, arms outstretched, voices crying, "Mama! Mama! Come back, Mama!" He rushed through the gloom, knocking aside stone towers, children screaming in frustration.

"There's the entrance!" Micah shouted. As they pressed into the moonlight, the trailing children vanished with prolonged sighs. Micah brought her out onto a ledge and embraced her. Kiyomi offered no resistance. Below, the roaring sea hurled itself against the cliff, while the sound of weeping carried from inside the grotto.

"Ai is not here. What am I going to do?"

"Where did you say a soul goes to enter the Pure Land?"

She looked up at him. "What?"

"You said a soul must cross a river and then go into a volcano."

"*Hai.* They must cross the Sanzu River and enter the Pure Land through Mount Osore."

"Where is this river?"

She brushed hair from her eyes. "Aomori prefecture in northern Honshū. Ai could not get there on her own."

"Maybe she had help."

Kiyomi blinked as she tried to imagine who might have helped her daughter.

"Banri or Sayoka?"

"I suppose … it's possible. But even if they led her to the river, Ai could not cross without me. Powerful forces prevent children from crossing without a parent."

Micah stared at the cliff wall. "We'll have to climb."

"Are you certain you want to do this?"

"We didn't come this far to fail. Now let's go find Ai."

Kiyomi pressed against him. "Thank you, Micah-san. Thank you."

Chapter Forty

A summer storm swept in from the sea after they left Kyu-Kudedo and set out across the Shimane Peninsula. Boiling grey clouds produced fat raindrops that pattered leaves and splashed into puddles. Kiyomi walked with her head low, seldom talking as they traveled into central Honshū. The experience inside the cave of lost children had shaken Kiyomi's confidence. Micah tried to lift her spirits by telling her stories about his past. He told her how he and Levi used to throw eggs at passing cars on Halloween, then ran like hell whenever an egg found its target. He shared how his face turned red inside Mrs. Smith's third grade classroom whenever a girl handed him a Valentine's Day card, and that he'd been too shy to ask anyone to the senior prom and ended up alone inside his bedroom listening to a Yankees game on the radio.

She listened without comment, but her eyes drew down after hearing the prom story, as if it touched her somehow. Micah had come to believe she might act this way forever, until the day they arrived at the Shinano River. Kiyomi stood on the riverbank watching a man and woman playing with two small children on a boat. After observing them for several minutes, she turned to Micah and said, "I have been having many thoughts. About Ai. About the war. About my life. And about you. You have suffered my silence long enough." He responded with a quick nod, which she accepted with a smile.

They journeyed through valleys shaded by giant camphor and red cedar trees, where moss turned everything green. Chrysanthemums the size of a man's fist blossomed in the underbrush. They trekked up mountains of granite into the heart of the sun. A golden eagle circled overhead, its majestic cry carrying over distant slopes. A rarely seen *raicho* appeared on a treetop. Kiyomi was pleased to spot the *raicho*, explaining it was a good omen to see a Thunderbird. Mountain shrines offered moments of quiet reflection. Here, she told him, all things that exist in time must perish, and the universe was an illusion. She said attachment to persons, places, or things must be fraught with sorrow and only through suppression of desire could humanity reach eternal peace. He wanted to tell her she was wrong and explain his desire for her in a way she might understand. He wanted to show her that eternal peace could be achieved through love, but remained silent.

The leaves on the maple trees turned red with the changing season. When touched by afternoon sun, the maples appeared to be on fire. They passed thatched villages tucked between hills, where farmers raced to bring in their rice harvest before winter arrived. Some nights they stopped to rest. He loved these moments, because Kiyomi sat pressed against him as if he were someone she had known all her life. She shared myths and tales of her homeland. She told him of the *yama-otoko*, giant mountain men who scared people when they showed up in villages. The river bottom weaver was a young woman who killed herself in a river to escape a cruel mother-in-law. Whenever the rain fell, one could hear her weaving beneath the water. Kiyomi explained how some of the bridges they crossed were jealous of longer or more famous bridges. The jealous bridges became angry whenever a person mentioned another bridge, and caused them some terrible misfortune. Standing before a fan-shaped waterfall hidden deep in the woods, Kiyomi related that each mountain in Japan had a guardian god, and each lake or stream was dedicated to a sylvan deity. The mountain deity commanded the thunder and lightning, wind and rain, clouds and sunshine. They spoke to people in different tones; some rumbling in the form of volcanoes, while others whispered in gentle breezes.

Days passed. Time slipped away from them. How long had it been since they left Hiroshima? Were they too late to save Ai? If Kiyomi shared his concerns, she never showed it. Her earlier despair was replaced with a steadfast resolve. She climbed mountains and hiked through shadowed woods without complaint. "We must be getting close," she said, while scanning the countryside.

They ventured out of the forest and onto a clearing. Ahead lay miles of rolling green hills. A cold wind stirred the grass. Iron-colored clouds smothered the sun and cast a pall over the land. Kiyomi massaged her arms and shivered. "Winter will be here soon."

Micah pointed at the cloud cover. "It might be here sooner than you think."

Freezing drizzle poured over them. Ice crystals peppered Kiyomi's hair like tiny diamonds.

Micah guided her toward a small building in the distance. As they drew closer, he saw it was a house with broken window coverings and a thatched roof in need of repair. "We can rest here."

The side door creaked open when he pulled on the handle. "Must be vacant," he said. Inside, holes dotted screens that had divided rooms. Mold grew on the edges of the tatami mats. The air smelled musty.

"I wonder what happened to the family who lived here."

"There's great sadness in this house," Kiyomi said, looking out one of the windows. "Someone must have died."

"Like us."

She nodded. "*Hai*. Like us."

Micah sat on a tatami mat with his back against a wall. Kiyomi lowered onto the mat beside him. She leaned against him, her head on his shoulder. Wind-driven sleet pummeled the latticed blinds.

"We must keep going, even if the rain continues."

"Yes," he agreed. "It can't be much farther."

"This trip has taken a lifetime," she said and sighed. "Every step brings me pain."

"I know, but we'll find Ai."

Wind whistled through holes in the ceiling. "Have you ever wondered what the Pure Land will be like?" he asked. "I mean, do you think there'll be houses and streets?"

"I have considered this," she said. "Here, we believe our bodies need air. We believe our hearts must pump blood. Why is this so? Because this is what we are used to? I feel the Pure Land will be similar to this. *Hai.* There will be houses and streets because we need there to be houses and streets. But I might be wrong. Some say the Pure Land is made of gold, but for what purpose? Why would spirits need a land of gold? It makes no sense."

"Are you excited to be reunited with your family?"

Kiyomi chewed her lip. "It's been so long since I last saw my parents, I doubt I'll recognize them."

"You'll be surprised."

"How did we end up here? A Japanese woman and an American man working together? Enemies."

"Former enemies."

She smiled. "*Hai.* Former enemies."

A dull ache settled in Micah's chest as he remembered his hatred of the Japanese. He had wanted to eradicate their race from the Earth. How foolish that seemed to him now.

"What are you thinking, Micah-san?"

"How much I've changed after living with you and Ai. You opened my eyes to a different reality and I'm grateful. Things I did before my death ... well ..." His gaze fell to his lap. "I'm sorry."

"Why must you apologize?"

"I want to help you, Kiyomi. If I could do more, I would."

"The past is the past and—"

"Karma."

She blinked. "What?"

"The things we do in our former lives determine our fate moving forward. Isn't that one of the principles of Buddhism?"

"Yes but—"

The door banged open and a Japanese soldier bathed in a bluish glow stepped into the house. A Samurai sword hung on his left side. His dark eyes went straight to Kiyomi, who hurried to her feet. Micah pushed off the floor to stand beside her, never taking his eyes off the stranger who continued to stare at Kiyomi. What did this man want? The soldier closed the door behind him. Micah tensed as he stepped closer. The soldier stopped, as if sensing the threat he presented, and put up a hand. He reached for the sword.

"Wait!" Micah shouted.

"No. Please," the soldier said. He placed the sword on the floor. "I'm not here to fight."

Micah stared at the soldier's face. Something about his eyes and the scar on his chin seemed familiar. *I know this man. He is Jikan, Kiyomi's husband.* What did Jikan want with Kiyomi? Even without his sword, Jikan couldn't be trusted.

"Why are you here?"

A sly grin lifted the corners of his mouth. "It's nice to see you too, Kiyomi-san."

Kiyomi stood erect with her chin raised.

"You've changed," Jikan said.

"The war has changed us all."

"*Hai.*" Jikan glanced at Micah, then back at her. "But it wasn't just the war that changed you." He gestured at the floor. "May I sit?"

Her eyes narrowed on his face. "If you must."

Micah remained standing until Jikan lowered onto his knees.

Jikan spread his hands over his thighs. "Tell me about—"

"Wait," Micah said. "In my country, introductions come first."

Jikan nodded. "*Hai.* Please excuse my rudeness, Micah-san."

"You know who I am?"

"*Hai.* And I know what you've done for Kiyomi. Thank you."

The tension left Micah's shoulders. "You're welcome ... Jikan-san."

Jikan smiled. "He's becoming more Japanese every day, *neh?*"

Kiyomi remained quiet. Her face revealed nothing.

Jikan turned serious. "Tell me, Kiyomi-san, what happened in Hiroshima?"

The creaking of the door intensified. Freezing rain splattered against the windows. Her fingers dug into the fabric of her *monpe* pants. "A bomb exploded. A powerful new weapon."

"*Hai.* What else?"

"The city ... was destroyed."

Jikan massaged the scar on his chin. "The entire city?"

"Everything."

"And my parents?"

Kiyomi's head bowed. "I'm sorry."

"And now you search for Ai."

Her head came up. "*Hai.* How did you—"

"You went to Kyu-Kudedo."

"*Hai.* Ai wasn't there."

"She was there."

"What do you mean?" Micah asked. "We searched the entire cave."

"I saw Ai crying in a dream. I went to Kyu-Kudedo and found her."

Kiyomi sat up straighter. "You found Ai?"

"*Hai.* I couldn't leave her, so I led Ai to the Sanzu River."

"You left her alone at the river?"

Jikan held her in his gaze. "Not alone. There were countless souls making the crossing and many children waiting on the shore of the river. She cannot cross the bridge without you, Kiyomi-san."

Datsueba?"

"*Hai.* The old hag is there, along with *Keneo.*"

"Excuse me," Micah said. "Would someone please explain what you're talking about?"

Jikan dipped his head. "*Hai.* So sorry. *Datsueba* and *Keneo* are demons who patrol the banks of the Sanzu. *Datsueba* strips the clothes off the dead and *Keneo* weighs the clothes on tree branches to judge their karma. *Datsueba* prevents children from crossing into the Pure Land."

"Then it's all true?" Kiyomi said.

Jikan nodded. "*Hai.* The stories are true."

"Then the Pure Land is real."

"It's real but ...."

"What?"

"We imagine the Pure Land as a Buddhist Heaven, *neh?* A place for Japanese spirits to spend eternity together. I don't believe Heaven is exclusive for Buddhists, nor do I believe the Pure Land is only for Japanese. Is that the afterlife we desire? Division and isolation? We cross the river and enter the Pure Land through Mount Osore. This is our portal. We might be surprised by what awaits on the other side."

"Ai must be scared."

"*Hai.* She knows you'll come for her, but there is one thing …"

"What? What is this one thing?"

"Ai cannot remain at the river forever. You must reach her as soon as you can."

"Or she will be taken to the underworld?"

"It's possible." Jikan let out a breath. "You're closer than you realize."

"How close?" Micah asked.

"Halfway between Miyako and Same. You could make it to the river in two days."

Kiyomi's face flushed. She turned toward Micah, her eyes open wide. "We are close."

Micah hesitated, his focus on Jikan, who stared at Kiyomi with a puzzled expression. Did he return to reclaim his place as Kiyomi's husband? If so, what was Jikan thinking as Kiyomi turned her attention toward him? Micah forced a smile to placate her. "That's fantastic news."

"Will you guide us to the river?" Kiyomi asked.

Jikan didn't respond, his gaze moving from Micah to her.

"Jikan-san?"

"*Hai.* I will do what I can. But now, I suggest we all rest for the journey ahead. The rain will be gone by morning."

"*Hai.* We should rest."

Jikan again searched both of their faces before bowing. "Good night, then." He stood and went to the far side of the room where he laid on his side, his back toward them.

Kiyomi reached out and took hold of Micah's hands. Her face glowed with excitement. "We're going to make it. We're going to find Ai."

"Yes, we are." Micah stared at the ground. "We should rest. Good night." He pulled back his hands and the cold wind roaring past the house seemed to blow right through the door and into his bones. He stretched out on a tatami mat. She sat nearby, looking at Jikan. Micah closed his eyes. It was proper that Kiyomi go to Jikan and yet, the idea of them resting side by side made Micah's body ache with jealousy. The floor creaked as she walked. Micah pictured her lowering next to Jikan and gnashed his teeth to fight off his growing misery. A rush of sudden warmth made him open his eyes. Kiyomi laid near him in open defiance of the marriage vow she had sworn to Jikan. Her eyelids fluttered shut and soon, her breathing quieted to a whisper. He smiled while watching rain slip through a hole in the roof.

Chapter Forty One

Kiyomi sat up and looked around the room. Micah stared out a window. He turned to face her. "Jikan left before dawn."

An idea came to her, which she quickly dismissed. "Did he say when he would return?"

"No. I asked him where he was going and he stood in the doorway with a smile on his face, then walked out into the rain."

A chill hovered inside the house, but the storm had passed and fractured sunlight beamed in through the blinds. "We can't wait for his return."

Micah went to the door. He grabbed the handle but hesitated. "Do you trust him? I mean, he shows up out of nowhere with this story about helping Ai, and you said yourself Jikan was never close to her."

Kiyomi joined him at the door. She detected jealousy in Micah's face and voice. Excitement tingled along her spine. She couldn't remember the last time a man became jealous over her. "*Hai*. I trust him. Why else would Jikan track me down in a storm? I've given him no reason to want revenge. And if revenge is on his mind, what could he do to me now? No. I'm certain he told the truth about Ai."

"All right," Micah said, opening the door. "According to Jikan, the river is two days away. We should get started."

To the east, the sun lay low, a shimmering orange flame on the horizon. The air was crisp, with autumn fading into memory.

The frozen ground crunched under their shoes. A blanket of ice frosted the surrounding hills, sparkling in the sunlight.

"Aren't your feet cold in those *geta*?"

"Japanese tradition conditions our bodies from a young age to withstand the cold and heat. This is how we can endure hot baths."

"I've always wondered about that."

"Was this while you spied on me in the bathing room?"

A blush rose in Micah's cheeks. "That was an accident."

"A most convenient accident for your eyes."

Micah pointed at a hill where a pair of deer stood. "Hey, look at those deer. Beautiful."

"Are you trying to change the subject?"

"I used to go hunting with Levi back home. I don't recall killing much of anything, but we had some good times. Yes, sir."

She found his evasiveness amusing. "You're right. The deer are beautiful."

The trail twisted through rolling hills before climbing into a dense forest of pine, maple, and beech trees. Heavy foliage blocked the sunlight. Branches twisted over the path like brown snakes. As she trekked, Kiyomi remembered her aunt teaching her about the Eightfold Path, the things a Buddhist must do to find Nirvana. Had she done enough to find enlightenment? She knew the Four Noble Truths. She had no illusions regarding herself and her place in the world. She wasn't frivolous with the truth. Her actions were proper. She didn't hurt living things. Her jobs never violated other steps on the Eightfold Path. She always strived for enlightenment, despite the obstacles she faced. Distracting thoughts were pushed from her head as soon as possible and she was alert to the truth. Kiyomi glanced over at Micah. She knew it pleased Micah when she chose to lie beside him instead of Jikan. It had pleased her as well. With this in mind, she said, "I've been thinking about what Jikan said last night."

"Which part?"

"About the Pure Land belonging to everyone. Do you believe this is possible?"

"I suppose. I mean, why would God segregate his children after death?"

Ice melted on the trail, leaving behind mud. Her *geta* squished in the soft ground. "I had an idea regarding the Pure Land."

"What's that?"

"After we find Ai, why don't you cross over with us?"

He slowed to a stop and studied her. "Cross into the Pure Land?"

"*Hai.*"

"You want me to go with you and Ai into the Pure Land?"

"If you'd rather not, I understand."

"No. No. I never said that. I mean ... well ... to be honest, I'm honored you asked."

"Then you agree?"

"What if Jikan is wrong? What if they won't have me?"

Kiyomi grabbed hold of his arm and leaned against him. "If I will have you, Amida will have you."

He smiled and patted her hand. "How can I refuse an offer like that?"

"You can't, which is why I made it."

Her heart seemed lighter and she feared it would rise into her throat, then escape through her mouth, sailing away toward the sun. The last time she had felt this way was on the night before the atomic bombing, while dancing with Micah on the bridge. So many ruined dreams. Not again. No. She wouldn't let anyone destroy what remained of her life. They would find Ai and cross over into the Pure Land. She deserved this. They all deserved this.

Night arrived. The curtain pulled back to reveal brilliant stars and a glowing moon. The frigid woods turned quiet. She offered her hand to Micah, which he accepted with a grin. An idea formed inside her mind: they could be lovers strolling toward an uncertain future. *Lovers.* The notion seemed both ludicrous and thrilling until she remembered number seven on the Eightfold Path: Keep the right mindfulness. No distracting thoughts. *I cannot afford to have this fantasy clouding my judgment, not when we're this close to finding Ai.*

A red dot cut through the darkness. "What do you suppose that is?" Kiyomi asked.

"I'm not sure."

As they drew closer, the light flickered. "I believe it's a fire," Micah said.

A man sat on a rock at the side of the trail with his back toward them. He stared into the wavering flames of a campfire. He turned as they drew closer. "I was wondering when you'd arrive."

Kiyomi squeezed Micah's hand and then released it. She stepped into the circle of light cast by the flames. "Hello, Jikan-san. I wasn't sure we'd see you again."

He rose from the rock and bowed. "I needed to scout ahead. How was your day?"

"Cold."

"*Hai.* Winter comes early this year." He gestured toward two rocks. "Please. Sit and warm yourselves."

Micah scowled at Jikan as he went by, and she knew he would always consider Jikan a rival. Micah sat and leaned forward to rest his elbows on his thighs. The fire revealed the resentment etched into his face. The crackling and popping of burning wood carried across the quiet night. They could sit this way for hours, staring into the fire, their thoughts locked behind their teeth. *This will not do.* Kiyomi shifted on the rock to get a better look at Jikan. "What happened in China?"

"In China?"

"*Hai.* You went missing, but you weren't killed."

Micah sat up straight. "He's not dead?"

"No."

Jikan remained focused on the flames. "How did you know?"

"You only appear at night. I suspect you're asleep at this moment, somewhere in China."

"You must think me dishonorable."

"Why would I think that?"

He closed his eyes and shook his head. "I was with the 16th Division of the Shanghai Expeditionary Force when we captured Nanjing."

"I've heard rumors."

Jikan opened his eyes. "The rumors are nothing."

"They're lies?"

"No. They're nothing because they cannot explain the brutality of what occurred. Our soldiers turned into savages. They raped women and children."

"Children?"

"*Hai*. Some younger than Ai."

"Did you—"

"No. Whatever you might think of me, I'm not the kind of man to take part in such a crime."

"But you did nothing to stop it," Micah said.

"I did nothing."

Jikan's eyes closed again. "We killed so many people, in the worst ways imaginable. Some were buried in the Ten-Thousand-Corpse-Ditch. Others dumped in the Yangtze River. A stack of corpses rose six feet at the north gate. At night, I hid from the slaughter while escaping into thoughts of home. I would have given anything to be back in Hiroshima."

"What did you do?" Kiyomi asked.

"I fled west, far from the war. I've been living on a farm in a small mountain village all these years. I have a wife, Huan, and a daughter, Mei. Huan is not attractive like you, Kiyomi-San, but she asks little of me. At first, I was afraid someone in the village would betray me. The longer the war dragged on, I worried less. I'm accepted in the village now. It will always be my home."

"You have a wife and daughter?"

"*Hai*. Are you upset with me?"

Burning embers sailed off into the night sky. She followed their progress until they vanished. "I'm happy for you."

"Our marriage would never have succeeded. You weren't the right woman for me."

"Because I wasn't compliant?"

He rocked back on the stone as a chuckle rumbled up from the pit of his stomach. "This is true; however, that's not the reason. We weren't a good match. You are better educated. You come from a successful family. If you hadn't given birth out of wedlock, your aunt and uncle would never have agreed to let you marry me."

"We cannot change what cannot be changed. The roots have died on the tree we planted."

"*Hai*, and I'm the one who killed them." Jikan let out a breath. "After the way I've treated you, helping Ai was the least I could do."

"Then you can lead us to the river?"

"You don't need me. Micah is a better man."

Even in the darkness, a shadow appeared to pass over Micah's face. "Don't go putting me on the altar of morality. The only difference between us is this; I killed from the air. I couldn't see their faces or hear their screams. I killed thousands with my bombs. Old people. Children. It made no difference to me at the time." Micah's hands balled into fists on his lap. "No. I'm most definitely not a better man."

Kiyomi knew Micah experienced guilt for participating in the fire-bombing raids, but she wasn't prepared to see him suffer so acutely.

Jikan held his hands toward the flames. "You'll spot others traveling to the river. Stay with them."

"We won't see you again?"

"No. You'll be settled in your new life tomorrow and I'll return to mine."

Chapter Forty Two

Jikan had told them to watch the sun. "When it takes a position directly ahead, swing westward. You'll pass through an ancient forest and over mountain streams before reaching Osorezan, and the Sanzu River. Keep a sharp eye, goblins and all manner of hellish creatures lurk in the woods. They'll try to stop you." Jikan's warning repeated inside Kiyomi's head as they walked. Micah stayed close, the tension of the moment affirmed in the fine wrinkles at the corners of his eyes. A fervent expectancy heightened inside her chest with each passing mile. Ai must be near and yet, for some reason, she felt farther away than ever.

Kiyomi recalled the dying embers of Jikan's fire in the cold night. They had talked for hours, long after Micah had fallen asleep. As she listened to Jikan's account of his life in China, followed by several apologies for the way he treated her, Kiyomi came to believe Jikan had restored his honor. At one point, Jikan gestured toward Micah and said, "You've asked him to join you in the Pure Land?"

"*Hai*. He deserves to find peace."

"There's more to your decision than helping Micah find peace, *neh*?"

"You ask difficult questions."

"They are only difficult if you make them so, Kiyomi-san."

With Micah at her side, she understood what Jikan had meant with his questions. Once they found Ai and crossed over into the

Pure Land, Micah would be a part of whatever future they were meant to experience. A perfect world awaited, where race and nationally meant nothing. Where the horror of war would be forgotten.

As they walked through the shadowed forest, Kiyomi stumbled and the ground rushed toward her face. Kiyomi's cheek slammed against the dirt, a shock of pain exploding through her. Micah knelt beside her. "Are you all right?"

"*Hai.*" She grabbed her throbbing ankle. "I stepped in a hole. Foolish."

He helped her stand. "Can you walk?"

"Why can't we be flying ghosts? Things would be so much easier."

They resumed their journey, her *geta* kicking up red and golden leaves scattered over the narrow trail. The forest closed in around them. Shadows deepened and Kiyomi shivered as the temperature dropped. She stopped and searched the gathering gloom. "I don't know where we are."

"Don't lose hope. It can't be much farther."

"It's so dark, how will we—"

A heavy crashing sound carried through the shadows. "What do you think that—"

"There!" Micah pointed.

A pair of glowing eyes stared at them. As she opened her mouth to speak, two creatures stepped out of the darkness. No taller than children, they resembled savage primeval men with cream-colored faces, unruly reddish hair and jaundiced eyes. "Goblins," she said, taking hold of his arm. "We must hurry!"

The goblins growled and hissed as they paced them from the trees. Kiyomi slowed to a stop.

"What is it?"

"Can you see the path?"

"It's too dark, but we've got to keep moving." Micah plunged forward, dragging her with him. A high-pitched cry, like the sound made by fighting cats, echoed from the woods.

"There are more of them!" she shouted.

The goblins drew closer. *It can't end like this*, she thought. *We're almost there. Ai is waiting.* Golden light bloomed overhead and the goblins screamed as the brightness poured over them. "The trail," Kiyomi said, pointing to a worn path.

"The light is from fireflies," Micah said. "But how can there be fireflies at this time of year?"

Kiyomi looked up at the undulating dots of color. "*Jizō.*"

"*Jizō?*"

"*Hai.* He must have sent the fireflies to help us."

Back on the trail, Kiyomi scanned the woods for more goblins. The fireflies remained, their light pointing the way. Figures appeared in her peripheral vision, plodding between the trees. Men and women, each surrounded by a bluish glow.

"Micah-san."

"I see them," he said. "The river can't be far."

The forest ended and the landscape turned grey and barren. A rancid odor, like rotten eggs, hit her. Kiyomi covered her nose. "What's that smell?"

Micah's nostrils flared. "Sulfur. I smelled the same thing when we toured the mud pots at Yellowstone. There's a volcano nearby."

"Mount Osore."

"Most likely."

An odd sound rose over the silence, like wind roaring out of the mountains. Thousands of spirits crowded the shore of the Sanzu River, some wailing and crying, some dashing about as if they had lost their minds. Ghost children cried for their mothers. Some hurried to pile stones into towers in an effort to accumulate enough karma to warrant crossing into the Pure Land. Horned demons wearing loin-cloths rushed between the stone towers, knocking them over with iron bars. *Datsueba*, the old hag, was busy stripping the clothes off spirits and tossing them to *Keneo*, a blood red demon, for weighing. When she had no one to strip, Datsueba ran along the shore waving her arms and shouting to drive anxious children from the river. Adult spirits crossed the river on bridges, while the less fortunate, who had committed great sins, attempted to wade across the *Sanzu*, some disappearing when turtle-like *Kappa* burst out of the water and snatched them. Others fell victim to giant horned serpents with dragon scales. She turned to Micah. "How are we going to find Ai?"

"We should make our way down the riverbank and call to her."

"We must be careful, otherwise, *Datsueba* will grab us and tear off our clothes for Keneo to weight."

Micah massaged his chin. "I hadn't considered that."

"We must stay together, agreed?"

"Agreed."

They fell in with a group of adults lined up to make the passage into the Pure Land. Others ran straight toward the river, bypassing children hovered over precious stone towers. *Datsueba* chased after these renegades, her ragged white dress flying out behind her, capturing most before they reached the water. She tore off their clothes with a swipe of her hand, leaving them naked and vulnerable, then tossed their clothes to *Keneo*, who draped them over the cypress branches. If the branch didn't bend under the weight, *Datsueba* ordered the person to join the line at the bridge. If the branch sagged, horned demons dragged them off into the forest.

A vein pulsed in Micah's neck.

"What's wrong, Micah-san?"

"They're being judged for their sins, right?"

"*Hai.* Those with bad lives are taken to Hell."

"We should avoid the old hag at all costs."

Reaching the spirit children, Kiyomi cupped a hand around her mouth and shouted, "Ai Oshiro! Ai Oshiro! Do you hear me?"

Dozens of children with pleading eyes closed in, clutching her clothes as they cried, "Mama! Mama! Can you help me?"

"This is like in the cave," Micah said.

"What can I do?"

Micah pulled a boy off Kiyomi. "She can't help you. She's not your mama."

One by one, the spirit children wilted from her presence like dying flowers, their mouths turned down, and tears welling in their eyes. "Not, mama. Not, mama," they said, and went back to stacking stones on their piles.

Kiyomi pushed her way through the throng of spirits. "Ai Oshiro, can you hear me? Ai-chan, answer me!"

Micah focused on *Datsueba*. "If she heads this way, we run toward the woods, got it?"

"*Hai.* I hope you're fast enough to keep up with me."

Angry grey clouds moved in from the north and a biting wind swept over the land. Kiyomi shivered and hugged herself. "So many lost souls," she whispered.

"Will they be stuck here forever?"

"We are taught a spirit must complete the journey into the Pure Land within forty-nine days. After that ..." Kiyomi closed her eyes. "Are we too late for Ai?"

"We have to keep looking."

An idea streamed through her mind and Kiyomi nodded. *Hai. This is what we must do.* She seized Micah's forearms. "Mio could see us."

"Yes, she could."

"And communicate with us."

"Where are you going with this?"

"There are women at the temple."

"What temple?"

"The Bodaiji Temple, built where Lake Usoriyama feeds into the river. The women are *Itako* like Mio-san. They've been trained to commune with the dead. Perhaps an *Itako* can make contact with Ai and tell us where she is." Kiyomi released his arms and sighed. "Or tell us if we're too late to save her."

"All right. It's worth a shot. We don't seem to be making much progress." He considered the woods.

"What are you thinking?"

"On missions, we'd fly parallel to the coast to avoid gun batteries. We should move back from the river. No need to risk an encounter with the old hag."

"*Hai.* Good plan, Micah-san."

Kiyomi followed Micah to the edge of the woods. As she studied the children laboring along the riverbank, a sense of apprehension grew inside her. What would happen if they didn't find Ai? How could she cross over into the Pure Land without her daughter?

She guided Micah in the direction of the lake, keeping an eye on the forest in case a demon or goblin should attack. Micah remained quiet, his body tense as if anticipating a goblin charge. The temple appeared on the horizon. "This temple is used to take care of the dead. The priests give them burial and perform ceremonies in their soul's favor."

"That makes sense, given the location."

A number of buildings comprised the temple compound, built on a foundation of crushed rock. The encompassing grey merged with the darkening sky to produce a bleak panorama. Toro lanterns lined both sides of a planked walkway that led to the *Butsuden*. Adding to the somber atmosphere was the barren land of jagged white and grey rocks on the opposite side of the river, where steam belched from sulfuric hot springs. Small *Jizō* statues dotted every hillock and rise, surrounded by *kazaguruma* left by grieving parents. The tiny bamboo and paper pinwheels hummed in the wind.

A number of priests wearing traditional robes milled about, oblivious to the turmoil within the nearby invisible world.

"Where now?" Micah asked.

"I'm not sure. The *Itako* aren't officially part of the temple." Kiyomi motioned with her chin toward the Butsuden. "Let's try over there."

Multiple voices whispered into her ears. Kiyomi slowed while trying to decipher their message. She recognized some of the people speaking to her. There was Banri and Sayoka, her aunt and uncle, and others she didn't know. *What do you want of me? What are you trying to tell me?*

"Are you all right?"

"Yes ... I ..." She massaged her temples, her fingers digging into flesh as the voices merged into a single message. "On the left side of the *Butsuden*. Go to the left."

She stepped onto the veranda surrounding the *Jizō-den* and turned left. The temple was built around *onsen*. Acidity from the lake turned the hot springs yellow. The stench of sulfur made her nostrils twitch. Kiyomi rounded a corner and paused. An old woman stood looking down at a steaming pool. She wore a white kimono and clutched a long black rosary made of soapberries.

Festooned to the rosary were old coins and the claws and bones of animals. Kiyomi turned to Micah. "We've found our *Itako*."

"Are you sure?"

"She is," the old woman said. "Come closer so I may see you better. My sees what my eyes cannot."

Kiyomi reached for Micah's hand as fear made her knees shake. She was desperate for answers, but would the *Itako* provide the answers she wanted to hear?

"I see you're holding hands with an American. Interesting."

"He's a friend," Kiyomi said.

"*Hai.* In times such as these, we all need friends, even the unexpected variety." She clutched her rosary and rattled the bones. "Are you here to cross into the Pure Land?"

"*Hai.* But that's not why we've come to talk with you."

"Something prevents you from crossing."

"You know what happened in Hiroshima?"

"*Hai.* Why do you think there are so many children gathered at the river?"

"When the bomb went off, my daughter, Ai, died."

"Before you?"

"*Hai.*"

"And you believe her soul is waiting for you? What makes you believe she is here?"

"My ... former husband ... brought her from Kyu-Kudedo."

The old woman thrust out her chin. "And why didn't he take your daughter into the Pure Land?"

"Well ... he's not her father, you see. And ..."

"Say it."

"He's not dead."

Crows on a nearby building cried out. Their shrill cawing pierced the air.

"What a lovely sound," the old woman said. "Don't you think so?"

"I don't like crows," Kiyomi whispered.

The *Itako* raised a palm toward the birds. The noisy cawing stopped. "People misunderstand crows. They can tell us a great deal if we open our minds to their message."

"We have searched along the riverbank. Could you try to communicate with Ai? I need to know if she's here."

"And if she's not? Are you prepared to leave this realm without her?"

Tears welled in Kiyomi's eyes. "I cannot answer that."

"I know you've considered the possibility."

"*Hai.* Living without Ai would be a nightmare from which I would never awaken. Will you help me? Please."

"I will help you, Kiyomi-san."

"How do you know my name?"

"The crows told me." She reached out and placed a hand over Kiyomi's hand. Cold radiated from her flesh. "I'm going to try and contact your daughter. Unless you're fluent in *Tsugaru,* you will not understand me. I need you to close your eyes and concentrate. Think about Ai. Let her fill your mind and take away your distress. Can you do this?"

Kiyomi gazed beyond the *Itako* to the mountains surrounding Lake Usori. The grey sky deepened the emerald color of the water. "*Hai.* I will do whatever it takes and am prepared for whatever the consequences might be."

"You've experienced the sorrow of two lifetimes, Kiyomi-san. Forgive me if I should add to your anguish."

"There will be nothing to forgive. You're not responsible for Ai's death."

"If you're ready, close your eyes and do what I told you."

Kiyomi glanced at Micah.

Micah nodded. "It'll be all right."

"I'm ready." Eyes closed, she pictured Ai's face in her mind. As she concentrated, the *Itako* chanted, her voice low and distant as if traveling through a tunnel. The tempo of the chanting increased, but the sound faded, growing softer and softer until at last Kiyomi heard nothing. She floated through a black void where light couldn't penetrate. The darkness drew her farther and farther from Osorezan. A strip of color broke through the void. Little by little, the blackness pulled back and the Motoyasu River appeared. Beyond the riverbed, the copper dome of the Industrial Promotion Hall shimmered. Two men fished on the far shore. Children swam and splashed each other, their laughter a heavenly song. *I've gone back. Hai. I've returned to an earlier time. To a Hiroshima that exists only in my memory. But why? Why am I here?*

"Mama."

Kiyomi whirled toward the voice. Ai stood behind her. She wore her red bathing suit and held a cone of flavored ice. Kiyomi covered her mouth. "Are you real? Are you with me?"

"You and Micah-san have traveled far to find me."

"Have I found you?" Kiyomi asked.

Ai took a bite of the ice and smiled. "No. Not yet."

"What does that mean?"

"I must go now. I love you, Mama." Ai evaporated like morning mist burned off by the sun.

She reached for her and held only air. "No! No! Come back to me. Ai-chan, please!"

Kiyomi opened her eyes and discovered she was on her knees. Micah knelt beside her with an arm draped across her shoulders.

"Are you all right?"

A whimper escaped her throat. "We're too late. I've lost her. I've lost Ai."

"No. It can't be."

Kiyomi brushed aside tears. "I saw her. In a vision. Then she left me."

"*Hai.* You had a vision," the *Itako* said, "but I spoke with her and I tell you, Ai is here."

"Are you certain?"

"I might be blind, but there are things only I can see."

"Let me help you up," Micah said.

"Where is she?"

"You'll find her at the river. Near the cypress tree where *Keneo* hangs the clothes."

"The place with the old hag?" Micah asked.

"*Hai.*"

"It's dangerous there."

The old woman shook her rosary at him. "*Hai.* It's dangerous. But you of all people should understand the nature of fear. Were you afraid when you flew on your bombing missions?"

"Yes. I was afraid."

"And still you continued. Any man who could face his own death surely could face *Datsueba*?"

He turned toward Kiyomi. "If that's where we must go, then so be it. I won't let you down."

Micah treated her better than any other man had and this confused her. He demanded nothing of her and yet, she felt a sense of obligation toward him. But it wasn't the thought of wearing his *On* that troubled Kiyomi. It was something more, something she couldn't define. She understood his feelings toward her, but what did her heart have to say on the matter? What did he mean to her? "Thank you, Micah-san. You've been most helpful."

"Leave," the old woman said and shooed them away.

"I cannot pay you," Kiyomi responded.

"Of course not, you're dead. Now go and find your daughter."

"Thank you," Kiyomi said and bowed.

They left the temple compound and advanced in the direction of *Keneo's* tree, passing through the ongoing chaos. Kiyomi steeled herself against the madness. *If I can handle the horrors of the atomic bomb, I can handle this.*

"Do you see Ai?" Micah asked.

"No, but the *Itako* said to look for her near *Keneo's* tree."

A goblin ran up to Kiyomi and seized her wrist. "Micah-san, help me!"

"Get off her!" Micah punched the goblin's face. The creature staggered and Micah hit it again. The goblin dropped to the ground, rolled over, then retreated with a screech. "Are you all right?"

Kiyomi rubbed the spot on her arm where the goblin had grabbed her. "My arm hurts, but I'll be fine." From the corner of her eye, she caught *Datsueba* watching. Would she strip off their clothes for *Keneo* to judge them? Would the branch on his cypress tree sag under the weight of her sins? "We must keep an eye on *Datsueba*."

Micah nodded. "I noticed her looking this way."

"We don't have time to play her game," Kiyomi said. "Not if we are going to find Ai."

"Where could she be?"

Kiyomi searched the faces of nearby children. "I don't know." Her shoulders slumped. What if the *Itako* was wrong? What if her vision of Ai in Hiroshima represented something more than the old woman implied. What if Ai had traveled into a new plane of existence? She could be lost in darkness, waiting for a rescue that would never occur.

"Kiyomi-san," Micah said, his voice deeper, more urgent. "*Datsueba* is coming this way. Should we run into the woods again?"

She wanted to run—but not for herself—for Micah. Did he deserve to be judged in this place where the spirits of Buddhists gathered before leaving the earthly realm behind?

"No. We won't flee again. We're here for Ai, and no one is going to keep us from finding her."

A subtle smile turned the corners of his mouth. "You're a strong woman. I've always admired that about you. I used to imagine what it would be like to be with you. To have you for a partner. But I never deserved a woman of your quality." He stared at his boots. "I fell in love with you. I don't know why I tell you this now. Please forgive me for clouding your thoughts."

His words swept through her like the winds of a typhoon, forever changing the topography of her heart. She wished she had time to consider the meaning of his desire and how to properly respond to him, but time was the one thing she didn't have. Not with *Datsueba* closing in and Ai nowhere in sight. She placed a hand on his wrist. "We must go to the tree. *Keneo* will do nothing to us until *Datsueba* arrives."

"Let's go."

She marveled at how quickly Micah moved past the subject of his affection and on to the serious issues they faced. He possessed many qualities a Japanese person would admire.

Keneo watched the branches of the cypress sag under the weight of a man's clothes. He faced the cowering spirit and ordered him to wade across the river. The man slunk off in the direction of the water. *Keneo's* eyes glistened as they approached. Behind them, *Datsueba* drew closer.

"What now?"

"Wait," Kiyomi said.

"What are we waiting for?"

A golden light spread over them. Inside the light, warmth caressed her skin. *Keneo* stepped back from the tree. *Datsueba* stopped advancing and turned around to flee. What made them retreat? A man wearing the simple robe of a monk stepped out of the radiance. His round face shined in the luminescence coming off a jewel carried in his left hand. Grey smoke rose from a staff held in his right hand. A halo levitated over his bald head. His eyes sparkled with kindness and compassion. Kiyomi dropped to her knees and bowed.

Micah leaned close to whisper. "Who is he?"

"*Jizō*."

"The deity who protects children?"

"*Hai*."

Jizō stopped before Kiyomi. "Look at me. Do not be afraid."

Kiyomi raised her head to stare into his eyes.

"You are Kiyomi-san from Hiroshima," he said. "You have come to find your daughter, Ai."

She chewed the inside of her lip, hesitant to respond in fear of what he might tell her. As if sensing her dilemma, Micah cleared his throat and said, "Yes. *Hai*. She is Kiyomi-san from Hiroshima, here to find her daughter."

Jizō turned to consider Micah. An amused expression passed over his face before he returned his focus to Kiyomi. He held out the glistening jewel in his hand. "This jewel can grant wishes. But I do believe you have already made your wish, Kiyomi-san, have you not?" He took hold of his robe. The edge of the robe appeared wet. "From the tears of children," he said in response to an unstated question. *Jizō* pulled back the robe. Ai cowered beneath the cloth.

Kiyomi's heart leaped inside her chest as she pushed off her knees. "Ai-chan! Ai-chan! You're here. Thank the gods."

"Mama! Mama!" Ai raced out from under *Jizō's* robe.

Kiyomi swept her into an embrace. "My baby. My baby. I thought I'd never see you again." She kissed Ai's forehead, cheeks, chin, nose, and lips. Tears rolled onto Kiyomi's cheeks. "Thank you for protecting my daughter." She cupped Ai's face in her hands. "I've missed you so much."

Ai grinned. "I've missed you too, Mama. Jikan found me in the cave. He brought me here."

"*Hai.* We met Jikan in the mountains."

Ai pulled back. "Micah-san! I knew you'd come after me."

Micah's face flushed. "Your mama did it all. I just kept her company."

Kiyomi shook her head. "Micah-san has been a great help to me."

"I knew it," Ai said. She glanced back at *Jizō.* "He rides on porpoises too."

Jizō stepped in front of Micah and held out the shimmering jewel. "You have not made your wish."

Micah touched his chest. "I get a wish?"

"Close your eyes and think of what you would like."

Kiyomi nodded. "Go ahead, Micah-san. Make your wish. You've earned it."

Micah hesitated, then closed his eyes. After a few seconds, he reopened his eyes and turned to *Jizō,* who smiled.

"Your wish is granted," *Jizō* said.

Kiyomi detected a trace of sadness in Micah's face as he thanked *Jizō.*

Jizō pointed the staff he carried toward the river. Thousands of flickering lights emerged. Ai pointed at the tiny golden specks. "Look, Mama. Fireflies."

Kiyomi's gaze followed the fireflies to the water, where they merged into a sparkling mass. The light intensified, glowing brighter and brighter, like staring into the noonday sun. Her eyes stung as she watched, and when she thought she must turn away, the brightness faded, leaving behind a vermillion drum bridge. The bridge they must cross into the Pure Land.

Jizō motioned them forward. "Go. Find peace."

Kiyomi brushed hair out of Ai's face. She couldn't believe she was holding her. The last time she held Ai, her lifeless body crumbled into ash. Never again. She would hold her forever this time. "Are you ready to go?"

Ai beamed. "Is Micah-san coming with us?"

"*Hai*. I have asked him to join us."

"We can play *janken*. But I'll win."

"You should let me win at least once."

Ai giggled behind a hand. "*Hai*. If that will make you feel better."

Kiyomi helped Ai to her feet and squeezed her hand, the joy of touching her filling Kiyomi with a sense of wonder. Micah came alongside and Ai held out her free hand. He stared at her hand, then up at Kiyomi. A fragile smile passed over his mouth and the aura of sadness that enveloped him left her confused. Micah accepted Ai's hand and Kiyomi said, "Hard to believe our journey is almost over."

"Almost over," he whispered.

Kiyomi paused at the foot of the bridge and glanced back at the world they would be leaving. Memories trickled through her mind like summer rain. She recalled her youth in Tokyo, shopping adventures with her aunt, and the excitement of starting school. Faces glided past, friends, neighbors, and boys she had desired. The Floating World offered forbidden romance, warm kisses, and firm hands caressing her flesh. And then there was Ai, taking her first breaths, capturing Kiyomi's heart with her trusting eyes. Her thoughts traveled to Hiroshima and tears acquired from a failed marriage. She blinked away this sorrow, replacing the pain with images of swimming in the river with Ai, the sun on their shoulders. The memories ended with Micah holding her as they danced.

"Are you all right, Mama?"

Kiyomi looked at her daughter with the confidence that their lives moving forward would be filled with love and laughter. "We should get going, *neh*?" She turned to Micah, who was staring up at the bridge. "Micah-san?"

"Thank you."

"What are you thanking me for?"

"For believing in me. For allowing me to be a part of your lives."

"We will have many more days together."

He looked at his shoes.

"Micah-san?"

His mouth struggled to form a smile. "Many more days."

The wooden bridge creaked beneath them. "Are we walking on fireflies?" Ai asked.

"We're walking on a bridge," Kiyomi answered.

"Did you not see the fireflies, Mama? Are your eyes tired from looking for me?"

Kiyomi chuckled. "*Hai* to both of your questions."

"I missed you, Mama."

"Were you scared all by yourself?"

"I wasn't by myself. There were many children inside the cave. And when Jikan left me during the day, a lady spoke to me from the sky. She told me not to be afraid."

"Oh? What was this woman's name?"

"Ameya. Do you know her?"

Kiyomi bit her lip. "*Hai*. She is my mother."

They reached the apex of the bridge and descended toward the far shore of the Sanzu River. Near the bottom, a blinding flash spread across the structure. Kiyomi shielded her eyes against the overpowering brightness. The light faded and a pulsating purple cloud floated down from the sky. Three figures stood on lotus pedestals. Gold and silver rays emanated from their bodies. She recognized the one in the middle as Amida and the others as his assistants, Kanzeon, and Mahasthamaprapta. The cloud settled and Amida gazed straight into her eyes. The faces of the Buddha held indescribable beauty and great wisdom. Flowing robes clothed their bodies. Dazzling gold and jeweled earrings and bracelets added to their luster. Amida's bare left arm extended downward, his thumb and forefinger touching, while his right hand was raised, also with his thumb and forefinger touching. Kiyomi knew from her uncle's teaching that this mudra suggested wisdom is accessible to all, and Amida's compassion was directed at those who could not save themselves. Kiyomi bowed.

"Close your eyes, Kiyomi-san," Amida instructed, his voice resonating like thunder, "and tell me what you see."

Kiyomi closed her eyes. "I see you, great Amida, and your assembly." She opened her eyes and found him nodding.

"I appear to believers with their eyes open or shut. It is good you can see me. However, you did not look to the west and contemplate me at the time of your death. You did not generate the thought of being born in the Pure Land."

"That was a mistake."

"And still, your faith has brought you here."

"One must possess sincerity, faith, and aspiration to be reborn in the Pure Land," Kanzeon said. "Do you possess these qualities? Remember, you represent not only yourself but your daughter as well."

Kiyomi looked at Ai, who smiled at the Buddha as if watching a theater performance and then at Micah, who fidgeted under their scrutiny. "*Hai*. I possess these qualities."

Mahasthamaprapta held up a finger. "There is a simple prayer that will demonstrate whether or not you are ready to make this passage. Do you know it? If so, could you recite it for us?"

Kiyomi drew in a breath and exhaled. "*NAMO O-MI-TO FWO*. I seek refuge in the Amitabha Buddha."

Amida nodded again. "You and your daughter may enter the Pure Land." He pointed at Micah. "He cannot join you."

Ai tugged on Kiyomi's shirt. "Mama?"

The world darkened around her, as if every shadow born throughout time converged at this moment. The same vibrating ache she suffered in her bones after the atomic bomb exploded returned. *This is wrong. It has to be wrong.* Micah faced her with a desperate certainty in his eyes. She refused to accept his capitulation and turned toward Amida. "Why can't he cross over? Is it because he's not Buddhist?"

"No. His faith in God is undeniable."

"Then what is it? Micah is a good man."

"Kiyomi, no."

"It's true," she said, facing him. "If you were a bad person you couldn't have seen this bridge. You would have seen a mountain of needles."

Amida spread the fingers on his raised hand to gain her attention. "To enter the Pure Land, a person's mind must be free of distractions. He is burdened with guilt for the sins he believes he has committed."

Kiyomi grabbed hold of Micah's arm. "What are these sins?"

He answered with silence, his face becoming a tortured mask. She blinked while searching his eyes for the reason he suffered, then pulled back at a sudden idea. "You were fighting for your country and your family. You did what you had to do. It was war. A war you didn't start."

"I used to believe that," he whispered, "but after the things I've seen, I understand my role in the senseless violence and cannot forgive myself."

Kiyomi remembered the prayers copied by Banri that were said to blow away sins and carry them to the bottom of the sea. If only she could recall the words. Kiyomi held her hands before her, palms pressed together. "Wise Buddha, I beg you. Can't you see his heart is pure? Why must he be punished for sins he never committed?"

Micah pressed closer. "Kiyomi, take Ai into the Pure Land. Find peace."

"No. You must free yourself of this guilt and join us."

"I've tried, but I can't. This is my burden to bear, not yours."

Micah took hold of her hands and held her in his gaze. She tried to think of a way to change his mind but said nothing. He squeezed her hands and released them. Kiyomi felt his absence immediately as he started back down the bridge. *Here is our wakare. Here is our parting.*

Ai yanked on her arm and wailed, "Can't you see it, Mama? Can't you see it? Don't let him go, Mama. Please, make him stay!"

Chapter Forty Three

Micah staggered off the bridge and turned to look back. The bridge had vanished into a fine mist. He recalled the wish he had made upon *Jizō's* jewel and took satisfaction in knowing Kiyomi and Ai were safe in the Pure Land, as it should be. Even so, his heart longed to be with them. But this was impossible. He could no more free his mind of guilt than the tides could free themselves of the moon's sway.

The warmth and love he experienced on the bridge didn't carry over into the realm of *Datsueba* and *Keneo*. Surely she would come for him now that he wasn't under *Jizō's* protection. He'd be stripped and judged by *Keneo*, the branch on his cypress tree snapping under the weight of Micah's sins. He remembered Kiyomi pleading with Amida to allow him passage. She remained convinced he had nothing to feel guilty about. Why did she believe this after what happened in Hiroshima? She knew he'd taken part in a similar evil, that he was responsible for the deaths of her aunt and uncle, and so many more.

He journeyed across the riverbed, past ghost children frantically piling up stones, and demons determined to ruin the children's chances for a better life. Scattered stones. Scattered dreams. The pain of loss never ending. Micah kept his head down, glancing back from time to time at *Datsueba*. To his surprise, she paid no attention to him, as if to demonstrate her disdain for the man who had thrown away his chance at Heaven.

As he entered the woods, Micah recognized the extent of his purgatory. He would live alone. Troubled. Unloved. Kiyomi's words lingered inside his mind. "You were fighting for your country and your family. You did what you had to do. It was war. A war you didn't start." Why couldn't he believe her? Yes, they were at war, and yes, he was following orders, but did this justify what he had done? He paused to stare at the darkening sky. Moonlight beamed through an opening in the trees and he could imagine Jacob's ladder rising in the white shaft of light. But even if it existed, he'd stay planted on the ground. If he couldn't enter the Pure Land with Kiyomi, he didn't deserve eternal peace.

Micah pressed onward, the black forest closing in around him. Glowing spirits trudged past, oblivious to his plight, headed in the direction of the Sanzu River. Red-faced goblins dogged his every step, mocking with shrill laughter, but he knew they wouldn't waste their time on someone who was already in Hell.

A piercing wind blew through the trees. Leaves scattered. Branches creaked. The wind became whispering voices. First, his mother saying, "You should have stayed with Levi. Why didn't you stay with Levi?" His father spoke next, his words measured and soothing. "I told you the war would take something from you, didn't I? You just never imagined the thing it would take was love." As Micah forded a chilly stream, Levi called to him. "The answers will come to you, little brother. Don't despair. People who haven't fought in a war could never understand what you're going through." Kiyomi's voice was the last one he heard, a gentle plea that drove him onto his knees. "You shouldn't have left us, Micah-san. We need you." He buried his face in his palms and cried, "I want to believe that. But how can I? How can I ask for forgiveness after what was done to you?"

Micah stared into the void. *Where am I going? I have no future. No reason for existing.* If he had a way of taking his own life, he would. A gun to the temple; the taste of bitter poison on his lips; or perhaps he would cast himself from a tall bridge, like the stones from his youth, like the plunge he took over Hiroshima, only, this time he wouldn't awaken. Kiyomi wouldn't be there to rescue him, to show him the nature of his sins.

Gnarled branches weaved together above the forest floor. He stumbled beneath the thick canopy, craving some semblance of color in a black and grey world. Jagged rocks stabbed at his shoes. Roots reached out to trip him. He had no idea where he was or the direction he traveled. After hours of struggling through a maze of trees, rocks, streams, and underbrush, Micah broke out of the forest. The night sky opened before him. Hands on his hips, he surveyed a landscape of hills dotted by an occasional tree. A distant roar reached him. Micah concentrated on the sound. The sea. Yes. He had been hearing this song his entire life.

Micah picked his way around boulders, the percussion of the waves intensifying with each step. He paused at the edge of a cliff and stared at the ocean below. His eyes swept the steep cliff, stopping on a house built on a leveled plain. Darkness enveloped the home, constructed in the style of a Japanese farmhouse with a thatched roof and veranda. Who would live in such a lonely place?

A serpentine path led to the building. The steep trail forced him to lean back as he descended, his boots digging into the dirt and scattering rocks. He arrived at the quiet house and stepped onto the veranda, wood creaking beneath him. A dried crab shell was nailed over the door. Had a fisherman lived here? A man like his grandfather, a son of the sea. Leaning against a beam, Micah contemplated the water. A sliver of amber wedged between the sea and night sky like the line of an advancing fire. His thoughts turned to Kiyomi and the expression on her face as he turned away on the bridge. He could only imagine how she must have felt at that moment, her sense of betrayal.

The house was unlocked. The rooms stood empty, host to shadows and the festering stench of ruin. It was the perfect place for a ghost. The brittle *tatami* mats crunched beneath his boots. He traced a finger across the torn paper screens. His mind ached, tortured by the idea of a future that would never belong to him. Easing onto a mat, he lay on his side and closed his eyes.

Chapter Forty Four

Warmth tingled across his face and Micah forced his eyes open. Dust motes swam in sunlight beaming through a broken window. He sat up. It took him a moment to orient to his surroundings, then memories came rushing back all at once. The scene on the bridge; his journey through the dark forest; arriving at this abandoned house. The reality of his situation made him want to slip into a comforting dream. Would he ever find peace, or would he live like a hermit with idle days spent watching sunrises and sunsets, or swim far into the ocean in the hope he might drown, while knowing this was impossible? He had constructed this prison from his shame, and there would be no escaping. His life had been wasted.

Micah pushed off the floor and stood. He walked across the room and went out onto the veranda. A crisp breeze blew in from the sea. Waves rolled onto a narrow strip of sand before retreating. The sun blazed in a cloudless sky bleached of color. A trail winding between serrated boulders led to the beach. A peaceful setting for anyone but him. Micah knew whenever he viewed the water, he'd be haunted by visions of ash and ruin.

What have I done? How many did I kill?

He closed his eyes and ground knuckles against his forehead. *Stop torturing yourself. No amount of remorse will bring them back.*

A sound carried on the wind. Micah's eyes snapped open.

Silence.

No. Wait. There it was again. Coming from behind the house. Laughter. Yes. The high-pitched laughter of a child.

Micah left the veranda. He started up the path that led to the top of the hill, then stopped. *This isn't possible. No. It's an illusion. I'm conjuring their presence the way Oda summoned a bottle of sake.* And yet, he knew this was no illusion, no trick meant to comfort his afflicted soul. Kiyomi stood on a cliff looking down at him. Ai sat beneath a nearby cypress tree. *What are they doing here? Something's wrong.* Ai smiled and waved. He forced himself to wave as questions raced through his mind. Kiyomi watched him approach through downcast eyes.

"Why aren't you in the Pure Land?" Micah stopped before her.

Kiyomi kept her gaze low. "Don't be angry."

"Of course I'm angry. I want you and Ai to be happy, not miserable like me." Micah massaged the back of his neck. "Why didn't you cross over?"

She raised her head. "I couldn't cross over."

"What? I heard Amida say that you and Ai could enter the Pure Land."

"*Hai.* Amida said this. But to enter the Pure Land, one must have an undisturbed mind. When you left us, my mind became disturbed. My thoughts traveled with you."

The idea he had cost them their chance at Heaven filled Micah with a terrible sadness. "I've hurt you again."

"You've never hurt us." Kiyomi touched him on the forearm. "You only helped."

"How can you say that? You and Ai wouldn't be here if not for me." Micah shook his head. "I never should have followed you to your house."

"Do you regret meeting me?"

"No. That's not what I meant."

She studied his face, the skin tightening and relaxing over her cheekbones. "There's another reason why we're here." Kiyomi released her hold on his arm and turned toward Ai. "In Japan, it's believed human relations are predestined by a red string tied by the gods to the pinky fingers of those who will find each other in life. The string might tangle or constrict, but it can never break. The two people thus connected will have an important story together. As you left us on the bridge, Ai said she could see this string connecting me to you. That's how we followed you to this place."

Micah pictured them journeying through the dark forest, Ai pointing to a red string that stretched into the night. If this myth was true, what did it mean? Kiyomi returned to stand in front of him, her expression strong, assured. "You might wonder if the connecting string means I'm in love with you. The answer is no."

His body slumped at the news, the hopes and dreams built up inside his mind dying. She smiled as he suffered. "What is it?" he asked.

Kiyomi glanced at Ai, then back at him. "I said I'm not in love with you. I never said I cannot learn to love you."

His eyes squeezed shut. When Micah looked at her again, it was through tears.

Kiyomi pressed against him. She wrapped her arms around his back and leaned forward until their foreheads touched. "We have come so far, you and I. Now, in this moment, I have come home to you."

Made in the USA
Middletown, DE
27 November 2020